Hans Christian Andersen's Fairy Tales

THE FARMER LIFTED THE LID A LITTLE AND PEEPED UNDER.

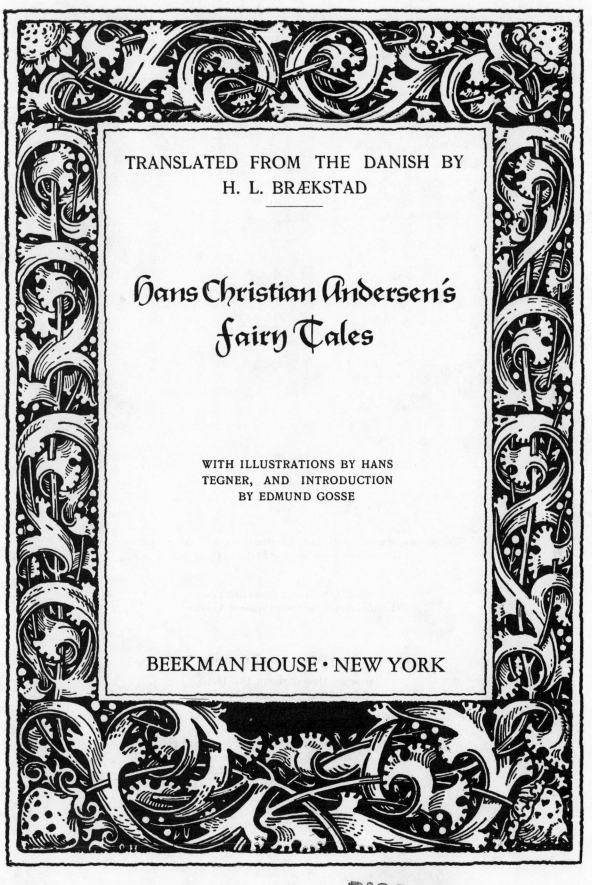

TRANSLATED FROM THE DANISH BY
H. L. BRÆKSTAD

Hans Christian Andersen's Fairy Tales

WITH ILLUSTRATIONS BY HANS
TEGNER, AND INTRODUCTION
BY EDMUND GOSSE

BEEKMAN HOUSE · NEW YORK

This book was originally published under the title Fairy Tales and Stories.
This edition is published by Beekman House,
a division of Crown Publishers, Inc.
a b c d e f g h
BEEKMAN HOUSE 1978 PRINTING
Manufactured in the United States of America

Library of Congress Cataloging in Publication Data

Andersen, Hans Christian, 1805-1875.
Hans Christian Andersen's Fairy tales.

Reprint of the 1900 ed. published by Century Co.,
New York under title: Fairy tales and stories.
SUMMARY: An extensively illustrated presentation of
42 well-known Andersen fairy tales.
1. Fairy tales, Danish.   [1. Fairy tales]
I. Tegner, Hans Christian Harald, 1853-   II. Title.
III. Title: Fairy tales.
PZ8.A54Hap 1978   [Fic]   78-11706
ISBN 0-517-26803-5

TO

H. R. H. THE PRINCESS OF WALES

BY SPECIAL PERMISSION.

CONTENTS

CONTENTS

LIST OF ILLUSTRATIONS

LIST OF ILLUSTRATIONS

LIST OF ILLUSTRATIONS

LIST OF ILLUSTRATIONS

LIST OF ILLUSTRATIONS

LIST OF ILLUSTRATIONS

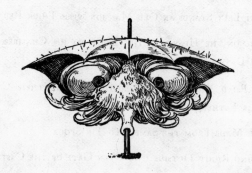

INTRODUCTION

Such an original species of writing as that in which Andersen excelled does not burst full-blown upon the world. It is the result of many experiments, many accidents, even, perhaps, of some blunderings. Andersen did not set out deliberately to be a teller of fairy stories, much less did he expect or desire to be mainly known as the composer of these *smaating*, as he called them, of these trifles or bagatelles. He set out in life intending to be a serious poet, a writer of five-act dramas, a novelist of passion and society. Almost to the very last he persisted in believing that the critics and the public had made a mistake, and that his ambitious works, in the conventional branches of the profession, were what he would really live by. "Don't you think," he said to me in a sort of coaxing whisper, toward the very close of his life—"don't you think that people will really come back to 'The Two Baronesses' when these *smaating* have had their day?" "The Two Baronesses" is an old novel of Andersen's, which I had not read, so I could only bend my eyes politely. But that was in 1874, and people have neither come back to "The Two Baronesses" nor forgotten "The Ugly Duckling" and "The Snow Queen."

Unwilling as he was to admit it, however, Andersen could not fail to be aware that the Fairy Tales were his real possession and treasure-trove. In 1862 he deigned to recollect how these stories came into existence, and his notes,—which I do not happen to have seen translated or even referred to,—although tantalizingly scanty, are very valuable. He put back the germ of his fairy-story telling to the year 1829, when he published, along with a little collection of his poems, a tale in prose called "The Dead Man." This was a treatment of one of the disquieting, half-humorous, half-melancholy legends which Andersen had heard when in his childhood he haunted the Odense workhouse and its old women. He deliberately tried to tell it in the tone of Musäus, a German author of the eighteenth century, who began by being an imitator of Richardson, and who ended as the first man to collect and retell, after a somewhat over-genteel fashion, the folk-tales of Germany. Musäus possessed no great talent, but it is interesting to see him, who set the Brothers Grimm and all the multitude of modern folk-lorists in motion on the one hand, giving the start-word in a very different direction to Andersen. For

INTRODUCTION

"The Dead Man"—which was quite a failure—was the story which, entirely rewritten, appeared in 1831 as "The Traveling Companion."

In Andersen's account of his journey in the Harz Mountains, published in 1831, there is to be found a story of an old king, who believed that he had never heard a lie, and therefore promised that the man who should first successfully tell him a falsehood should receive the princess, his daughter, and half his royal kingdom. Here the fairy-tale tone is clearly perceptible, but it has not yet discovered its form or its final character. But in 1835 there appeared a little pamphlet,—the originality and importance of which it would be difficult to appraise too highly,— "Fairy Tales Told for Children." This precious pamphlet of sixty-one pages contained four tales, "The Tinder-Box," "Little Claus and Big Claus," "The Princess and the Pea," and "Little Ida's Flowers." These four stories are included in the present collection, and the reader may find it interesting to detach these, with a view to observing what we may call Andersen's primitive manner in the evolution of a fairy tale.

There was one peculiarity in these stories which startled a Danish ear, and led at first to almost universal reproof by the critics, and neglect by cultivated readers. Like the other literatures of Europe, and more than some,—more than our own, for instance,—the poetry and prose of Denmark were held at that time in the bondage of the proprieties. An author still had to consider not merely what he should, but also what he should not say. There was little attempt to reproduce, even in comedy, the actual daily speech of citizens, but something more polished, more rhetorical, more literary, in fact, was put into the lips of even vulgar persons before they could be permitted to speak in public. It would not be easy to make an Englishman or a Frenchman understand how startlingly lax and puerile the conversations in these little stories of Andersen's appeared; perhaps a German would realize it more. It was the first time that children and uneducated people of the lower middle class had been allowed to speak in Danish literature, and their naïvetés and their innocent picturesqueness were at first an absolute scandal. Conceive what Johnson and Burke would have thought of "Alice's Adventures in Wonderland," and you have a parallel to the effect of "Little Claus and Big Claus" upon academic Denmark.

But in this first typical specimen there were differences to be observed. "The Tinder-Box" and "The Princess and the Pea" are not of the same class as "Little Ida's Flowers." Nothing of its kind could be more exquisite than the last, and Andersen never excelled its lightness and brightness of fancy, its intimate recognition of the movement of a child's imagination. Only a great poet could have written it—only the great poet who subsequently wrote so many other pure fairy tales of the same enchanting innocence and ebullience. But that poet needed not to have had Andersen's peculiar training. As a matter of fact, "Little Ida's

Flowers" was composed in consequence of hearing the small daughter of Thiele make remarks about the plants in the Botanic Gardens of Copenhagen; remarks the delicious artlessness of which so delighted Andersen that he noted them down, and reproduced them in the setting which we all know so well. This is an example of the side of Andersen's genius on which he most closely approaches Lewis Carroll.

If from this lovely fantasia we turn to the other three stories, we see something different, something more entirely original, and suggestive of a more surprising departure. These also were suggested to Andersen by matters lurking in his recollection. He never, perhaps, absolutely invented the material of his tales. But these were legends the crude germ or kernel of each of which he had heard long ago, in his unparalleled childhood — fragments of the prejudice and ignorance and mother-wit of the untaught peasant mind. These were atoms of folk-lore left sticking to his memory from the days when he went weeding in the garden of the lunatic asylum, or strolled along among the hop-pickers at Bogense. These worn fragments of a primitive age, shapeless and unsuggestive to any less penetrating imagination than his, Andersen redeemed from their low uses, and clothed again with his fancy and his humanity.

The next little collection, that of 1836, contained three, and that of 1837 only two stories. It appeared in these that Andersen had become a little shy of his old, direct folk-lore. He had put forth his discovery, and the world had proved averse to it. Here was "The Traveling Companion," in its remodeled form, which, indeed, was actual folk-lore; but the others belonged to the modern, the invented, or, as we English may roughly call it, the Alice section of the stories. "The Naughty Boy" came out of Anacreon; "The Emperor's New Clothes," remarkable as showing the first complete development of Andersen's satiric irony, from Spanish sources. In "Thumbeline" and "The Little Mermaid" we have pure fairy tales, works of literary fancy, unattached to any genuine folk-lore. The last mentioned, however, was the earliest of all Andersen's tales to become widely popular. It was in "The Wild Swans," of 1838, that he first dared to come back to actual Danish legend. By this time he had begun to conquer his public, and he now went on writing as it happened to please him best. Oddly enough, he himself was never perfectly converted. To the last, and in the presence of his immortal little masterpieces, he continued to be slightly scandalized at the liberties he had persuaded himself to take with classical Danish.

Perhaps there never existed a more remarkable instance of the adaptation of extraordinary circumstances to the purposes of a unique genius than was seen in the case of the early training of Andersen. His childish days had been spent in strange places, in still stranger company. He must have been about five years of age when he went with his parents to dine with the jailer of the common prison in Odense. Two prisoners waited at table, but Hans Christian could eat nothing; his brain was full of all the stories of robbers and dungeons and enchanted castles that he had ever heard of, and he had to be put to bed. But when he was left alone, he characteristically tells us, he forgot to be frightened, for he turned the whole incident into a wonderful fairy tale. How he played about in the corridors of the madhouse, and how a beautiful lunatic nearly frightened him to death, is well known; but this is an incident which could have happened, one is inclined to say, to no poet but Andersen. He has given us a most curious account of the long hours he used to spend in the old women's ward of the poorhouse at Odense, and how he offered to sketch the internal economy of any one of the ancient ladies, with chalk, on the door of the room. With these and other ingenuities he so diverted them that they declared with one voice that so clever a child was not long for this world. But, in their turn, to this ignorant, freakish, wild little boy, the old women told stories, legends of troll and water-sprite, ghost and goblin and wizard, such as in those days the uninstructed imagination of the Scandinavian peasant teemed with.

When the child was eleven, his father, the gentle, consumptive young cobbler, fell deadly sick. Already Andersen had gained a reputation as a clever, uncanny boy ("he is cracked, like his grandfather," people said in Odense); accordingly when his father was very ill, his mother sent him out at night to walk by the river, "for," she said, "if thy father is to die this time, thou wilt meet his ghost." The poor frightened child came home, having seen nothing, and his mother's superstition was assuaged; but the third day after that her husband did die. Little Andersen and his mother watched with the corpse, and all night long a cricket chirped; till at last the mother sat up and cried to it, "You need not call to him; he is dead!" In this amazing old-world atmosphere of terror and spiritual bewilderment was the delicate and nervous brain of this great modern poet nurtured, and we must not forget it if we would understand in what manner he was prepared for the composition of the Fairy Tales.

It may be said that in his address to his imaginary audience Andersen never advanced beyond what he recalled of his own childhood in those loose, undisciplined and fruitful years when it was doubtful whether he would become a tailor's apprentice or a super at a provincial theater. It is to what he recollected of his own dimly-luminous mind before he set out for Copenhagen, in 1819, that he addressed, in later life, the ingenuous language of his tales. Hence he uses the simplest words, the most concrete images, is occupied with the rudest tastes and the humblest ambitions. If he wishes to conjure up power, it is always in the person of an old king, generally a peasant in intelligence and experience, but known to be a king by his wearing a golden crown and an ermine robe, and by his carrying a scepter. So, if he wishes to suggest wealth, he uses none of its symbols or evidences, but quantities of bullion — bars of gold, 'or bags of minted money. The child's want of clear distinction between the seen and the unseen, the experienced and the impossible; its naïve acceptance of animals and flowers, and even of the winds and the stars and the inanimate domestic objects around it, as creatures allied to itself, with which it may be in mutual comprehension, the dullest of which, in fact, is more in sympathy with it than an ordinary "grown-up person,"—all this was realized by Andersen with a clairvoyance which becomes almost supernatural when we recollect that no previous writer had ever seriously dreamed of it, and that this was a little chamber of literature into which even Shakspere had never forced his way.

It has taken the world sixty years to become perfectly assured that Andersen, in his own best line, is an author of the very highest originality, that—given the particular *genre*—he is as great in it as Milton or—shall we say?—Molière in his. Nothing less than this can be claimed for Andersen,—absolute supremacy in his own special field. Only one man perceived this fact, however, at first. This was the Dane, Johan Ludvig Heiberg, the acutest critic of Northern Europe in those years, who, though hitherto not well affected to Andersen's writings, told him bluntly as soon as he had read "The Princess and the Pea," that here he had struck at last into the road that leads to immortality. But the excellent Frederika Bremer could only wish that "The Little Mermaid" had been brought down to the level of a young child's apprehension, and most of what were considered the "best judges" of that age were shocked at the humor which gives the very salt of life to the fairy tale, which, without it, is apt to be a little mawkish. Andersen's autobiography is full, perhaps over full, of instances of want of appreciation of his writings by those from whose praise he anticipated the most pleasure. But the children soon took up the matter themselves, and paid him an abundant and enthusiastic devotion which dragged their elders along with it.[1]

There can be little doubt that one peculiarity of Andersen's imagination especially endeared him to the minds of the children. A child is like a savage in its calm acceptance of incongruous elements, in the ease with which it passes over essential difficulties of tone and plane. Andersen's art consists largely of the adroitness with which he blends together ideas which in the real world cannot be conceived of in combination or even in relation. He is unique, for instance, in his mingling of images from the Christian religion and from primitive forms of superstition. When "The Traveling Companion," for example, opens, Johannes is at the parish church, and the people are singing a hymn. But in the tower of the old church a brownie or *nisse* is squatting, and it waves its red cap at him. He follows the bells through the forest, and with a good conscience enters another little church, listening to the word of God. This does not pre-

[1] For the facts of Andersen's life, the reader may be referred to Mr. R. Nisbet Bain's excellent "Biography," 1895, a work collected entirely from Danish sources.

vent him from presently enjoying the gambols of the elves in the woodland. He is a good little modern boy, living in a quiet parish, among God-fearing people, but the mountain opens before him and he enters without surprise the great hall where the king of the trolls sits under a canopy of pink spiders' webs, and listens to the choir of great black grasshoppers playing on Jews' harps. But he is the same sober Christian lad as ever, and in due time overthrows all his enemies by his honesty and sagacity. Here the mixture of spiritual ideas is bewildering, if we only persuade ourselves to realize it, and involves an incongruity which no other teller of fairy stories allows himself to undertake. In one of Grimm's stories, for instance, or of Asbjörnsen's, we have trolls, and wicked princesses, and imps with enormous noses, but they are not mixed up with the singing of hymns in church and preparing for a first communion. But in the mind of a child this or any incongruity is possible, and the mind of Andersen was exactly like that of a child. Hence, even when his topsy-turvy world is most startling, we are never scandalized. Probably no one was ever found to accuse Andersen of profanity.

A somewhat similar moral incongruity would not be quite so easy to condone, if we were inclined to take a very high ground. The soldier in "The Tinder-Box" cuts off the head of the old woman and steals her treasures with shocking ingratitude, yet with complete impunity. His ultimate good fortune even springs directly from his crime. The behavior of the merchant's son to the Turkish princess in "The Flying Trunk" was deplorable, but Andersen does not seem to regret it. Little Claus can hardly be said to live up to any recognized standard of morals in his relation to Big Claus. But all this is very characteristic of the childish instinct. Life to a child is a phantasmagoria, and thanklessness and rapine and murder are amusing shadows which the unsubstantial human figures throw as they dance in the flicker of the firelight. It is precisely the absence of any priggishness in this respect, and the daring with which he sets himself against all the obvious school-room axioms of conduct that help to make up the astounding fascination of Andersen. His very savagery endears him to the little innocent barbarians of the nursery.

It was a favorite exercise with Andersen to read aloud his fairy tales, soon after they were written, to some fortunate friend. The number of those who can say that they have enjoyed this privilege must now be growing small. In England it must be extremely small, for Andersen's latest visit to this country was paid in 1857. The present writer, therefore, is tempted to believe that there is some little rarity, at least, in the experience which he is able to relate, and the more so from a particular which will be presently mentioned. Only on a single occasion did Hans Christian Andersen read to me one of his unpublished fairy tales, and, indeed, I had not the honor of knowing him until he had given to the world the main bulk of his productions. But in the summer of 1872 I had the happiness of listening to "The Cripple." At that time Andersen had a suite of rooms in Copenhagen, but he was much more frequently to be found at the mansion of some friends just outside the fortifications, called Rolighed or "Quietude." This house had been the residence of several interesting people, among others of no less a person than Örsted. It was now owned by a wealthy and liberal merchant, Mr. Moritz Melchior, who had rebuilt it, and who had turned it into a miniature of Rosenborg Castle, with a tower, and with high balconies overlooking the Sound.

In this house Andersen was so constantly welcome that a portion of it — three or four charming rooms — was set apart entirely for his service, and he came and went in them without constraint. "Rolighed" is the subject of Andersen's latest poem, in which he says:—

> "My home of homes, where behind the slope of elder-bushes
> My life regained its sunshine and my harp its tone,
> To thee I bring with gratitude this blithe song of mine!"

It was here, in his bright room open to the east, with the long caravan of ships going by in the Sound below, "like a flock of wild swans," as he said, with the white towns of Malmö and Landskrona sparkling on the Swedish coast, and the sunlight falling on Tycho Brahe's island, that Andersen proposed to recite to me a new fairy tale. He read in a low voice, which presently sank to almost a hoarse whisper; he read slowly, out of mercy to my imperfect apprehension, and as he read he sat beside me, with his amazingly long and bony hand — a great brown hand, almost like that of a man of the woods — grasping my shoulder. As he read, the color of everything, the twinkling sails, the sea, the opposite Swedish coast, the burnished sky above, kindled with sunset. It seemed as if Nature herself were flushing with ecstasy at the sound of Andersen's voice.

When he had finished, he talked to me a little about the story, and confided to me that he intended this, "The Cripple," to be his last. He was very much pleased with it; he thought it summed up all his methods, and that in a certain sense it presented symbolically his lesson, his imaginative message, to mankind. The reader may not recollect this story, since it is far from being the best known of Andersen's tales; nor is it really one of the most characteristic, for there is nothing supernatural or fantastic about it. It has, therefore, not been included in this collection. It presents a little complicated episode of humble manners. A gardener and his wife have five children, of whom the eldest, a fine boy, has the misfortune to be a bed-ridden cripple. The parents, worthy, narrow people, live engrossed in their materialistic interests, and when some one from whom a present is expected gives the cripple a book, they ungraciously say to one another, "He won't get fat on that." But it is a book of fairy tales, and the boy's whole spiritual life is awakened by the vistas these open for him in every direction. He finds two simple and direct parables, which he reads over and over again to his parents, and their hearts, too, are humanized and melted. Finally, a little dark bird, like the Emperor of China's nightingale, is presented to him, and in a supreme nervous effort to save its life the cripple regains the use of his own limbs. In this story Andersen intended to sum up the defense of fairy tales and of their teller. It was to be a sort of *apologia* for his whole poetical career, and he told me that it would be the latest of his writings. In this matter his mind afterward changed, for later in the same year, 1872, he composed "Auntie Toothache," inspired by his own sufferings, and it is with this story that the long series of his fairy tales ultimately closed with the original.

He gradually realized that his work was done. In a most pathetic letter to me, on New Year's Day, 1875, he admitted that we must look for nothing more, that his bag of magic was emptied. After a long illness, however, his physical health seemed in large measure restored, and at the completion of his seventieth year, great festivities were arranged at Copenhagen and at Odense. The whole nation, from the Royal family down to the peasants in the country villages, kept Andersen's birthday as a holiday, and this attention soothed and pleased him. But his vital energy was now fast ebbing. He began to suffer great torture from an obscure complaint which puzzled the doctors. It was interesting that when he was dying Andersen expressed a curiosity to study the ancient Indian fables which are identified with the mythical name of Bidpai, and the death-bed of the greatest modern fabulist was strewn with translations and commentaries of his earliest fellow-craftsman of Hindustan. At last, on the 4th of August, 1875, he fell asleep in the room at Rolighed, where we were sitting when he read me "The Cripple" three years before. And out of that peaceful slumber he never woke again. His laborious and beautiful life had been the most enchanting of his fairy tales. It closed at last in honor and serenity. It will probably be centuries before Europe sees again a man in whom the same peculiar qualities of imagination are blended. She can never see one more blameless in his life, or inspired by an aim more delicate and guileless.

EDMUND GOSSE.

THE NIGHTINGALE

THE NIGHTINGALE WAS INDEED A GREAT SUCCESS.

THE NIGHTINGALE

IN China, you know, the emperor is a Chinaman, and all those he has about him are Chinamen. The story I am going to tell you happened many years ago, but just on that account it is worth hearing, before it is forgotten. The emperor's palace was the most magnificent in the world, built entirely of the finest porcelain. It was very costly, but so fragile that it would hardly stand being touched, so one had to be careful.

In the garden were to be seen the most wonderful flowers; to the most beautiful of them were fastened silver bells, which tinkled all the time, so that no one should pass by without noticing the flowers. Indeed, everything in the emperor's garden was cleverly thought out; and it was so big that the gardener himself did not know where it ended. If you kept on walking, you came to a most beautiful forest, with lofty trees and deep lakes. The forest went right down to the deep blue sea; great ships could sail right in under its branches, and in these lived a nightingale, which sang so exquisitely that even the poor fisherman, who had so many other things to attend to, would rest on his oars and listen to him when he went out at night to pull in his nets. "How beautiful it is!" he would say; but he had to look after his nets, and forgot the bird. Yet, when he was singing again next night, and the fisherman came there, he said the same thing: "How beautiful it is!"

Visitors came from all parts of the world to the emperor's city, and admired it, as well as the palace and the garden; but when they came to hear the nightingale, they all said: "He is the best of all!"

And on their return home they spoke of all they had seen, and the learned wrote many books about the city, the palace, and the garden, but they did not forget the nightingale, which they praised beyond everything; and those who could write poetry wrote the most beautiful poems, all about the nightingale in the forest by the deep blue sea.

These books went all over the world, and at last some of them reached the emperor. He sat in his golden chair and read and read; every moment he nodded his approval, for it pleased him to read the splendid descriptions of the city, the palace, and the garden. "But the nightingale is the best of all!" said the books.

"What's this?" said the emperor, "the nightingale! I don't know anything at all about him! Is there such a bird in my empire, and, fancy! in my garden, too. I have never heard of him. To think one has to find out such things from books."

And so he called his chamberlain, who was such a grand personage that when any one inferior to himself in rank ventured to speak to him or ask him a question, he only answered " P," and that really did not mean anything.

"There is, I hear, a most remarkable bird here, called a nightingale!" said the emperor; "they say he is the best thing in my great empire. Why have I never been told anything about him?"

"I have never heard him mentioned before," said the chamberlain; "he has never been presented at court——!"

"It is my wish that he shall appear here this evening and sing before me!" said the emperor. "It seems the whole world knows what I possess, and I know nothing about him!"

"I have never heard him mentioned before," said the chamberlain; "I shall look for him, I shall find him——!"

But where was he to be found? The chamberlain ran up and down all the staircases, through the halls and corridors; not one of those he met had heard of the nightingale; and the chamberlain ran back to the emperor again, and said it must all be a fable, invented by those who wrote the book. "Your Imperial Majesty must not believe all that is written. It is fiction, or what is called the black art!"

"But the book in which I have read it," said the emperor, "has been sent me by the great and mighty Emperor of Japan, and it cannot therefore be a falsehood. I will hear the nightingale! He must be here this evening! He shall have my most gracious patronage. And if he does not come, the whole of the court shall have their stomachs punched after they have had their supper!"

"Tsing-pe!" said the chamberlain, and again he ran up and down all the staircases, and through all the halls and corridors; and half the court ran after him, for they did not like the idea of having their stomachs punched.

And inquiries were made right and left after the wonderful nightingale which all the world knew of, but of which the court knew nothing.

At last they came across a poor little girl in the kitchen. She said: "Oh, yes! the nightingale! I know him well. How he can sing! Every evening they let me take home some leavings from the table for my poor sick mother, who lives down by the shore; and when I feel tired on my way back, and rest in the forest, I hear the nightingale sing. He brings tears to my eyes; it is just as if my mother was kissing me!"

"My little kitchen-maid," said the chamberlain, "I will get you a permanent place in the kitchen, and permission to see the emperor eat, if only you can take us to the nightingale. He has been commanded to appear at court this evening."

And so they all set out for the forest, where the nightingale used to sing, and half the court went with them. As they walked along a cow began lowing.

"Ah!" said one of the courtiers, "there he is! What wonderful strength for such a small creature to possess! I have certainly heard him before!"

"No, that's the cows lowing!" said the little kitchen-maid. "We are still far from the place."

Some frogs now began croaking in a pool.

"Beautiful!" said the palace-dean; "now I hear him; it sounds just like tiny church bells!"

"No, that's the frogs!" said the little kitchen-maid. "But I think we shall soon hear him!"

Just then the nightingale began to sing.

"There he is!" said the little girl. "Listen, listen! and there he sits!" and she pointed at a little gray bird up among the branches.

"Is it possible?" said the chamberlain; "I never imagined he would be like that! How common he looks! He must have lost his color at seeing so many grand folks here!"

"Little nightingale!" cried the little kitchen-maid quite loudly, "our gracious emperor

would like so much to hear you sing before him."

" With the greatest pleasure ! " said the nightingale, and began to sing in good earnest.

" It sounds like crystal bells," said the chamberlain ; " and how he does use his little throat !   It is most remarkable that we have never heard him before.   He will be a great success at court ! "

" Shall I sing once more before the emperor ? " said the nightingale, believing that the emperor was present.

" My excellent little nightingale ! " said the chamberlain, " I have great pleasure in commanding you to appear at a court festival this evening, where you shall enchant his Imperial Majesty with your charming singing ! "

" It sounds best in the greenwood," said the nightingale ; but he was quite willing to go when he heard that the emperor wished it.

At the palace everything had been polished and smartened up.   The walls and floors, which were all of porcelain, shone in the light of many thousands of golden lamps.   The most beautiful flowers with tinkling bells were placed along the corridors ; there was such a running to and fro, and such a draught, that all the bells were set tinkling, until at last one could not hear one's self speak.

In the middle of the great hall, where the emperor sat, a golden perch had been fixed, and on this the nightingale was to sit.   The whole court was present, and the little kitchen-maid had got permission to stand behind the door, for she was now a real kitchen-maid by title.   All were dressed in their best finery, and all were looking at the little gray bird, at which the emperor was nodding his head.

And the nightingale sang so beautifully that tears came into the emperor's eyes, and rolled down his cheeks, and then the nightingale sang still more beautifully ; his song went straight to every one's heart, and the emperor was so happy, and said that the nightingale should have his golden slipper to wear round his neck.   But the nightingale declined the honor with thanks ; he had already received sufficient reward.

" I have seen tears in the emperor's eyes," the nightingale said ; " that is the greatest reward you can give me.   An emperor's tears possess wonderful virtue.   Heaven knows I have been sufficiently rewarded ! " And so he sang again with his sweet, blessed voice.

" That 's the most lovely coquetry I know of ! " said the ladies all around ; and so they took water in their mouths so that they might make a warbling sound when anybody spoke to them, believing that they also were nightingales ; even the footmen and chamber-maids made it known that they too were satisfied — and that is saying a great deal, for they are the most difficult of all to please.   Yes, the nightingale was indeed a great success.

He was now to remain at court, to have his own cage, with liberty to take a walk twice a day, and once at night.   He had twelve footmen to attend upon him, all of whom had a silk ribbon which was fastened to his leg, and which they all held tightly. There was no pleasure at all in that kind of outing.

The whole city was talking of the wonderful bird, and when two of the inhabitants met, one would merely say "Nightin—," and the other "gale," and then they sighed and understood each other. Yes, the children of eleven buttermen were named after him, but not one of them could sing a note.

One day a large parcel arrived for the emperor, and on the outside was written: "Nightingale."

"Here we have a new book about our celebrated bird!" said the emperor; but it was not a book, it was a small mechanical toy, which lay in a box — an artificial nightingale, which had been made to look exactly like the living one, but was set with diamonds, rubies, and sapphires. As soon as the artificial bird had been wound up, it began to sing one of the songs of the real bird, while the tail moved up and down, sparkling with silver and gold. Around its neck hung a small ribbon on which was written: *The Emperor of Japan's nightingale is poor compared with the Emperor of China's.*

"It is beautiful!" exclaimed all; and he who had brought the artificial bird received at once the title of "Imperial Nightingale-Carrier-in-Chief."

"Now they must sing together! What a duet it will be!"

And so they had to sing together; but they did not get on well, for the real nightingale sang in his own way, while the artificial bird was dependent upon its barrels.

"It 's not its fault," said the musical director; "it keeps time beautifully, and sings quite in my style." So the artificial bird was to sing alone. It had just as much success as the real bird, and then it was so much prettier to look at; it glittered like diamond bracelets and brooches.

It sang the same piece thirty-three times over, and still it was not tired; the audience would have liked to hear it from the beginning again, but the emperor thought that the living nightingale ought also to sing a little — but where was he? Nobody had noticed that he had flown out through the open window, away into his green forest.

"But what 's the meaning of this?" said the emperor; and all the courtiers began abusing the nightingale, saying he was a most ungrateful creature.

"But we have the best bird after all!" they said; and so the artificial bird had to sing again, and they heard the same piece for the thirty-fourth time, but still they did not know it, for it was rather difficult to learn, and the musical director was loud in his praises of the bird; nay, he even protested that it was better than the real nightingale, not only as regards its attire, and its many beautiful diamonds, but also with regard to its internal arrangements.

"For you must know, ladies and gentlemen, and, above all, your

Imperial Majesty, that with the real nightingale you can never be sure of what is coming; but with the artificial bird everything has been arranged beforehand. So what is coming, will come, and nothing else. Everything can be accounted for; it may be ripped open and will show what human thought and skill can do; you may see how the barrels are placed, how they are worked, and how one thing is the result of another."

"That's exactly what we have been thinking!" they all said. And the musical director got permission to show the bird to the people on the following Sunday. "They should also hear it sing," said the emperor. And they heard it, and were as pleased as if they had got too merry on strong tea, for that's quite Chinese, you know. They all exclaimed, "Oh!" and held up their forefingers and nodded their heads; but the poor fisherman, who had heard the real nightingale, said: "It sounds pretty enough, and it is very like the other; but there's something wanting, I can't tell exactly what!"

The real nightingale was banished from the land.

The artificial bird was placed on a silk cushion close to the emperor's bed; all the presents which it had received, the gold and the precious stones, lay round about it, and its title had been raised to "Singer of the Imperial Toilet-table," to rank number One on the left side, for the emperor considered that the side nearest the heart was of most importance—for even an emperor has his heart on the left side.

And the musical director wrote five-and-twenty volumes about the artificial bird; they were very learned and long, and full of the most difficult Chinese words, and everybody said that they had read them and understood them, for otherwise they would, of course, have been stupid, and would then have had their stomachs punched.

In this way a whole year passed by; the emperor, the court, and all the other Chinamen knew by heart every little note in the artificial bird's song, but just on that account they liked it best; they could now join in the song themselves, which they did. The boys in the street sang "Ze-ze-ze! Cluck-cluck-cluck!" and the emperor sang the same.—Yes, it was really delightful!

But one evening, when the artificial bird was singing its best, and the emperor lay in bed listening to it, something inside the bird went "pop"; a spring had broken, and, "whir-r-r," round went all the wheels, and then the music stopped.

The emperor jumped out of bed at once and called for his physician; but how could he be of any help? Then they fetched the watchmaker, and after a great deal of talking and a long and careful examination he got the bird into something like order, but he said it must not be used so much, for the pinions were so worn — and it was not possible to put in new ones— that one could not be sure of the music. This caused a great deal of sorrow in the land. Only once a year did they venture to let the

THE EMPEROR FELT AS IF SOME ONE WAS SITTING ON HIS CHEST. HE OPENED HIS EYES,
AND THEN HE SAW IT WAS DEATH.

artificial bird sing, and that was almost too often; but then the musical director made a little speech, full of difficult words, and said it was just as good as ever — and so it was, of course, just as good as ever.

Five years had passed, when the whole of the country was threatened with a very great affliction, for the people were really fond of their emperor, and now he was ill, and it was said he was not expected to live.

A new emperor had already been chosen, and the people stood outside in the street and asked the chamberlain how it fared with their emperor.

"P!" he said, and shook his head. The emperor lay pale and cold in his large and gorgeous bed. All the court thought he was dead, and every one ran off to greet the new emperor; the footmen rushed out to gossip about it, and the chamber-maids gave a great coffee-party at the palace.

All the floors of the halls and the corridors had been covered with carpets, so that no footsteps should be heard, and therefore it was so silent, so quiet there. But the emperor was not dead yet; pale and stiff he lay in his splendid bed, with the long velvet curtains and the heavy golden tassels; high above, a window stood open and the moon shone in upon the emperor and the artificial bird.

The poor emperor could scarcely breathe; he felt as if some one was sitting on his chest. He opened his eyes, and then he saw it was Death, who was sitting on his chest and had put on his golden crown, and held in one hand the emperor's golden saber and in the other his gorgeous banner, while round about were strange faces peering forth from among the folds of the large velvet bed-curtains; some of them were horrible, others kind and gentle-looking — they were the emperor's evil and good deeds, which were looking at him, now that Death sat over his heart.

"Do you remember that?" whispered one after the other. "Do you remember that?" And then they told him of so many things that the perspiration stood out on his brow.

"That I never knew!" said the emperor. "Music, music! The big Chinese drum!" he cried, "so that I may not hear all they say!"

And they went on, while Death sat nodding just like a Chinaman to everything they said.

"Music, music!" cried the emperor. "You blessed, little golden bird! Sing, do sing! I have given you gold and precious things, I have myself hung my golden slipper round your neck. Sing, do sing!"

But the bird remained silent; there was no one to wind it up, and it could not sing until this was done; but Death kept on staring at the emperor with his great hollow eyes, and everything was so still, so terribly quiet around them.

Suddenly the most lovely song was heard close to the window; it was the little, living nightingale, which sat outside on a branch; he had heard of the emperor's illness, and had therefore come to sing to him of life and hope; and as he sang the specters grew paler and paler, the blood began to course more and more rapidly through the emperor's weak body, and Death himself listened and said: "Go on, you little nightingale, go on!"

"Yes, if you will give me that splendid golden saber! Yes, if you will give me that costly banner! Will you give me the emperor's crown?"

And Death gave each of the precious things for a song, and still the nightingale went on singing. He sang of the quiet churchyard, where the white roses grow, where the elder-tree perfumes the air, and where the fresh grass is moistened by the tears of those left behind; then Death began to long for his garden, and floated like a cold white mist out through the window.

"Thanks, thanks!" said the emperor. "You heavenly little bird, I knew you well! I banished you from land and realm, and yet you have driven away with your song the horrible visions from my bed, and Death from my heart! How shall I reward you?"

"You have rewarded me!" said the nightingale. "I drew tears from your eyes the first time I sang before you; I shall never forget that! Those are the jewels that bring joy to a singer's heart; but go to sleep now, and grow well and strong. I will sing to you."

And he sang—and the emperor fell into a sweet sleep; so gentle and refreshing was that sleep.

The sun was shining in through the windows at him, when he awoke hale and hearty; none of his servants had as yet returned, for they thought he was dead, but the nightingale still sat and sang.

"You must stay with me always!" said the emperor. "You shall only sing when you please, and the artificial bird I will break into a thousand pieces."

"Do not do that!" said the nightingale. "It has done what it could. Keep it as before. I cannot settle down and live in the palace; let me come when I like; I will then sit on the branch outside the window in the evenings and sing to you, so that you can be happy and be inspired with fruitful thoughts. I will sing to you about those who are happy and about those who suffer; I will sing about the good and the evil around you which are kept hidden from you, for the little song-bird flies far around to the poor fisherman, to the peasant's roof, to every one, far away from you and your court. I love your heart better than your crown, and yet the crown has a fragrance of sanctity about it!—I will come, I will sing to you!—But one thing you must promise me."

"Everything!" said the emperor, as he stood there in his imperial robes, which he had himself put on, pressing the golden saber to his heart.

"One thing I beg of you! Do not tell any one that you have a little bird that tells you everything, and then all will go still better with you!"

And then the nightingale flew away. The servants came in to look after the dead emperor — yes, there they stood, and the emperor said: "Good morning!"

THE JUMPERS

THE JUMPERS ARRIVE AT THE KING'S PALACE.

THE JUMPERS

THE flea, the grasshopper, and the spring-goose[1] once wanted to see which of them could jump highest, and so they invited the whole world and everybody else who might care to see that kind of sport. When the three entered the room, all thought they were splendid specimens of jumpers.

"Well, I'll give my daughter to the one who jumps highest!" said the king; "for it would look so mean to let these people jump for nothing!"

The flea stepped forward first; he had such nice manners and bowed on every side, for he had the blood of grand ladies in his veins, and had been accustomed to associate only with human beings, which means a great deal.

Next came the grasshopper; he was certainly very much bigger, but he bore himself fairly well for all that, and wore a green uniform, the one he was born with. Moreover, as he said, he was connected with a very old family in the land of Egypt, and was highly esteemed here at home.

[1] An old-fashioned toy formerly much used in Denmark. It is made from the breast-bone of a goose, and, with the aid of a peg, some string, and cobblers' wax, can be made to jump.

He had been taken straight from the fields and put into a house of cards, three storeys high, all made with court-cards, with the colored side turned in; there were both doors and windows, all cut out in the waist of the Queen of Hearts. " I sing so well," he said, "that, on hearing me, sixteen native crickets, that had been chirping since they were born, but never had a house of cards, fretted themselves even thinner than they were!"

Both the flea and the grasshopper were thus able to give a good account of themselves, and saw no reason why they should not marry a princess.

The spring-goose did not say anything; people said of him that he thought all the more, and as the palace-dog only sniffed at him, it was a

THE GRASSHOPPER JUMPED RIGHT ONTO THE KING'S FACE.

guarantee that the spring-goose was of good family. The old alderman, who had got three orders for holding his tongue, assured them that he knew the spring-goose possessed the gift of prophesying; one could tell by his back, whether the winter would be mild or severe, and that was more than you could see by the back of the man who writes the almanacs.

"Well, I sha'n't say anything!" said the old king; "but I generally go about and have my own opinion of things."

Everything now depended upon the jumping. The flea jumped so high that no one could see him, so they said he had not jumped at all, which was rather mean.

The grasshopper jumped only half as high, but he jumped right onto the king's face, which, the king declared, was most disagreeable.

The spring-goose stood still a long time, thinking to himself; the people at last began to believe that he could not jump at all.

"I only hope he isn't ill!" said the palace-dog, and sniffed at him again, when — wh'st! with a jump, a little sideways, he sprang right into the lap of the princess, who was sitting on a low, golden footstool.

Then the king said; "The highest jump is to jump at my daughter, for that's just the clever part of it. It requires brains to get an idea like that, and the spring-goose has shown that he has brains. He has a mind of his own!"

And so he got the princess.

" I jumped highest after all!" said the flea. " But it does n't matter! Let her keep that stuck-up bit of a goose with the peg and the cobblers' wax! I jumped highest, anyhow; but I find it is necessary in this world to have substance, if one is to be noticed!"

And so the flea went abroad and enlisted, and there they say he was killed. The grasshopper settled down in a ditch just outside, and pondered over the way things were really managed in this world, and he also said: " Yes, substance is the thing, substance is the thing!" And then he went on singing his own melancholy ditty; and it is from that we have taken this story, which may not be true, although it is printed.

THE SPRING-GOOSE SPRANG RIGHT INTO THE PRINCESS'S LAP.

THE TRAVELING COMPANION

JOHANNES LAY ON HIS KNEES BY THE BED AND KISSED HIS DEAD FATHER'S HAND.

THE TRAVELING COMPANION

POOR Johannes was in great distress, for his father was very ill and was not expected to live. There was no one in the little room but the two; the lamp on the table was on the point of going out, and it was getting late in the evening.

"You have been a good son, Johannes," said the sick father; "God will help you on in the world"; and he looked at him with his mild, earnest eyes, drew a deep breath and died—it seemed as if he had only gone to sleep. But Johannes wept; he had now no one dear to him in the whole world, neither father nor mother, sister nor brother. Poor Johannes! He lay on his knees by the bed and kissed his dead father's hand, and wept many bitter tears; but at last his eyes closed and he fell asleep with his head resting on the hard edge of the bedstead.

Then he dreamed a strange dream; he saw how the sun and the moon were courtesying to him and he saw his father hale and hearty again and heard him laugh, as he always laughed, when he was in really good humor. A beautiful maiden with a golden crown on her long, lovely hair, held out her hand to Johannes, and his father said: "Do you see what a lovely bride you have got? She is the most beautiful in all the world." Then he awoke and the beautiful vision vanished; his father lay dead and cold on the bed and poor Johannes was left all by himself!

The following week the dead man was buried and Johannes walked close behind the coffin. He could no longer see the kind father who had loved him so much; he heard how they shoveled the earth down upon the coffin, of which he could now only see the last corner, but the next shovelful of earth which was thrown down into the grave hid that also from his view, and then he felt as if his heart would break under the weight of his great sorrow. Around him they were singing a hymn; it sounded so beautiful, and the tears came into his eyes; he wept, and this was a relief to him in his distress. The sun shone brightly on the green trees just as if it wanted to say: "You must not be so sad, Johannes! Do you see how beautiful the blue sky is? Your father is now up there, and is praying to the kind God that it may always fare well with you."

"I will always be good," said Johannes, "and then I shall go to heaven to my father. What joy it will be when we see each other again! How much I shall have to tell him, and he will show me so many things and teach me all about the glories of heaven, just as he taught me here on earth. Oh, what a joy that will be!"

Johannes pictured it so vividly to himself that he smiled while the tears were still running down his cheeks. The little birds sat in the chestnut-trees, twittering: "quivit, quivit!" They were so pleased and happy, although they had come to the funeral, but they seemed to know that the dead man was in heaven, that he had wings larger and much more beautiful than theirs, and that he was now happy, for he had been a good man here on earth, and all this made them happy. Johannes saw how they flew away from the green trees far out into the world, and then he felt a longing to fly away with them also. But first he made a large wooden cross to put on his father's grave, and when he brought it there in the evening he found the grave was strewn with sand and decked with flowers; this had been done by people who, although strangers to him, had greatly respected his dear father, who was now dead.

Early next morning Johannes packed his little bundle and hid his whole inheritance, which consisted of fifty dollars and a couple of smaller silver coins, in his belt, with which he was now going to set out into the world. But first he went to his father's grave in the churchyard, repeated the Lord's Prayer and said: "Farewell, my dear father! I will always try to be a good man, and so you may well ask the kind God that it may go well with me!"

Out in the fields, through which Johannes passed, all the flowers were standing so fresh and lovely in the warm sunshine, and they nodded with the wind just as if they wished to say: "Welcome into the green fields! Isn't it beautiful here?" But Johannes turned round once more to have a look at the old church where he was christened when quite a little child, and where he had gone every Sunday with his old father to worship and sing hymns. Then, high up in one of the openings of the church tower, he saw the little brownie with his pointed red cap standing, shading his face with his uplifted arm, so that the sun should not shine in his eyes. Johannes nodded farewell to him, and the little brownie waved his red cap, laid his hand on his heart, and kissed his hand to him many times to show him that he wished him all possible good and a safe and prosperous journey.

Johannes then began to think of all the fine things he would now get to see in the great and glorious world, and walked on farther and farther, farther than he had ever been before; he did not know any of the towns through which he passed, or the people he met; he was now far away among strangers.

The first night he had to lay down and sleep under a haystack out in the fields; he had no other bed. But he thought it was quite grand;

the king could not have it much finer. The whole of the field with the rivulet, the haystack and the blue heavens above, made a most beautiful bedchamber. The green grass, with the little red and white flowers, was the carpet, the elder bushes and the wild rose hedges were bouquets of flowers, and for a wash-hand basin he had all the rivulet with the clear, fresh water, where the rushes courtesied to him and said both "Good evening" and "Good morning." The moon was a fine, big lamp, high up under the blue vault, without any risk of setting fire to the curtains. Johannes might sleep on in peace, which he did; he did not wake up till the sun rose and all the little birds were singing all around him: "Good morning! Good morning! Are you not up yet?"

The bells were ringing for church; it was Sunday. The people were on their way to hear the sermon and Johannes went with them, sang a hymn, and listened to the word of God; it seemed to him as if he were in his own church, where he had been christened, and had sung hymns with his father.

In the churchyard there were many graves, and on some of them the grass had grown high. Johannes then thought of his father's grave, which in time would look like these, now that he could not weed it and keep it in order. He sat down and plucked the grass from the graves, raised up the wooden crosses which had fallen down, and put back in their places the wreaths which the wind had blown away from the graves, for he thought: "Perhaps some one will do the same to my father's grave now that I cannot do it!"

Outside the churchyard gate stood an old beggar, leaning upon his crutch; Johannes gave him the small silver coins he had, and proceeded on his way, happy and pleased, into the wide world.

Toward evening the weather became terribly bad, and Johannes hurried on to get under shelter, but very soon the dark night set in; just then he at last reached a little church which lay quite by itself on the top of a hill. The door was fortunately ajar and he stole inside; here he would remain till the bad weather was over.

"I'll sit down here in a corner!" he said, "I am quite tired and sorely in want of a little rest!" And so he sat down, folded his hands and said his evening prayer, and in less than no time he was asleep and had begun to dream, while it thundered and lightened outside.

When he awoke it was midnight; the bad weather was over and the moon shone in upon him through the windows. In the middle of the aisle stood an open coffin with a dead man in it, for he had not yet been buried. Johannes was not afraid, for he had a good conscience, and knew that the dead do not harm anybody; it is living, wicked people who molest their fellow-creatures. Two such wicked men were standing close to the dead man, who had been placed inside the church before he was buried; they were evilly disposed toward him, and would not let him lie

in peace in his coffin, but wanted to throw him outside the church door
—poor, dead man!

"Why do you do that?" asked Johannes; "it is very bad and wicked!
Let him rest in Christ's name!"

"What nonsense!" said the two wicked men; "he has made a fool of
us! He owes us money, which he could not pay, and now that he is dead,
we shall not get a penny. Therefore we will have our revenge; he shall
lie like a dog outside the church door!"

"I have no more than fifty dollars," said Johannes, "that is the whole
of my inheritance; but I will willingly give you the money if you will
promise me on your honor to leave the poor dead man in peace. I shall
be able to get on without the money; I have strong and sound limbs, and
God will always help me."

"Well," said the horrible men, "if you will pay his debt, we shall not
do anything to him, that you may be sure of!" And so they took the
money that Johannes gave them, laughed quite loudly at his good-hearted-
ness and went their way; but Johannes put the dead body right again in
the coffin, folded its hands, took leave of it, and went away quite contentedly through the great forest.

Round about him, where the moon shone in between the trees, he
saw graceful little elves playing about quite merrily; they did not let themselves be disturbed, for they knew he was a good, unoffending creature.
It is only wicked people who are not allowed to see the elves. Some of
them were not bigger than one's finger, and had their long, golden hair
fastened up with golden combs; they were rocking, two and two, on the
large dewdrops, which had settled on the leaves and the long grass. Sometimes the dewdrops rolled off, when the elves would fall down between the
stalks of the long grass, and then there was a regular outburst of laughter
and merriment among the tiny little people. It was a rare frolic! They
were singing, and Johannes plainly recognized all the pretty songs which
he had learned when a little boy. Large and gaudy-colored spiders, with
silver crowns on their heads, were spinning from one hedge to another
long, hanging bridges and palaces which, when the fine mist settled on
them, looked like shining crystal in the clear moonlight. This lasted until the sun rose. Then the little elves crept into the flower buds, and the
wind caught hold of their bridges and palaces, which then sailed off
through the air like big cobwebs.

Johannes had just got out of the forest when a strong, manly voice
called out just behind him, "Hullo, comrade! Where are you going?"

"Out into the wide world," said Johannes. "I have neither father
nor mother; I am only a poor boy, but God will help me."

"I 'm also going out into the wide world," said the strange man.
"Shall we two keep each other company?"

"Yes, certainly!" said Johannes, and so they went on together. They soon came to like one another very much, for they were both good people. But Johannes found that the stranger was much wiser than he. He had been nearly all over the world, and could tell him about every possible thing in existence.

The sun stood high in the heavens when they sat down under a big tree to eat their breakfast. Just then an old woman came along the road. She was very old and walked quite bent, leaning upon a crutch, and carrying on her back a bundle of firewood, which she had gathered in the forest. Her apron was fastened up, and Johannes saw three big rods, made of ferns and willow-twigs, projecting from it. Just when she was quite close to them, her foot slipped; she fell and gave a loud scream, for she had broken her leg—the poor old woman.

Johannes proposed at once that they should carry her home to where she lived, but the stranger opened his bag, took out a jar and said he had a salve in it which could at once make her leg sound and well, so that she could walk home herself, just as if she never had broken it. But in return he wanted her to make him a present of the three rods she had in her apron.

"That's being well paid!" said the old woman, nodding her head quite strangely; she did not like very much to part with her rods; but on the other hand it was not very pleasant to lie there with a broken leg, so she gave him the rods, and as soon as he had rubbed the salve on her leg the old crone got on her legs and was able to walk even better than before. That was a proof of what the salve could do; but then it was not to be got at a chemist's either.

"What are you going to do with those rods?" asked Johannes of his traveling companion.

"They'll make three fine nosegays," said he, "just the sort I like, for I am a funny fellow, you know!"

And so they walked on for some distance.

"How the clouds are gathering!" said Johannes, pointing straight before them; "what awful, heavy clouds!"

THEY SAT DOWN UNDER A BIG TREE TO
EAT THEIR BREAKFAST

"No, they are not clouds," said his traveling companion, "they are mountains, beautiful, great mountains, where you can get high up above the clouds into the pure air! It is delightful, I can assure you! To-morrow we shall be a good bit on our way out into the world!"

They were not so near to them as they thought; they had to walk a whole day before they reached the mountains, where the dark forests grew straight up toward the heavens, and where there were stones as big as a whole town; it certainly was hard work to get right across them, and therefore Johannes and his traveling companion went into an inn to get a good rest and gather strength for the journey on the morrow.

Down in the large bar parlor in the inn a great many people were assembled, for there was a man there with a puppet-show; he had just put up his little theater, and the people sat all round the room to see the play, but right in front of all an old fat butcher had taken a seat, the best of all; his big bulldog (ugh! how fierce he looked) sat by his side and stared like everybody else.

Now the play began; it was a pretty piece with a king and a queen in it; they sat on a velvet throne and had golden crowns on their heads and long trains to their robes, which, of course, they could very well afford. The most beautiful wooden dolls with glass eyes and big mustaches were standing at all the doors, and were opening and shutting them, so that some fresh air could get into the room. It was a beautiful play, and it was not at all tragic, but just as the queen stood up and walked across the floor, the big bulldog,— goodness knows what he could have been thinking about,— but as he was not kept back by the fat butcher, he made a spring right on to the stage, seized the queen round her slender waist, and one could hear her going "crick-crack!" It was really terrible!

The poor man, who managed the whole show, became very frightened, and was so sorry for his queen, for she was the most beautiful doll he had, and now that ugly bulldog had bitten her head off; but afterward when the people had gone away, the stranger, who was in Johannes's company, said he would soon put her right, and so he brought out his jar and rubbed the doll with the salve, with which he helped the poor old woman that broke her leg. No sooner had the doll been rubbed than she was all right again; yes, she could even move all her limbs of her own accord; it was not at all necessary to pull her by the string; the doll was just like a living being, except that she could not speak. The man who owned the little puppet-show was greatly pleased; now he need not hold this doll at all by the string, for she could dance by herself. None of the other dolls could do that.

Afterward, when night came on and all the people had gone to bed, some one began to sigh so heavily, and continued sighing so long, that everybody got up to see who it could be. The man who had the show went to his little theater, for it was from there the sighing came. All

THE KING LED JOHANNES OUT INTO THE PRINCESS'S GARDEN. IN EVERY TREE HUNG THREE OR
FOUR SKELETONS OF PRINCES WHO HAD WOOED THE PRINCESS.

the wooden dolls lay mixed up together, the king and all his yeomen were sighing most pitifully, and staring with their big glass eyes, for they wanted so much to be rubbed a little, just like the queen, so that they too might be able to move about of themselves. The queen went down at once on her knees and held up her beautiful crown, while she begged: "Take it, oh, take it! But rub my consort and my courtiers!" The poor man who owned the theater and all the dolls could not help weeping, for

THE QUEEN WENT DOWN ON HER KNEES AND HELD UP HER CROWN, BEGGING, "TAKE IT, OH, TAKE IT!"

he really felt sorry for them; he promised the traveling companion at once that he would give him all the money he took at his show the next evening if he would only rub four or five of his finest dolls, but the traveling companion said he would not ask for anything but the big saber which the man wore by his side, and when he got it he rubbed six of the dolls, who at once began dancing, which they did so beautifully that all the girls, the real, living girls, who were looking on, took to dancing as well. The coachman and the cook, the footmen and the chamber-maid, and all the strangers danced; even the fire-shovel and the tongs wanted to join in the dance, but they toppled over at the very first jump they made — yes, it was indeed a merry sight!

Next morning Johannes and his traveling companion went away from all of them and continued their journey across the lofty mountains and through the large pine-forests. They got so high up that the church towers far down below them looked at last like small red berries among all the green, and they could see a long way off, for many, many miles off, far away to places where they had never been. Johannes had never before seen so much of the beauties of this lovely world all at once; the sun shone so warm through the fresh blue air, he heard the huntsmen blow their bugles among the mountains, so beautifully and gaily, that the tears came into his eyes with joy and he could not help saying: "I feel as if I could kiss you, dear Lord, because you are so kind to us all, and have given us all the loveliness there is in the world!"

The traveling companion also stood with folded hands, looking out over the forest and the cities that lay bathed in the warm sunshine. Just then they heard the most wonderful and lovely music over their heads; they looked up and saw a large white swan soaring above them in the air; it was very beautiful, and it sang as they never before had heard a bird sing; but the song grew fainter and fainter, the bird bent its head and dropped quite slowly down at their feet, where it lay dead — poor, beautiful bird!

"Two such beautiful wings," said the companion, "as white and large as those which this bird has, are worth a deal of money! I 'll take them with me! You can now see it was a good thing I took the saber!" and with one blow he cut off both wings of the dead swan, which he wanted to keep.

They now traveled for many, many miles across the mountains, till at last they saw before them a great city, with over a hundred steeples, which shone like silver in the sunshine. In the middle of the city was a splendid marble palace, with a roof of red gold, and here lived the king.

Johannes and his companion would not go straight into the city, but stopped at the inn outside it, so that they might make themselves tidy, for they wanted to look respectable when they got into the streets. The landlord told them that the king was such a good man, that he never did any injustice or harm to any one, either in one way or another, but as for his daughter — well, heaven preserve us, she was a very wicked princess indeed! Beauty she possessed enough, — no one could be more beautiful and fascinating than she, — but what good could that be? She was a wicked witch, who was the cause of so many handsome princes having lost their lives. She had given permission to all men to woo her; everybody might come and try his luck, whether he was a prince or a beggar, that did not matter as far as she was concerned; the suitor would only have to guess three things which she would ask him. If he guessed rightly she would marry him, and he should be king of the whole country when her father died; but if he could not guess the three things she would order him to be hanged or beheaded—so cruel and wicked was this beautiful princess! Her father, the king, was much distressed at all this, but he could not forbid her wicked proceedings, for he had once said he would have nothing at all to do with her love affairs; she might do just as she pleased. Every prince who came and tried his luck at guessing, in order to win the princess, was sure to fail, and so he was hanged or beheaded; they had all been warned in time, and, of course, they need not have gone a-courting. The old king was so grieved at all this misery and wretchedness that he lay on his knees a whole day every year with all his soldiers, and prayed that the princess might mend her wicked ways; but she was not at all in the humor for that! All the old women, who were fond of spirits, colored it quite black before they drank it. That was the way in which they mourned, and what more could they do?

"What a terrible princess!" said Johannes; "she really ought to be birched, that might do her some good. If only I were the old king, I would whip her till she was sore all over her body!"

Just then they heard the people outside shouting "hurrah!" The princess was on her way past the house; she was really so beautiful that everybody forgot how wicked she was, and therefore they cried "hurrah!" Twelve beautiful maidens, all dressed in white silk dresses and with golden tulips in their hands, rode by her side on coal-black horses. The princess herself had a snow-white horse, decked with diamonds and rubies; her riding habit was woven of pure gold, and the whip she held in her hand looked like a sunbeam. The golden crown on her head glittered as if it were set with small stars from the heavens, and her mantle was made of thousands of beautiful butterflies' wings, but nevertheless she herself was much more beautiful than all her clothing.

As soon as Johannes saw the princess his face became as red as blood, and he could scarcely utter a word, for the princess was the exact image of the beautiful maiden with a golden crown about whom he had dreamed the night his father died. He thought her so beautiful that he could not help falling in love with her. Surely it could not be true that she was a wicked witch who would hang or behead people if they could not guess what she was thinking about. "Everyone is allowed to woo her," he said, "even the poorest beggar. I will go up to the palace; I cannot help myself!"

They all said he should not do it; it was sure to go with him as with all the others. His traveling companion dissuaded him from it also, but Johannes thought he would be all right, so he brushed his boots and coat, washed his hands and face, combed his beautiful yellow hair, and went all by himself into the city and up to the palace.

"Come in!" said the old king, when Johannes knocked at the door.

Johannes opened it, and the old king in his dressing-gown and embroidered slippers came to meet him; he had the crown on his head and carried the scepter in one hand, and the golden apple in the other. "Wait a bit," he said, and put the apple under his arm, so that he could hold out his hand to Johannes. But as soon as he heard he was a suitor for his daughter's hand he began to cry so violently that both the scepter and the apple fell on the floor, and he had to dry his tears on his dressing-gown — poor old king!

"Do n't think of it," he said, "you 'll fare as badly as all the others. Now just come and see!" and so he led Johannes out into the princess's pleasure garden. There a terrible sight met his eyes. In every tree hung three or four princes, who had wooed the princess, but had not been able to guess what she had been thinking of. Every gust of wind made the skeletons rattle, so that the little birds were frightened away and never dared to come into the garden; all the flowers were fastened up to human bones, and in the flower-pots were placed grinning skulls. That was certainly a strange garden for a princess.

"Here you can see!" said the old king, "it will fare with you as with all the others you see here. Let it therefore be! You really make me unhappy, for I take it so much to heart!"

Johannes kissed the hand of the good old king and said that things would come all right, for he was very much in love with the lovely princess.

At this moment the princess herself came riding into the palace yard with all her ladies; they therefore went out to meet her and say "Good morning" to her. She was really very beautiful; she held out her hand to Johannes, who now could not help loving her more than ever; she could not be the cruel, wicked witch that all the people said she was. They all went into the hall, where little pages offered them sweetmeats and ginger-nuts, but the old king was so distressed that he could not touch anything at all; besides, the ginger-nuts were too hard for him.

It was then arranged that Johannes should come up to the palace again next morning; the judges and the whole council would then be assembled and hear how clever he was at guessing. If he got on well the first time, he was to come twice more, but as yet no one had ever succeeded in guessing right the first time, and so they lost their lives.

Johannes was not at all anxious as to how he would fare; he was quite pleased and only thought of the beautiful princess, and believed firmly that God would help him, but how, he did not know, nor did he want to think of it either. He went dancing along the high road on his way back to the inn, where his companion was waiting for him.

Johannes never tired of telling him how nice the princess had been to him and how beautiful she was; he was already longing greatly for the next day, when he was to go to the palace and try his luck at guessing.

But his companion shook his head and was greatly troubled. "I am very fond of you!" he said, "we might still have kept together for a long time, and now I am going to lose you already! Poor, dear Johannes! I could almost cry, but I will not disturb your happiness on the last evening, perhaps, we are to be together. We will be merry, quite merry! To-morrow when you are gone, I can cry!"

All the people in the city had soon got to know that a new suitor for the princess's hand had arrived, and there was therefore great sorrow among

THE TRAVELING COMPANION FLEW BEHIND THE PRINCESS AND KEPT ON WHIPPING HER
WITH HIS ROD.

them. The playhouse was closed, all the women who sold cakes and sweets in the streets tied black crape round their sugar-pigs, and the king and the parsons lay on their knees in the church; there was such lamenta-tion, for Johannes would surely not fare better than all the other suitors.

In the evening the traveling companion brewed a large bowl of punch and told Johannes that now they were going to be really merry and drink the health of the princess. But when Johannes had drunk two glasses, he became so sleepy that it was not possible for him to keep his eyes open, and at last he fell asleep. His companion then lifted him quite gently from the chair and laid him on the bed, and when it was quite dark he took the two large wings which he had cut off the swan, tied them fast to his shoulders, and the biggest rod which he had got from the old woman who fell and broke her leg, he put in his pocket; he then opened the window and flew over the city straight to the palace, where he hid himself in a corner up under the window which led into the princess's bedchamber.

Everything was quiet all over the town; the clock now struck a quarter to twelve, the window was opened and the princess, with long black wings on her shoulders and dressed in a large white cloak, flew away over the city to a great mountain; but the traveling companion, who had made himself invisible so that she could not see him, flew behind her and kept on whipping her with his rod till there were actually signs of blood where he had struck her. Ugh! what a journey through the air! The wind caught hold of her cloak so that it spread out on all sides just like a big sail on a ship, and the moon shone through it.

"How it hails! How it hails!" the princess said at every blow she got from the rod, and well she deserved them all. At last she reached the mountain and knocked for admission. There was a rumbling sound like the roll of thunder, and then the mountain opened and the princess went in. The traveling companion followed her, for no one could see him as he was invisible. They went through a great long passage where strange lights were seen sparkling on the walls; over a thousand glowing spiders were running up and down the walls, shining like fire. They then came to a great hall, built of silver and gold; red and blue flowers as large as sun-flowers shone from the walls, but no one could pluck any of these flowers, for the stems were horrible poisonous snakes, and the flowers were fiery flames, which blazed out of their mouths. The whole of the ceiling was covered with shining glow-worms and azure blue bats, which were flapping away with their thin wings; it was quite a wonderful sight. In the middle of the hall was a throne, supported by the skeletons of four horses with harness made of red, fiery spiders; the throne itself was of milk-white glass, and the cushion for sitting on consisted of little black mice biting each other's tails. Above it was a canopy of rose-colored spiders' webs, studded with beautiful little green flies, which sparkled like diamonds. On the throne sat an old troll with a crown on his ugly head and a scepter in his hand. He kissed the princess on the forehead and let her sit by his side on the costly throne, and then the music began. Great black grasshoppers played on Jews' harps, and the owl struck herself on the stomach, for she had no drum. It was a funny concert! Little brownies with will-o'-the-wisps in their caps danced round the hall. Nobody could see the traveling companion; he had taken a place just behind the throne and could hear and see everything. The courtiers, who now came into the hall, looked nice and grand enough, but any one with his wits about him could see what they really were. They were nothing more or less than broomsticks with cabbage heads on their ends to which

JOHANNES UNTIED HIS HANDKERCHIEF AND SHOWED THE PRINCESS THE UGLY HEAD OF THE TROLL.

the troll had given life, as well as their embroidered clothes.   But this did not matter much after all, for they were only used for show.

After there had been some dancing the princess told the troll that she had got a new suitor, and asked therefore what she should think of for the suitor to guess when he came to the palace next morning.

"Just listen," said the troll, "I 'll tell you something.   You must think of something very easy, for then he won't guess it at all!   Think of one of your shoes.   He won't guess that.   Then have his head cut off, but don't forget when you come here to-morrow night to bring his eyes with you, for I want to eat them!"

The princess courtesied quite low, and said she would not forget the eyes.   The troll then opened the mountain for her and she flew home again, but the traveling companion followed behind and whipped her so hard with the rod that she groaned heavily at the severe hailstorm, as she thought, and made all the haste she could to get back to her bedchamber through the window, but the traveling companion flew back to the inn, where Johannes was still asleep, took off his wings and lay down on his bed, for he might well be tired.

It was quite early in the morning when Johannes awoke; his companion also got up and told him he had had a very wonderful dream in the night about the princess and one of her shoes, and he therefore begged Johannes to be sure to ask her if she might not have been thinking of one of her shoes.   For that was what he had heard from the troll in the mountain, but he would not tell Johannes anything about that; he begged him only to ask if she had been thinking of one of her shoes.

"I may as well ask about one thing as another," said Johannes; "it may be quite true what you have dreamt, for I always believe that God will be sure to help me!   But still I will say farewell to you, for if I guess wrong I shall never see you any more!"

They then kissed each other and Johannes went into the city and thence straight to the palace.   The whole hall was filled with people; the judges sat in their easy chairs, with eider-down cushions at the back of their heads, for they had so much to think about.   The old king stood up and dried his eyes with a white handkerchief.   The princess now entered the hall; she was still more lovely than the day before and greeted everybody in the most friendly manner, but to Johannes she gave her hand and said: "Good morning to you!"

Johannes was now to guess what she had been thinking of.   Goodness, what a kind look she gave him!   But no sooner had she heard him say the one word "shoe," than she turned as pale as death and trembled all over; but that could not help her, for he had guessed right.

My gracious!   How glad the old king was!   He turned a somersault that made every one stare, and all the people clapped their hands at him and Johannes, who had now guessed right the first time.

The traveling companion was beaming with delight when he got to know how successful Johannes had been; but Johannes folded his hands and thanked God, who, no doubt, would also help him on the second and third occasions.   Next day the guessing was to begin again.

In the evening things happened in just the same way as on the previous one.   When Johannes was asleep, the traveling companion flew behind the princess to the mountain and birched her still more than on the last occasion, for now he had taken two of the rods with him.   No one saw him, while he heard everything.   This time the princess was going to think of her glove, and this he told to Johannes, just as if it had come to him in a dream.   Johannes was thus once more able to guess right, and there were in consequence great rejoicings at the palace.   The whole court began turning somersaults, just as they had seen the king do on the first day, but the princess lay on a sofa and would not speak a word.   All now depended on whether Johannes could guess right the third time.   If all went well he would have the beautiful princess and inherit the whole kingdom when the old king was dead; if he guessed wrong he would lose his life, and the troll would eat his beautiful blue eyes.

The evening before the third trial Johannes went early to bed, said his prayers, and slept quite peacefully; but his companion fastened the wings to his back, and the sword to his side, and took all the three rods with him and flew off to the palace.

The night was pitch dark and a storm was raging, so that the tiles flew off the houses, and the trees in the garden, on which the skeletons were hanging, swung to and fro like reeds before the wind; every moment there were flashes of lightning and the thunder rolled as if in one continuous clap which lasted the whole of the night.   The window was now thrown open and the princess flew out; she was as pale as death, but she laughed at the bad weather and thought it was not bad enough; her white cloak whirled round in the air like a large sail, but the traveling companion whipped her so hard with his three rods that the blood trickled down on the ground, and at last she was scarcely able to fly any farther.   But at length she got to the mountain.

"It is hailing and blowing," she said; "never have I been out in such weather."

"Yes, one can have too much of a good thing," said the troll.   The princess then told him that Johannes had guessed right again the second time; if he should succeed again the next day he would win, and she would never be able to come to him in the mountain any more, and never be able to try her hand at witchcraft as before; and therefore she was quite distressed in her mind.

"He shall not guess it," said the troll; "I will think of something that has never entered his head, or else he must be a greater troll than I.   But now we will make merry!"   And so he took the princess by both hands, and they danced round with all the little brownies and will-o'-the-wisps in the room; the red spiders ran quite merrily up and down the walls, and the fiery flowers seemed to throw out sparks of fire. The owl beat the drum, the crickets chirped, and the grasshoppers played on the Jews' harp. It was, indeed, a merry ball!

After they had danced enough, the princess had to think of getting home, or else she might be missed at the palace. The troll said he would go with her, and they would then be together for a little while longer. So away they flew in the bad weather, while the traveling companion lashed their backs with all his three rods till they were worn into shreds; never before had the troll been out in such a hail-storm. Outside the palace he said farewell to the princess and whispered to her at the same time: "Think of my head"; but the traveling companion heard it sure enough, and just at the moment when the princess was slipping through the window into her bed-chamber, and when the troll was going to turn back, he seized him by his long black beard, and with his saber cut off the ugly head of the troll close to the shoulders, so quickly that the troll did not even see him. The body he threw into the sea to the fishes, but the head he only dipped into the water and then tied it up in his silk handkerchief, took it with him home to the inn and lay down to sleep.

Next morning he gave Johannes the handkerchief, but told him that he must not open it till the princess asked him what she was thinking of.

There were so many people in the large hall of the palace that they were standing up against one another like radishes tied up in a bundle. The council sat in their chairs with their soft cushions, and the old king had put on new clothes, and the gold crown and scepter had been polished up, till everything looked quite grand; but the princess was quite pale and wore a coal-black dress, as if she were going to a funeral.

"What have I been thinking of?" she said to Johannes, who at once untied the handkerchief and became quite frightened himself when he saw the ugly head of the troll. All the people shuddered, for it was a terrible sight, but the princess sat like an image in stone, and could not utter a single word. At last she rose and gave Johannes her hand, for he had now guessed right enough. She did not look at anybody, but sighed quite deeply: "Now you are my master! This evening we will celebrate our wedding!"

"That's what I like!" cried the old king, "that's what we like to see!" All the people shouted "hurrah!" the military band played in the streets, the bells were rung, and the women who sold cakes took the black crape off their sugar-pigs, for now there was joy in the land. Three whole roasted oxen, filled with ducks and fowls, were placed in the middle of the market-place, where every one might cut a piece for himself; the fountains ran with the finest wine, and all who bought a penny cake at the bakers' got six large buns into the bargain, and they were buns with raisins in them.

In the evening the whole town was illuminated, and the soldiers fired salutes with guns and the boys with percussion caps, and there was eating and drinking, and clinking of glasses, and a running about at the palace, and a long way off one could hear them singing:

> So many pretty girls I see,
> All ready for a swing about,
> The drummer's march they wait with glee;
> Come, fair one, trip it in or out,
> Trip it and dance — ankle and knee —
> Till shoe and sole part company.

But the princess was still a witch, and did not at all care for Johannes. This the traveling companion was aware of, and he therefore gave Johannes three feathers from the swan's wings and a little bottle with a few drops of some liquid in it, and told him that he should let a large tub, filled with water, be placed near the bridal bed, and when the princess was about to get into bed he should give her a gentle push so that she should fall into the water, and he should then duck her three times, after having first thrown in the feathers and the drops from the little bottle, and she would be freed from the spell of witchcraft she was under and come to love him very much.

Johannes did all that his companion had advised him to do. The princess screamed loudly when he ducked her under the water, sprawled about in his grip, and was turned into a large coal-black swan with flashing eyes; the second time, when she came up above the water, the swan had become white, with the exception of a single black ring round the neck. Johannes muttered a pious prayer and ducked the bird for the third time under the water, and the next moment it was changed into the most beautiful princess. She was more lovely than ever, and she thanked him with tears in her beautiful eyes for having freed her from the spell of the troll.

Next morning the old king and the whole court came to offer their congratulations, which lasted till far into the day. Last of all came the traveling companion; he had his stick in his hand and his knapsack on his back. Johannes kissed him many times and asked him not to go away; he must remain with him, for he was the cause of all his good fortune. But the traveling companion shook his head and said in a kind and friendly tone: "No, my time is now up. I have only paid my debt to you. Do you remember the dead man whom the wicked men wanted to disturb? You gave everything you possessed that he might have peace in his grave. The dead man was I!"

And the next moment he was gone. The wedding lasted a whole month. Johannes and the princess loved one another very much, and the old king lived to see many happy days, and he let his wee little grandchildren ride on his knee and play with his scepter; but Johannes was king over the whole country.

THE MONEY-PIG

THE MONEY-BOX WAS MADE IN THE SHAPE
OF A PIG, AND HAD THE USUAL
SLIT IN ITS BACK.

THE MONEY-PIG

THERE was such a lot of toys in the nursery; on the top of the chest of drawers stood the money-box. It was made of clay in the shape of a pig, and had the usual slit in its back, but this slit had been made bigger with a knife, so that silver dollars could also be put into it; two of these had already passed through, besides many other kinds of money. The money-pig was so stuffed that he could not rattle any longer, and that is the highest a money-pig can attain to. There he stood on top of the chest of drawers and looked down upon everything in the room; he knew well enough that with what he had in his stomach he could buy the whole lot of them, and that's what is called having confidence in oneself.

The other toys thought the same, although they did not say so; there were other things to talk about. The top drawer was partly open, and there a large doll appeared; she was rather old, and had had her neck riveted. She looked round and said: "Shall we play men and women? It 'll be something for a change." And then there was a commotion! Even the pictures on the wall turned themselves round; they knew that they had another side as well, but they did not turn round just for the sake of contradicting.

CRASH! THERE HE LAY ON THE FLOOR, ALL IN BITS AND PIECES, WHILE THE MONEY ROLLED ABOUT.

It was midnight; the moon shone through the window and provided lighting for nothing. Now the fun was going to begin; everything in the room had been invited, even the perambulator, which, after all, only belonged to the commoner kind of toys. "Everyone is good enough in his own estimation," it said; "we cannot all be of noble birth! Somebody must make himself useful, as they say."

The money-pig was the only one who got a written invitation; he stood too high, they all thought, to hear them if they spoke to him. He did not send word, either, whether he was coming, for he did not turn up. If he was to take any part in it he would have to enjoy it up there from his own point of view. They would make their arrangements accordingly, and so they did.

The little toy-theater was at once placed so that he could look straight into it; they wanted to begin with a play, and afterward there were to be tea and mental exercises, but they commenced with the latter. The rocking-horse talked about training and thoroughbreds, the perambulator about railways and steam power—all of which were matters connected with their occupations, and which they could discuss. The parlor clock talked about politics—tick-tick! it knew the time of the day, but it was said that it did not go correctly. The bamboo cane stood there, proud of its ferrule and silver button, because it was mounted both at top and toe; in the sofa lay two embroidered cushions; they looked very pretty and stupid.

And then the play was to begin.

All were seated and looked on; they had been requested to rap, crack, and rattle, according as they were pleased. But the riding-whip said he would never rap to old people, only to those who were not engaged to be married.

"I'll crack to all and everything!" said the percussion cap. "One has to be in some place, after all!" thought the spittoon; this was the kind of thoughts they had in their minds as they sat at the play. The piece was not of much account, but it was well performed; all the actors turned their colored side to the audience, for they had only been made to be seen on the one side and not on the other. They all played excellently; they came right out in front of the stage; their strings were too long, but this made them all the more noticeable. The doll with the riveted neck became so excited that the rivets got loose, and the money-pig became so excited in his way that he made up his mind to do something for one of them, to put him in his will as the one who should be publicly buried with him, when the time came.

It was such a treat that they gave up tea and went on with mental exercises, which they called playing men and women, and there was no harm in that, for they were only playing—and everyone was thinking about himself and what the money-pig thought; but the money-pig's thoughts went farthest, for he was thinking about his will and burial and when it would come to pass—always sooner than you expect it! Crash!—and there he lay on the floor, all in bits and pieces, while the money danced and rolled about; the smaller pieces whirled round and round, and the bigger ones rolled along the floor, particularly one of the silver dollars, who wanted to see the world in earnest. And so he did, and so did all the rest; the pieces of the money-pig were thrown into the pail, but next day on the top of the chest of drawers stood a new money-pig of clay; as yet there was not a penny in him and so he could not rattle. In this respect he was like the other, and this was at any rate a beginning, so with this we will come to an end.

THE GALOSHES OF FORTUNE

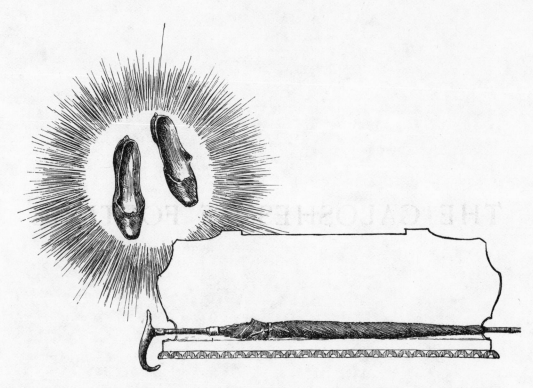

THE GALOSHES HAD THE PROPERTY OF INSTANTLY TRANSPORTING ANY ONE WHO
PUT THEM ON, TO WHATEVER PLACE, OR TIME, HE WISHED.

THE GALOSHES OF FORTUNE

I. THE BEGINNING

IN Copenhagen, in one of the houses in Östergade, not far from Kongens Nytorv,[1] a large party was being given; for you know you must have a party now and then, and then you are done with it, and can expect to be invited in return.

One half of the company already sat at the card-tables, and the other

---

[1] A large public square in the center of Copenhagen. Östergade is the principal thoroughfare leading from it.

half were waiting to see what would be the result of the remark of the lady of the house: "Well, we must now think of something!"

So far they had got, and the conversation was carried on as best it could. Amongst other things it turned on the Middle Ages. Some considered that period of far greater interest than our times, and Mr. Knap, the councilor, defended this opinion so warmly, that the hostess at once took his side, and both declaimed against Professor Örsted's words in the almanac about old and modern times, in which our age is given the preference.

The councilor looked upon the times of King Hans[1] as the most delightful and happy of all.

During this discussion, which was not interrupted except for a moment by the arrival of the newspaper, in which there was nothing worth reading, we will betake ourselves to the anteroom, where the coats and cloaks, umbrellas, and galoshes had been left.

Here were sitting two maids, one young and one old; one might have thought they had come to fetch their mistresses, some old maiden lady or widow, but if one looked at them a little closer one would soon have seen that they were not ordinary servant-girls; their hands were too delicate, their movements were too stately for that, and their clothes were of quite a peculiar, bold cut. They were two fairies; the youngest was not Fortune herself, but lady's maid to one of the ladies of the bed-chamber, who distributes the smaller gifts of fortune. The older looked very austere; she was Care, who, in her own exalted person, always goes her own errands, for then she knows they will be properly executed.

They were telling one another where they had been that day; she, who was the messenger of Fortune, had only been on some unimportant errands; she had, she said, saved a new hat from a shower of rain, had procured an honest man a bow from some grand nonentity, and such like, but what she had still to perform was something quite unusual.

"I must tell you," she said, "it is my birthday to-day and in honor of it I have been intrusted with a pair of galoshes which I am to give to the world. These galoshes have the virtue of instantly transporting any one who puts them on, to that place or that time in which he would prefer to be; and every wish with regard to place and time will at once be fulfilled, so that mankind will at last be happy down here!"

"So you may think!" said Care. "I think they will be very unhappy and will bless the moment they get rid of the galoshes."

"Whatever do you mean?" said the other fairy. "I will now place the galoshes near the door, and some one will put them on by mistake, and will thus become the fortunate one!"

This was the conversation they held.

[1] 1481 — 1513.

II. WHAT HAPPENED TO THE COUNCILOR

It was late. Councilor Knap, deep in meditation on the times of King Hans, was on his way home, but fate had so ordained it that instead of his own galoshes, he had put on the galoshes of fortune, in which he now stepped out into Östergade. By the magic power of the galoshes, however, he was now put back to the days of King Hans, and his feet went right into the mire and mud of the street, for in those days the streets were not paved.

THE COUNCILOR SAW A LARGE FIELD BEFORE HIM, WITH A FEW BUSHES HERE AND THERE, AND A BROAD STREAM FLOWING THROUGH IT.

"How terribly dirty the street is!" said the councilor. "The whole pavement has vanished and all the lamps are out!"

The moon had not yet risen high in the sky, and the weather was somewhat misty, so that everything around him was buried in the darkness. At the next corner, however, hung a lantern in front of an image of the Madonna, but it gave hardly any light; the councilor only discovered it when he stood just under it, and his eyes fell upon the painted picture of the Mother and the Child.

"That 's probably some traveling show," he thought, "where they have forgotten to take in the sign."

A couple of men in the dress of the period passed him by.

"What curious clothes they wear! They must be coming home from a masquerade."

Suddenly there came the sound of fifes and drums, and flaming torches threw a bright light around; the councilor stopped and saw a wonderful procession coming toward him. First of all came a band of drummers, who were beating their drums right merrily, and after them followed halberdiers with bows and cross-bows. The most important person in the procession was a man of clerical appearance. The councilor asked in astonishment what it all meant and who that person might be.

"The Bishop of Zealand!" was the answer.

"Good gracious, what can the bishop be up to?" said the councilor with a sigh, shaking his head. "Surely it could not be the bishop!" Pondering on thus, and without looking to the right or the left, he walked along Östergade and crossed Höibro-place. The bridge to the open place in front of the palace was not to be seen; he caught a glimpse of a low-lying bank of a river, and came finally to two men who were sitting in a boat.

"Does your honor want to be ferried across to the island?" they asked.

"Across to the island?" said the councilor, who did not know, of course, in what period he was now moving. "I have to get to Lille Torvegade, out at Christianshavn."

The men stared at him.

"Only tell me where the bridge is!" he said. "It is a disgrace that the lamps are not lighted here, and it is as dirty and muddy as if one were wading in a bog!"

The longer he talked to the boatmen, the more unintelligible they appeared to him.

"I can't understand your Bornholm jargon!" he said at last in an angry voice, and turned his back upon them. He could not find the bridge, and there was no sign of a railing. "It is a scandalous state of things!" he said. Never had he been so disappointed with his existence as this evening. "I think I'll take a coach," he thought. But where were the coaches? Not one was to be seen. "I shall have to go back to Kongens Nytorv; there must be some coaches there, otherwise I shall never get out to Christianshavn!"

He then set off through Östergade and had almost got to the end of it, when the moon made her appearance.

"Good gracious! What scaffolding is that they have put up here?" he exclaimed when he saw the eastern gate, which at that time stood at the end of Östergade.

At last he found a wicket and through this he got out to what is now our Kongens Nytorv, but which at that time was a large field, with a few bushes here and there. A broad canal or stream flowed through the field, and on the opposite bank stood some miserable wooden huts used by the skippers from Halland in Sweden, after whom the place was called Hallandsaas.

"Either I see a Fata Morgana, as they call it, or I am tipsy!" wailed the councilor. "What can this be? What can this be?"

He turned back again, in the full belief that he was ill. When he

IT WAS ONE OF THE TAVERNS OF THOSE DAYS. A NUMBER OF PEOPLE, CONSISTING OF
SKIPPERS, CITIZENS, AND LEARNED PERSONAGES WERE SITTING THERE.

got into the street he looked more closely at the houses; most of them were built of timber and plaster, and many had only thatched roofs.

"No, I am not at all well!" he sighed, "and I drank only one glass of toddy, but it does not agree with me. Besides, it was very wrong to give us toddy and hot salmon; I shall just mention it to Madame. I wonder if I should go back and tell them how I feel? But it would look so bad, and they may have gone to bed."

He began looking for the house, but it was not to be found.

"This is really terrible! I cannot recognize Östergade. There is not a shop to be seen. Only old, miserable shanties, just as if I were in Roskilde or Ringsted. Alas, I am ill! It's no use being timid. But where in all the world is the house? It is no longer the same. But the people are still up. Oh, I must be quite ill!"

He then pushed against a half-open door, through which the light shone out. It was one of the taverns of those days, a kind of beer-house. The room had the appearance of the Holstein parlors, and a number of people, consisting of skippers, Copenhagen citizens, and a couple of learned personages, were sitting there in deep discourse over their mugs, and paid little attention to the councilor who came in.

"I beg your pardon," said the councilor to the landlady, who came toward him; "I have been taken very ill. Can you get me a coach to Christianshavn?"

The woman looked at him and shook her head, whereupon she spoke to him in the German language. The councilor thought she did not understand Danish, and therefore repeated his request in German; this and his dress confirmed the woman in her belief that he was a foreigner. She soon understood that he was ill, and gave him a jug of water, which was brought from the well and was somewhat brackish in taste.

The councilor rested his head on his hand, drew a deep breath, and wondered at all the strange things around him.

"Is that this evening's 'Daily News'?" he asked for the sake of saying something, as he saw the woman move a large sheet of paper.

She did not understand what he meant, but handed him the paper; it was a wood-cut, representing a Fata Morgana seen in the ancient city of Cologne.

"It is very old," said the councilor, and he became quite cheerful at coming across such an ancient print. "How did you become possessed of this rare copy? It is very interesting, although it is altogether a fable. We explain such aërial visions as being Northern lights which they have seen; probably they are produced by electricity."

Those who sat nearest to him and heard his remarks, looked at him in surprise, and one of them rose to his feet, took off his hat respectfully, and said, with the most serious expression: "You are surely a very learned man, monsieur!"

"Oh, no," answered the councilor; "I can only discuss things in general, as one ought to do."

"*Modestia* is a great virtue," said the man, "otherwise I must say to your speech *mihi secus videtur*, yet will I here willingly suspend my *judicium*."

"May I ask whom I have the pleasure of speaking with?" asked the councilor.

"I am a baccalaureus in the Holy Writ!" answered the man.

This answer was sufficient for the councilor; the title corresponded to the dress in this case. "He must be an old village schoolmaster," he thought, "a quaint old fellow, such as one can still find over in Jutland."

"This is no *locus docendi*," the man began, "yet I would ask you to condescend to speak. You are, no doubt, deeply versed in the classics?"

"Yes, indeed," answered the councilor; "I like to read old instructive books, but I also like the modern ones, except 'Every-day Stories,' of which we have enough in real life."

"'Every-day Stories?'" asked our baccalaureus.

"Yes, I mean the new romances we have."

"Ah!" said the man, with a smile, "they are very entertaining, and are read much at court; the king is especially fond of the romance of 'Sir Iffven and Sir Gaudian,' which treats of King Arthur and the Knights of the Round Table; he has had many pleasantries over it with his noble lords."[1]

"I have not yet read that," said the councilor, "it must be quite a new book, which Heiberg has published."

"No," said the man, "it is not published by Heiberg, but by Godfred von Ghemen!"

"Oh, is that the author?" said the councilor; "it is a very old name. Why, it is that of the first printer Denmark ever had!"

"Yes, he is our first printer," replied the man; and so the conversation went on fairly well. One of the good citizens then spoke about the terrible plague which had raged a couple of years before, referring, of course, to the plague of 1484; the councilor thought they spoke about the cholera,[2] and so the discourse went on quite satisfactorily. The freebooter expedition of 1490 was of such recent date, that they could not help referring to it; the English freebooters had seized the ships in the roadstead, they said, and the councilor, who had made a special study of the events of 1801,[3] joined in quite appropriately with his denunciations of the Eng-

---

[1] Holberg tells in his "History of Denmark" that King Hans, one day when he had been reading the romance of King Arthur, was jesting with the well-known Ove Rud, of whom he was very fond. "Sir Iffven and Sir Gaudian, of whom I read in this book," said he, "must have been remarkable knights. Such knights we do not have any more nowadays!" To this Ove Rud answered: "If there were many such kings as King Arthur, there would also be many knights like Sir Iffven and Sir Gaudian."

[2] Copenhagen was visited by a terrible outburst of cholera in 1831.

[3] When the English fleet under Sir Hyde Parker, Lord Nelson, and others, defeated the Danish fleet in the roadstead of Copenhagen.

lish. The rest of the conversation, however, did not proceed so well; every moment it gave rise to misunderstandings on both sides; the old baccalaureus was very ignorant, and the simplest observations of the councilor appeared to him too bold and too fantastic. They stared at each other, and when matters became too complicated, the baccalaureus spoke in Latin, thinking he would be better understood, but it was of no use.

"How do you feel now?" asked the landlady, pulling the councilor by the sleeve. He now came back to his senses, for while he had been talking he had forgotten what had taken place before.

"BLESS ME!" SAID THE COUNCILOR, "HAVE I BEEN LYING HERE IN THE STREET, DREAMING?"

"Gracious goodness! where am I?" he exclaimed, feeling quite giddy at the thought of it.

"We'll have some claret! And some mead and some Bremen beer!" cried one of the guests, "and you shall drink with us!"

Two girls came into the room; one of them had on a cap of two colors. They poured out the drink and courtesied; the councilor felt a cold shudder down his back.

"What does this mean? What does this mean?" he asked; but he had to drink with them. The men paid every attention to the good councilor, who was in despair, and when one of them told him that he was tipsy, he did not at all doubt the man's words; he only asked them to get him a droshky, and then they thought he spoke Russian.

Never before had he been in such rough and vulgar company. "One would think the country had gone back to heathen times," he said to himself; "this is the most terrible moment of my life!" Just then it struck him that he would stoop down under the table and creep across to the door and try to get away, but just as he had got to the door the others discovered what he was about; they seized him by the legs, when luckily for him the galoshes came off, and—with that the whole spell was broken.

The councilor saw quite plainly a lamp burning brightly just in front of him, and behind it a large house. He recognized it as well as the house next door to it. It was Östergade, such as we all know it; he was lying with his feet toward a gateway and opposite to him sat the night watchman asleep.

"Bless me! Have I been lying here in the street, dreaming?" he said. "Yes, this is Östergade! How delightfully light and bright! It is terrible to think how one glass of toddy could have affected me!"

Two minutes afterward he sat in a carriage, which drove him to Christianshavn, thinking of the anxiety and anguish he had gone through, and praised with all his heart the happy reality—our own times—which, with all their shortcomings, were far better than the period of which he had just had a glimpse; and that, I think, was very sensible of the councilor.

III. THE WATCHMAN'S ADVENTURE

"Why, here's a pair of galoshes!" said the night watchman. "They must belong to the lieutenant who lives up there. They are lying close to the gate!"

The honest man would gladly have rung the bell and left the galoshes, for there was still a light to be seen in the house, but he did not like to awaken the other people in the house, and so he let it be.

"It must be very warm to have a pair of these things on!" he said. "How soft the leather is!" He put them on and they fitted him exactly. "What a funny world this is! Now there's the lieutenant, he might lie in his warm bed, but do you think he does? No, he will keep pacing up and down the room. Ah, he is a happy man! He has neither wife nor youngsters! Every evening he goes out to some party. I only wish I were he, then I should be a happy man!"

The moment he uttered this wish the magic power of the galoshes he had put on took effect; the watchman passed over into the lieutenant's body and mind. There he stood, up in the room, holding between his fingers a small rose-colored paper, on which was a poem, written by the lieutenant himself; for who has not, at some time or other in his life, been in the mood to write poetry, and if you then write down your thoughts, then you have the verses. On this paper was written:—

WERE I BUT RICH!

Were I but rich! This was my constant prayer
When scarce an ell in length — without a care.
Were I but rich, a captain I would be,
With saber, plume, and coat so brave to see.
Then came the day when fortune smiled on me:
A captain was I — but a poor man still!
For such was heaven's will.

THE WATCHMAN SAT DOWN AGAIN AND BEGAN NODDING. HE HAD STILL THE
GALOSHES ON HIS FEET.

In youth's first flash I sat at eventide,
A sweetheart maid of seven by my side;
For I had many fairy tales to tell,
And legends rare; but as for wealth — ah, well!
She cared not but for elf or goblin's spell.
Then was I rich, but not — heaven knows! — in gold,
    Or silver coins untold.

Were I but rich is still my prayer to heaven.
Though now grown tall, I love the maid of seven,
So good is she, so sweet, so fair to see.
Would that she knew my heart's wild fantasy!
Would that she, as of yore, could care for me!
But I am poor, and so my lips are sealed,
    My love is unrevealed.

Were I but rich in comfort and repose,
My pain I would not to the world disclose.
If you, my love, can understand, then read
This as a mem'ry of the past. Yet heed!
'T were best, perhaps, your heart were hard indeed!
I 'm poor, alas! my future dark and drear,
    But may God bless you, dear!

Yes, these are the kind of verses one writes when one is in love, but a sensible man does not let them get into print. Lieutenant, love, and poverty form a triangle, or perhaps, rather, the one half of the broken die of fortune. The lieutenant himself felt this keenly, and therefore leaned his head against the window frame and sighed deeply.

"The poor watchman in the street is far happier than I! He does not know what I call privation! He has a home, a wife, and children, who weep with him in his sorrows and rejoice with him in his joys! Oh, I should be happier than I am, if I could change places with him, for he is much happier than I am!"

At the same moment the watchman became again a watchman, for it was through the galoshes of fortune that he had become the lieutenant, but then, as we have just heard, he felt still less contented, and preferred to be what he really was. So the watchman was a watchman once more.

"It was a terrible dream, but funny enough!" he said. "I thought I was the lieutenant up there, and I did not like it at all. I missed the wife and the youngsters, who are always ready to hug me to death!"

He sat down again and began nodding; he could not quite get rid of the dream, and he still had the galoshes on his feet. Just then a falling star shot across the heavens.

"There it goes!" he said, "but there are plenty more. I should like to have a look at those little things a little nearer, especially the moon, for she is not likely to slip through one's fingers. The student for whom my wife does the rough washing, says that when we die we fly from one planet to the other. That 's a story, but it would be great fun, if it were true. I wish I could just take a little leap up there, and my body could remain here on the steps!"

There are certain things in the world one has to be careful about saying, but one ought to be still more careful if one has got the galoshes of fortune on one's feet. Just listen what happened to the watchman.

As far as we human beings are concerned, nearly all of us know the great speed which can be obtained by steam; we see it on the railways and on the steamers crossing the seas. Yet the speed thus obtained is like the pace of the sloth or the snail compared with the rapidity with which light travels; it flies nineteen million times faster than the best race-horse. And yet electricity is still more rapid. Death is an electric shock which we receive in the heart, and on the wings of electricity the liberated soul flies away. A ray of sunlight takes eight minutes and some seconds for its journey over ninety-five millions of miles; with the express speed of electricity a soul needs some minutes less to do the same journey. The distance between the planets is no greater for the soul than the distance between the houses of friends in the same town, even if they are quite close to one another. But this electric shock to the heart costs us the use of our body here below, unless, like the watchman, we happen to have the galoshes of fortune on our feet.

In a few seconds the watchman had traversed the distance of two hundred and fifty thousand miles to the moon, which, as we know, is of a much lighter substance than our earth, and as soft as new-fallen snow, as we might say. He found himself on one of the numerous circular mountains which we know from Dr. Mädeer's large map of the moon. I suppose you have seen this? Inside the ring the mountain formed a caldron with steep sides, about five miles deep; at the bottom of the caldron lay a town, which had the same appearance as the white of an egg poured into a glass of water, with towers, and cupolas, and galleries, like waving sails, all transparent and floating in the thin air. Our globe floated like a large fiery ball above his head.

There were many beings to be seen, most probably what we should call human beings, but they looked quite different to us; they had a language of their own, but although no one could expect the watchman's soul to understand it, it did so for all that.

The watchman's soul understood the language of the inhabitants of the moon very well. They discussed about our globe, and explained their doubts as to its being inhabited; the air there, they said, must be too thick for any sensible dweller on the moon to live in. They considered that the moon alone was inhabited by living beings, and was, after all, the only globe on which the ancient peoples of the planets had ever lived.

But we will have a look at Östergade, and see how the body of the watchman fares.

He sat lifeless on the steps; his pipe had fallen out of his hand, and his eyes were staring up at the moon after his honest soul, which was roaming about there.

"What 's o'clock, watchman?" asked a passer-by. But no answer came from the watchman, and the passer-by pulled his nose quite gently; the body lost its balance and fell full length on the ground — the man was dead to all appearance. The stranger, who had pulled the watchman's nose, was greatly frightened — the watchman was dead, and dead he remained. The matter was reported to the authorities, and early in the morning the body was removed to the hospital.

The watchman's soul would have had anything but an easy task if it had come back and — as in all possibility it would have done — had looked for the body in Östergade, but without finding anything. Most likely it would first have inquired at the police-station, and afterward proceeded to the office of the "Public Advertiser" to advertise for it among lost articles, and finally to the hospital. It may, however, be some comfort to us to know that the soul is at its best when it acts by itself; the body only makes it stupid.

As has already been mentioned, the watchman's body was removed to the hospital, where it was brought into the cleansing room, and the first thing they did was, of course, to pull off the galoshes, when the soul had to return to the body; it made straight for it, and all at once there was life in it. The watchman assured everybody that he had passed the most terrible night in his life; not if he were paid half a dollar would he go through the same experience again, but now it was happily all over.

He was discharged the same day, but the galoshes were left at the hospital.

IV. A HEAD IN DIFFICULTY. A RECITATION.
A MOST UNUSUAL JOURNEY

Every inhabitant of Copenhagen knows what the entrance to the Frederiks Hospital is like, but as some non-residents in all probability may read this story, we will give a short description of it.

The hospital is separated from the street by a very high railing, the solid iron bars of which are so wide apart, that, as the story goes, some of the very thin students have squeezed themselves through and paid their little visits into the town. The part of the body which was found most difficult to get through was the head, and consequently the small heads were here, as is often the case in this world, the most lucky.

This will suffice as an introduction.

One of the young students, of whom we need only say that he had a big head, was on duty this evening; the rain was pouring down, but in spite of these two obstacles he must try to get out, if only for a quarter of an hour. He did not think it was worth while to take the lodge-keeper into his confidence, when he could slip between the bars.

There lay the galoshes which the watchman had forgotten — he little thought they were the galoshes of fortune — they would come in very handy in this weather, and so he put them on. The question was now whether he could squeeze himself through the bars, a thing he had never tried before.

There he stood. "I wish I could get my head through!" he said, and the next moment his head, big as it was, slipped easily and safely through the bars, all thanks to the galoshes. He had still to get his body through, but there he stood in a fix.

"I'm too fat!" he said; "I thought my head would have been the worst! I sha'n't be able to get through."

He then attempted to pull back his head quickly, but all of no avail. He could move his neck comfortably, but that was all. His first feeling was one of anger, next he felt his spirits sinking below zero. The galoshes of fortune had brought him into this terrible fix, and unfortunately he never thought of wishing himself free; he only tried to extricate himself, but was not able to move from the spot. The rain was pouring down, and not a living being was to be seen in the street. He could not reach the bell; how was he to get loose? He foresaw that he might be kept there till the early morning, when they would have to send for a smith to get the bars filed through, but that would take some time, and in the meantime the boys of the Blue School opposite would be about and stirring, and all the inhabitants of Nyboder[1] would be passing and see him standing in the pillory; there would be such a crowd of people as had not been seen since the giant agave was shown last year.

"Ugh! the blood is rushing to my head! I shall go mad! Yes, I

The sailors' quarter in Copenhagen.

am going out of my mind! Oh, that I were free again! I should then be all right."

That is what he should have said sooner, for the very next moment after he had expressed the wish, his head was free, and he rushed back quite dazed with the fright the galoshes of fortune had given him.

We must not imagine that this was the end of the matter, no — there were worse things still to come.

The night passed and the following day as well, but no messenger came for the galoshes.

In the evening an entertainment was to be given in the little theater in Kannike lane. The house was crammed; among the recitations was a new poem, which we will listen to. The title was:—

GRANNY'S SPECTACLES

My Granny's wisdom's known to great and small;
In olden days, I have no doubt at all,
They would have burned her for a witch. For she
Knows everything that happens; she can see
Right into next year—aye, and farther, too;
But, tell you *all* she knows—no, that she will not do.
I wonder what will happen here next year!
The great events I'd like to see—to hear
All that's in store for me, for Art, for King,
And Country; but, alas! one cannot bring
My Granny to disclose such things as these.
Yet one day I did plague her so, and tease,
That she relented, after I had got
A scolding (for she loves me!) which was rather hot!

"For once your wish I'll gratify," said she,
And handed me her spectacles. "Now see!
You must find out a place—no matter where—
A place where many people go, and there
Stand where you best can overlook the throng.
Put on my glasses; then you'll see ere long
The people like a pack of cards laid out.
From them you may foretell the future without doubt."

I thanked my Granny, and ran off to see
If I could find where that strange place could be.
"Where many people go?" The Promenade?
'T is chilly there! The High Street's quite as bad,
And muddy too! The Theater, then? Why, this
Is just the thing for me—an evening's bliss!
Well, here I am! I first salute all here.
Permit me through my Granny's "specs" to peer,
That I may see—no, do not run away!—
If like a pack of cards you look. I may

Foretell the future thus.   Do you assent?
No answer!   Then your silence is consent.
By way of recompense, with you I'll share
The hidden secrets which the wondrous cards lay bare.

Now we shall see what fate the cards foretell
For you, for me, for King and Country.   Well!
                              (*He puts on the spectacles.*)
Yes, it's quite true!—Ah, that's a funny sight!
I only wish that you could see it quite
As well as I!   But what a lot of beaux,
And Queens of Hearts!   Of these there are long rows,
The black ones over there are Clubs and Spades—
I soon shall see them all, both men and maids!
The Queen of Spades, I see, has only eyes
For one, the Knave of Diamonds—a prize!
Oh, this inpection makes my head turn quite!
There's such a heap of money here to-night,
And strangers, too, from far across the seas!
Yes, but we do not wish to know such things as these
Of Nobles and of Commons!—Well, "The Times"—
But that I must not breathe of in my rhymes!
To injure that great paper I've no wish,
So I'll not take the best bone from the dish!
The theater, then?   The latest play?   But no!
The manager's my friend; 't is better so!

The future that awaits me?   Ah! one's fate
Concerns oneself: one learns it soon or late.
What's this I see?   In truth, I hardly know;
You'll see it when it happens.   On I go!
Who's happiest among us here just now?
That I can tell you easily.   I trow
The happiest is——.   No, it might embarrass,
And possibly the others it might harass!
Well—will this gentleman live longer than
The lady?   That 't were ruder still to scan!
Shall I, then, tell of——? No! of——? No! of——? No
Of——?   Ah!   I hardly know myself what I should show!
So easy 't is to wound, I'm quite put out.
Yet wait!   I'll tell you what you think about
My powers of prophecy—no pains I'll spare!
You think—I beg your pardon?   Everywhere
You think that, as my promise I have broke,
My undertaking only ends in smoke.
And so I hold my peace, most honored sirs and dames;
I'll own you may be right—but trust that no one blames.

The poem was excellently recited, and the reciter met with a great
success.   Among the audience was the student from the hospital, who
appeared to have forgotten his adventure of the night before; he had

put on the galoshes because they had not been called for, and as the streets were very dirty he thought they would be of great service to him.

He liked the poem very much.

The idea took his fancy; he thought he would like to have a pair of spectacles of that sort; if one used them properly one might perhaps look right into people's hearts. That would really be more interesting, he thought, than to see what was going to happen next year, for one was sure to get to know that—but about the other matter one could never get to know anything. "I can just imagine to myself all the gentlemen and ladies in the front row. If one could only look straight into their hearts!—there would, of course, have to be some opening to see through, as if you were looking into a shop. How my eyes would like to roam about in these shops!

"In yon lady's heart I should no doubt find a large millinery establishment! The next lady's is empty, but it would be none the worse for a little cleaning; but there are sure to be some shops of stability! Alas, yes!" he sighed, "I know of one where everything is genuine, but there is already a shopman there, and he is the only useless thing in the whole shop!

"From some of them I should hear, 'Please walk in!' Yes, I should like to step inside, just as a beautiful, fleeting thought passes through the heart!"

This was sufficient for the galoshes; the student disappeared altogether, and a most unusual journey began through the hearts of the spectators in the front row. The first heart he entered was that of a lady, but he thought he had suddenly been transported to an orthopædic institution, which they call the place where the doctors take away human deformities and make people straight; he was in the room where the plaster casts of the deformed limbs hang on the walls, but with this difference, that at the insti-tution the casts are taken when the patients arrive, but in this heart they were taken and preserved after the worthy people were gone. They were the casts of female friends, their bodily and mental defects, which were here preserved.

He quickly passed into another female heart; this appeared to him like a large sacred church, where the white dove of innocence was hovering over the high altar. He would gladly have gone down on his knees, but he had to proceed farther on his way to the next heart. He still heard the tones of the organ, and felt as if he himself had become a new and better man, and was worthy to enter the next sanctuary, which showed him a poor garret with a sick mother; but through the open window shone God's warm sun, and from the little wooden box on the roof hung lovely roses, while two azure blue-birds sang of the joys of childhood, and the sick mother prayed for blessings on her daughter.

He next crept on all fours through a well-stocked butcher's shop: it was meat and nothing but meat he came across; it was the heart of a rich, respectable man, whose name was sure to be found in the directory.

He then entered the heart of this man's wife: it was an old dilapitated dove-cote; the husband's portrait was used as a weather-cock, which was connected with the doors in such a way that they opened and shut as the husband veered round.

Afterward he entered a glass cabinet, like the one we have in Rosenberg Castle, only the glass magnified everything to an incredible degree. In the middle of the floor sat a Dalai Lama, the insignificant "I" of the person surprised at seeing his own greatness.

Then he fancied himself in a narrow needle-case, full of sharp needles, and he could not help thinking it must be the heart of an old maid; but that was not the case; it was quite a young officer, with many orders, a man of spirit and heart, as they said.

The poor student came out of the last heart in the row in quite a confused condition; he was not able to collect his thoughts and could only believe it must have been his too vivid imagination which had run away with him.

"Good gracious!" he sighed, "I must have a tendency to madness! Besides, it is insufferably hot in here! the blood is rushing to my head!" And now he remembered his great adventure of the previous evening; how his head had stuck fast between the iron railings of the hospital. "That 's where I must have caught it!" he thought. "I must do something at once. A Russian bath would be a good thing. I wish I were lying on the uppermost shelf of one."

And so he found himself lying on the uppermost shelf in a vapor bath, but he was lying with all his clothes on, in his boots and with the galoshes on; the hot drops of water from the ceiling were dripping onto his face.

"Ugh!" he cried, and sprang down from the shelf to get a shower-bath. The attendant uttered a loud cry on seeing a person with all his clothes on in the bath.

The student had, however, sufficient presence of mind to whisper to him: "It is a wager"; but the first thing he did when he got to his own room was to get a large blister on the back of his neck, and another down his back, in order to draw out the madness. Next morning his back was quite raw; and that was all *he* gained by the galoshes of fortune.

V. THE TRANSFORMATION OF THE CLERK

In the meantime the watchman, whom we are not likely to have forgotten, bethought himself of the galoshes, which he had found and taken with him to the hospital; he called there for them, but as neither the lieutenant nor anybody else living in the street would own them, he took them to the police station.

"They look exactly like my own galoshes!" said one of the clerks in the office, looking at them and placing them beside his own. "It requires more than a shoemaker's eye to know one pair from another!"

A constable now came in with some papers for the clerk, who turned round to talk to him; but when he had done with him and again looked at the galoshes, he was quite uncertain whether it was the pair on the left or on the right which belonged to him. "It must be the soiled ones that are mine!" he thought; but he was mistaken, for they were the galoshes of fortune; besides, why should not the police be mistaken sometimes? He put on the galoshes, stuck some papers in his pocket and some others under his arm; he had to take them home to read them through and copy them. But it happened to be Sunday morning, and as the weather was fine he thought that a walk as far as Frederiksberg would do him good; and off he went.

No one could be a more steady and diligent person than this young man. We hope he will enjoy his little walk; it will do him a great deal of good after so much sitting. At first he only walked on without thinking of anything, and the galoshes had therefore no opportunity of showing their magic power.

In the avenue he met an acquaintance, a young poet, who told him that he was going to set out on his summer trip next day.

"So you are off again!" said the clerk; "you are a lucky man to be so free. You can fly wherever you like, while we others are chained by the foot!"

"But the foot is fixed to the tree that gives you bread," said the poet. "You need not trouble for the morrow, and, when you grow old, you get a pension.

"But you are best off," said the clerk; "to sit and write verses is a pleasure. The whole world says pleasant things to you, and, besides, you are your own master. You should try sitting in court and attending to the trivial matters there."

The poet shook his head, and the clerk shook his also; each of them stuck to his own opinion, and so they parted. "They are a peculiar race of people, these poets!" said the clerk; "I should like to enter into such a nature, to become a poet myself. I am sure I should not write such whimpering verses as the others do! This is truly a spring day for a poet! The air is so wonderfully clear, the clouds are so magnificent, and the trees and greensward smell so sweet. Ah! I have not felt like this for many years!"

We can already notice that he had become a poet; not that it was noticeable in his appearance, for it is foolish to suppose that a poet is different from other people, among whom you may find far more poetical natures than in many of the great poets we recognize. The difference is simply that the poet has a better intellectual memory; he can retain the idea and the feeling till they are clearly and plainly embodied in words, which the others cannot do. But to be transformed from a commonplace nature to a more highly gifted one is always a wonderful transition; and that is what happened to the clerk.

"What a delicious fragrance!" he said; "how it reminds me of the violets at Aunty Loue's! Ah! I was a little boy then! Bless me, I have not thought of that for many a day! The good old lady! She lived just behind the Exchange. She always kept a twig or a couple of green shoots in water, no matter how severe the winter was. The scent of the violets pervaded the whole room, while I put hot copper pennies against the frozen window-panes to make peep-holes.

"What an interesting view it was! Out in the canal lay the ice-bound ships, quite deserted by their crews; a screaming crow was the only living creature on board. But when the spring came, a busy life began; amid singing and cheering the ice was sawed in pieces, the ships were tarred and rigged, and set sail for foreign lands; but I remain here, and must always remain sitting here in the police office, and see others taking out their passports to go abroad. That's my lot, alas, alas!" he sighed deeply, but stopped suddenly. "Bless me, what is the matter with me? I have never thought or felt like this before. It must be the spring air. I feel both anxious and happy."

He felt in his pocket for his papers. "These will give me something else to think about," he said, and let his eyes wander over the first page. "'Sigbrith, an Original Tragedy in Five Acts,'" he read. "What's this?— and it's in my own handwriting! Have I written this tragedy? 'The Intrigue on the Ramparts, or the Day of Prayer'—a vaudeville. Where can I have got this from? Somebody must have put it in my pocket! Why—here's a letter!" It was from the manager of the theater; the plays were rejected, and the letter was not at all politely worded. "H'm, h'm!" said the clerk, and sat down on a bench; his imagination was all alive, and his heart was quite tender; unconsciously he seized hold of one of the nearest flowers; it was a simple little daisy; the flower told him in a minute what would take a botanist many lectures to explain. It told him about the myth of its birth, about the power of the sunlight, which expanded its delicate leaves and made it so fragrant. He then thought of the struggles of life, which likewise awaken feelings in our hearts. Light

"THE UPPER WINDOW IS OPEN," SAID THE CANARY. "FLY! FLY AWAY!"

and air courted the flower, but light was the favored one; it leaned toward the light; if this vanished the flower rolled its leaves together, and went to sleep embraced by the air. "It is the light which adorns me," said the flower; "but the air gives you the breath of life!" whispered the voice of the poet.

Close by stood a boy, striking with his stick into the muddy ditch; the drops of water spurted up amongst the green branches, and the clerk thought of the millions of invisible animalcules in the drops which were cast so high in the air, that in proportion to their size it would be the same as if we were whirled up high above the clouds.

As the clerk thought of this, and the great change that had taken place in him, he smiled and said: "I must be asleep and dreaming. It is most remarkable in any case. How naturally one can dream, and at the same time know it is only a dream! I wish I could remember it to-morrow, when I wake up; just now I seem to be quite unusually fit for anything. I can see everything so clearly, and feel so wide awake and bright, but I am sure that if I recollect anything of it to-morrow, it will only be nonsense; I have experienced it before. It is just the same with all the wise and splendid things one learns and says in dreams, as with the gold of supernatural beings, when you receive it, it is bright and sparkling, but by daylight it is only stones and withered leaves. Alas!" he sighed, quite sadly, looking at the birds that were singing and hopping from branch to branch, "they are far better off than I. To fly — that must be a splendid gift of nature — happy is he who is born with it! Yes, if I were to wish to change into anything, it would be into a little lark."

At the same moment the tails and sleeves of his coat grew into wings, his clothes turned into feathers, and the galoshes into claws. He noticed this quite plainly, and laughed to himself: "Well, now I can see I am dreaming. But never have I dreamed anything so foolish before"; and he flew up among the green branches and began to sing; but there was no poetry in his song, for the poetical nature was gone. The galoshes, like every one who does his business thoroughly, could only do one thing at a time; he wanted to be a poet, and he became one; now he wanted to be a little bird, but on changing into this his former characteristics disappeared.

"This is very funny indeed!" said he. "In the daytime I sit in the police office among the most voluminous documents, and at night I dream I am flying about as a lark in Frederiksberg Garden; one could write quite a comedy about it."

He then flew down into the grass, turned his head from one side to the other, and struck his beak at the pliant blades of grass, which, in proportion to his present size, appeared to him as large as the branches of the North-African palms.

The next moment everything around him became as black as the darkest night; it seemed to him as if some enormous object had been thrown over him. It was a large cap which a boy from Nyboder had thrown over the bird; a hand was pushed in under the cap, and the clerk was seized round the back and wings so that he squeaked. In his first fright he cried aloud: "You impudent whelp! I am a clerk in the police office!" But to the boy it only sounded like "tweet, tweet!" He gave the bird a tap on its beak and walked off with it.

In the avenue he met a couple of school-boys of the better class, that is to say, as far as their station in life was concerned, but as regards intellect, they belonged to the lowest class in the school. They bought the bird for fourpence, and in this way the clerk was brought back to Copenhagen to a family which lived in Gothers Street.

"It is a good thing that I am dreaming," said the clerk, "otherwise I should become quite angry. First I was a poet, now I am a lark. Ah! it was that poetical spirit in me that transformed me into this little creature. It is a wretched state of affairs, especially when one falls into the hands of boys. I should like to know how all this is going to end."

The boy took him into a very elegant room; a stout smiling lady received them, but she was not at all pleased at the common field-bird, as she called the lark, being brought into the house; still she would allow it just for one day, but they would have to put the bird into the empty cage over by the window. "Perhaps it will please Polly," she said, smiling at a large green parrot which was swinging majestically on her ring in the pretty brass cage. "It's Polly's birthday," she said, in her foolish, naïve way, "and the little field-bird has come to congratulate her."

Polly did not answer a single word, but went on swinging to and fro in her majestic way; but a pretty canary, which had been brought there last summer from his warm, balmy home, began to sing loudly.

"You squealing thing!" said the lady, and threw a white handkerchief over the cage.

"Tweet, tweet!" sighed the bird, "what a terrible snowstorm!" and settled down in silence with a sigh.

The clerk, or the field-bird, as the lady of the house called him, was put in a little cage close to the canary and not far from the parrot. The only sentence which Polly could scream out, and which often came in most comically, was: "Come, let us be human!" Everything else she screamed was as unintelligible as the twittering of the canary; but not to the clerk, who was now himself a bird; he understood his comrades very well.

"I used to fly under the green palms and the blossoming almond-tree!" sang the canary. "I used to fly with my brothers and sisters over the gorgeous flowers and over the crystal lake, where the plants waved to and fro. I also saw many beautiful parrots who told me the funniest stories, ever so long and ever so many."

"But they were wild birds!" answered the parrot, "they had no education. No, come, let us be human! Why don't you laugh? If our mistress and all the strangers can laugh at it, why don't you do so as well? No, come, let us be human!"

THE NEXT MOMENT HE WAS THE CLERK ONCE MORE, BUT HE FOUND HIMSELF
SITTING ON THE TABLE IN HIS ROOM.

"Do you remember the pretty girls, who danced under the awning near the blossoming trees? Do you remember the sweet fruits and the cooling juice of the wild plants?"

"Oh, yes!" said the parrot, "but I am much better off here! I have good food, and am treated in the most friendly way; I know I have a good head, and want for nothing more. Come, let us be human! You have the soul of a poet, as they call it; I have sound knowledge and wit. You possess genuis, but no discretion; you indulge in those high natural tones of yours, and therefore they cover you up! They dare not treat me like that! Oh, no, I cost them a good deal more! I impress them with my beak and can crack a joke. Wit! wit! wit! Come, let us be human!"

"Oh, for the warm and balmy land of my birth!" sang the canary. "I will sing about your dark, green trees, about your calm bays, where the branches kiss the bright surface of the water; I will sing about the joys of my resplendent brothers and sisters, where the cactus grows."

"Do stop those whimpering tones!" said the parrot. "Say something that'll make one laugh. Laughter is a sign of the highest intellectual development. Can a dog or a horse laugh? No, they can weep, but it is only given to man to laugh. Ho, ho, ho!" laughed the parrot, adding his witty saying: "Come, let us be human!"

"You little gray Danish bird," said the canary, "you, too, are a prisoner! It must be cold in your forests, but you have liberty there, at any rate! Fly away! They have forgotten to close your cage, and the upper window is open. Fly! Fly away!"

And the clerk did so, and the next moment he was out of the cage; just then the half-open door, leading to the next room, creaked, and the cat with its green, glistening eyes crept stealthily into the room and started in pursuit of him. The canary fluttered in its cage and the parrot flapped its wings and screamed: "Come, let us be human." The clerk was in a terrible fright, and flew away through the window and over the houses and streets, till at last he was obliged to rest a little.

The house opposite seemed familiar to him; the window stood open, he flew in. It was his own room. He perched on the table. "Come, let us be human!" he said, mimicking the parrot without thinking of what he said; and the next moment he was the clerk once more, but he found himself sitting on the table.

"Good gracious!" he said, "how did I get up here and fall asleep in this way! That was an uneasy dream I had! What a lot of silly nonsense it was."

VI. THE BEST THING THE GALOSHES BROUGHT

Early in the morning of the following day, as the clerk still lay in bed, there came a knock at his door; it was his neighbor on the same floor, a theological student, who came into the room.

"Will you lend me your galoshes?" he asked, "it's so wet in the garden, but the sun is shining brightly and I should like to smoke a pipe down there!"

He put on the galoshes and soon found himself in the garden. There was only a plum-tree and a pear-tree, but even such a small garden is greatly prized in Copenhagen.

The student walked up and down the path; it was only six o'clock; he heard the horn of the mail coach in the street.

"Ah, to travel! to travel!" he exclaimed, "after all, that is the most delightful thing in the world! That is the highest goal of my ambition! Then all this restlessness which I feel would subside. But I must go far, far away! I should like to see beautiful Switzerland, to travel in Italy, and—"

It was a good thing that the galoshes began to apply their magic power at once, or else he would have gone too far away altogether, both for his own convenience and ours. He was now on his travels, in the midst of Switzerland, packed together with eight other people inside a diligence, his head ached, he felt a weary pain in his neck, and his feet, which were swollen and pressed by his boots, had gone to sleep. He was in a half-sleeping, half-waking condition. In his right-hand pocket he had his letter of credit, and in his left-hand pocket his passport, and in a small leather bag, which he wore on his breast, some louis d'or were sewed up; every time he dozed off, he thought that one or the other of these valuable things had been lost, and would therefore awake with a feverish start, and the first movement his hand would make was a triangular one from the right to the left and up to his breast, to feel if he had them still in his possession. Umbrellas, sticks, and hats were swinging to and fro in the net above, and to a certain extent shut out the view, which was highly impressive; he just glanced at it while his heart sang what at least one poet whom we know, has sung in Switzerland, but which has not as yet been printed:—

> Here, 'neath the splendor of Mont Blanc,
> With awe-filled heart, my love, I wander,
> Were purse as full as heart—then long
> And happy days we'd live and squander!

The scenery around was grand, impressive, and gloomy; the pine forests looked like the tops of heather on the lofty rocks, the summit of which was hidden in clouds of mist. It began to snow and the wind blew cold.

"Ugh!" he sighed, "I wish we were on the other side of the Alps! Then we should have summer, and I should have drawn out the money for my letter of credit. I am so anxious about this money, that I do not enjoy Switzerland! Oh, that I were on the other side!"

And he was on the other side, far down into Italy, between Florence and Rome.

The lake of Thrasimene lay like a sheet of flaming gold in the sunset between dark-blue mountains; here, where Hannibal defeated Flaminius, the vines now grew peacefully, clutching each other by their green fingers; and pretty, half-naked children were tending a herd of coal-black swine under a clump of fragrant laurels near the roadside. If we could reproduce such a picture accurately every one would exclaim: "Glorious Italy!" but neither the theological student nor any of his traveling companions in the diligence said anything of the kind.

Thousands of venomous flies and mosquitoes swarmed into the coach, the passengers trying in vain to beat them off with sprigs of myrtle; the flies stung in spite of all their exertions; there was not a person in the coach whose face was not swollen and red from their bites. The poor horses looked like carrion; the flies clung in big swarms to them, and it was only a momentary relief when the driver got down and scraped off the insects. The sun was now setting; a sharp, icy cold pervaded all nature; it was not at all pleasant, but all around the hills and clouds assumed the most lovely green tint, so clear, so bright; well, take a trip there and see for yourself; that is better than reading a description of it! It was a glorious sight! The travelers thought so too, but their stomachs were empty, their bodies tired, and all that their hearts yearned for was quarters for the night.

But what would they be like? The passengers were looking far more eagerly for these than for the beauties of nature.

The road passed through an olive wood; it seemed to the student as if he was driving between the knotty willows in his own country. Here stood the lonely inn, outside which a dozen crippled beggars were stretched; the strongest of them looked like "hunger's eldest son just come to the years of manhood," as Marryat says. The others were either blind, or had withered legs, and crept about on their hands, or gaunt arms with fingerless hands. It was real misery, dragged out from its rags.

"Eccellenza, miserabili!" they moaned, as they stretched out their disabled limbs. The landlady herself, with bare feet, uncombed hair, and dressed in a dirty blouse, received the guests. The doors were tied up with string, and the floors in the room presented the appearance of a broken-up roadway paved with bricks; bats were flying about under the ceilings, and the stench——

"She might lay the table down in the stables!" said one of the passengers, "there we should know what it was we were breathing!"

The windows were opened to let in a little fresh air, but quicker than this came in the gaunt arms, and the everlasting whines of "miserabili, Eccellenza!"

On the walls were many inscriptions, half of which were invectives against *la bella Italia*.

The meal was now served; it consisted of some watery soup, seasoned with pepper and rancid oil, the same kind of oil being also used for the salad; musty eggs and fried cock's-combs were the principal dishes. Even the wine had a disagreeable taste; it was like a black draught!

All the trunks were placed against the door for the night, and one of the travelers was to keep watch while the others slept. This fell to the lot of the theological student. Oh, how suffocating the air was in the room! The heat was oppressive, the mosquitoes were buzzing about and stinging, while the "miserabili" outside were heard whining in their sleep.

"Yes, traveling is all very well!" sighed the student, "if only one was not troubled with a body! If that could rest and the spirit fly! Wherever I go I feel a void which oppresses my heart; I want something better than the momentary, yes, something better — in fact, the best. But where and what is it? I think, however, I know what I really want. I want to reach a happy goal, the happiest of all!"

No sooner had he spoken these words than he was in his own home, the long white curtains were drawn across the window, and in the middle of the room stood a black coffin in which he was lying in his peaceful sleep of death. His wish had been fulfilled, the body rested, the spirit had fled. The truth of Solon's words, "Call no man happy until he is in his grave," were here again confirmed.

Every dead body is a sphinx of immortality. Nor did the sphinx in this black coffin solve what the living being two days before had written:

> Oh, mighty Death, thy silence strikes me dumb!
> 'T is but the churchyard graves that hear thy tread!
> Our thought that scales the heavens, must it come
> To naught? Is grass the only rising of the dead?
>
> The world knows nothing of our greatest pain:
> Thou wert in solitude unto the end!
> In life worse presses upon heart and brain
> Than heavy clods that on thy coffin-lid descend!

Two figures were moving about in the room; we know them both. They were the two fairies, Care and the messenger of Fortune; they were bending over the dead body. "Do you see," said Care, "what fortune your galoshes brought mankind after all?"

"They brought, at least, a lasting benefit to him who sleeps here," answered Fortune's messenger.

"Oh, no," said Care. "He passed away by his own wish; he was not called. His intellectual power here was not strong enough to raise the treasures yonder, which he, according to his destiny, had to raise. I will do him an act of kindness."

She then pulled the galoshes off his feet; the sleep of death was over, the dead man came to life again, and raised himself.

Care vanished, and with her the galoshes; she, no doubt, considered them her property.

AUNTY TOOTHACHE

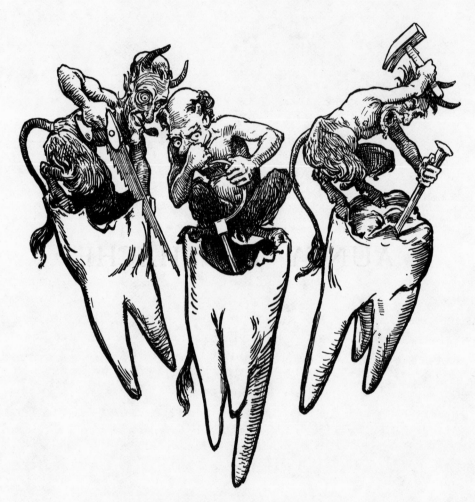

A GRAND ATTACK OF TOOTHACHE WAS COMING ON.

AUNTY TOOTHACHE

WHERE did we get this story?
Would you like to know?
We got it from the tub in which the waste paper is kept.

Many a good and rare old book has found its way to the butterman's and the grocer's, not to be read, but to be used as packing paper for starch and coffee, or to wrap up salted herrings, butter, and cheese. Manuscripts and letters also find their way to the tub.

We often throw into the waste-paper tub what ought not to go there.

I know a grocer's assistant, the son of a butterman; he has risen from serving in the cellar to serving in the front shop, and is a well-read person, his reading consisting of the matter, printed and written, found on the paper he used for packing. He has an interesting collection; and in this are to be found many important official documents from the waste-paper baskets of several busy and absent-minded officials, a few confidential letters from one lady friend to another — bits of scandal which were to go no further, and were not to be mentioned by any one. He is a living salvage-institution for not an inconsiderable portion of our literature, and his collection covers a wide field; he has the run of his parents' shop and that of his present master, and has there saved many a book, or leaves of a book, well worth reading more than once.

He has shown me his collection of printed and written matter from the waste-paper tub; the most valuable has come from the butterman's. I noticed a couple of leaves from a large exercise book; the unusually clear and neat handwriting attracted my attention at once.

"That 's what the student wrote," he said; "the student who lived opposite here and died about a month ago. One can see he must have suffered terribly from toothache. It is very interesting reading. This is only part of what he wrote; there was a whole book and more besides; my parents gave the student's landlady half a pound of soft soap for it. This is all I have been able to save."

I borrowed it, I read it, and now I give it to the world.

The title was:

AUNTY TOOTHACHE

I

Aunty used to give me sweets when I was a little boy.

My teeth did not suffer; they were not injured; now I am older, and I am a student; still she goes on spoiling me with sweets, and says I am a poet.

I have something of the poet in me, but not enough. Often when I go about the streets, it seems to me as if I am walking in a big library; the houses are the bookshelves; and every floor is a shelf with books. There stands a story of every-day life; next to it a good old comedy, and scientific works in all branches, and here are books of good reading and books of bad reading. Over all this wealth of literature I can dream and philosophize.

There is something of the poet in me, but not enough. No doubt many people have just as much of it in them as I, yet they do not carry a badge or a necktie with the word "Poet" on it. They and I have been endowed with a divine gift, a blessing great enough to satisfy oneself, but altogether too insignificant to be portioned out again to others. It comes like a ray of sunlight, and fills one's soul and thoughts; it comes like a fragrant breeze, like a melody which one knows but without remembering whence it comes.

The other evening I sat in my room and felt inclined to read, but I had no book, no paper. Just then a leaf, fresh and green, fell from the lime-tree, and the breeze carried it in through the window to me.

I examined the many veins in it; a little insect was crawling across them, as if it were making a thorough study of the leaf. This led me to think of all the wisdom that we men lay claim to; we also crawl about on a leaf, our knowledge being limited only to that; yet we are ready to deliver a lecture on the whole tree—the root, the trunk, and the crown; the great tree—God, the world, and immortality;—and of all this we know only the little leaf.

As I was sitting meditating thus, I received a visit from Aunty Milly.

I showed her the leaf and the insect, and told her of all the thoughts they had awakened in me, whereat her eyes sparkled.

"You are a poet!" she said; "perhaps the greatest we have. If I should live to see this, I would gladly lie down and die. Ever since Rasmussen the brewer's funeral you have astonished me with your powerful imagination."

This is what Aunty Milly said, and then she kissed me.

Who was Aunty Milly, and who was Rasmussen the brewer?

II

We children always called our mother's aunt "Aunty"; we had no other name for her.

She gave us jam and sweets, although they were very injurious to our teeth; but the dear children were her weakness, as she used to say. It was a shame to deny them a few sweets, when they were so fond of them.

And that 's why we loved aunty so much.

She was an old maid, and as far back as I can remember she was always old. She seemed always to be the same age.

In earlier years she had suffered a great deal from toothache, and was always talking about it; and so it happened that her friend, Mr. Rasmussen, the brewer, called her Aunty Toothache, just to show his wit.

He had left off brewing some years before, and was now living upon the interest of his money, and used to come and visit aunty. He was older than she, and had no teeth at all — only some black stumps.

When a child he had eaten too much sugar, he told us children, and that 's how he came to look as he did.

Aunty could surely never have eaten sugar when she was young, for she had the most beautiful teeth.

She took great care of them, and she did not sleep in them at night — so Rasmussen the brewer said. The children knew that this was said in malice, but aunty declared he did not mean anything by it.

One morning, after breakfast, she told us of a terrible dream she had had in the night, and that one of her teeth had fallen out.

"That means," she said, "that I shall lose a true friend!"

"Was it a false tooth?" asked the brewer with a smile; "if so, it can only mean that you will lose a false friend!"

"You are a rude old man!" said aunty, angrier than I have ever seen her before or since.

Afterward she told us that her old friend had only been teasing her; he was the noblest being on earth, and when he died he would become one of God's angels in heaven.

I thought a good deal of this transformation, and wondered whether I should be able to recognize him in this new character.

When aunty and he were young people, he had proposed to her. She had taken too long to think it over, and had settled down all by herself and become an old maid, but always remained his true friend.

And then Rasmussen died.

He was conveyed to his grave in the most expensive hearse, and was followed by a great number of people, many with orders and in uniform.

Aunty stood dressed in mourning by the window, together with all of us children, except our little brother whom the stork had brought a week ago.

The hearse and the procession had just passed, the street was empty, and aunty wanted to go away from the window, but I did not want to; I was waiting for the angel, Rasmussen the brewer; for had n't he now become one of God's bewinged children, and would n't he appear now?

"Aunty," I said, "don't you think he will come now? Or, when the stork again brings us a little brother, won't he then bring us the angel Rasmussen?"

Aunty was quite overwhelmed by my flight of imagination, and said: "That child will become a great poet!" And this she kept on repeating all the time I went to school, and even after I was confirmed and had become a student.

She was, and is, to me the most sympathetic of friends, both in my poetical and dental troubles, for I have attacks of both.

"Only write down your ideas," she said, "and put them in the table drawer! That 's what Jean Paul did; he became a great poet, though I don't admire him; he does not excite one. You must be exciting, and I know you will!"

During the night I lay awake, full of longings and anguish, full of desire and anxiety to become the great poet that aunty saw and perceived in me; I went through all the agonies of a poet! But there is a still greater agony — toothache; it was grinding and crushing me, and I became a writhing worm, with a poultice of sweet herbs and mustard plaster round my face.

"I know all about it," said aunty. There was a sorrowful smile on her lips, and her white teeth glistened.

*　　　*　　　*　　　*

But I must begin a new chapter in my own and my aunt's history.

III

I had removed to new lodgings, where I had been living a month. I was telling aunty about them.

I live with a quiet family; they do not trouble themselves about me, even if I ring three times. Otherwise it is a noisy house, full of sounds and disturbances caused by the weather, the wind, and the people. I live just over the gateway; every cart that drives out or in makes the pictures on the walls move to and fro. The gate bangs and shakes the whole house, as if there was an earthquake. If I am in bed the shocks go right through all my limbs, but they say that is strengthening to the nerves. If it blows, and it is always blowing in our country, the long window-hooks outside swing to and fro, and strike against the wall. The bell in the neighbor's yard rings with every gust of wind.

The people living in the house come home at all hours, from late in the evening till far into the night; the lodger just above me, who in the daytime gives lessons on the trombone, comes home last of all, and does not go to bed till he has taken a short midnight promenade with heavy steps and iron-heeled boots.

We have not double windows, but there is a broken pane in my room, over which the landlady has pasted some paper; but the wind blows through the crack for all that, and produces a sound something like a buzzing wasp. It is the kind of music which sends one to sleep. If at last I fall asleep, I am soon awakened by the crowing of the cocks. From the cellarman's hen-coop the cocks and hens announce that morning is approaching. The small ponies, which have no stable, but are tied up in the store-room under the staircase, kick against the door and the boarding whenever they move their legs.

The day dawns; the porter, who lives with his family in the garret, comes thundering down the stairs; his clogs clatter along the passages, the gate bangs and the house shakes, and, when all this is over, the lodger above begins his gymnastic exercises; he lifts a heavy iron ball in his hand, but, as he is not able to hold it, it is constantly falling on the floor, while at the same time the young folks in the house, who go to school, come tearing along, screaming with all their might. I go to the window and open it to get some fresh air, which I consider most refreshing when I can get it, and when the young woman in the back building is not washing gloves in soap-suds, by which work she makes a living. Otherwise it's a nice house, and I live with a quiet family!

This was the account I gave aunty about my lodgings, only it was in a more lively style; the spoken word has a fresher sound than the written.

"You are a poet!" cried aunty. "Only put down all you have said, and you will be as good as Dickens. Well, to me, of course you are much more interesting. You paint when you speak. You describe the house you live in as if one saw it before one's eyes. It makes me shudder. Go on with your work. Put some living beings into it — some people, beautiful men and women, and — especially unhappy ones."

I wrote down my description of the house as it now stands, with all its faults, and included only myself. There was no plot in it. That comes later on.

IV

It was in the winter, late at night, after theater hours; it was terrible weather; a snow-storm was raging, so that one could hardly get along.

Aunty had gone to the theater, and I went to take her home; but it was difficult enough to get along by one's self, to say nothing of helping any one else.   All the carriages were engaged.   Aunty lived in the out-skirts of the town, while my lodgings were close to the theater.   If it had not been for this, we should have had to take refuge for a time in a sentry-box.

We trudged along in the deep snow with the snow-flakes whirling around us.   I had to lift her, support her, and push her along.   Only twice did we fall, but we fell on soft ground.

We reached my gate, where we shook off some of the snow.   On the stairs also we shook some off, but there was still enough almost to cover the floor of the anteroom.

We took off our outer wraps and galoshes, and everything else we could divest ourselves of.   The landlady lent aunty dry stockings and a night-cap; she would be sure to want it, said the landlady, for, as she rightly added, it would be impossible for my aunt to get home that night; and so she asked her to make use of her parlor, where she would make a bed for her on the sofa, in front of the door leading into my room, which was al-ways kept locked.

And aunty agreed to the arrangement.

The fire burned in my stove, the tea urn came on the table, and the little room began to look cozy, if not quite so cozy as aunty's, where in the winter time there are thick portières before the door, thick curtains before the windows, and double carpets on the floor, with three layers of thick paper underneath.   One sits there as if in a well-corked bottle, full of warm air; still, as I have said, my room also was pleasant and warm, while outside the wind was whistling.

Aunty talked and talked; the days of her youth came back; the brewer returned — all her old memories were revived.

She could remember when I got my first tooth, and how the family rejoiced.

My first tooth! The tooth of innocence, shining like a little drop of milk — the milk-tooth!

The first had come, then came more — a whole row, side by side, at the top and at the bottom, the prettiest of children's teeth; but only the first ones, not the real ones, which have to last one's whole lifetime.

They also appeared, and the wisdom-teeth as well, the fuglemen in the row, born in pain and great tribulation.

They disappear again, every one of them; they disappear before the time of service is up — the very last one has gone, and it is not a day for rejoicing; it is a day for mourning.

So one begins to feel old, although one is young at heart.

Such reflections and such conversations are not pleasant.   Yet we came to talk about all this; we went back to the days of my childhood, and talked and talked.   It was twelve o'clock before aunty went to rest in the room close by.

IT WAS MISTRESS TOOTHACHE, HER TERRIBLE HIGHNESS! . . . I FELT AS IF
A RED HOT AWL PASSED THROUGH MY CHEEKBONE.

"Good night, my dear child," she said. "I shall sleep as if I lay in my own four-poster."

And she slept peacefully; but peace did not reign either within the house or without. The storm rattled the windows, struck the wall with the long, dangling iron hooks, and rang the neighbor's bell in the back-yard. The lodger up-stairs had come home. He was still taking his nightly promenade up and down the room; he then kicked off his boots, and went to bed and to rest; but he snores, so that any one with good ears can hear him through the ceiling.

I found no peace, no rest; nor did the weather take any rest; it was unusually lively. The wind howled and sang in its own way; my teeth also began to be lively and they hummed and sang in their way. A grand attack of toothache was coming on.

Draughty gusts came from the window. The moon shone through the window upon the floor; the light came and went as the clouds rolled by in the stormy weather. There was an unceasing change of light and shadow, until at last the shadow on the floor began to take shape. I stared at the apparition, and felt an icy cold gust against my face.

On the floor sat a thin, long figure, just like what a child would draw with a pencil on its slate; something like a human being—a single thin line formed the body, another line or two made the arms, and the legs were only indicated by a single line for each, and the head by angular lines.

The figure soon became more distinct; it was draped with a very thin and fine kind of stuff, clearly showing that the figure was that of a woman.

I heard a buzzing sound. Was it she or the wind, which was buzzing like a hornet through the crack in the pane?

No, it was she, Mistress Toothache! Her terrible highness, *Satania Infernalis!* Heaven deliver and preserve us from her visits!

"How cozy it is here!" she buzzed; "these are nice quarters— marshy ground, boggy ground! Here the gnats have been buzzing with poison in their stings; I have a sting, and it must be sharpened on human teeth. Those over in the bed shine so brightly. They have defied sweet and sour things, heat and cold, nutshells and plum-stones; but I shall shake them to their roots, I shall stretch them on the rack, and feed their roots with draughty winds and chilly blasts!"

They were terrible words!—She is a terrible visitor!

"So you are a poet!" she said. "Well, I'll coach you in all the meters of toothache! I'll thrust iron and steel into your body! I'll seize all the fibers of your nerves!"

I felt as if a red-hot awl passed through my cheek-bone; I writhed and twisted in my bed.

"A splendid row of teeth to play upon! just like an organ!" she said. "We shall have a grand concert on Jews'-harps, with kettle-drums and trumpets, piccolo-flute, and trombone in the wisdom-tooth! Grand poet, grand music!"

And then she started the performance.

She looked terrible, although one did not see more of her than her hand, the shadowy, gray, ice-cold hand, with the long, thin, pointed fin-

gers; each of them was an instrument of torture; the thumb and the fore-finger were pincers and wrench, the middle finger ended in a pointed awl, the ring finger was an auger, and the little finger a squirt with gnat's poison.

"I 'll teach you the right meter!" she said. "A great poet must have a great toothache, a little poet a little toothache!"

"Oh, consider me then a little poet!" I prayed. "Consider me nothing at all! And I am not a poet; I have only fits of poetry like fits of toothache. Leave me, oh leave me!"

"Will you acknowledge, then, that I am mightier than poetry, philosophy, mathematics, and all the music?" she said. "Mightier than all these notions that are painted on canvas or hewn in marble? I am older than any of them. I was born close to the Garden of Paradise, just outside, where the wind blew and the wet toadstools grew. It was I who made Eve put on clothes in the cold weather, and Adam also. There was manifestation of power in the first toothache, I can tell you!"

"I believe it all," I said. "But leave me, oh leave me!"

"Yes, if you will give up being a poet, never put verse on paper, slate, or any kind of writing material, then I will let you off; but I shall come again, my poet!"

"I swear!" I said; "only let me never see or feel you any more!"

"See me you shall, but in a more substantial shape, in a shape more dear to you than I am at present. You shall see me as Aunty Milly, and I will say: 'Write poetry, my dear boy! You are a great poet, perhaps the greatest we have!' But if you believe me, and you begin to write poetry, then I will set music to your verses, and play them on your mouth-organ. You dear child! Remember me, when you see Aunty Milly!"

And then she vanished.

At parting I received something like the thrust of a red-hot awl **through** my cheek-bone, but it soon subsided. I felt as if I were gliding **along** the smooth water; I saw how the white water-lilies, with their **large** green leaves, bent and sank down under me; how they withered and perished, and how I sank with them; how I was set free and found peace and rest.

"To die, to melt away like snow!" resounded in the water; "to evaporate into air, to sail away like the clouds!"

Great shining names and inscriptions on waving banners of victory, the letters patent of immortality, written on the wing of an ephemera, shone down to me through the water.

The sleep was deep, a sleep without dreams. I did not hear the whistling wind, the banging gate, the neighbor's noisy bell, or the gymnastics of the lodger.

What happiness!

Then came a sudden gust of wind, so that the locked door to aunty's room burst open. Aunty jumped up, got dressed, and came into my room.

I slept like one of God's angels, she said, and had not the heart to wake me.

I awoke later on and opened my eyes, but did not remember that aunty was in the house; but I soon remembered it — and also my toothache vision.

Dream and reality were blended.

"I suppose you did not write anything last night after we said good-night?" she said. "I wish you had; you are my poet, and shall remain so!"

I thought that she smiled somewhat slyly. I did not know if it were the Aunty Milly who loved me, or the terrible one to whom I had made the promise of last night.

"Have you written any poetry, dear child?"

"No, no!" I shouted. "Are you really Aunty Milly?"

"Who else?" she said. It was really Aunty Milly.

She kissed me, got into a carriage, and drove home.

I jotted down what is written here. It is not in verse, and it shall never be printed.

Here ended the manuscript.

My young friend, the grocer's assistant, could not find the missing sheets; they had gone out into the world like the papers round the salted herrings, the butter, and the soft soap; they had fulfilled their destiny!

The brewer is dead, aunty is dead, the student is dead, he whose sparks of genius went into the tub. *Nota bene*—everything goes into the tub. This is the end of the story—the story of Aunty Toothache.

THE TINDER-BOX

THE WITCH HOISTED THE SOLDIER UP FROM THE HOLLOW TREE.

THE TINDER-BOX

A SOLDIER came marching along the high road: one, two! one, two! He had his knapsack on his back and a sword by his side, for he had been in the wars, and he was now on his way home. He met an old witch on the road; she was a hideous-looking creature; her under-lip hung right down upon her breast.

"Good evening, soldier," she said. "What a fine sword, and what a big knapsack you have got. You are a real soldier! You shall have as much money as you want."

"Thank you, old witch," said the soldier.

"Do you see that tree?" said the witch, pointing at the tree which stood beside them. "It is quite hollow inside. You must climb to the top, where you will see a hole through which you can let yourself slide down, and get far down into the tree. I 'll tie a rope round your waist, so that I can pull you up again when you call me."

"What shall I do down in the tree, then?" asked the soldier.

"Fetch money," said the witch. "You must know that when you get to the bottom of the tree you will find yourself in a large corridor; there is plenty of light there, for over a hundred lamps are burning there. You will then see three doors, which you can open; the keys are in the locks. When you get into the first chamber, you will see, in the middle of the floor, a large chest, on the top of which a dog is sitting; he has a pair of eyes as large as tea-cups, but you must not mind that. I will give you my blue-chequered apron, which you must spread out on the floor, then go quickly and take the dog, put him on my apron, open the chest, and take as many pennies as you like. They are all of copper; but if you would rather have silver, you must go into the next chamber; there a dog is sitting with a pair of eyes as large as mill-wheels, but you must not mind that; put him on my apron, and help yourself to the money. If, however, you want gold, you can have that as well, and as much as you can carry, if you will go into the third chamber. But the dog that sits on the money-chest there has eyes as big as the Round Tower.[1] That 's the right sort of dog, I can tell you. But you must not trouble yourself about that. Only put the dog on my apron, and he won't harm you, and take as much gold as you like from the chest."

"That 's not at all bad," said the soldier. "But what shall I give you, old witch? For you are sure to want something, I should say."

"No," said the witch, "not a single penny will I have. You shall only bring me an old tinder-box, which my grandmother forgot the last time she was down there."

"Ah, indeed! Let me get the rope round my waist," said the soldier.

"Here it is," said the witch, "and here is my blue-chequered apron."

The soldier then climbed up into the tree, let himself plump down into the hole, and stood now, as the witch had said, in the great corridor below, where the many hundred lamps were burning.

So he opened the first door. Ugh! there sat the dog with eyes as large as tea-cups, staring at him.

"You are a nice fellow," said the soldier. He put the dog on the witch's apron, and took as many copper pennies as he had room for in his pocket; he then closed the chest, put the dog back again, and went into the second chamber. Ah! there sat the dog with eyes as big as mill-wheels.

"You should n't look so hard at me," said the soldier; "it might hurt your eyes." And so he put the dog on the witch's apron; but when he

[1] A well-known tower in Copenhagen.

THE SOLDIER LIFTED THE DOG DOWN ON THE FLOOR AND OPENED THE CHEST.

saw all the silver money in the chest, he threw away all the copper money he had, and filled his pocket and his knapsack with silver only.

He then went into the third chamber. But oh, how horrid! The dog in there had really eyes as big as the Round Tower, and they went round in his head like two wheels!

"Good evening!" said the soldier, and touched his cap, for such a dog he had never seen before; but, after having looked at him for a while, he thought he had had enough of that, so he lifted the dog down on the floor and opened the chest. Great heavens! what a lot of gold! He could buy the whole of Copenhagen, and all the sugar-pigs from the sweetstuff women out of it, as well as all the tin soldiers, whips, and rocking-horses in the world. Yes, there was plenty of money, sure enough.

The soldier now threw away all the silver shillings he had filled his pocket and his knapsack with, and took gold coins instead; all his pockets, his knapsack, his cap, and his boots were filled, so that he could scarcely walk. Now he had plenty of money! He put the dog back on the chest, slammed the door to, and cried up the tree:

"Pull me up, old witch!"

"Have you got the tinder-box with you?" asked the witch.

"Why, no!" said the soldier. "I had forgotten all about it"; and so he went and fetched it. The witch hoisted him up, and there he stood again on the high-road, with his pockets, boots, knapsack, and cap full of money.

"What are you going to do with the tinder-box?" asked the soldier.

"That has nothing to do with you," said the witch; "you have got your money! Give me the tinder-box!"

"Nonsense!" said the soldier; "just tell me at once what you are going to do with it, or I 'll draw my sword and cut your head off!"

"No!" said the witch.

The soldier then cut her head off. There she lay. But he tied up all his money in her apron, carried it on his back like a bundle, put the tinder-box in his pocket, and set out straight for the town.

It was a fine town; he put up at the best inn, ordered the very best rooms, and the dishes he was fond of; for now he was rich, since he had so much money.

The servant who was going to clean his boots thought, of course, they were funny old boots for such a rich gentleman to wear, for he had not yet bought himself new ones. The next day, however, he got new boots and fine clothes; and now the soldier looked like a fine gentleman, and the people told him all about the grand things in their town, and about the king, and what a beautiful princess his daughter was.

"Where can one get to see her?" asked the soldier.

"She is not to be seen at all," they all said; "she lives in a big palace of copper, with many walls and towers round about it. No one but the king can go in and out there, because it has been predicted that she will be married to quite a common soldier, and that the king will not hear of."

"I should like to see her," thought the soldier; but that, of course, he would not be permitted to do.

So he began leading a merry life; he went to the theater, drove in the king's park, and gave a deal of money to the poor, which was very good of him. He knew from past experience how terrible it was to be without a penny.

He was now rich, had fine clothes, and a number of friends who all said he was a 'jolly fellow,' a real cavalier, and this the soldier liked much to hear. But as he went on paying out money every day and received none at all in return, he was at last left with only two pennies, and was obliged to give up the pretty rooms he had been living in, and to move to a small, tiny garret, right under the roof, where he had to brush his own boots and to mend them with a darning-needle; and none of his friends came to see him, for there were so many stairs to walk up!

One dark evening he found he was not even able to buy himself a candle, when suddenly he remembered that there was a candle-end in the tinder-box, which he had taken out of the hollow tree into which the witch had helped him. He brought out the tinder-box and the candle-end, but as soon as he struck fire and the sparks flew from the flint, the door was burst open, and the dog, whom he had seen down under the tree, and who had eyes as large as tea-cups, stood before him and said: "What are master's orders?"

"Hullo! what's this?" said the soldier; "this is a jolly tinder-box, if I can get what I want in this way. Bring me some money!" he said to the dog; and off the dog went; and the next minute he was back again, holding a large bag full of money in his mouth.

The soldier now knew what a splendid tinder-box it was. If he struck it once, the dog who was sitting on the chest with the copper money came; if he struck it twice, the one who had the silver money appeared; and if he struck it thrice, the one who had the gold came.

So the soldier moved down into his pretty rooms again, put on his fine clothes, and then all his friends knew him at once, and appeared to be very fond of him.

One day he thought to himself: it's very strange one cannot get a sight of that princess! She is so very beautiful, they all say! But what can be the good of that, when she must always sit inside that great copper palace with the many towers. Shall I never be able to see her, I wonder. Where is my tinder-box? He struck a light, and there stood the dog with eyes as large as tea-cups!

It's in the middle of the night, I know," said the soldier, "but I should like so much to see the princess, only for a moment!"

THE SOLDIER COULD SEE THROUGH THE WINDOW HOW THE PEOPLE WERE HURRYING OUT OF THE
TOWN TO SEE HIM HANGED.   HE HEARD THE DRUMS GOING AND SAW THE SOLDIERS MARCHING.

The dog was out of the room in an instant, and before the soldier could give it a thought, he saw him returning with the princess, who was sitting on the dog's back asleep. She was so lovely, that any one could see she was a real princess; the soldier could not help it, he had to kiss her, for he was a true soldier.

The dog then ran back again with the princess, but when the morning came and the king and queen were having their cup of tea, the princess said she had had such a wonderful dream in the night about a dog and a soldier. She had ridden upon the dog and the soldier had kissed her.

"That's a pretty story, I must say!" said the queen.

One of the old court-ladies was then set to watch by the princess's bedside next night, to see if it really had been a dream, or what it might be.

The soldier was longing terribly to see the beautiful princess again, and in the night the dog came for her; he took her on his back and ran as fast as he could, but the old lady put on spring-heeled boots and ran behind, keeping up the same pace as they. When she saw them disappear in a big house, she thought to herself: "Now I know where it is," and made a big cross on the gate with a piece of chalk. She then went home, and soon afterward the dog came back with the princess; but when he saw that a cross had been put on the gate where the soldier lived, he took a piece of chalk and make a cross on all the gates all over town; this was clever of him, for now the court-lady could not find the right gate, since there were crosses on all of them.

Early next morning the king and the queen, the old court-lady and all the officers went to see where the princess had been to.

"There it is!" said the king, when he saw the first gate with a cross on it.

"No, my dear, there it is!" said the queen, who saw another gate with a cross.

"But here is one, and there is one!" said all of them; wherever they looked there were crosses on the gates. So they knew it would be of no use to go on searching any farther.

But the queen was a very clever woman, who could do something more than ride in a carriage. She took her large pair of gold scissors, cut out a large piece of silk and made a nice little bag, which she filled with small fine buckwheat groats. This she tied to the princess's back, and when this was done, she cut a little hole in the bag, so that the groats should run out along the ground the whole of the way the princess went.

In the night the dog came again; he took the princess on his back and ran with her to the soldier, who was so deeply in love with her, and who wished so much he had been a prince, that he might make her his wife.

The dog did not notice that the groats were running out of the bag all the way from the palace right up to the soldier's window, where he climbed up along the wall with the princess. In the morning the king and the queen could easily see where their daughter had been, and so they took the soldier and put him in prison.

There he sat. Ugh, how dark and miserable it was! And the people said to him: "To-morrow you will be hanged." That was not pleasant to hear, and he had forgotten his tinder-box at home in the inn. Next

THE THREE DOGS DANCED IN FRONT OF THE KING'S CARRIAGE AND CRIED "HURRAH!"

morning he could see through the iron bars in the little window how the people were hurrying out of the town to see him hanged. He heard the drums going and saw the soldiers marching. All the inhabitants were running about; amongst them was a shoemaker's boy with a leather apron and with slippers on his feet; he galloped past at such a rate, that one of his slippers flew off right against the wall, where the soldier sat peering out through the iron bars.

"Hey, you shoemaker's boy! You need not be in such a hurry," said the soldier to him, "there 'll be nothing going on till I come! But won't you run across to where I have been living and fetch my tinder-box, and I 'll give you twopence? But you 'll have to use your legs!" The shoemaker's boy was glad to earn the twopence, and rushed off to fetch the tinder-box; he gave it to the soldier, and—well, now you shall hear all about it.

Outside the city a great gallows had been erected, and round about stood the soldiers and many hundred thousand people. The king and the queen sat in a gorgeous throne right opposite the judge and the whole court.

The soldier was already standing at the top of the ladder, but as they were going to place the halter round his neck, he said that they always allowed a poor sinner to have an innocent wish granted before he suffered his punishment. He would so like to smoke a pipe of tobacco; it would be the last pipe he would get in this world.

The king would not say no to that, and so the soldier took the tinder-box and struck a light, once, twice, thrice! and there stood all the dogs, the one with eyes as large as tea-cups, the one with eyes like mill-wheels, and the one who had eyes as large as the Round Tower.

"Now help me, so that I sha'n't be hanged!" said the soldier, and then the dogs rushed at the judges and the whole court, seized one by the legs and one by the nose, and threw them many fathoms up in the air, so that they fell down and were dashed to pieces.

"I will not!" said the king, but the biggest dog seized both him and the queen and threw them after all the others. Then all the soldiers grew frightened, and all the people shouted: "Little soldier, you shall be our king and marry the beautiful princess!"

So they placed the soldier in the king's carriage, and the three dogs danced in front of it and cried "hurrah!" and the boys whistled through their fingers, while the soldiers presented arms. The princess left the copper palace and became queen, which she liked very much. The wedding lasted eight days, and the dogs sat at the table and looked on in astonishment with their big eyes.

LITTLE IDA'S FLOWERS

"MY POOR FLOWERS ARE QUITE DEAD!" SAID LITTLE IDA.

LITTLE IDA'S FLOWERS

"MY poor flowers are quite dead!" said little Ida. "They were so beautiful last night, and now all the leaves are hanging down quite faded! Why are they doing that?" she asked the student, who sat on the sofa. She was very fond of him; he could tell the most beautiful stories and cut out the funniest pictures, such as hearts with little damsels who danced, and flowers, and large castles with doors that could be opened; he was indeed a merry student!

"Why do the flowers, look so poorly to-day?" she asked again, and showed him a whole bouquet which was entirely faded.

"Don't you know what's the matter with them?" said the student. "The flowers were at a ball last night, and that's why they hang their heads!"

"But flowers cannot dance!" said little Ida.

"Oh, yes," said the student, "when it is dark and we are asleep, they run about quite merrily; almost every night they hold a ball!"

"Can't children go to those balls?"

"Yes," said the student, "as tiny daisies and lilies of the valley."

"Where do the prettiest flowers dance?" asked little Ida.

"Haven't you often been outside the gate of the great palace, where the king lives in summer, and where there is a beautiful garden with many flowers? You have seen the swans, which swim toward you when you want to give them bread crumbs. They hold real balls out there, I can tell you!"

"I was there in the garden yesterday with my mother," said Ida; "but all the leaves had fallen off the trees, and there were no flowers at all! Where are they? Last summer I saw so many!"

"They are in the palace," said the student. "You must know that as soon as ever the king and all the court move into the town, the flowers at once run away from the garden up to the palace and make merry. You ought to see that! Two most beautiful roses take a seat on the throne, and then they are king and queen. All the red cockscombs range themselves by their side and stand bowing; they are the chamberlains. Then all sorts of lovely flowers arrive and then they have a great ball; the blue violets represent little midshipmen, and dance with hyacinths and crocuses whom they call young ladies. The tulips and the large tiger-lilies are the old ladies; they see that the dancing is done well and that everything is properly conducted!"

"But," asked little Ida, "does n't any one do anything to the flowers for dancing in the king's palace?"

"There is no one who really knows anything about that," said the student. "Sometimes the old keeper who looks after the palace out there, comes round at night, but he has a large bunch of keys, and as soon as the flowers hear the keys rattle, they are quite quiet and hide themselves behind the long curtains and peep out.

"'I can smell that there are some flowers in here!' says the old keeper, but he cannot see them."

"That 's great fun," said little Ida, clapping her hands. "But should n't I be able to see the flowers either?"

"Yes," said the student, "just remember when you go there again to peep in through the window, and you are sure to see them. I did so to-day, and there lay a long yellow daffodil on the sofa, stretching herself and imagining herself to be one of the ladies of the court!"

"Can the flowers in the Botanical Gardens also go there? Can they go such a long way?"

"Yes, of course!" said the student, "for they can fly if they like. Have n't you seen the beautiful butterflies, red, yellow, and white; they almost look like flowers, and that is what they once were. They have flown from the stalks right up into the air, flapping with their leaves as if they were little wings. And as they behaved well, they were allowed to fly about in the daytime also, and were not obliged to remain at home and sit still on the stalk, and so the leaves became real wings at last. You have seen that yourself! It may be, however, that the flowers in the Botanical Gardens have never been to the king's palace, and do not know that they have such a merry time at night out there. I will therefore tell you something which will greatly surprise the botanical professor, who lives next door—you know him, don't you? When you go into his garden, you must tell one of the flowers that there is going to be a great ball at the palace, and he again will tell it to all the others, and then they will all fly off. When the professor comes into the garden there will not be a single flower left, and he will not be able to make out what has become of them."

"But how can the flower tell it to the others? The flowers cannot talk!"

"That 's true!" answered the student, "but they make signs to one another. Have n't you seen when the wind blows a little that the flowers nod to one another and move all their green leaves? They understand it as plainly as if they spoke!"

"Can the professor understand their language?" asked Ida.

"Yes, of course! He came down into his garden one morning and saw a big nettle making signs with its leaves to a beautiful red carnation; it said, 'You are so lovely, and I am so fond of you.' The professor does not like such goings on, so he gave the nettle a slap across its leaves, for they are its fingers, you know; but he stung himself, and since then he never dares to touch a nettle."

"How funny!" said little Ida with a laugh.

"What ideas to put into the child's head!" remarked the tiresome counselor, who had come on a visit and was sitting on the sofa. He did not like the student and was always grumbling when he saw him cutting out the funny, comic pictures, sometimes a man hanging on a gallows and holding a heart in his hand, for he had been a destroyer of hearts, sometimes an old witch riding on a broom and carrying her husband on her nose. The counselor did not like that, and so he would say as he had done just now: "What ideas to put into the child's head! It is pure imagination!"

But it seemed to little Ida that what the student had told her about her flowers was very amusing, and she thought a great deal about it. The flowers hung their heads, because they were tired of dancing all the night; they must be poorly. So she carried them with her to a nice little table where she kept all her toys and the whole drawer was full of pretty things. In the doll's bed lay her doll Sophia, asleep, but little Ida said to her: "You must really get up, Sophia, and be content with lying in the drawer to-night; the poor flowers are poorly and they must lie in your bed; perhaps they will then get well again!" And so she took the doll, who looked very cross but did not say a single word, because she was angry at not being allowed to keep her bed.

Ida put the flowers in the doll's bed, pulled the little quilt over them, and said they must lie quiet and she would make tea for them, so that they might get well again and be able to get up in the morning. She then drew the curtains closely round the little bed, so that the sun should not shine in their eyes.

The whole evening she could not help thinking about what the student had told her, and when she had to go to bed herself, she felt she must first go behind the curtains which hung before the windows, where her mother's lovely flowers were standing, both hyacinths and tulips, and then she whispered quite softly, "I know you are going to a ball to-night!" but the flowers appeared as if they understood nothing and did not move a leaf, but little Ida knew — what she knew.

When she had got into bed she lay for a long time thinking how nice it would be to see the beautiful flowers dance at the king's palace.

"I wonder if my flowers really have been there?" And so she fell asleep. In the course of the night she awoke; she had been dreaming about the flowers and the student, whom the counselor used to scold for putting silly ideas into her head.   It was quite quiet in the bedroom where Ida was lying; the night-lamp was burning on the table and her father and mother were asleep.

"I wonder if my flowers are now lying in Sophia's bed," she said to herself, "how I should like to know!"   She raised herself a little and looked toward the door, which was half open; in there lay the flowers and all her toys.   She listened, and it appeared to her as if she heard some one playing the piano in the next room, very softly, and more beautifully than she had ever heard it before.

"I expect all my flowers are now dancing in there!" she said, "how I should like to see them!"   But she dared not get up for fear of waking her father and mother.   "If they would only come in here," she said; but the flowers did not come, and the music continued to play so beautifully that she could not resist it any longer,—it was too entrancing,—so she crept out of her little bed and went quite softly to the door and looked into the room.   Oh, what an amusing scene met her sight!

There was no night-lamp in there, but still it was quite light; the moon was shining through the window right into the middle of the room! It was almost as light as day.   All the hyacinths and tulips were standing in two long rows along the floor; there were none at all in the window, where only empty pots were to be seen.   Down on the floor the flowers were dancing most gracefully round and round, doing the chain quite correctly and holding each other by their long green leaves as they swung round.   And over at the piano sat a large yellow lily whom little Ida was sure she had seen last summer, for she remembered so well that the student had said: "How she is like Miss Lina!" but they all laughed at him then. But now Ida really thought that the long yellow flower was like Miss Lina, and had just the same manners when playing, putting her large yellow head first on one side and then on the other, and nodding it to keep time with the music.   No one noticed little Ida.   She then saw a large blue crocus jump right onto the middle of the table, where the toys were standing, and walk straight up to the doll's bed and pull aside the curtains; there lay the sick flowers, but they got up directly and nodded their heads to the others to show that they also wanted to join in the dance.   The old incense-burner with the broken under-lip stood up and bowed to the pretty flowers; they did not appear at all ill, they jumped down among the others and looked so pleased.

Just then it seemed as if something fell down from the table.   Ida looked that way; it was the Shrove-tide rod,[1] which had jumped down; it thought it also belonged to the flowers.   It was really very pretty; at the top sat a little wax doll, which had just the same kind of broad hat on her

[1] The Shrove-tide rod is generally a three-branched flower-decoration, made of paper, about twelve to eighteen inches in height.

DOWN ON THE FLOOR THE FLOWERS WERE DANCING MOST GRACEFULLY ROUND AND ROUND,
HOLDING EACH OTHER BY THEIR LONG, GREEN LEAVES.

head as the counselor wore; the Shrove-tide rod and its three red wooden legs jumped right into the midst of the flowers and stamped quite loudly; it was dancing the mazurka, and this the other flowers could not dance because they were too light and could not stamp.

All at once the wax doll on the rod began to grow bigger and bigger, whirled round above the paper flowers, and called out quite loudly: "What ideas to put into the child's head! It is pure imagination!" And then the wax doll looked exactly like the counselor with the broad hat, and was just as yellow and cross as he, but the paper flowers struck him across his

THE FLOWERS LED SOPHIA INTO THE MIDDLE OF THE FLOOR AND DANCED WITH HER,
SOME OF THEM FORMING A CIRCLE ROUND HER.

thin legs; and he shrank and shrank till he became a little wee bit of a wax doll again.   He looked so very funny, little Ida could not help laughing! The Shrove-tide rod went on dancing and the counselor had to dance as well; there was no help for it, he had to dance whether he made himself big and long, or became the little yellow wax doll with the big black hat. Then the other flowers interceded for him, especially those that had been in the doll's bed, and at last the Shrove-tide rod stopped dancing.

At that moment there was a loud knocking in the drawer where Ida's doll Sophia lay among the other toys; the incense-burner ran to the edge of the table, laid himself flat down upon his stomach and managed to get the drawer pulled out a little; whereupon Sophia sat up and looked quite surprised.

"There's a ball here!" she said; "why hasn't any one told me?"

"Will you dance with me?" asked the incense-burner.

"You are a nice one to dance with, I'm sure!" she said, and turned her back upon him. So she sat down on the drawer and thought that one of the flowers would be sure to come and engage her, but no one came; then she coughed, hem! hem! hem! but no one came for all that. The incense-burner danced all by himself, and he didn't do it at all badly!

As none of the flowers seemed to notice Sophia, she let herself fall with a thump from the drawer right down on the floor, and caused quite a commotion; all the flowers came running round her asking if she had hurt herself, and they were all so nice to her, especially the flowers that had been lying in her bed. But she had not hurt herself at all, and all Ida's flowers thanked her for her beautiful bed, and said they loved her very much; they led her into the middle of the floor, where the moon was shining, and danced with her, while the other flowers formed a circle round them. Sophia was now very pleased and said they might keep her bed; she did not at all mind lying in the drawer.

But the flowers said: "We are very much obliged to you, but we cannot live very long! To-morrow we shall be quite dead, but tell little Ida she must bury us in the garden where the canary bird is lying; then we shall grow up again in the summer and be prettier than ever!"

"No, you must not die!" said Sophia, and then she kissed the flowers.

Just then the door of the next room flew open, and a lot of beautiful flowers came dancing in. Ida could not make out where they came from; they must be all the flowers from the king's palace. First of all came two lovely roses, with their little golden crowns; they were the king and the queen. Then came the most beautiful stocks and carnations, bowing on all sides; they had brought music with them. Large poppies and peonies were blowing pea-shells till they were quite red in the face. The blue-bells and the little white snowdrops tinkled as if they had bells on. The music was very funny! Then there came many other flowers, and they all danced; the blue violets and the red hearts-eases, the daisies and the lilies of the valley. And all the flowers kissed one another; it was such a pretty sight!

At last the flowers said good night to each other and little Ida stole back to her bed, where she dreamed of all that she had seen.

When she got up next morning, she went at once to the little table to see if the flowers were still there. She pulled aside the curtains of the little bed, and there they all lay, but they were quite faded, more so than they were the day before. Sophia lay in the drawer, where she had put her; she looked very sleepy.

"Can you remember what you were to tell me?" said little Ida, but Sophia looked very stupid and did not say a single word.

"You are not at all kind," said Ida, "and yet they all danced with you." So she took a little cardboard box, on which were painted beautiful birds; she opened it and put the dead flowers into it.

"That will make a pretty coffin for you!" she said, "and when my Norwegian cousins come here, they shall help me to bury you in the garden, so that you can grow up next summer and be prettier than ever!"

Her Norwegian cousins were two fine boys, whose names were Jonas and Adolph; their father had given them each a new cross-bow, and they had brought these with them to show Ida. She told them about the poor flowers that were dead, and they were allowed to bury them. Both the boys went first with their cross-bows on their shoulders, and little Ida followed behind with the dead flowers in the beautiful box. A little grave was dug in the garden. Ida first kissed the flowers and then laid them in the box in the grave, while Adolph and Jonas shot with their cross-bows over it, for they had neither guns nor cannons.

ELDER-TREE MOTHER

THE FLOWERS OF THE ELDER-TREE SMELLED SO SWEETLY.

ELDER-TREE MOTHER

THERE was once a little boy who had caught a cold through getting his feet wet. No one could make out how he had managed
to get them wet, for the weather was quite fine. His mother
undressed him and put him to bed, and had the tea-urn brought in to
make a nice cup of elder-tea for him, for that warms the body so well!
Just then the amusing old gentleman, who lived at the top of the house,
came in through the door; he lived by himself, for he had neither wife
nor children, but he was so very fond of children and could tell so many
fairy tales and stories that it was a pleasure to listen to him.

"You must drink your tea, now," said the mother to the little boy,
"and then perhaps you shall hear a fairy tale!"

"If one could only think of something new!" said the old man with
a friendly nod. "But how did the little fellow get his feet wet?" he
asked.

"Yes, where did he get them wet?" said the mother. "No one can
make it out."

"Will you tell me a story?" asked the boy.

"Yes, if you can tell me exactly how deep the gutter is in the little
street where your school is. I must know that first."

"Just half way up to my knee," said the boy, "but then I have to stand in the deepest part!"

"Ah, that 's where we have got our wet feet!" said the old man; "I ought now to tell you a fairy tale, but I don't know any more!"

"But you can make up one," said the little boy. "Mother says that you can make a story out of everything you look at or touch!"

"Yes, but those tales and stories are no good; no, the real ones come of themselves—they knock at my forehead and say, 'Here I am!'"

THE LID GRADUALLY LIFTED ITSELF AND LARGE BRANCHES OF THE ELDER-TREE SHOT
FORTH FROM THE URN, EVEN THROUGH THE SPOUT.

"Will one knock there soon?" asked the little boy, and his mother laughed, put the elder-tea into the urn and poured boiling water over it.

"Do tell me a fairy tale, do!"

"Yes, if only it would come of itself, but the real fairy tale only comes when it is in the right humor and likes to come— But stop!" he suddenly exclaimed. "There 's one! Mind! There 's one now in the tea-urn!"

The little boy looked at the tea-urn; the lid gradually lifted itself and large branches of the elder-tree with fresh white elder flowers shot forth from the urn, even through the spout, and spread themselves out on all sides, always growing larger and larger, till they formed the most beautiful elder-tree—in fact, a great tree, which extended right to the little boy's bed and pushed the curtains aside. How it blossomed, and how fragrant it was! In the middle of the tree sat a pleasant-looking old woman in a strange dress; it was quite green, just like the leaves of the elder-tree, and was trimmed with large white elder flowers; one could not see at once whether it was made of cloth or of living green plants and flowers.

"What is the name of the old lady?" asked the little boy.

"Well, the Romans and the Greeks called her a dryad," said the old man, "but we do not understand the meaning of that name. In Nyboder they have a better name for her; there she is called 'Elder-Tree Mother,' and it is to her you must now give all your attention. Listen, and look at the beautiful elder-tree!

UNDER THE TREE SAT AN OLD SAILOR AND HIS OLD WIFE. ELDER-TREE MOTHER SAT IN THE TREE AND LOOKED SO PLEASED.

" Just such a large tree stands in full bloom out at Nyboder! It grew there in the corner of the yard of a poor little cottage; under this tree one afternoon, in the most delightful sunshine, sat two old people. They were an old, old sailor and his old, old wife; they were great-grandparents and were soon to celebrate their golden wedding, but they could not quite remember the date. Elder-tree mother sat in the tree and looked so pleased, just as she does now. 'I know when the golden wedding is!' she said, but they did not hear it; they were talking about the old days.

"'Yes, do you remember,' said the old sailor, 'when we were quite youngsters and used to run about and play together? It was in this very yard where we are now sitting! We put twigs into the ground and made a garden.'

"'Yes,' said the old woman, 'I remember it well! We watered the twigs, and one of them was from an elder-tree, and it took root, shot forth green shoots, and has now become the great tree under which we old people are sitting.'

"'Yes, of course!' said he, 'and over in the corner stood the water-butt, in which I used to sail my ship, which I had made myself. How it did sail! But I soon came to sail in quite a different style!'

"'Yes, but first we went to school and learned something!' she said. 'And then we were confirmed; we both cried, I remember. But in the afternoon we went hand and hand up the Round Tower, and looked out upon the world over Copenhagen and the Sound; then we went to Frederiksberg, where the king and queen sailed about in the canals in their beautiful boats.'

"'But I soon came to sail about in quite a different style, and for many years, far away on long voyages!'

"JUST AS I WAS STANDING THERE READING YOUR LETTER, SOME ONE PUT HIS ARM ROUND MY WAIST—"

"'Yes, I often wept for you!' she said; 'I thought you were dead and gone and lying rolling about at the bottom of the sea! Many a night have I got up to look at the weather-cock to see if the wind had shifted; it had shifted, of course, but you did not come. I remember so clearly how the rain was pouring down one day, when the dustman came outside the house where I was in service, and I came down with the dustbin, and was standing by the door. What terrible weather it was! Just as I was standing there, the postman came up and gave me a letter! It was from you. How it had traveled about! I snatched it and read it! I laughed and I cried! I was so happy! You wrote that you were in the hot countries, where the coffee grows! How delightful it must have been there! You told me so much and I could see it all before me, while the rain was pouring down and I was standing there with the dust-bin. Just then some one put his arm round my waist ——'

"'Yes, and you gave him such a box on the ear, that it sent him flying!'

"'Well, I did n't know it was you! You had arrived as early as your letter; and you looked so handsome,—of course, you are so still,—you had a long, yellow-silk handkerchief in your breast-pocket and a black, glazed hat! You were so grand! But, gracious me, what terrible weather it was, and what a state the streets were in!'

"'Then we got married!' he said; 'do you remember? And then our first little boy came, and then Marie, and Nils, and Peter, and Hans Christian!'

"'Yes, and all of them have now grown up and become respectable people, whom everybody likes!'

"'And then their children again; and they have little ones too!' said the old sailor. 'Yes, they are great-grandchildren, and chips of the old block! But it seems to me it was about this time of the year we were married!'

"'Yes, this is the day of your golden wedding!' said elder-tree mother, as she put her head straight in between the two old people, and they thought it was the neighbor's wife who nodded to them; and they looked at one another and took each other by the hand. Soon after came their children and grandchildren, who all knew it was the golden-wedding day; they had already been there in the morning to offer their congratulations, but the old people had forgotten that, although they remembered so well everything that had happened many years ago. The elder-tree smelled so sweetly and the sun, which was setting, shone right into the faces of the old people, which were quite fresh and ruddy, and the youngest of the grandchildren danced around them and shouted gleefully that to-night there would be great doings — that they were going to have hot potatoes! And elder-tree mother in the tree nodded her head and shouted 'hurrah!' with all the others."

"But that is not a fairy tale!" said the little boy, who had been listening to it.

"Well, you ought to know!" said the old man, who had been telling the story; "but let us ask elder-tree mother!"

"That was not a fairy tale!" said elder-tree mother, "but now it is coming! Out of real life grow the most wonderful fairy tales; otherwise my beautiful elder-tree could not have sprung from the tea-urn." And then she took the little boy out of bed and held him to her bosom, and the elder-tree branches, which were full of blossoms, closed around them, till at last they seemed to sit in an arbor, thickly covered with leaves and flowers — and away it flew with them through the air. What a delightful trip! Elder-tree mother had suddenly become a beautiful young girl, but her frock was of the same green stuff and was trimmed with the same white flowers which elder-tree mother had worn; in her bosom she had a real elder flower and round her yellow, curly hair a whole wreath of elder flowers; her eyes were large and blue—it was a pleasure to look at her! She and the boy kissed each other; they were of the same age and felt the same happiness. They went hand in hand out of the arbor, and were now standing in the beautiful flower garden of their home. On the

THE ELDER-TREE BRANCHES CLOSED AROUND THEM TILL THEY SEEMED TO SIT IN AN ARBOR, AND AWAY IT FLEW WITH THEM THROUGH THE AIR.

fresh lawn the father's stick was tethered to a peg; to the little ones there was life in that stick; as soon as they set themselves astride it, the bright knob turned into a horse's head with a long, black, flowing mane, and four strong legs shot out from the stick. The animal was powerful and high-spirited, and they flew at full gallop round the lawn—hurrah!— "Now we'll ride many miles away," said the boy; "we'll ride to the old manor-house, where we were last year!" And they rode round and round the lawn, while the little girl, who, as we know, was no one else but elder-tree mother, kept crying out: "Now we are in the country! Do you see the farmer's house with the big baking-oven sticking out like a giant egg in the wall facing the road? The elder-tree spreads its branches over it, and the cock struts about and scratches the ground for the hens; look how proudly he holds himself! Now we are near the church. It lies high up on the hill behind the great oak-trees, one of which is half dead! Now we are near the smithy where the fire burns in the forge and half-naked men strike the red-hot iron with their hammer, so that the sparks fly all over the place. Away, away to the old manor-house!"

And everything which the little girl, who sat behind him on the stick, spoke of, flew rapidly past them, and the boy saw it all, although they were only galloping round the lawn. Then they played on a sidewalk and marked the outline of a little garden in the ground, and she took the elder flower out of her hair and planted it there; it grew up exactly like the one which the old couple had planted in Nyboder, when they were young, which has already been told. They went hand in hand just like the old people had done as children, but they did not go up the Round Tower or to Frederiksburg Garden; no, the little girl took the boy round the waist and flew with him all over Denmark. It was spring, and the summer came, and it was autumn, and the winter came, and thousands of pictures were reflected on the boy's eyes and heart, while the little girl sang to him: "This you will never forget!" And during their whole flight the elder-tree smelled sweet and delicious; he noticed, of course, the smell of the roses and the fresh beeches, but the fragrance from the elder-tree became still sweeter, for its flowers hung near the little girl's heart, and he often leaned his head on it during their flight.

"How beautiful it is here in the spring!" said the little girl, as they stood in the beechwood where all the shoots were fresh and green, and where the fragrant green woodruff lay at their feet, and the pale-pink anemones looked so beautiful among the green. "Oh, that there might always be spring in the fragrant Danish beechwoods!"

"How beautiful it is here in the summer!" she said, as they flew past the old manor house of the middle ages, the red walls and pointed gables of which were reflected in the moats where swans were swimming about and looking up the old shady avenue. In the fields the corn stood waving like a sea, the ditches were full of red and yellow flowers, and the hedges with wild hops and budding convolvuluses, and in the evening the moon rose, large and round, while the scent from the hayricks in the meadows filled the air with sweetness. "It can never be forgotten!"

"How beautiful it is here in the autumn!" said the little girl, as the heavens became loftier and of a darker blue; the forests glowed with the most beautiful colors in red, yellow, and green; the hounds rushed past while whole flocks of wild birds flew screeching over the burial mounds, where the blackberry bushes hung over the old stones. The sea was blue-black, dotted with white sails, and in the barn sat old women, girls, and children picking hops into a big tub; the young folks sang ditties and the old ones told fairy tales about brownies and trolls. "It could not be better!"

"How beautiful it is here in the winter!" said the little girl as all the trees stood covered with hoar frost, looking like white corals. The snow creaked under foot as if all the people were wearing new boots, and from the sky fell one shooting star after another. In the parlor the Christmas tree was lighted; there were presents, and all were in good spirits. In the country the violin was heard in the peasant's parlor; and there were scrambles for slices of apples. Even the poorest child said: "It is beautiful in winter-time!"

Yes, it was delightful! The little girl showed the boy everything, while the elder-tree filled the air with scent, and the red flag with the white cross was waving, the flag under which the old sailor in Nyboder had sailed! And the boy grew up and was going out into the wide world, far away to the hot countries where the coffee grows; but when they parted the little girl took an elder flower from her breast and gave it to him to keep. It was placed in his hymn-book, and whenever he opened the book in foreign lands, it always opened at the place where the flower lay, and the more he looked at it the fresher it grew; he seemed to breathe the air of the Danish woods, and between the leaves of the flowers he could plainly see the little girl peeping out with her clear blue eyes, and then she whispered: "How beautiful it is here in spring, in summer, in autumn, and in winter," while a hundred pictures passed before him.

Thus many years had passed and he was now an old man and sat with his wife under the blossoming tree; they held each other by the hand, just as great-grandfather and great-grandmother had done out at Nyboder, and like them, talked about the old days and of the golden wedding; the little girl with the blue eyes and the elder flowers in her hair was sitting up in the tree, nodding to them both, and saying: "To-day it is the golden wedding-day!" And then she took two flowers from his wreath and kissed them; they shone first like silver, and then like gold, and when she placed them on the heads of the old couple, each flower became a golden crown. There they both sat, like a king and queen, under the fragrant tree, which looked exactly like an elder-tree; and he told his old wife the story about elder-tree mother, just as it had been told him, when he was a little boy, and they both thought there was so much in it, which resembled their own and these parts they liked best.

"Yes, that 's how it is!" said the little girl in the tree. "Some call me elder-tree mother, others call me a dryad, but my proper name is 'Memory'; it is I who sit in the tree which goes on growing and growing. I can remember; I can relate. Let me see if you still have your flower!"

And the old man opened his hymn-book and there lay the elder flower as fresh as if it had just been put there, and Memory nodded, and the two

ELDER-TREE MOTHER TOOK TWO FLOWERS FROM HER WREATH AND PLACED THEM ON THE HEADS
OF THE OLD COUPLE, WHEN EACH FLOWER BECAME A GOLDEN CROWN.

old people with their golden crowns sat in the red glow of the setting sun; they closed their eyes, and—and then the story came to an end!

The little boy lay in his bed; he did not know whether he had been dreaming, or whether he had been listening to the story. The tea-urn stood on the table, but no elder-tree was growing out of it, and the old man, who had been telling the story, was just on the point of going out at the door, which he did.

"How beautiful it was!" said the little boy. "Mother, I have been to the hot countries!"

"Yes, I can quite believe that!" said the mother; "when one has drunk two brimful cups of elder-tea, one may well think one has been to the hot countries!" And she covered him up well, so that he should not take cold. "You must have slept while I sat disputing with him whether it was a story or a fairy tale!"

"And where is elder-tree mother?" asked the boy.

"She is in the tea-urn," said the mother, "and there she had better stay!"

THE BROWNIE AT THE
BUTTERMAN'S

THE STUDENT LIVED IN THE GARRET.

THE BROWNIE LIVED ON THE
GROUND FLOOR.

THE BROWNIE AT THE BUTTERMAN'S

HE was a student of the good old sort; he lived in the garret and possessed nothing. The butterman, who was also one of the good old sort, lived on the ground floor and owned the whole house. The brownie stuck to him, for he always got a dish of porridge every Christmas eve with a big lump of butter in the middle. The butterman could well afford this, so the brownie settled down in the shop, where there was much to learn.

One evening the student came in through the back door to buy some candles and cheese; he had no one to send, so he went himself. He got what he asked for and paid for it, and the butterman and his wife nodded "good night" to him—she, by the by, could do more than nod to people, for she was gifted with a glib tongue—and the student nodded in return, but stopped to read the piece of paper in which the cheese was

125

wrapped.   It was a leaf torn out of an old book, which ought not to have been torn to pieces; it was an old book full of poetry.

"There is more of it over there!" said the butterman.   "I gave an old woman some coffee-beans for it; if you'll give me fourpence you can have what there is left of it."

"Thanks!" said the student, "let me have it instead of the cheese!   I can eat my bread and butter without anything to it; it would be a sin to let the whole of the book be torn into bits and pieces.   You are an excellent man, a practical man, but poetry you don't understand, any more than the tub yonder."

This was rather rude of him to say, especially as far as the tub was concerned, but the butterman and the student both laughed, for it was only said in fun, of course.   But the brownie was annoyed that any one should dare to say such things to a butterman, who had a house of his own, and sold the best butter.

As soon as it was night and the shop was closed, and all, with the exception of the student, had gone to bed, the brownie went into the bedroom and took the wife's tongue—she had no use for it when she was asleep—and whatever object in the room he put it on, received voice and speech, and could express its thoughts and feelings just as well as the mistress of the house.   But only one object at a time could make use of it, which was a blessing, for otherwise they would all have been speaking at once.

And the brownie put the woman's tongue on the tub, in which the old newspapers were kept.   "Is it really true," asked the brownie, "that you don't know what poetry is?"

"Of course I do," said the tub.   "It is what you find at the bottom of the pages in newspapers and cut out.   I should say I have more of it inside of me than the student, and I am only a simple tub compared with the butterman."

And the brownie put the tongue on the coffee-quern; how it rattled away!   And he put it on the butter-firkin and the money-drawer—all were of the same opinion as the tub, and what all are agreed about one must respect.

"I 'll just pay out that student!" said the brownie, as he went quietly up the kitchen stairs to the garret, where the student lived.   He had a light burning, and the brownie peeped through the keyhole and saw that the student was reading in the ragged book from the shop down-stairs. But how light it was in there!   Out of the book shot forth a clear ray of light, which grew into a trunk—into a mighty tree, which rose high in the air and spread its branches out over the student.   Every leaf was fresh and every flower was a beautiful girl's head, some with dark, sparkling eyes, others with clear blue eyes.   Each fruit was a shining star and then there was such a wonderfully lovely sound of song and music.

Such splendor the little brownie had never dreamed of, much less seen or experienced.   And so he remained standing on tip-toe, peeping and peering through the keyhole till the light was put out.   The student had, no doubt, blown out his candle and gone to bed; but the little brownie stood there nevertheless, for he could still hear the beautiful soft melody, a delightful cradle-song for the student, who had lain down to rest.

THERE THE LITTLE BROWNIE SAT, ILLUMINATED BY THE BURNING HOUSE OPPOSITE, HOLDING IN HIS HANDS HIS RED CAP IN WHICH THE TREASURE LAY.

"It is really wonderful here!" said the little brownie. "I never should have thought it — I think I will stop with the student!"   And he began to think it over, and reasoned quite sensibly with himself, and then he sighed: "But the student has no porridge!" and so he went away.   He went down to the butterman's shop again, and it was a good thing he did, for the tub had quite exhausted the mistress's tongue, by discussing all it contained from one point of view and was just about to turn round to repeat it from another, when the brownie came to take back the tongue to its owner.   But the whole of the shop, from the money-drawer to the firewood, had from that time the same opinion as the tub, and they respected it to such an extent and had such confidence in it, that when the butterman afterward read about "Art" and "The Drama" in his evening paper, they all believed it came from the tub.

But the little brownie could not sit quiet and listen any longer to all the wisdom and arguing down in the shop. As soon as the light shone out from the garret, he felt as if the rays were strong ropes which drew him up there; and he had to go and peep through the keyhole, and then a feeling of vastness came over him, such as we experience at the sight of the rolling ocean when the storm sweeps over it, and he burst into tears. He did not know why he cried, but he found some comfort in these tears. How wonderfully delightful it must be to sit with the student under that tree, but it could not be—he would have to be content with the keyhole. There he was standing on the cold landing, while the autumn wind blew down through the trap-door in the loft above him. It was so cold, so very cold; but the little brownie only felt it when the light in the garret was put out, and when the tones of the music died away. Ugh! How he shivered! He then crept down again to his snug little corner where it was so pleasant and comfortable! And when the Christmas porridge came with a big lump of butter in the middle—ah, then the butterman's was the best place after all.

But in the middle of the night the brownie was awakened by a terrible noise against the shutters, caused by the people outside knocking and thundering away at them, while the watchmen were blowing their whistles. A big fire had broken out, and the whole street was enveloped in flames. Was the fire in this house, or in the neighbor's? Where? It was a terrible moment! The butterman's wife was so bewildered that she took her gold earrings out of her ears and put them in her pocket, in order to save something; the butterman ran to fetch his bonds and shares, and the servant girl to save her silk mantilla, which she had just managed to buy out of her savings. Every one wanted to save the best they possessed, and the brownie became possessed by the same desire; in a couple of bounds he was up the stairs and in the student's garret. The student was standing quite calmly at the open window, looking at the fire which was raging in the house opposite. The little brownie seized the wonderful book that was lying on the table, put it inside his red cap, and held it tightly to his bosom with both hands. The most valuable treasure in the house had been saved, and he rushed off with it, right out upon the roof, to the top of the chimney. There he sat, illuminated by the burning house opposite, and holding his hands on his red cap in which the treasure lay. Now he knew where his sympathies lay, and to whom he really belonged; but when the fire had been put out and he was himself again — well: "I shall have to divide myself between the two," he said, "I cannot quite give up the butterman because of the porridge!"

And, after all, it is only human! We all of us go to the butterman — for the sake of the porridge.

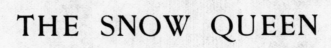

THE SNOW QUEEN

THERE WERE TWO LITTLE WINDOWS OPPOSITE EACH OTHER
ON THE ROOFS OF THE HOUSES.

THE SNOW QUEEN

THE FIRST STORY

WHICH TREATS OF THE MIRROR AND THE BROKEN PIECES

WELL, now let us begin! When we have got to the end of the story, we shall know more than we do at present. It is all about a wicked troll, the worst of them all, the Devil. One day he was in a really good humor, for he had made a mirror which had this virtue, that everything good and beautiful which was reflected in it would shrink to almost nothing, but all that was worthless and hideous appeared only too distinctly, and was even magnified. The most beautiful landscapes looked like boiled spinach, and the best of people looked hideous, or were seen standing on their heads with no stomach to their bodies; the faces were so distorted that no one could recognize them, and, if one had a freckle, in the mirror it was sure to spread all over one's nose and mouth. "It is most amusing," said the Devil. If a good, pious thought passed through a person's mind it was reflected so hideously in the mirror that the chief of the trolls had to laugh at his crafty invention. All those who went to the troll-school—for he kept such a one—went about telling everybody that a miracle had happened; now at last one could see what the world and mankind really looked like. They ran about with the mirror till at last there was not a country or a human being that had not been reflected and distorted in it. And now they wanted to fly up to heaven with it and mock at the angels and the Lord. The higher they flew with the mirror the more distorted and ridiculous the reflections became, till they could scarcely hold it for laughter. Higher and higher they flew, nearer to God and the angels; then the mirror trembled so violently in its distortions that it slipped from their hands and fell down to the earth, where it broke into hundreds of millions and billions of pieces. But just on that account it caused greater misfortune than before, for some pieces were hardly as big as a grain of sand and these flew about all over the world, and when they got into people's eyes they stuck there and made everything appear to them topsy-turvy, or made them only see the wrong side of things, for every piece had retained the same power as the whole mirror. Some people even got a small piece into their hearts and this was the most terrible of all; these hearts became like lumps of ice. Some of the pieces were so large that they could be used for window-panes, but it was scarcely worth looking at one's friend's through these panes; other pieces were used for spectacles, and when people put on these spectacles to see aright and be just, then things went all wrong; the Evil One laughed till his sides ached—he felt so awfully tickled. But small pieces of glass were still flying about in the air. Now we shall hear!

KAY MANAGED TO GET HIS SLEDGE FASTENED TO THE LARGE ONE, AND AWAY
HE WENT WITH IT.

THE SECOND STORY

A LITTLE BOY AND A LITTLE GIRL

In the middle of the big town, where there are so many houses and
people that there is not room enough for every one to have a little garden,
and where most people must therefore be content with growing flowers in
pots, there were, however, two poor children who had a garden somewhat
bigger than a flower-pot. They were not brother and sister, but they
were just as fond of one another as if they had been. Their parents lived
close to each other; they lived in two garrets, where the roof of the one
house adjoined that of the neighboring one, with the gutter running
between them along the eaves. There were two little windows opposite
each other in the roofs of the houses; you had only to step across the gutter
to get to one window from the other.

Outside each window the parents had placed a large wooden box in which they grew vegetables for their own use, and a little rose-tree, one in each box, which thrived well.   The parents had now placed the boxes right across the gutter, so that they almost reached from one window to the other and looked exactly like two flower beds.   The creepers of the sweet-pea hung down over the sides of the boxes, and the rose-trees shot long branches which twined themselves around the windows while others clustered together; it was almost like a triumphal arch of flowers and leaves.   As the boxes were very high and the children knew that they must not climb up there, they were often allowed to step outside and sit on their small footstools under the rose-trees, and there they could play splendidly.

In the winter-time these pleasant hours came to an end.   The windows were often frozen all over, but then they heated copper pennies on the stove and placed the warm coin against the frozen pane, and thus got a splendid peephole, so round, so round; and then from behind would peep a bright gentle eye, one from each window, they were those of the little boy and the little girl.   He was called Kay, and she, Gerda.   In the summer-time they could get to each other with one jump; in the winter they had first to go down many stairs and then up many stairs, while the snow was falling outside.

"It 's the white bees that are swarming!" said the old grandmother.

"Have they also a queen-bee?" asked the little boy, for he knew that there was such a thing among the real bees.

"That they have!" said the grandmother; "she is generally where the swarm is thickest.   She is the largest of them all and never settles on the ground, but flies up to the black clouds again.   Many a winter night does she fly through the streets of the town looking in through the windows, and the frost on the panes then becomes most wonderful, and looks like flowers."

"Yes, I have seen that!" said both the children, and then they knew it was true.

"Can the Snow Queen come in here?" asked the little girl.

"Let her only come," said the boy, " I 'll put her on the warm stove and then she 'll melt."

But the grandmother smoothed his hair and told him some other stories.

In the evening when little Kay was at home and half-undressed, he climbed up on the chairs by the window and looked out through the little hole; he could see the snowflakes falling outside, and one of them, the largest of all, settled on the edge of one of the flower-boxes.   The snowflake grew larger and larger till at last it became a full-grown woman, dressed in the most delicate white gauze; it looked as if it was composed of millions of star-like flakes.   She was very beautiful and graceful, but she was made of ice, dazzling, glittering ice; still, she was alive, her eyes sparkled like two bright stars, but there was no repose or rest in them. She nodded toward the windows and beckoned with her hand. The little boy was frightened and jumped down from the chair, and just then it seemed as if a large bird flew past outside the window.

Next day it was clear frosty weather, and then came the thaw, and at last the spring; the sun shone, the green shoots burst forth, the swallows built their nests, the windows were opened and the two little children were again sitting in their little garden high up in the gutter on the roof.

The roses blossomed most beautifully that summer; the little girl had learned a hymn, in which there was something about roses, and that made her think of her own roses, and so she sang it to the little boy, who also joined in, and together they sang:

"The roses grow in the valley,
Where the Christ-Child we shall see."

And the little ones held each other by the hand, kissed the roses, and looked up at God's bright sunshine, and spoke to it as if the Christ-Child were there. What beautiful summer days they were, what a blessing to be near the fresh rose-trees, which seemed never to cease blossoming.

Kay and Gerda sat looking in the picture book of animals and birds, when just at that moment the clock in the great church tower struck five. Kay exclaimed: "Oh dear! I feel as if something had stabbed my heart! And now I 've got something into my eye!"

The little girl put her arms round his neck; he blinked his eye, but no — there was nothing to be seen.

"I think it is gone!" he said; but it was not gone. It was one of the glass pieces from the mirror, the troll-mirror, which you no doubt remember, the horrible mirror, in which everything great and good that was reflected in it became small and ugly, while everything bad and wicked became more distinct and prominent and every fault was at once noticed. Poor Kay had got one of the fragments right into his heart. It would soon become like a lump of ice. It did not cause him any pain, but it was there.

"Why do you cry?" he asked. "And you look so ugly! There is nothing the matter with me! Fie!" he cried suddenly, "that rose is worm-eaten! And look! why, it is quite crooked! They are ugly roses after all, just like the boxes they are in!" And then he kicked the box with his foot, and knocked off two roses.

"Kay, what are you doing?" cried the girl; and when he saw her fright he knocked off another rose and rushed through his window away from the good little Gerda.

When afterward she brought out the picture book he said it was only fit for babies, and if the grandmother began to tell stories he was always sure to put in an *if*, and if he saw his opportunity he would go behind her, put on a pair of spectacles, and talk like her; he could mimic her exactly, and make people laugh at him. He could soon talk and walk like all the people in the whole street. Everything that was peculiar and unattractive to them he was sure to imitate, and then people said: "That boy must have a clever head!" But it was the piece of glass he had got in his eye and the piece of glass that had stuck in his heart that caused all this; that was the reason he teased even little Gerda, who loved him with all her heart.

He no longer cared for the old games, he was now only interested in what he considered was more sensible, thus, one winter day, when the snow was falling, he brought a large magnifying glass and held out the tail of his blue coat and let the snowflakes fall upon it.

"Just look through the glass, Gerda!" he said; and every snowflake was magnified and looked like a splendid flower or star with many points, and a most beautiful sight it was!

"Do you see how curious it is?" said Kay, "how much more interesting than real flowers? And there is not a single fault in them; they are quite perfect, if only they do not melt away!"

Shortly afterward Kay appeared with thick gloves on, and his sledge on his back, and shouted into Gerda's ears: "I have got leave to go sledging in the great square, where all the boys are playing"; and off he went.

Many of the boldest boys on the playground used to fasten their sledges to the peasants' carts, and in this way they got a good ride. It was a merry time! While the fun was at its height a large sledge came driving past; it was painted all white, and a person was sitting in it wrapped in a white fur coat and with a white fur cap. The sledge drove twice round the square and Kay managed to get his own little sledge fastened to it, and away he went with it. They went faster and faster right through the next street; the driver turned round and nodded in a friendly way to Kay, as if they were old acquaintances. Every time Kay wanted to set free his sledge, the driver nodded again to him, and so Kay remained on the sledge and soon they drove out of the gate of the town. The snow then began to fall so heavily that the little boy could hardly see a hand before him as they rushed onward; then suddenly he let go the rope, to get loose from the large sledge, but it was of no use, his little sledge stuck fast to the other and they sped on as quickly as the wind. He then cried out aloud, but nobody heard him; the snow fell fast and furious, and the sledge flew onward, while now and then it gave a jump, as if they were rushing over ditches and hurdles. He became quite frightened and wanted to say the Lord's Prayer, but could only remember the multiplication table.

The snowflakes became larger and larger, till at last they looked like big white fowls; suddenly they ran aside and the great sledge stopped and the person who had been driving stood up; the coat and the cap were entirely of snow. It was a lady, very tall and erect and dazzlingly white, it was the Snow Queen.

"We have got on quickly!" she said, "but you are shivering with cold! Creep in under my bearskin!" Then she put him beside her in the sledge and wrapped the skin round him, and he felt as if he were sinking into a snowdrift.

"Do you feel cold still?" she asked, as she kissed him on his forehead. Ugh! it was colder than ice, it went right through his heart, which was already half frozen; he felt as if he were going to die — but only for a moment, and then he was quite well again and did not feel the cold around him any more.

"My sledge! Don't forget my sledge!" This was the first thing he remembered; it was tied to one of the white fowls, which came rushing on behind them with the sledge on its back. The Snow Queen kissed Kay once more, and then little Gerda, and the grandmother, and all at home passed out of his mind altogether.

"I shall give you no more kisses," she said; "or I should kiss you to death!"

Kay looked at her; she was very beautiful; a more intelligent or lovely face he could not imagine; she did not now appear to him to be of ice as when she sat outside the window and beckoned to him. In his eyes she was perfect, and he did not feel the least afraid of her; he told her he knew mental arithmetic even in fractions, and how many square miles and inhabitants there were in all countries, to all of which she smiled. But he felt he did not know enough after all, and he looked up into the great space above, whereupon she flew with him high up on the black cloud, while the storm whistled and roared; it seemed as if it were singing old ballads. They flew over forests and lakes, across the ocean and many countries; below them the cold blast scoured the plains, the wolves howled and the snow sparkled, and over them flew the black, screeching crows, while the moon shone bright and clear, and by its light he beheld the long, dreary winter's night — by day he slept at the feet of the Snow Queen.

THE THIRD STORY

THE WITCH'S FLOWER GARDEN

BUT how did little Gerda fare when Kay did not return? Where could he be? Nobody knew; nobody could give any tidings of him. The boys could only tell that they had seen him tie his little sledge to another large and splendid sledge which drove down the street and out through the town gate. No one knew where he was; many tears flowed and little Gerda cried long and bitterly; then they said that he was dead, that he had been drowned in the river which flowed past close to the town; oh, they were indeed long, dark winter days.

Then came the spring with the warm sunshine.

"Kay is dead and gone," said little Gerda.

"I don't believe it!" said the sunshine.

"He is dead and gone," she said to the swallows.

"We don't believe it!" they answered, and at last little Gerda did not believe it either.

"I will put on my new red shoes," she said one morning, "those which Kay has not seen, and then I will go down to the river and ask it about him!"

It was quite early; she kissed her old grandmother, who was asleep, put on the red shoes, and went out quite alone through the town gate toward the river.

"Is it true that you have taken my little playmate? I will make you a present of my red shoes if you will give him back to me."

And she thought the waves nodded to her strangely. She then took her red shoes, the most precious she had, and threw them both out into the river, but they fell close to the bank and the little billows soon carried them ashore to her. It seemed as if the river would not take the dearest treasure she had because it could not give back little Kay to her; but then she thought she had not thrown the shoes out far enough, and so she climbed into a boat which was lying among the rushes, and went right to the farthest end of it and threw the shoes into the water. But the boat was not fastened, and its motion as she got into it sent it adrift from the bank. As soon as she noticed this she hastened to get out, but before she could jump ashore the boat was an arm's length from the bank and now it drifted still faster.

Little Gerda now became quite frightened and began to cry, but no one heard her except the sparrows, and they could not carry her ashore; but they flew along the banks of the river, singing as if to comfort her: "Here we are! Here we are!" The boat drifted with the current, while little Gerda sat quite still in her stockinged feet; her little red shoes were floating along behind, but they did not overtake the boat, which drifted more quickly ahead.

The banks on both sides of the river were pretty; there were beautiful flowers, old trees, and green slopes with sheep and cows, but not a human being was to be seen.

"Perhaps the river is carrying me to little Kay," thought Gerda; and then she became more cheerful and stood up in the boat, looking for many hours at the beautiful banks of the river, till she came to a large cherry orchard where there was a little house with strange red and blue windows and a thatched roof, and outside stood two wooden soldiers who presented arms to all who sailed past.

Gerda called out to them; she thought they were living beings, but of course they did not answer. She was drawing near to them; the current was driving the boat right against the shore.

Gerda called out still louder, when an old—very old—woman came out of the house, leaning upon a crook; she wore a big sun-bonnet with a broad brim painted all over with the most lovely flowers.

" You poor little child ! " said the old crone ; " how did you get into the strong, rapid current, and drift so far out into the wide world ? " And the old woman went right out into the water, hooked her crook fast into the boat, pulled it ashore and lifted little Gerda out of it.

Gerda was glad to get on land again, but was a little afraid of the strange old woman.

" Come, tell me who you are and how you came here ! " she said.

And Gerda told her everything, the old woman shaking her head all the time and only muttering " Hem ! Hem ! " When Gerda had told her all and asked her if she had not seen little Kay, the woman said he had not passed by there, but he would, no doubt, be coming that way ; she had better be of good cheer and taste her cherries and see her flowers— they were much prettier than any picture book. Each of them had a story to tell. She then took Gerda by the hand and went into the little house, locking the door after her.

The windows were high up near the ceiling and the panes were red, blue, and yellow ; the daylight shone through them in such a strange way in all sorts of colors. On the table stood the most delicious cherries, and Gerda ate as many as she liked, for she was not afraid to touch them. And while she was eating, the old woman combed her hair with a golden comb, till the glossy hair hung in beautiful yellow curls round the pleasant little face, which was as round and as fresh as a rose.

"I have really been longing for such a pretty little girl as you ! " said the old woman. " You will soon see how well we shall get on together, we two ! " And as she went on combing little Gerda's hair, the more Gerda forgot her playmate, little Kay, for the old woman was learned in witchcraft, but she was not one of the wicked witches. She only practised witchcraft for her own amusement, and did so now because she wanted to keep little Gerda. She therefore went out into her garden and stretched out her crook toward all the rose-trees, and, beautifully though they blos- somed, she caused them all to sink into the dark ground and no one could see where they had been standing. The old woman was afraid that if Gerda saw the roses she would think of her own and then remember little Kay and run away.

She now led Gerda out into the flower garden. Oh, how fragrant and lovely it was there ! Every imaginable flower of every season was here in full bloom ; no picture book could be more variegated and beautiful. Gerda ran joyously about and played till the sun went down behind the lofty cherry-trees. Then she was put to sleep in a splendid bed with new silk quilts stuffed with blue violets, and there she slept and dreamed as hap- pily as any queen on her wedding-day.

Next day she again played with the flowers in the warm sunshine, and thus many days passed. Gerda knew every flower, but numerous as they were she seemed to feel there was one missing, but she did not know which it was. Then, one day, as she sat looking at the old woman's sunbonnet with the painted flowers, she noticed that the prettiest of them all was a rose. The old crone had forgotten to take it off her bonnet when she buried the rose-trees in the ground. But that is the way when you don't keep your wits about you!

"What! are there no roses here?" cried Gerda, as she ran among the flower beds, looking and searching, but there were none to be found.

She then sat down and cried, but her hot tears happened to fall just where a rose-tree had sunk into the ground, and when the warm tears moistened the soil the tree shot up suddenly in full bloom, just as when it had disappeared. Gerda embraced it, kissed the roses, and thought of the lovely roses at home, and then of little Kay.

"Oh, how I have been losing my time!" said the little girl. "Why, I was going to find Kay! Do you know where he is?" she asked the roses. "Do you think he is dead, and lost to us?"

"He is not dead," said the roses. "We have been under the ground, where all the dead are, but Kay was not there!"

"Thank you," said little Gerda, and she went to the other flowers and looked into their cups and asked: "Do you know where little Kay is?"

But all the flowers were standing in the sunshine, dreaming the fairy tale of their own lives. Gerda heard many — very many — of these stories, but none of the flowers knew anything about Kay.

And what did the orange-lily say?

"Do you hear the drum? Rat! Tat! There are only two sounds — always Rat! Tat! Listen to the women's funeral dirge! Listen to the priest's cry! The Hindoo woman is standing in her long red robe on the funeral pile, the flames are enveloping her and her husband's dead body; but the Hindoo woman is thinking of the living being in the circle around her, of him whose eyes burn hotter than the flames, and the fire which penetrates sooner to her heart than the flames which will soon burn her body to ashes. Can the flames of the heart die in the flames of the funeral pile?"

"I cannot understand it all!" said little Gerda.

"That is the story of my life," said the orange-lily.

What does the convolvulus say?

"Over the narrow mountain path looms an old castle; the ivy is climbing, leaf by leaf, up along the old red walls and around the balcony, on which stands a beautiful girl; she bends over the balustrade and looks down the road. No rose is fresher than she; no apple-blossom carried away from the tree by the wind could float more gracefully than she. How her magnificent silk robe rustles! She murmurs: "Will he not come?"

"Is it Kay you mean?" asked little Gerda.

"I am only thinking about the fairy tale of my life, my dream," answered the convolvulus.

What does the little snowdrop say?

"Between the trees hangs a long board suspended between ropes; it is a swing, and two lovely little girls, in frocks white as snow, and with long green-silk ribbons fluttering from their hats, are sitting in it, swinging to and fro. Their brother, who is bigger than they, stands on the swing with one arm round the rope to steady himself, for in one hand he has a little bowl and in the other a clay pipe; he is blowing soap-bubbles. The swing goes backward and forward and the bubbles fly about, constantly changing their color. The last bubble is still hanging at the end of the pipe, swaying to and fro in the wind. A little black dog, as light as the bubbles, sits up on his hind legs and wants to get on the swing; but it never stops, and the dog falls, barks, and becomes angry; they tease him, the bubbles burst — a swinging board, the picture of a bursting bubble is my song."

"It may be very pretty, all that you tell me, but you speak in such a sad voice, and do not mention Kay at all! What do the hyacinths say?"

"There were three beautiful sisters, fair and delicate; one was dressed in red, the other in blue, and the third in white; hand in hand they danced near the silent lake in the bright moonshine. They were not elfin-maidens, they were the daughters of mankind. There was a sweet fragrance in the air as the maidens disappeared into the wood; the fragrance became stronger — three coffins, in which lay the beautiful maidens, glided away from the thicket across the lake; shining glow-worms flew about like little floating lights. Were the dancing maidens asleep or were they dead? The fragrance of the flowers tells us they are corpses; the evening bell is tolling for the dead!"

"You make me quite sad," said little Gerda. "Your perfume is so strong, I cannot help thinking of the dead maidens! Alas! is little Kay really dead after all? The roses have been under the ground, and they say no!"

"Ding, dong!" rang the bells of the hyacinths. "We are not tolling for little Kay; we do not know him. We are only singing our own song, the only one we know!"

And Gerda went to the buttercup which shone forth among the bright-green leaves.

"You are a bright little sun," said Gerda. "Tell me, if you know, where I can find my playmate." And the buttercup shone so brightly and looked up at Gerda. What song would the buttercup sing? It was not to be about Kay either.

"The sun was was shining so warmly, on the first day of spring, into a little courtyard; the rays glided down along the neighbors' white wall, and close by grew the first yellow flowers, sparkling like gold in the warm sunlight. The old grandmother sat outside in her chair, her grand-daughter, the poor, good-looking servant-girl, came home from a short visit; she kissed her grandmother. There was gold, the gold of the heart, in that blessed kiss. Gold on the lips, gold on the ground, gold high above in the early morning hour! There, that is my little story!" said the buttercup.

"My poor old grandmother!" sighed Gerda. "She must be longing for me, and be anxious about me, just as she was about little Kay. But I shall soon be home again, and then I'll bring Kay with me. It is no use asking the flowers; they only know their own song, they cannot give me any tidings!" And so she fastened up her little frock, so that she might run the faster; but the narcissus caught her by the leg as she sprang over it. She stopped, looked at the long flower and said:

"Perhaps you know something?" And she bent down close to it. What did she say?

"I can see myself! I can see myself!" said the narcissus. "Oh, what a perfume! Up in the little garret stands a little dancer, half dressed; sometimes she stands on one leg, and sometimes on two—she kicks at the whole world; she is only a phantom. She pours water out of the teapot onto a piece of cloth which she holds in her hand; it is her corset. Cleanliness is a virtue! Her white dress hangs on a peg, and that has also been washed in the teapot and dried on the roof! She puts it on and ties a saffron-colored handkerchief round her neck, so that her dress should look all the whiter. How high she kicks! Look how well she poises on one stem! I can see myself! I can see myself!"

"I don't care for that at all!" said Gerda; "it isn't worth telling me!" And then she ran toward the far end of the garden.

The gate was shut, but she fumbled with the rusty latch till it gave way and the gate flew open, and then little Gerda ran out, barefooted, into the wide world. She looked back three times, but no one was pursuing her; at last she could run no longer and sat down on a large stone, and when she looked round she discovered that the summer was over, and that it was late in the autumn; one could not see that in the beautiful garden where there was always sunshine, and flowers of every season of the year were always in full bloom.

"Gracious goodness! how I have been delayed!" said little Gerda; "the autumn has set in, so I dare not rest!" And she rose to proceed on her journey.

Oh! how sore and tired her little feet were; everything looked so bleak and damp round about; the long willow leaves were quite yellow, and the dew dripped like water from them. Leaf after leaf fell; the blackthorn alone bore fruit, but it was so sour and bitter that it set one's teeth on edge. Oh, how gray and gloomy the wide world looked!

THE FOURTH STORY

THE PRINCE AND PRINCESS

GERDA was obliged to sit down and rest again, when a large crow came hopping across the snow just opposite to where she was sitting. The crow looked at her for some time, turning his head from one side to the other, and at last he said: "Caw! Caw! Goo' day! Goo' day!" He could not pronounce the words any better, but he was kindly disposed toward the little girl and asked her where she was going all alone out into the wide world. Gerda understood the word "alone" very well and felt how much it meant, and so she told the crew the story of her life and asked him if he had not seen Kay.

The crow nodded quite thoughtfully and said: "Perhaps I have! Perhaps I have!"

"What? You don't say so!" cried the little girl, and she almost hugged the crow to death, so violently did she embrace him.

"Gently, gently!" said the crow. "I dare say it may be little Kay! But he has no doubt forgotten you by this time for the princess!"

"Does he live at a princess's?" asked Gerda.

"Well, yes!" said the crow; "but I find it rather difficult to speak your language. If you understand the crows' language I shall be able to tell it you better."

"No, I have not learned it!" said Gerda; "but grandmother knows it. I only wish I had learned it."

"It does not matter!" said the crow. "I will tell you as well as I can, but I am afraid it will be badly done after all." And so he told what he knew.

"In the kingdom where we are now sitting lives a princess who is very wise, but then she has read all the newspapers in the world and forgotten them again; so wise is she! The other day she was sitting on the throne,—and that is not so very pleasant, people say,—when she happened to hum a song which began with 'Why should I not marry!' 'Yes, there is something in that,' she said, and then she made up her mind to marry; but she wanted a husband who understood how to answer when spoken to, not one, in fact, who could only stand and look grand, for that was so tiresome.

"She then summoned all her maids-of-honor, and when they heard what was her will they were greatly pleased. 'We are so glad to hear that!' they all said. 'We were just thinking about the same thing the other day!' You can believe every word I tell you," said the crow; "I have a tame sweetheart at the palace who goes all over the place, and she has told me all about it!"

His sweetheart was, of course, a crow; for birds of a feather flock together, so a crow wants a crow for his mate.

"The newspapers at once appeared with a border of hearts with the princess's initials; it was there announced that every good-looking young man would be received at the palace and allowed to speak with the princess, and he who by his speech showed himself most at ease there and spoke most fluently would be chosen by the princess for her husband. Well!" said the crow, "you must believe me, it's as true as I sit here. The people came in crowds to the palace, and there was much crushing and running to and fro; but no one was successful either on the first or the second day. They could all speak well enough when they were out in the street, but when they came through the palace gate and saw the guards in silver and the lackeys in gold, standing on the staircases, and the great illuminated halls, they lost their heads altogether. And when they stood before the throne where the princess was sitting, they did not know what to say except the last word she had uttered, and she did not care to hear that said over again. It seemed as if the people, while in the room, had partaken of some narcotic, and were in a state of stupor till they got out into the street again; then they could talk and no mistake! There was a whole row of them from the town gate to the palace. I went in myself to have a look," said the crow. "The people were both hungry and thirsty, but they did not get as much as a glass of luke-warm water in the palace. Some of the more prudent had taken sandwiches with them, but they did not give any to their neighbors; they thought: 'Let him look hungry, and then the princess will not have him!'"

"But Kay, little Kay!" asked Gerda. "When does he come? Was he in the crowd?"

"Patience! patience! We are just coming to him. It was on the third day that a small person, without horse or carriage, came marching quite cheerfully right up to the palace, his eyes shone like yours, he had beautiful long hair, but was otherwise poorly dressed."

"That was Kay!" cried Gerda in great delight. "Oh, now I have found him!" And she clapped her hands.

"He had a little knapsack on his back!" said the crow.

"No, that must have been his sledge," said Gerda; "for he had the sledge with him when he left home!"

"That may be," said the crow. "I did not take particular notice, but I heard from my sweetheart that when he came in through the palace gate and saw the life guards in silver and the lackeys in gold on the staircases he was not in the least abashed; he nodded to them and said, 'It must be very tedious to stand on the staircase; I prefer to go inside.' The halls were all ablaze with lights. Counselors and excellencies were walking about in their bare feet, carrying golden vessels; it was enough to strike any one with awe. His boots creaked dreadfully, but he was not a bit frightened."

"That must have been Kay!" said Gerda, "I knew he had new boots; I have heard them creak in grandmother's room."

"Yes, they did creak," said the crow; "but he went boldly straight up to the princess, who was seated on a pearl as large as a spinning-wheel, and all the maids-of-honor with their maids and maids' maids, and all the gentlemen-in-waiting with their servants and servants' servants, who again kept page-boys, were standing round about the hall, and the nearer they stood to the door the prouder they looked. One could hardly look at the page-boys of the servants' servants, who always went about in slippers, so proud did they look standing in the doorway."

"It must be terrible!" said little Gerda. "And did Kay get the princess after all?"

"If I had not been a crow, I would have taken her myself, although I am engaged. He is said to have spoken as well as I do, when I speak the crows' language, at least that's what my sweetheart tells me. He looked a bold and handsome youth as he stood there; but he had not come to woo the princess, only to hear some of her wisdom. He was quite pleased with her and she with him."

"Yes, that must have been Kay!" said Gerda, "he was so clever; he could do mental arithmetic even in fractions! Oh, will you not take me to the palace?"

"Well, that is easily said!" said the crow. "But how shall we manage it? I will speak with my sweetheart about it; she can give us some advice, no doubt, for I must tell you such a little girl as you will never be permitted to get right inside!"

"Yes, I shall!" said Gerda. "When Kay hears I am there he will come out at once and fetch me!"

"Wait for me at the stile over yonder!" said the crow, with a twist of his head as he flew away.

It was not till late in the evening that the crow returned.

"Caw! Caw!" he croaked. "My sweetheart sends you her kind love, and here is a piece of bread for you; she took it from the kitchen, there is plenty of bread there, and you must be hungry! You cannot possibly get into the palace—for, look, you are barefooted! The guards in silver and the lackeys in gold would not allow it; but don't cry, you shall get in somehow. My sweetheart knows a little back staircase which leads up to the bedroom, and she knows where she can find the key!"

And they went into the garden and along the long avenue where the leaves were falling one after the other; and when the lights in the palace were extinguished, one by one, the crow led little Gerda to a back door, which stood ajar.

Oh, how Gerda's heart was beating with anxiety and longing! She felt as if she were about to do something wrong, while she only wanted to know if little Kay was there. Yes, it must be he; she could see his clever eyes, his long hair, and could even see how he smiled, just as when they used to sit under the roses at home. He would surely be glad to see her when he heard what a long way she had come for his sake, and how grieved they all were at home because he did not come back. Oh, what fear and what joy!

They were now on the stairs, where a small lamp was burning on the top of a cupboard; in the middle of the room stood the tame crow, turning her head in all directions and staring at Gerda, who curtseyed as her grandmother had taught her to do.

"My sweetheart has spoken so nicely about you, my young lady," said the tame crow; "your *vita*, as they say, is really very touching! If you will carry the lamp, I will go on in front. We will go straight ahead, for we shall meet no one this way."

"I fancy there is somebody coming behind us," said Gerda, as she felt something sweep past her. Shadows of horses with flying manes and the thin legs of huntsmen, and ladies and gentlemen on horseback seemed to glide past her on the wall.

"They are only dreams," said the crow; "they come to fetch the thoughts of our royal folks to go a-hunting, which is just as well, for then you can look at them in their beds all the better.   But I hope, when you have risen to a post of dignity and honor, that you will show you have a grateful heart!"

"Oh, it is n't worth talking about!" said the crow from the forest.

They now entered the first room, the walls of which were hung with rose-colored satin and artificial flowers; the dreams were already rushing past them, but they swept on at such a great speed that Gerda could not see the royal personages.

Each room was more magnificent than the last; it was enough to bewilder any one.   They were now in the bedroom, the ceiling of which was like a large palm-tree with leaves of the most costly glass, and in the middle of the room hung in a silken cord two beds, resembling lilies; the one in which the princess lay was white, the other was red; and it was in this that Gerda was to look for little Kay.   She pulled aside one of the red leaves and then saw a brown neck.   Oh, that must be Kay!   She called his name aloud and held the lamp over him,— the dreams came rushing back into the room on horseback, — he awoke, turned his head, and — it was *not* little Kay.

They only resembled each other about the neck, but the prince was a young and very handsome man.   The princess peeped out from her lily-white bed and asked what was the matter.   Little Gerda then began to cry and told them her whole story and all that the crows had done for her.

"Poor little creature!" said the prince; and the princess praised the crows, telling them that they were not at all angry with them, but that they must not do it again.   In the meantime they should receive a reward.

"Would you like to have your freedom and fly away?" asked the princess, "or would you like an appointment as crows to the court, with all the leavings of the kitchen as your perquisites?"

And both the crows curtseyed and asked for the appointments, for they thought of their old age, and said: "It would be so nice to know that we are provided for," as they put it.

And the prince got out of his bed and let Gerda sleep in it, and more he could not do.   She folded her little hands and thought: "How kind men and animals are to me!"   And then she closed her eyes and fell into a sweet sleep.

All the dreams came flying back into the room; they now looked like angels, drawing a little sledge in which Kay was sitting nodding to her.   But it was only a dream, and therefore it was all gone as soon as she awoke.

The following day she was dressed from top to toe in silk and velvet; she received an invitation to remain in the palace and enjoy herself, but she only asked for a small coach and a horse, and a little pair of shoes, and she would again set out into the wide world to find Kay.

And she not only got the shoes, but a muff, and exquisite clothes, and when she was ready to start a new coach of pure gold was waiting for her at the door. The prince and princess's coat-of-arms on the coach shone like a star; the coachman, the footman, and the postillions, for there were postillions too, wore gold crowns on their heads. The prince and princess helped her into the coach and wished her success. The crow from the forest, who was now married, accompanied her for the first ten miles. He sat by her side, for he could not bear riding backwards; while the other crow stood in the gateway flapping her wings; she did not accompany them, for she had suffered from headache since she had been definitely attached to the court and had too much to eat. The inside of the coach was stocked with fancy cakes, and under the seat were fruits and gingerbread nuts.

"Farewell! farewell!" cried the prince and princess, and little Gerda wept, and the crow wept. Thus the first miles passed, and then the crow also bade her farewell, and this was the saddest parting of all. The crow flew up into a tree and flapped his black wings as long as he could see the coach, which sparkled like bright sunbeams.

THE FIFTH STORY

THE LITTLE ROBBER GIRL

THEY drove through the dark forest, but the coach shone like a bright light, the glare of which hurt the eyes of the robbers in the forest, who could scarcely bear it.

"It's gold! It's gold!" they cried as they rushed out and seized hold of the horses. They killed the little postillions, the coachman, and the footman, and dragged little Gerda out of the coach.

"She is so fat and nice! She has been fed on nuts!" said the old robber woman, who had a long bristly beard and eyebrows, which hung down over her eyes. "She is as good as a little fatted lamb! Ah, how nice she'll taste!" And so she pulled out her bright knife, the glitter of which was terrible to behold.

"Oh, dear!" the woman shouted just at that moment; she had been bitten on the ear by her own little daughter, who was hanging on her back and was as wild and ungovernable as could be. "Oh, you wicked brat!" said the mother, who could not find the time just then to kill Gerda.

"She must play with me!" said the little robber girl. "She must give me her muff and her pretty frock, and sleep with me in my bed!" And then she bit her mother again so that she jumped into the air and twirled round and round, while all the robbers laughed and said:

"Look how she is dancing with her brat!"

"I want to get into the coach!" said the little robber girl; and she would and must have her own way, for she was such a spoiled and self-willed child. She and Gerda sat up in the coach, and away they went over stock and stone far into the forest. The little robber girl was just as big as Gerda, but much stronger and more broad-shouldered; her skin was dark and her eyes quite black; they looked almost melancholy. She took little Gerda round the waist and said: "They shall not kill you, as long as I do not get angry with you! You are a princess, I suppose?"

"No," said little Gerda, and told her about everything she had gone through, and how fond she was of little Kay.

The robber girl looked earnestly at her, gave a little nod with her head, and said: "They shall not kill you, even if I get angry with you, for then I would rather do it myself." And so she dried Gerda's tears and put both her hands into the beautiful muff, which was so soft and warm.

The coach now stopped; they were in the middle of the courtyard of a robbers' castle, the walls of which were cracked from top to bottom, and where ravens and crows flew in and out of the open holes, and the big bulldogs, which looked as if they could swallow a man, jumped high in the air, but they did not bark, for that was prohibited.

In the large old smoky hall a big fire was burning in the middle of the stone floor; the smoke ascended to the ceiling and had to find a way out for itself; a large caldron of soup was boiling on the fire, and both hares and rabbits were being roasted on spits before it.

"You shall sleep here with me and all my little animals to-night!" said the robber girl. They had something to eat and drink, after which they went over into a corner where there was some straw and blankets. On some laths and poles above their heads were sitting about a hundred pigeons, which all appeared to be asleep, but they turned their heads a little when the little girls came into the room.

"They are all mine," said the little robber girl, and quickly seized hold of one of the nearest, holding it by the feet and shaking it so that it flapped its wings. "Kiss it!" she cried, and dashed it into Gerda's face. "There are the wood-pigeons!" she went on, and pointed to a hole high up on the wall, with a number of laths nailed across it. "Those two are a couple of rascals from the woods. They would fly away directly if they were not properly shut up; and here is my old sweetheart Ba!" she said, as she tugged at the antlers of a reindeer, who had a bright copper ring round his neck and was tied up. "We have to look closely after him, too, else he would also run away from us. Every evening I tickle his neck with that sharp knife of mine, of which he is terribly afraid!" And the little girl pulled out a long knife from a crevice in the wall and drew it across the reindeer's neck; the poor animal kicked out with its legs, and the robber girl laughed and then pulled Gerda into bed with her.

"Do you take the knife to bed with you?" asked Gerda, looking somewhat scared at it.

"I always sleep with a knife," said the little robber girl. "One never knows what may happen. But tell me again what you have already told me about little Kay and why you went out into the wide world." And Gerda told her story over again, while the wood-pigeons were cooing up in their cage and the other birds slept. The little robber girl put her arm round Gerda's neck and held the knife in her other hand, and slept so soundly that one could hear her; but Gerda could not close her eyes at all, for she did not know whether she was to live or die. The robbers sat round the fire, singing and drinking, while the old woman turned somersaults. Oh, it was a horrible sight for the little girl!

Then the wood-pigeons suddenly cried, "Coo! Coo! we have seen little Kay! A white fowl carried his sledge while he sat in the Snow Queen's sledge as they drove through the forest and we lay in our nests; her icy breath killed all the young ones except us two. Coo! Coo!"

"What are you saying up there?" cried Gerda. "Where was the Snow Queen going? Do you know anything about it?"

"She was going to Lapland, no doubt, for there is always snow and ice. Just ask the reindeer who is fastened to the rope over there."

"Yes, there is ice and snow there," said the reindeer. "It is a glorious place. There you can freely roam about in the great glittering valleys. There the Snow Queen pitches her summer tent, but her stronghold is near the North Pole on the island called Spitzbergen!"

"Oh, Kay! little Kay!" sighed Gerda.

"You must lie quiet," said the robber girl, "else you will feel my knife in your body!"

In the morning Gerda told her everything that the wood-pigeons had said, and the little robber girl looked quite serious, but nodded her head and said, "It does n't matter! it does n't matter! Do you know where Lapland is?" she asked the reindeer.

"Who should know better than I?" the reindeer said, its eyes sparkling with excitement. "I was born and bred there; there I used to scour the snow-fields."

"Just listen," said the robber girl to Gerda. "You see all the men are gone, but mother is still here and will be for some time, but later in the morning she takes a drink out of the big bottle over there, and afterward she takes a little nap; then I'll do something for you!"

She now jumped out of bed, threw her arms round her mother, pulled her mustache, and said, "Good morning, my own sweet nanny-goat!"

And the mother snapped her nose till it was both red and blue, but it was all done out of pure love.

When the mother had had her drink out of the bottle and was taking a little nap, the robber girl went across to the reindeer and said, "I should like very much to tickle you a good many times still with my sharp knife, for then you are so funny; but never mind, I will undo your rope and set you free so that you may set out for Lapland; but you must use your legs and carry this little girl for me to the Snow Queen's castle, where her play-mate is. You heard, of course, what she said, for she spoke loud enough, and you were listening."

The reindeer jumped for joy. The robber girl lifted little Gerda on its back and took care to tie her fast, and even to give her a little cushion to sit on. "I don't mind giving them back to you," she said, "but here are your fur-lined boots, for you will find it cold up there; I must keep the muff, though, it is so pretty. All the same you shall not feel cold. Here are mother's large woolen gloves, which will reach right up to your elbows. Put your hands in! Now they look just like my ugly mother's!"

And Gerda wept for joy.

"I don't like to see you whimpering," said the little robber girl. "You must look pleased and happy now. Here are two loaves and a ham for you, so that you shall not starve."

The provisions were fastened to the reindeer's back, and the little robber girl opened the door and called all the big dogs into the room, after which she cut the rope with her knife and said to the reindeer, "Be off! But look well after the little girl."

And Gerda stretched out her hands with the large gloves toward the robber girl and said, "Farewell." And the reindeer set off and flew across bushes and logs of trees, through the big forest, over bogs and steppes, as fast as ever he could. The wolves howled and the ravens croaked. "Whizz! Whizz!" was heard in the sky, which was covered with fiery-red streaks.

"They are my old friends the Northern lights!" said the reindeer. "Look how they shine!" And so he ran still faster, by night and by day. The loaves were eaten, and the ham too, when they came to Lapland.

THE SIXTH STORY

THE LAPWOMAN AND THE FINWOMAN

They stopped before a miserable little hut; the roof went right down to the ground, and the door was so low that the family had to creep on all fours when they wanted to go out or in. There was nobody at home except an old Lapwoman, who was cooking fish over a train-oil lamp. The reindeer told her the whole of Gerda's story, but only after having first told his own, which he considered was more important, and Gerda was so benumbed with cold that she was not able to speak.

"Ah, poor creature!" said the Lapwoman, "then you still have far to go! You must travel four hundred miles into Finmark, for that is where the Snow Queen spends her summer and burns blue lights every evening. I will write one or two lines on a dried codfish, as I have no paper, and give it to you for the Finwoman up there; she can give you better information than I."

And when Gerda had become warm and had had something to eat and drink, the Lapwoman wrote a few words on a dried codfish, told Gerda to look well after it, and tied her fast to the reindeer again, and off he went at full speed. "Whizz! whizz!" was heard, while up in the heavens the most beautiful blue Northern lights were blazing the whole night; and then they came to Finmark and knocked at the chimney of the Finwoman's hut, for it had not even a door.

It was so terribly hot inside that the Finwoman herself went about almost naked; she was small and dirty-looking. She loosened little Gerda's clothes at once, took off her big gloves and boots, or else it would have been too hot for her in the hut, put a piece of ice on the reindeer's head, and then began to read what was written on the codfish. She read it three times and then she knew it by heart, after which she put the fish into the pot, which was boiling on the fire, for it could very well be eaten, and she never wasted anything.

The reindeer first told his own story and then little Gerda's, and the Finwoman blinked with her knowing eyes, but did not say anything.

"You are so wise," said the reindeer; "I know you can bind all the winds in the world with a piece of thread; when the skipper loosens one knot he gets fair wind, if he loosens the second a stiff gale springs up, and if he loosens the third and the fourth it will raise such a storm that the forests are blown down. Will you not give the little girl a potion so that she will get twelve men's strength and be able to overcome the Snow Queen?"

"Twelve men's strength!" said the Finwoman. "Well, that would n't be of much use!" And then she went to a shelf and took down a large roll of skin, which she unrolled; it was inscribed with strange characters, which the Finwoman began reading, and went on with it till the perspiration fell in drops from her forehead.

But the reindeer begged again so hard for little Gerda, and Gerda, with tears in her eyes, looked so entreatingly at the Finwoman, that the eyes of the latter again began to blink, and, leading the reindeer into a corner, the Finwoman put some fresh ice on his head and whispered:

"Little Kay is with the Snow Queen sure enough, and finds everything there according to his mind and liking, believing it is the finest place in the world; but that comes of his having a glass splinter in his heart and a little speck of glass in his eye. They must be got out or he will never be himself again, and the Snow Queen will retain her power over him!"

"But can't you give little Gerda something to drink so that she may become strong enough to overcome all this?"

"I cannot give her greater power than she already possesses. Do you not see how great it is? Do you not see how men and animals must serve her, how she, barefooted, has got on so safely through the world? She must not be told by us of her power; it is seated in her heart, where it will remain; it consists in her being such a sweet and innocent child.   If she cannot obtain access herself to the Snow Queen, and remove the bits of glass from little Kay, we cannot help her.   Two miles from here the Snow Queen's garden begins; carry the little girl there and put her down by the great bush which stands full of rich berries in the snow.   Don't stop there long gossiping, but make haste back here."   And the Fin-woman lifted little Gerda up on the reindeer, who set out as fast as he could.

"Oh, I have n't got my boots! I have n't got my gloves!" cried little Gerda as soon as she felt the biting cold; but the reindeer dared not stop; he ran till he came to the great bush with the red berries.   There he put Gerda down and kissed her mouth, while big bright tears ran down the animal's cheeks, and then he trotted back as quickly as he could.   There stood poor Gerda without shoes and without gloves in the midst of the terrible ice-cold Finmark.

She ran as fast as her legs could carry her, when she encountered a whole regiment of snowflakes; but they did n't fall down from the sky, which was quite bright and full of shining Northern lights.   The snow-flakes ran along the ground and grew larger the nearer they came; Gerda well remembered how big and weird they had appeared to her when she looked at them through the magnifying glass, but now they were certainly much bigger and more terrible; they were alive and were the outposts of the Snow Queen.   They had the most wonderful shapes: some of them looked like great, ugly porcupines, others like coils of snakes putting forth their heads, and others again like small fat bears with bristling hairs; all were dazzlingly white, all were living snowflakes.

Little Gerda then said the Lord's Prayer; the cold was so great that she could see her own breath, it seemed like a jet of steam issuing from her mouth; her breath grew thicker and thicker and formed itself into little bright angels, who grew larger and larger as soon as they touched the ground.   They all had helmets on their heads, and spears and shields in their hands; their numbers increased every moment, and when Gerda had finished her prayer there was a whole legion around her.   They struck at the terrible snowflakes with their spears and shattered them into a hundred pieces, and little Gerda could then proceed safely and cheerfully on her way.   The angels patted her feet and hands so that she did not feel the cold so much, and she walked on rapidly toward the Snow Queen's castle.

But we will now first see how Kay is faring.   He certainly was not thinking of little Gerda, and least of all that she might be standing outside the castle.

THE SEVENTH STORY

WHAT HAD HAPPENED IN THE SNOW QUEEN'S CASTLE AND WHAT HAPPENED LATER ON

THE walls of the castle were made of the drifting snow, and the windows and doors of the cutting winds; there were over a hundred halls, according to how the snow had been drifting, the largest of which extended for many miles. All were lighted by the bright Northern lights; but how vast and empty, how icy cold and dazzling white they all were! There were never any amusements here, not even a little bears' ball, for which the storm could have supplied the music, and at which the ice bears could have danced on their hind legs and shown their elegant manners; there were never any little card parties, with slaps on the snout and pattings of paws; never any cozy little coffee parties and gossiping at Miss White-Fox's. The vast halls of the Snow Queen's castle were cold and deserted. The Northern lights shone so brightly, and the rays could be seen so distinctly, that they might be counted both when they were highest in the heavens and when they were at their lowest. In the middle of the empty and endless snow-hall was a frozen lake, which had cracked into a thousand pieces, but every piece was so exactly like the other that it formed a complete work of art. In the center of the lake sat the Snow Queen when she was at home; she used to say that she sat in the "mirror of reason," and that it was the only one and the best in this world.

Little Kay was quite blue, almost black with cold, but he did not feel it, for had she not kissed away his susceptibility to cold, and was not his heart almost a lump of ice? He was dragging some flat pieces of ice which he placed in all manner of ways, as he wanted to form something out of them; just like when we arrange small pieces of wood into figures, which we call a Chinese puzzle. Kay was forming some very intricate figures: it was the ice game of reason. In his eyes the figures were very remarkable and of the highest importance; the cause of this was the piece of glass which stuck in his eye! He formed complete figures which represented a written word, but he was never able to form the word he most wanted. It was the word "Eternity," and the Snow Queen had said: "If you can solve that figure, you shall be your own master, and I will make you a present of the whole world and a pair of new skates." But he could not.

"I will now fly away to the hot countries!" said the Snow Queen. "I want to peep down into the black caldrons!" They were the volcanoes, Etna and Vesuvius, as they are called. "I want to whiten them a little! It's quite necessary; it will do good on the top of lemons and grapes!" And away flew the Snow Queen, and Kay sat quite alone in the large empty hall, which was many miles long, and looked at the pieces of ice and pondered and pondered till he groaned; he sat quite stiff and motionless, one would have thought he was frozen.

Just then little Gerda entered the castle through the great gate where a biting wind was raging, but she said her evening prayers, and the wind went down, as if it wanted to go to sleep. She stepped into the great, empty, cold rooms,—when suddenly she saw Kay; she knew him, flew to him, threw her arms round his neck and held him fast as she cried: "Kay! dear little Kay! So I have found you at last!"

But he sat quite motionless, stiff and cold. Then little Gerda began to cry and wept hot tears which fell upon his breast; they penetrated to his heart, and thawed the lump of ice and consumed the little piece of glass in there. He looked at her, and she sang:

> The roses grow in the valley,
> Where the Christ-Child we shall see!

Then Kay burst into tears; he cried so that the splinter of glass rolled out of his eye; he recognized her and shouted joyfully: "Gerda!

dear, little Gerda! Where have you been so long? And where have I been?" And he looked all around him. "How cold it is here! How great and empty it all seems here!" And he clung to Gerda, while she laughed and cried for joy. Their delight was so great that even the blocks of ice began to dance about for joy, and when they were tired and settled down they formed themselves into the very word which the Snow Queen had said that he must find out if he were to become his own master, and that she would then make him a present of the whole world and a pair of new skates.

And Gerda kissed his cheeks and their bloom came back again; she kissed his eyes and they shone like her own; she kissed his hands and feet and he became hale and hearty. The Snow Queen might return when she chose; his warrant of release stood written there in sparkling blocks of ice.

And they took each other by the hand and wandered out of the great castle; they talked of grandmother and of the roses on the roof, and wherever they went the winds lay down to rest, and the sun shone forth. When they came to the bush with the red berries they found the reindeer waiting for them; he had a young reindeer cow with him, whose udders were full of milk; she gave the young folks a warm drink, and kissed them on the mouth. They then carried Kay and Gerda, first to the Finwoman, where they warmed themselves in her hot room and where they got to know everything about the journey home; then to the Lapwoman, who had made new clothes for them and got her sledge ready for them.

And the two reindeer ran side by side and accompanied them to the border of the district; here the first green shoots were to be seen, and here they took leave of the reindeer and the Lapwoman, and they all said, "Farewell." And then the first little bird began to twitter, and the forest was full of green shoots. Out of the forest came a young girl with a bright red cap on her head and pistols in front of her, riding on a beautiful horse, which Gerda knew at once; it was one of the team which had been harnessed to the golden coach. It was the little robber girl, who had got tired of staying at home, and was now going first to the North, and afterward in some other direction if it was not to her liking; she knew Gerda at once and Gerda knew her, and they were both delighted.

"You are a nice fellow to be running after!" she said to little Kay; "I should like to know whether you deserve that anybody should run to the end of the world for your sake!"

But Gerda patted her cheeks and asked about the prince and princess.

"They have gone to foreign lands," said the robber girl.

"And where is the crow?" asked little Gerda.

"The crow is dead," she answered. "The tame sweetheart is now a widow and goes about with a bit of black worsted round her leg, complaining and wailing most pitifully, but it is all humbug! But tell me now how you fared and how you got hold of him!"

And Gerda and Kay both told her all that had happened.

"And snipp-snapp-snurr-bassellurr!" said the robber girl, taking them both by the hand and promising them that should she ever pass through their town, she would be sure to pay them a visit, and then she rode off into the wide world. But Kay and Gerda walked on hand in hand, and as they proceeded the spring became more and more lovely with flowers and green foliage; the church bells were ringing and they recognized the lofty steeple and the big town — it was the one in which they lived. They entered the town and found their way to their grandmother's door; they went up the stairs, and into the parlor, where everything was in the same place as before. The clock said, "Tick! tick!" and the hands moved on as usual; but as they passed in at the door they discovered that they had become grown-up people. The roses on the roof could be seen in full bloom through the open windows, and there were the little footstools; Kay and Gerda sat down, holding each other by the hand; they had forgotten the cold, empty splendor of the Snow Queen's castle as if it were a distressing dream of the past.

Grandmother was sitting in the bright sunshine, reading aloud from the Bible: "Except ye become as little children, ye shall in no wise enter into the Kingdom of God."

And Kay and Gerda looked into each other's eyes, and all at once they understood the old hymn:

> The roses grow in the valley,
> Where the Christ-Child we shall see!

There they both sat, grown up, yet children in heart, and it was summer — the warm, blessed summer.

THE SWINEHERD

THE PRINCE MADE A PRETTY CALDRON WITH BELLS ALL AROUND IT.

THE SWINEHERD

THERE was once upon a time a poor prince who had a kingdom which was very small, but quite big enough to get married upon, and married he would be.

It was rather bold of him, to be sure, that he should dare to say to the emperor's daughter: "Will you have me?" But he did do it, for his name was renowned far and wide, and hundreds of princesses would have said, "Yes," and thanked him into the bargain; but do you think she did?

Now you shall hear.

On the grave of the prince's father there grew a rose-tree—oh, such a lovely rose-tree! It blossomed only every fifth year, and then it bore only a single rose, the fragrance of which was so sweet that every one who smelled it forgot all his cares and troubles. And then he had a nightingale which could sing as if every possible melody was fixed in its little throat. This rose and this nightingale the princess should have, and they were therefore both put into two large silver caskets and sent to her.

The emperor ordered the presents to be carried into the large hall, where the princess was playing at "receiving visitors" with her maids of honor,—they had nothing else to do,—and when she saw the large silver caskets with the presents she clapped her hands with joy.

" If it were only a little pussy cat ! " she exclaimed — but it was only the lovely rose.

" Oh, how beautifully it is made ! " said the maids of honor.

" It is more than beautiful ! " said the emperor ; " it is pretty ! "

But when the princess put out her hand to feel it she very nearly burst out crying.

" Fie, papa ! " she said. " Why, it is not an artificial one, it is a real one ! "

" Fie," said all the court, " it is a real rose ! "

" Let us first see what there is in the other casket before we get angry ! " remarked the emperor, and so the nightingale was brought out. It sang so beautifully that no one could have anything to say against it at the time.

" *Superbe ! Charmant !* " exclaimed the maids of honor ; they all spoke French, the one worse than the other.

" How that bird reminds me of our late beloved empress's musical box ! " said an old cavalier. " Ah, yes ! it is quite the same tone, the same execution."

" Yes ! " said the emperor, and he began to cry like a little child.

" I should n't have thought it was a real bird ! " said the princess.

" Yes, it is a real bird," said they who had brought it.

" Well, you may let that bird fly," said the princess, and she would on no account allow the prince to come and present himself.

But he did not let himself be disheartened ; he blackened his face, pulled his cap down over his eyes, and knocked at the gate.

" Good day, Emperor ! " he said ; " can you find something for me to do here in the palace ? "

" Well, there are so many that come here to ask for a place ! " said the emperor ; " but wait a bit — I want some one who can look after pigs. We have got a good many of them.'

And so the prince was engaged as imperial swineherd. He got a miserable little room near the pigsty, and there he had to remain. He sat working all day and toward evening he had made a pretty little caldron, with bells all round it, and as soon as the caldron boiled the bells rang out so prettily and played the old melody :

> " Oh, thou darling Augustin,
> All 's lost and gone ! "

But the most remarkable thing about it was that, when one put one's fingers into the steam that came from the caldron, one could at once smell what kind of dinner was being prepared in every kitchen in the town. That was quite a different thing to the rose.

The princess soon came walking past with all her maids of honor, and when she heard the melody she stopped and looked quite pleased, for she

THE MAIDS OF HONOR WERE SO TAKEN UP WITH COUNTING THE KISSES THAT
THEY DID NOT NOTICE THE EMPEROR.

could also play " Oh, thou darling Augustin "; it was the only tune she could play, and that she played with one finger.

" Why, that 's the one I play! " she said. " This must be a well brought up swineherd. Just go and ask him the price of the instrument."

And so one of the maids of honor had to run in, but first she put on her wooden clogs.

" What will you take for that caldron ? " asked the maid of honor.

" I want ten kisses from the princess for it! " said the swineherd.

" Gracious goodness! " said the maid of honor.

" Well, I sha'n't take less! " said the swineherd.

" Well, what does he say ? " said the princess.

" I really cannot tell you," said the maid of honor, " it is too dreadful!"

" Then you may whisper it! " said the princess, and the maid of honor whispered it.

" He is very rude! " said the princess, and walked away at once. But when she had gone some distance the bells rang again so prettily:

> "Oh, thou darling Augustin,
> All 's lost and gone!"

" Listen! " said the princess; "just ask him if he will take ten kisses from my maids of honor."

" No, thank you," replied the swineherd; "ten kisses from the princess, or I keep my caldron."

" How tiresome! " said the princess; "but you ladies will have to stand in front of me, so that nobody can see me."

And the maids of honor stood round her and spread out their skirts, and so the swineherd got the ten kisses and she got the caldron.

Well, now they had a merry time of it! The pot was kept boiling the whole evening and all day long; there was not a kitchen in the whole town but what they knew what was being cooked there, at the chamberlain's as well as at the shoemaker's.

The maids of honor danced about and clapped their hands.

" We know who is going to have sweet soup and pancakes. We know who is going to have porridge and cutlets. How interesting it is!"

" Highly interesting! " said the first lady of honor.

' Yes, yes, but hold your tongues, for I am the emperor's daughter!"

" Gracious goodness! " said all of them.

The swineherd, that is to say the prince—but of course they did not know he was anything but a real swineherd—did not let a day pass without doing something, and so he made a rattle, which, on being swung round, played all the waltzes, galops, and polkas known from the creation of the world.

"That is *superbe!*" said the princess as she passed by; "I have never heard a more beautiful composition! Listen! Just go in and ask him the price of the instrument; but I sha'n't kiss him."

"He wants a hundred kisses from the princess!" said the maid of honor who had been in to ask him.

"I think he is crazy!" said the princess, and so she walked away, but when she had gone some distance she stopped. "We ought to encourage

"OH, WHAT A MISERABLE CREATURE I AM!" CRIED THE PRINCESS.

art," she said, "and I am the emperor's daughter. Tell him he shall have ten kisses like yesterday, and the rest he can have from my maids of honor!"

"But we would rather not!" said the maids of honor.

"That's all nonsense," said the princess; "if I can kiss him, surely you can do so as well. Remember I give you your board and wages." And so the maid of honor had to go in to the swineherd again.

"A hundred kisses from the princess," he said, "or each keeps his own!"

"Stand before me!" she said, and all the maids of honor placed themselves around while he kissed the princess.

"What is that crowd doing down there by the pigsty?" asked the emperor, as he stepped out on the balcony; he rubbed his eyes and put on his spectacles. "Why, it is the maids of honor at some of their tricks. I shall have to go down there!" And so he pulled up his slippers at the back; for they were shoes which were trodden down at the heel.

Gracious goodness! what a hurry he was in!

As soon as he came down into the courtyard, he began to walk quietly; the maids of honor were so taken up with counting the kisses in order that there might be fair play — that he should not get too many, but at the same time not too few — they did not notice the emperor. He raised himself on the tips of his toes.

"What does this mean?" he exclaimed, when he saw them kissing, and he hit them on the head with his slipper, just as the swineherd got his eightieth kiss. "Off you go!" shouted the emperor, for he was angry, and both the princess and the swineherd were expelled from his empire.

There she was sitting, crying, while the swineherd was scolding and the rain pouring down.

"Oh, what a miserable creature I am!" cried the princess; "if only I had taken that handsome prince! Oh, how unhappy I am!"

And the swineherd went behind a tree, rubbed the blacking off his face, threw aside the dirty clothes, and stepped out in his princely dress, looking so handsome and grand that the princess could not help courtesying to him.

"I have learned to despise you!" he said, "You would not have an honest prince! You did not understand the rose and the nightingale, but you could kiss the swineherd for the sake of a musical toy! Now you can make the best of it!"

And so he went into his kingdom, shut the door after him, and bolted it; she could now stand outside and sing:

"Oh, thou darling Augustin,
All 's lost and gone!"

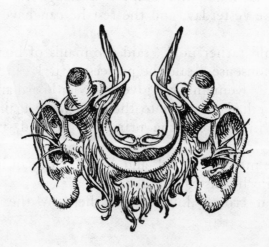

THE SWEETHEARTS

THE TOP COULD SEE THE BALL FLYING HIGH UP IN THE AIR LIKE A BIRD.

THE SWEETHEARTS

A TOP and a ball were lying together in a drawer among some other toys, and the top said to the ball: "Shall we not be sweethearts, since we are together in the same drawer?" But the ball, which was made of morocco, and thought just as much of herself as any fine lady, would not give any answer to such a proposal.

Next day the little boy who owned the toys came and painted the top red and yellow, and knocked a brass nail into the middle of it; the top looked quite splendid as it was spinning round.

"Look at me!" he said to the ball. "What do you say now? Shall we not be sweethearts? We should suit one another so well; you could jump and I dance. No one could be happier than we two!"

"Do you think so?" said the ball; "you know, I suppose, that my father and mother were morocco slippers and I have a cork in my body?"

"Yes, but I am made of mahogany," said the top, "and the sheriff himself turned me; he has a lathe of his own, and he took great pleasure in making me."

"But can I depend on that?" said the ball.

"May I never be whipped again if I tell a lie!" answered the top.

"You speak very well for yourself!" said the ball, "but I cannot accept you; I am as good as engaged to a swallow. Every time I fly up in the air he puts his head out of his nest and says: 'Will you? Will you?' And in my heart I have already answered, 'Yes,' so that it is as good as a betrothal; but I will promise you that I shall never forget you!"

"Well, there is n't much comfort in that!" said the top; and so they did not speak to each other again.

Next day the ball was taken out; the top could see her flying high up in the air like a bird, till at last he could not see her at all. Each time she came back, but as she touched the ground she always made a high bound; that was done either because she longed to jump again or because she had a cork in her body. The ninth time the ball disappeared and did not return; the boy looked and searched for her, but she was gone.

"I know where she is," sighed the top; "she is in the swallow's nest, and has married the swallow."

The more the top thought about her the more he became infatuated with her; just because he could not get her his love increased — that she should have chosen another made it only the more annoying. So the top whirled round and hummed, but was always thinking of the ball, who in his imagination became more and more beautiful. Thus several years passed by, and so it was now an old love.

And the top was no longer young. But one day he was gilded all over; never before had he looked so splendid — he was now a golden top, and whirled about till you could hear him humming far off. Yes, it was a grand sight! But suddenly he bounded too high and — he was gone!

They looked and searched everywhere, even down in the cellar, but the top could not be found.

Where could he be?

He had jumped into the dust-bin, where there were all sorts of rubbish — cabbage-stalks, sweepings, and gravel that had been washed down through the gutter.

"Well, I seem to have got into a nice place! My gilding will soon come off here. But what wretched creatures have I fallen amongst?" he said, looking askance at a long cabbage-stalk which had been plucked of all its green, and a curious round thing which looked like an old apple. But it was not an apple; it was an old ball which had been lying for many years up in the gutter under the roof, and through which the water had been oozing.

"Thank Heaven, here is one of one's own class, whom one can speak to!" said the ball, looking at the gilt top. "I am, strictly speaking, of morocco, sewed by maidenly hands, and have a cork in my body, but no one would think it, to look at me. I was very near getting married to a swallow, but then I fell into the gutter, and there I have been lying for five years with the water oozing through me. It is a long time, believe me, for a maiden!"

But the top did not say anything. He was thinking of his old sweetheart, and the more he heard, the clearer it became to him that it was she.

Just then the servant girl came to empty the dust-bin: "Hullo! there's the gilt top!" she exclaimed.

And the top was again brought into the house and became an object of esteem and appreciation. But nothing more was heard of the ball, and the top never spoke of his old love; love soon dies when one's sweetheart has been lying for five years in a gutter with the water oozing through her; in fact, one would never know her again when one met her in the dust-bin.

THE PINE-TREE

FAR IN THE FOREST STOOD A PRETTY PINE-TREE.

THE PINE-TREE

FAR in the forest stood a very pretty pine-tree; it had plenty of space;
the sunshine could reach it and it had plenty of air. Round about
grew many bigger companions, both pines and firs; but the little
pine-tree was in such a hurry to grow, it did not think of the warm sunshine and the fresh air. It did not even trouble itself about the peasant
children who ran about chattering when they came to gather wild strawberries and raspberries.

They would often come with a whole jar full of berries, or with the
strawberries threaded on a straw, and sit down by the little tree and exclaim: "Oh, what a pretty little one!" The pine did not at all like
this. The next year it was a long joint taller, and the following year it

had grown still a joint longer, for you can always tell by the joints on a pine-tree how many years it has been growing.

"Oh, if I were only such a big tree as the others!" sighed the little tree, "then I might spread my branches out far around me, and from the top look out over the whole world! The birds would then build their nests among my branches, and when the wind was blowing I could make my bow just as grandly as the others over there!"

It took no pleasure in the sunshine, in the birds, or the red clouds which sailed over it morning and evening.

If it happened to be winter, and the snow lay glittering white all around it, a hare would often come running along and jump right over the little tree — oh, it was irritating! But two winters passed, and in the third the tree had grown so big that the hare had to run round it. "Oh, to grow, to grow, to become big and old, that is the only thing worth living for in this world!" thought the tree.

In the autumn the wood-cutters always came and felled some of the largest trees. This was done every year, and the young pine-tree, which had now grown fairly big, trembled at the thought of it; for the big noble trees fell to the ground with a crash and a groan, the branches were cut off, the trees looked quite naked, long, and lanky — they could hardly be recognized. They were then put on carts and drawn by horses out of the forest.

Where were they going? What was going to be done with them?

In the spring, when the swallows and the storks came, the tree asked them: "Do you know where they have been taken to? Did you meet them?"

The swallows did not know anything, but the stork, looking serious, nodded his head and said: "Yes, I think so. I met many new ships on my way from Egypt. They had stately masts. I think I may say they were your trees, for there was a smell of the pine about them. I bring you greetings from them; they looked stately, quite stately."

"Oh, if I were only big enough to fly across the ocean! But what is the ocean and what is it like?"

"Well, that's too long a story to explain," said the stork, and walked away.

"Rejoice in your youth," said the sunbeams; "rejoice in your fresh growth and the young life you possess."

And the wind kissed the tree and the dew wept tears over it; but the pine-tree did not understand that.

As Christmas-time was drawing near, many young trees were cut down; some of them were not even as big or as old as the pine-tree which was so restless and impatient, and always wanting to get away. These young trees, which were always the most beautiful, were not denuded of their branches; they were placed on a cart and drawn by horses out of the forest.

"Where are they going to?" asked the pine-tree. "They are not bigger than I; there was even one which was much smaller. Why were they allowed to keep all their branches? Where are they being taken to?"

"We know! we know!" twittered the sparrows. "We have looked in at the windows down in the town! We know where they are going to! Ah! they are going to the greatest glory and splendor one can think of. We have looked in at the windows and seen that they are placed in the middle of the warm room and decorated with most beautiful things—gilt apples, honey-cakes, toys, and many hundreds of candles."

"And then?" asked the pine-tree, trembling in all its branches. "And then? What happens then?"

"Well, we have n't seen anything else. It was really wonderful!"

"I wonder if I came into existence to have such a glorious career?" cried the pine-tree in exultation. "That would be even better than going across the ocean. How painful this longing is! If only it were Christmas! Now I am tall and have big branches like those which were taken away last year. Oh, how I wish that I was already in the cart, that I was in the warm parlor with all that glory and splendor around me! And then? Well, then something still better must follow, something still more glorious. But what? Oh, how I suffer! How I am longing! I do not know myself what has taken possession of me."

"Rejoice in us," said the air and the sunshine; "rejoice in your fresh youth in the open!"

But the tree did not at all rejoice. It grew and grew; green, dark green, it stood there winter and summer; people who saw it said: "There 's a fine tree!" And at Christmas-time it was the first to be felled. The ax cut deeply into its marrow; the tree fell to the ground with a sigh; it felt a pain, a faintness; it was unable to think of any happiness; it was sad at parting from its home, from the spot where it had sprung up; it knew it would never again see the dear old comrades, the little bushes and the flowers round about, perhaps not even the birds. To take leave of all this was not at all pleasant. The tree came to itself only when it was being unloaded in the yard and heard a man say: "That 's a beauty! That 's the one we 'll use!"

Two grandly dressed servants then came and carried the pine-tree into a large, beautiful room. On the walls around hung portraits, and near the great stove stood Chinese vases with lions on the lids. There were rocking-chairs, silken sofas, large tables covered with picture-books and toys,—many hundred dollars' worth,—at least that 's what the children said. And the tree was placed in a great tub filled with sand, but nobody could see it was a tub, for it was covered up with some green cloth and was standing on a large, brightly colored carpet. How the tree trembled! What was going to take place? Both the servants and the ladies of the house were busy decorating it. On the branches they hung little nets cut out of colored paper; each net they filled with sweets; gilt apples and walnuts hung from it as if they had grown there, and over a hundred red, blue, and white little candles were fastened to the branches.   Dolls, which looked exactly like live beings—the tree had never seen any before— hung suspended from the green branches, and at the very top of the tree was fixed a great star of tinsel gold; it was splendid, it was quite magnificent.

"To-night," they all said; "to-night it will look glorious!"

"Oh," thought the tree, "I wish it were evening! If only the candles could be lighted soon! And what will happen then? Will the trees from the forest come and look at me? Will the sparrows fly past the window? I wonder if I shall grow fast here and remain decorated winter and summer."

Yes, it seems to know all about it; but it suffered from a terrible barkache from all the longing, and barkache is just as bad for a tree as a backache is to us.

The candles were now lighted.   What joy, what splendor! the tree trembled in all its branches at the sight of it, so that one of the candles set fire to a branch and singed it badly.

"Goodness gracious!" cried the young ladies, and set to work in all haste to put out the fire.

The tree did not even dare to tremble.   Oh, it was terrible!   It was so afraid of losing any of its finery that it was quite beside itself in all this splendor, when suddenly the folding doors were opened and a crowd of children rushed into the room as if they were going to upset the tree; the older people followed in a more dignified manner.   The little ones stood quite silent, but only for a moment, then they shouted again till the room rang; they danced round the tree, and one present after another was plucked from it.

"What are they doing?" thought the tree. "What 's going to happen?" The candles were beginning to burn down to the branches, and were then put out one after the other. The children were now allowed to strip it; they rushed at it so that all its branches creaked, and had it not been fastened to the ceiling by the top and the golden star, it would have been overturned.

The children danced round the room with their pretty toys; nobody looked at the tree except the old nurse who was looking about between the branches, but it was only to see if a fig or an apple had been forgotten.

"A story! a story!" cried the children, and dragged a fat little man toward the tree.   He sat down just under it.   "For then we shall be in the greenwood," he said, "and it may please the tree to listen to the story; but I will tell you only one story.   Will you have the one about Ivede-Avede, or that one about Lumpy-Dumpy, who fell down the stairs, but after all came on the throne and married the princess?"

THE FOLDING DOORS WERE OPENED AND A CROWD OF CHILDREN RUSHED INTO THE ROOM;
THE OLDER PEOPLE FOLLOWED IN A MORE DIGNIFIED MANNER.

" Ivede-Avede ! " cried some, " Lumpy-Dumpy ! " cried others. There was such a crying and shouting, only the pine-tree remained quite silent and thought: "Am I not to join in it, not do anything at all ? " It had already been in it and had done all it should do.

And the man told them about Lumpy-Dumpy, who fell down the stairs, and after all came on the throne and married the princess. " The princess ! " The children clapped their hands and cried : " Go on ! go on ! " They wanted to hear " Ivede-Avede " also, but they got only " Lumpy-Dumpy." The pine-tree stood quite silent and thoughtful: the birds in the forest had never told such stories. " Lumpy-Dumpy fell down the stairs and got the princess after all. Ah, well ! that 's the way of the world," thought the pine-tree, believing it was all true because it was such a nice old man who had told it. "Ah, well, who knows ! perhaps I may fall down the stairs too and marry a princess." And it looked forward with pleasure to being decorated again next day with lights and toys, with gold and fruits.

"To-morrow I shall not tremble," it thought. "I 'll enjoy myself thoroughly in the midst of all my glory. To-morrow I shall again hear the story about Lumpy-Dumpy and perhaps the one about Ivede-Avede."

And the tree remained quiet and thoughtful the whole night.

In the morning the man-servant and the chambermaid came into the room.

"Now the fun is going to begin again ! " thought the tree; but they dragged it out of the room, up the stairs and into the garret, and there they put it away in a dark corner where the daylight could not reach. "What is the meaning of this?" thought the tree ; " I wonder what I am going to do here, and what I shall hear ? " And it leaned against the wall and stood thinking and thinking. It had plenty of time to do so, for days and nights passed and nobody came near it, and when somebody at last came it was only to put some big boxes away in the corner. The tree stood quite hidden and one would think it had been quite forgotten.

"Now it 's winter outside ! " thought the tree. "The ground is hard and covered with snow and they cannot plant me; therefore I suppose I must stand here in the shelter till the spring. How thoughtful! How kind people are ! If it were only not so dark here and so terribly lonely ! Not even a little hare ! It was so jolly out there in the forest, when the snow was on the ground, and the hare was running about; yes, even when he jumped over me, but I did not like it at the time. Up here it is terribly lonely !"

"Squeak, squeak ! " said a tiny mouse just then, and crept out of its hole; and then came another. They sniffed at the pine-tree and crept up among its branches.

"It is terribly cold ! " said the little mice. "Otherwise it 's very nice here ! Don't you think so, you old pine-tree ? "

"I am not at all old!" said the pine-tree; "there are many much older than I."

"Where do you come from?" asked the mice, "and what do you know?" They were so dreadfully inquisitive. "Tell us about the prettiest spot on earth. Have you been there? Have you been in the larder, where there are cheeses on the shelves and hams hanging from the ceiling, where one can dance on tallow candles, and where one goes in thin and comes out fat?"

"I don't know anything about that," said the tree; "but I know the forest, where the sun shines and where the birds sing." And then it told them everything from its youth onward, and the little mice had never heard anything like it before; they listened attentively and said:

"Dear, dear! How much you must have seen! How happy you must have been!"

"I?" said the pine-tree, and thought over what it had been telling them. "Well, they were very jolly times, after all!" And then it went on to tell them about Christmas Eve, when it was decorated with cakes and candles.

"Ah!" said the little mice, "how happy you must have been, you old pine-tree!"

"I am not at all old," said the tree; "it is only this winter that I came from the forest. I am in my full prime, I am only a little stunted in my growth."

"How delightfully you do tell stories!" said the little mice, and the next night they came with four other little mice, to hear the tree tell stories; and the more it went on telling the more distinctly it remembered everything, and it thought to itself: "They were very jolly times, after all! But they may come again, they may come again! Lumpy-Dumpy fell down the stairs and still got the princess; perhaps I can get a princess too." And the pine-tree thought of a pretty little birch-tree which grew out in the forest and which to the pine-tree was as good as a real princess.

"Who is Lumpy-Dumpy?" asked the little mice. And then the pine-tree told them the whole story; it remembered every single word of it, and the little mice were so delighted with it that they were ready to jump to the top of the tree. The following night there came a great many more mice and on the Sunday even two rats; but they said the story was not funny, and the little mice were sorry to hear this, for now they also thought less of it.

"Do you know only that one story?" asked the rats.

"Only that one," answered the tree. "I heard it on the happiest evening of my life, but I did not then know how happy I was."

"It's a very poor story! Don't you know any one with bacon and tallow candles in it — any story from the larders?"

"No," said the tree.

"Ah, well, thanks all the same," answered the rats, and went off to their holes.

The little mice also disappeared at last, and the tree sighed: "It was rather pleasant to have the tiny little mice sitting round me and listening to what I told them! Now that's all over as well! but I shall take care to enjoy myself when I am brought out again!"

But when did that happen? Well, early one morning some people came and rummaged about in the garret; the boxes were moved about and the tree was dragged out of its corner and thrown somewhat roughly on the floor, but one of the men dragged it toward the staircase where there was bright sunshine.

"Now life is beginning again!" thought the tree as it felt the fresh air and the first sunbeam—and then it found itself in the yard. Everything happened so quickly that the tree forgot to take a look at itself. There was so much to see all round. The yard adjoined the garden, where everything was in full bloom; the roses hung so fresh and fragrant over the little palings; the linden-trees were in blossom, and the swallows flew about and said: "Quirre-virre-vit, my husband's come home!" but it was not the pine-tree they meant.

"Now I shall enjoy life!" it shouted joyously, spreading its branches far out; alas! they were all withered and yellow, and it was lying in a corner amongst weeds and nettles. The tinsel star was still fixed on the top and glittered in the sunshine.

Two of the merry children who had danced round the tree at Christmas and been so fond of it were playing in the yard. The smallest rushed at it and tore off the golden star.

"Just look what is still sticking to the ugly old Christmas-tree!" he said, and began trampling upon the branches till they crackled under his feet.

And the tree looked at all the splendor and freshness of the flowers in the garden and then at itself, and wished it had remained in its dark corner in the garret. It thought of its bright young days in the forest, of the merry Christmas Eve, and of the little mice which had listened so pleased to the story about Lumpy-Dumpy.

"It's all over!" said the poor tree. "If I had only enjoyed myself when I had the chance! It's all over! All over!"

And the servant man came and chopped the tree into small pieces; it made quite a large bundle. It blazed up brightly under the large copper kettle, and sighed so deeply that every sigh was like the report of a small gun, and the children who were at play came in and seated themselves in front of the fire, looked at it and shouted, "Pop! pop!" But at each report, which was really a deep sigh, the tree was thinking of a summer day in the forest, or a winter night out there while the stars were shining.

It thought of Christmas Eve and Lumpy-Dumpy, the only story it had heard and knew how to tell — and so the tree was burned to ashes.

The boys were playing in the yard, and the youngest was wearing the tinsel star on his breast, which the tree had worn on the happiest evening of its existence. Now all that had come to an end, and so had the tree; and the story as well came to an end, to an end — and so do all stories!

"THE WILL-O'-THE-WISPS ARE IN TOWN," SAID
THE WOMAN FROM THE MARSH

"THE WILL-O'-THE-WISPS ARE IN TOWN! TAKE CARE OF YOURSELVES!"

"THE WILL-O'-THE-WISPS ARE IN TOWN," SAID THE WOMAN FROM THE MARSH

THERE was a man who once knew very many new fairy tales, but now they had slipped from his memory, he said. The fairy tales which used to come of themselves and visit him did not come any more and knock at his door, and why did they not come? True enough, the man had not been thinking of them for years and days, and had not been expecting they would come and knock again; but most probably they had not been near him at all, for abroad there was war, and in his country the sorrow and distress which war carries with it.

The storks and the swallows came back from their long journey; they had not been thinking of any danger, but when they arrived they found their nests were burned, the dwellings of men and the wicket-gates out of order or even gone, the horses of the enemy trampling over the old graves. They were hard and gloomy times; but even they must come to an end.

And now they had come to an end, the people said; still the fairy tales did not knock at the door or give any sign of themselves.

"They are dead and gone, I suppose, with all the others," said the man.

But fairy tales never die.

And more than a year passed and he began to long sorely after them.

"I wonder if the fairy tales will ever come back and knock at my door?" And he remembered so vividly in how many forms they had come to him, sometimes young and fair, like the spring itself, as a beautiful young maiden with a wreath of woodruff in her hair and a branch of the beech in her hand, while her eyes shone like deep forest lakes in the bright sunlight; at other times they had come in the shape of a peddler who had opened his box of wares and let the silken ribbons fly about with their verses and inscriptions of old memories; but most delightful of all, however, were the occasions when they came as "old Granny," with silver-white hair and eyes so large and clear, who could tell so well about the times of old, long before the princesses spun yarn upon golden spindles, about the times when dragons and serpents lay outside the maidens' bowers and kept guard. She would then tell her stories so vividly that all who listened to her saw black spots dancing before their eyes, the floor became black with human blood; it was terrible to behold and listen to, and yet so fascinating, for it was such a long time since it had all happened.

"Will she ever knock at my door again?" said the man, and stared at the door till black spots appeared before his eyes and on the floor; he did not know if it was blood or the black crape from the dark, gloomy days gone by.

And as he sat there the thought struck him that the fairy tales might have hidden themselves somewhere, like the princess in the very old fairy tales, and were waiting to be discovered; if she were found, she would arise and shine with renewed splendor, more glorious than ever.

"Who knows? Perhaps she has hidden herself among the straw that was thrown near the brink of the well. Take care! Be careful! Perhaps she has hidden herself inside a dried flower which has been put inside one of the large books on the shelf."

And the man went and opened one of the newest books, full of information and knowledge, but no flowers lay there. There one could read about Holger Danske; and the man read that the story was invented and composed by a monk in France, that it was a romance which had been "translated and printed in the Danish language," that Holger Danske had never existed, and could consequently never come back again, as we have so long been singing and would so gladly believe. As with William Tell, so with Holger Danske—they were only myths, which could not be depended upon; and all this was set forth in the book with great wisdom.

"Well, I shall believe what I believe," said the man; "no plantain grows where no foot has trodden."

And he shut the book, put it back on the shelf, and went over to the fresh flowers in the window; perhaps the fairy tales had hidden themselves inside the red tulips with the golden-yellow edges, or in the fragrant rose, or in the highly colored camellia. There was sunlight among the leaves, but no fairy tales.

The flowers which stood here in the time of sorrow were far more beautiful; but they were cut off, every one of them, and made into wreaths and placed in the coffins, and over them the flag was spread.

Perhaps the fairy tales were buried with those flowers! But the flowers must have known of it, and the coffin would have been aware of it, the soil around it would have noticed it, every little blade of grass that shot forth would have told of it. For fairy tales never die!

"Perhaps they have been here and knocked at my door, but who had ears or eyes for them in those times?" People looked gloomily, sadly, and almost angrily at the spring sunshine, at the twittering birds, and all the budding foliage; yes, even the tongue could no longer sing the old, popular, ever-fresh melodies—they were consigned to oblivion with so many other things that were dear to our hearts. The fairy tales may have been here and knocked, but no one has heard them; they were not welcomed, and so they have gone away.

"I will set out to find them. Out into the country. Out into the woods by the open shore."

Out in the country lies an old manor-house with red walls, pointed gables, and with a flag waving from the tower. The nightingale is singing under the delicately fringed beech leaves, while he looks at the blossoming apple-trees and believes that they are bearing roses. Here in the summer sun the bees are busily fluttering about, and swarming and humming round their queen.

The autumn storms have much to tell about the wild chase, about the generations of mankind, and the leaves of the forest which sweep over the land. At Christmas time the wild swans sing from the open lake, while in the old manor-house the folks are gathering round the fireside to listen to songs and legends.

Down in the old part of the garden, where the great avenue of wild chestnut-trees allures one with its twilight, the man who was looking for the fairy tales was walking about. Here the wind had some time ago whispered into his ears the story of "Valdemar Daa and his Daughters." Here the dryad in the tree, the mother of fairy tales, had herself told him "The Last Dream of the Old Oak-Tree." Here in grandmother's time there were only clipped hedges; now only ferns and nettles grow there, spreading themselves over scattered fragments of old statues of stone; moss was growing in their eyes, but they could see just as well as before, while the man who was in search of the fairy tales could not; he could not see the fairy tales. Where were they?

Hundreds of crows flew over his head and the old trees, screaming "Kra! Kra!"

And he went from the garden across the moat into the alder-grove, where there was a little six-sided cottage with poultry- and duck-yards. In the middle of the room sat the old woman who looked after everything and knew exactly when each egg was laid, and knew every chicken that came out of the eggs. But she was not the fairy tales which the man was in search of; that she could prove by her certificate of Christian baptism and of vaccination, both of which were lying in her chest of drawers.

Some distance off, though not far from the house, is a hill with red hawthorn and laburnum; there lies an old tombstone, which was brought there many years ago from the churchyard in the town, in memory of one of the honorable councilors of the town, his wife, and his five daughters, all with folded hands and in ruffs, standing round him, hewed in stone. One could look so long at these figures that they seemed to have an effect upon one's thoughts, and these again seemed to influence the stone, so that it began telling stories about old times; at least, that is what happened to the man who was in search of the fairy tales. As he now came upon the spot, he saw a living butterfly sitting right on the forehead of the councilor's effigy in stone; the butterfly flapped its wings, flew some little distance, and settled down again close to the tombstone, as if to show what was growing there. Four-leaved clovers grew there; there were altogether seven of them, close to one another. If luck comes, it comes in abundance. He gathered the clovers and put them in his pocket. Luck is as good as ready money, but a new, delightful fairy tale would be much better, thought the man; but he did not find it there.

The sun went down, large and red; in the meadows vapors were rising; the woman from the marsh was brewing.

Later on in the evening the man was standing alone in his room, looking out into the garden over the meadows, the marshes, and the strand; the moon shone brightly, a mist was lying over the meadow, making it look like a great lake, which it had really been at one time. There were legends about it, and in the moonlight the legends seemed to take shape. The man then thought of what he had been reading when in town, that William Tell and Holger Danske had not existed; but still they remain in the traditions of the people, just like the lake over yonder —living evidence of the legends. Yes, Holger Danske will come back again. As he was standing there, buried in thought, something struck heavily against the window. Was it a bird, a bat, or an owl? One does n't open windows for such visitors when they knock.

The window flew open of itself, and an old woman looked right in at the man.

"Hullo!" he exclaimed. "Who are you? How can you look through a window on the first floor? Are you standing on a ladder?"

"You have got a four-leaved clover in your pocket," she said; "in fact, you have seven in all, and one of them is a six-leaved one."

"Who are you?" asked the man.

"The woman from the marsh," she said,—"the woman from the marsh, who brews. I was busy brewing, the tap was in the barrel, but one of the little imps from the marsh pulled out the tap for mischief, and I threw it right up here against the house and it struck against the window. Now the beer is running out of the barrel, and that won't do anybody any good."

"But do tell me," said the man.

"Yes, yes, only wait a little," said the woman from the marsh. "I have got something else to look after now," and then she was gone.

THE WINDOW FLEW OPEN OF ITSELF, AND AN OLD WOMAN LOOKED RIGHT IN
AT THE MAN.

The man was just closing the window when the woman again appeared.

"Now I am done," she said; "but half the beer I shall have to brew over again to-morrow, if the weather is suitable. Well, what was it you wanted to ask about? I came back again, because I always keep my word, and you have in your pocket seven four-leaved clovers, one of which is a six-leaved one; that commands respect; it is a decoration which grows by the roadside, but which cannot be found by every one. What is it you want to ask about? Don't stand there like a silly dolt. I must be off soon, to look after my tap and my barrel."

And the man asked after the fairy tales—whether the woman from the marsh had seen them on her way.

"By the big brew!" said the woman, "have you not had enough of fairy tales? I thought most people had had enough of them. There are other things to be looked after, and other things to mind. Even children have got beyond them. Give the little boys a cigar and the little girls a new crinoline—they care much more for these. Listen to fairy tales! No, indeed, there are other things to be looked after, much more important things to be done!"

"What do you mean by that?" asked the man. "And what do you know about the world? You see only frogs and will-o'-the-wisps."

"You had better beware of the will-o'-the-wisps," said the woman; "they are out. They have been let loose. Let's talk about them! Come and see me in the marsh, where I am wanted; there I'll tell you all about it, but make haste, while your seven four-leaved clovers, with the six-leaved one, are fresh, and while the moon still stands high."

And away went the woman from the marsh.

The clock struck twelve in the clock-tower; before it struck a quarter past the man was down in the yard, and had passed through the garden and stood in the meadow. The mist had disappeared, and the woman from the marsh had stopped brewing.

"You've been a long time coming," said the woman from the marsh. "Witches get on faster than men, and I am glad I was born a witch."

"What have you got to tell me now?" asked the man. "Is it something about the fairy tales?"

"Can you never get farther than to ask about them?" said the woman.

"Then is it about the poetry of the future that you can tell me?" asked the man.

"Don't begin with any of your grand phrases," said the woman, "and I'll be sure to answer you. You think only of poetry,—you ask only about fairy tales, as if they were the mistress of everything. She is the oldest, but she is generally taken for the youngest. I know her well enough! I have also been young, and that's no child's complaint. I was once a pretty elfin maid, and have danced with the others in the moonlight. I have listened to the nightingale and have walked in the woods, and met the fairy-tale maiden who was always gadding about. Sometimes she would take up her quarters for the night in a half-blown tulip, or in a globe-flower. At other times she would steal into the church and wrap herself up in the black crape which hung round the candles on the altar."

"You seem to be well informed," said the man.

"Well, I should say I know as much as you!" said the woman from the marsh. "Fairy tales and poetry—well, they are like two yards of the same piece of stuff; they may go and bury themselves where they like! All their ideas and talk can be brewed over again and be had much better and cheaper. You shall have them from me for nothing. I have a whole cupboard full of poetry in bottles. It is the essence, the best part of it; both the sweet and the bitter herb. I keep everything that people want of poetry in bottles, so that I can put a little on my hand-kerchief on Sundays to smell."

"You speak of very wonderful things," said the man. "Have you poetry in bottles?"

"More than you can stand," said the woman. "You know, I suppose, the story of 'The Girl Who Trod on the Loaf so that She Might not Dirty Her New Shoes'? It is both written and printed."

"I have told it myself," said the man.

"Well, then you must know it," said the woman; "and you must know that the little girl sank straight into the ground to the woman from the marsh, just as the devil's great-grandmother came on a visit to see the brewery. She saw the girl as she was sinking, and asked if she might have her to put on a pedestal, in remembrance of the visit. She got her, and I got a present which is of no use to me—a medicine-chest, a whole cupboard filled with poetry in bottles. Great-grandmother told me where the cupboard should stand, and there it is still standing. Just look! You have your seven four-leaved clovers in your pocket, of which one is a six-leaved one, so you will be sure to see it."

And sure enough, in the middle of the marsh was lying something like the stump of a big alder-tree; it was great-grandmother's cupboard. It was open to the woman from the marsh and to everybody from all countries, and at all times, she said, if they only knew where the cupboard was standing. It could be opened at the front and at the back, and at every side and all the corners,—a most ingenious piece of work,—and yet it only looked like the stump of an old alder-tree. The poets of all countries, especially of our own country, were re-manufactured here. Their minds were elaborated, criticized, renovated, concentrated, and then put into bottles. With great instinct, as it is called when you do not want to say genius, great-grandmother had seized upon that in nature which seemed to partake of the flavor of this or of that poet, had put a little devilry to it, and then she had his poetry in bottles for all time to come.

"Let me have a look," said the man.

"Yes, but there are more important things to listen to," said the woman from the marsh.

"But now we are at the cupboard," said the man, and looked into it. "Here are bottles of all sizes. What is there in this one? And in this?"

"This is what they call May-dew," said the woman. "I have not tried it, but I know that if you pour only a small drop of it on the floor, you have at once before you a beautiful woodland lake, with water-lilies, flowering rushes, and wild mint. You need pour only two drops upon an old exercise-book, even on those from the lowest class in the school, and the book becomes a sentimental comedy which is good enough to be performed, and over which people would be sure to fall asleep, so strong is the perfume of it. It is supposed to be out of compliment to me that the label on the bottle bears the inscription, 'The Brew of the Woman from the Marsh.'

"Here stands the bottle of 'Scandal.' It looks as if there were only dirty water in it; and it is dirty water, but with effervescing powder of town gossip, three ounces of falsehood, and two grains of truth, stirred about with a birch-twig, not taken from a rod that has been in pickle or fresh from the bleeding back of sinners; no, taken right from the broom which has been used to sweep the gutter with.

"Here is the bottle with 'Pious Poetry,' set to psalm tunes. Every drop has a ring about it, like the slamming of the gates of hell, and has been prepared from the blood and sweat of the penitent. Some say it is only the gall of the dove, but doves are the gentlest of creatures; they have no gall, people say who do not know their natural history.

"Here stood the bottle of all bottles,—it took up half the cupboard,— the bottle with 'Stories of Every-day Life.' It was covered over both with bladder and hogskin, for it would n't do to lose any of its strength. Every nation could here get its own soup; it all depended on how you turned and shifted the bottle. Here was old German blood-soup, with robber-dumplings; also thin cottagers'-soup, with real court officials, who lay like carrots at the bottom, while philosophical fat floated on the top. There was English governess-soup, and the French *pôtage à la coq*, made from cocks' legs and sparrows' eggs, in Danish called cancan-soup; but the best of all the soups was Copenhagen-soup. That 's what the family said.

"Here, in a champagne-bottle, 'Tragedy' used to stand; it could go off with grand effect, and that was necessary. 'Comedy' looked just like fine sand to throw in people's eyes—that is to say, the refined comedy; the coarser was also to be found in bottle, but consisted only of play-bills of future productions, the most attractive of which were the titles of the pieces. There were capital titles for comedies, such as: 'Dare You Spit on the Watchworks?' 'One On the Jaw,' 'The Darling Ass,' and 'She is Dead Drunk.'"

The man stood musing, but the thoughts of the woman from the marsh went further; she wanted to put an end to it all.

"I suppose you have seen enough now of the medicine-chest," she said, "now you know what there is in it; but there is something more important that you ought to know, and which you don't know—the will-o'-the-wisps are in town. That is of far greater importance than

"I HAD ALL THE TWELVE NEW-BORN WILL-O'-THE-WISPS IN MY LAP."

poetry and fairy tales. I ought to hold my tongue about it, but this must be the work of Providence, or fate—something which has taken possession of me, something that sticks in my throat; it must come out. The will-o'-the-wisps are in town. They have been let loose. You mortals had better beware!"

"I don't understand a word of it," said the man.

"Be good enough to sit down on the cupboard," she said; "but don't fall into it and break the bottles—you know what there is in them. I will tell you of the great event; it happened only yesterday, and it has happened before. This one has still three hundred and sixty-four days to run. You know, of course, how many days there are in the year?"

And the woman from the marsh began her story.

"There were grand doings out here in the marsh yesterday. There was a children's party. A little will-o'-the-wisp was born here—in fact, there were twelve of them born to the same family, and to them it is given to become mortals if they choose, and to appear, act, and command as if they were human beings. It is a great event in the marsh, and therefore all the will-o'-the-wisps, male and female,—for there are also females amongst them, but they are never mentioned,—were dancing like little lights all over the marshes and meadows. I sat on the cupboard there and had all the twelve new-born will-o'-the-wisps in my lap; they shone like glow-worms, and were already beginning to jump and increase in size every minute, so that before a quarter of an hour had passed they all began to look just as large as if they were fathers or uncles. Now it is an old established law and privilege that when the moon stands in the sky just as she did yesterday, and the same wind blows which blew yesterday, it is decreed and granted to all the will-o'-the-wisps who are born in that hour and in that minute to become mortals, and through the whole year to exercise their power everywhere, one and all of them. The will-o'-the-wisp may run at large all round the country and the whole world as well, if he is not afraid of falling into the sea or being blown out in a heavy gale. He can enter into a human being, talk to him, and make any movement he likes. The will-o'-the-wisp can assume any form whatever, man or woman, and can talk and act in their spirit, but according to his own notions of extremes, so that he arrives at any result he wishes. But in the course of the year he must know and understand how to lead three hundred and sixty-five mortals astray,—and that he must do in grand style, —to lead them astray from truth and righteousness; then he will rise to the highest position a will-o'-the-wisp can attain—that of becoming fore-runner to the devil's state chariot, with a fiery-yellow coat and the flames shooting out of his throat. That 's enough to make the mouths of the common will-o'-the-wisps water!

"But there is some danger and a good deal of work to be done by an ambitious will-o'-the-wisp who intends to play such a rôle. If a mortal discovers who he is, and can blow him away, he is done for, and has to return to the marsh; and if a will-o'-the-wisp is seized with a longing to return to his family and abandon his mission, then he is also done for, and can no longer burn brightly; he will soon go out and cannot be lighted again. And if the year comes to an end and he has not by that time led three hundred and sixty-five mortals astray from the path of truth, and from everything that is good and beautiful, he is condemned to take up his abode in decayed wood and shine without being able to move, and that is the most terrible punishment that can befall a sprightly will-o'-the-wisp. I knew all this, and I told it all to the twelve little will-o'-the-wisps whom I had on my lap, and they became wild with joy. I told them that the easiest and most comfortable way was to give up all ambition and not to think of doing anything; but the young lights would not listen to this — they already saw themselves arrayed in the fiery-yellow coats, with the flames shooting out of their throats.

"'Remain with us!' said some of the elder ones.

"'Go and play your tricks on mankind,' said the others. 'They dry up our meadows; they have invented a system of drainage. What will become of our descendants?'

"'We want to shine, to dazzle!' said the new-born will-o'-the-wisps; and so the matter was settled.

"And now they gave a ball which was to last only a minute; it could not very well be less. The elfin maidens whirled round three times with all the others, so that they should not be thought proud, for they generally prefer to dance by themselves. Then the christening presents were distributed — playing at 'ducks and drakes' as it was called. Presents were thrown about like pebbles across the marsh lake. The elfin maidens gave the end of their veils. 'Take it,' they said, 'and then you will know all the higher dances, the most difficult figures and turns; when you are in a dilemma you will know how to deport yourself correctly, and can show yourself in the very best society.' The night raven taught each of the young will-o'-the-wisps to say: 'Bravo, bravo, bravo!' and to say it at the right moment, and that is a great gift which brings its own reward. The owl and the stork had also something to say, but it was not worth talking about, they said, and so we shall not mention it. 'King Waldemar's wild chase' was just flying past across the marsh, and when the grand company heard of the goings on they sent as a present a couple of fine dogs which could run as fast as the wind, and could easily carry from one to three of the will-o'-the-wisps. Two old witches, who got their living by riding, were also present at the feast; they taught the young will-o'-the-wisps the trick of slipping in through the keyholes; when you know this it is the same as if all doors are open to you. They offered to take the young will-o'-the-wisps to town, which they knew well. They usually rode through the air on their own long black hair, in which they had made a knot in order to sit firmly, but now they sat astride the dogs from the wild chase, and took in their laps the young will-o'-the-wisps which were going to town to beguile and lead mortals astray. Whist! Off they went! All this happened last night. Now the will-o'-the-wisps are in town, now they have begun, but how and in what way? Ay! Can you tell me that? I have a weather prophet in my big toe, which always has something to tell me."

"Why, it is a regular fairy tale!" said the man.

"Yes, but it is only the beginning of one," said the woman. "Can you tell me how the will-o'-the-wisps are now behaving and disporting themselves, and what shape they have assumed to lead mortals astray?"

"I think," said the man, "that a whole romance might be written about the will-o'-the-wisps—a romance in twelve volumes, one about each will-o'-the-wisp; or perhaps a popular drama would be still better."

"You ought to write it," said the woman, "or, rather, leave it alone."

"Yes, that is more pleasant and comfortable," said the man; "and then one does not run the risk of being sat upon by the papers, which is often as unpleasant for us as for the will-o'-the-wisp to lie in decayed wood, shining and not daring to say a word."

"It is all the same to me," said the woman; "but rather let the others write—those who can write, and those who cannot. I will give them an old tap from my barrel, which will open the cupboard with the bottles of poetry; in these they may find whatever they are short of. But you, my good man, seem to have inked your fingers quite sufficiently and to have arrived at that time of life and maturity when you should not be running after fairy tales every year. There are now far more important things to be done. You understand, of course, that there is mischief brewing?"

"The will-o'-the-wisps are in town," said the man. "I have heard it and I understand it, but what do you want me to do? I should get an overhauling if I said to people: 'Look, there goes a will-o'-the-wisp in a respectable coat!'"

"They also go about in petticoats," said the woman. "The will-o'-the-wisp can assume all kinds of shapes and appear in all sorts of places. He goes to church, but not for religious reasons; perhaps he has taken up his quarters in the parson. He speaks on election days, not for the sake of the state or the country, but for his own sake; he is an artist, both in the color-pot and in the theatrical pot, but if he comes into power, there will be an end to it. I go on talking and talking, but I must say and speak out what is sticking in my throat, even to the detriment of my own family, though I am supposed to be the woman who is to save mankind. It is not of my own free will, or for the sake of the medal, I can assure you. I do the maddest thing I can: I tell it to a poet and then the whole town soon gets to know it."

"The town will not take it to heart," said the man. "It will not affect a single person. They will believe that I am telling them a fairy tale when I tell them with the most serious face: 'The will-o'-the-wisps are in town, as the woman from the marsh says. Take care of yourselves!'"

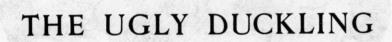

THE UGLY DUCKLING

A DUCK WAS SITTING ON HER NEST TO HATCH HER LITTLE DUCKLINGS.

THE UGLY DUCKLING

IT was beautiful out in the country, for it was summer-time. The corn was yellow, the oats green; the hay had been made up into ricks down in the green meadows, where the stork was walking about on his long red legs and talking away in Egyptian, for that was the language he had learned from his mother. Round about the corn-fields and meadows were large woods, and in the middle of the woods were deep lakes. Oh, it was indeed beautiful out in the country!

In the midst of the sunny landscape lay an old manor-house with a deep moat around it, and between the wall and the water grew large burdocks, which had attained such a height that little children could stand upright under the tallest of them. It was just as wild there as in the depths of the wood. A duck was sitting on her nest to hatch her little ducklings, but she was almost getting tired of it, for it took such a long time, and she seldom received any visitors. The other ducks preferred swimming about in the moat to climbing up and sitting under a burdock gabbling to her.

At last one egg after another began to crack, and "Peep! peep!" said the little ducklings; all the yolks had become living creatures and were popping out their heads.

"Quack! quack!" said the duck, and away they rushed as fast as they could, looking about them on all sides under the green leaves; their mother let them look around as much as they liked, for green is good for the eyes.

"How big the world is!" said all the young ones, for they had now more space to move about in than when they lay in the egg.

"Do you think this is the whole world?" said the mother. "It stretches far away on the other side of the garden, right up to the parson's field, though I have never been there. I hope you are all here," she said, as she stood up. "No, I have n't got you all; the biggest egg is still there. How long is this going to last? I am getting tired of it." And so she settled down again.

"Well, how are you getting on?" said an old duck, who came to pay a visit.

"This egg takes such a long time!" said the duck on the nest; "it won't break! But now you must look at the others. They are the finest ducklings I have seen. They are all like their father, the wretch! He never comes to see me."

"Let me see the egg that won't break," said the old duck. "You 'll find it is a turkey's egg. That was the way I was once deceived, and I had a lot of worry and anxiety with those youngsters, for they are afraid of the water. I may tell you, I could not get them to take to it. I quacked and snapped, but it was all of no use. Let me see the egg; yes, it's a turkey egg! Leave it, and teach your other children to swim."

"I 'll sit on it just a little longer," said the duck. "I have now been sitting on it so long that I may as well go on for some days longer."

"Just as you like," said the old duck, and away she went.

At last the large egg broke. "Peep! peep!" said the youngster as he rolled out of the shell; he was very big and ugly. The duck looked at him: "You are a terribly big duckling, to be sure," she said; "none of the others look like you. I wonder if it is a young turkey, after all. Well, we shall soon find that out. Into the water he shall go, even if I have to push him in myself."

The next day the weather was most beautiful; the sun was shining upon all the green burdocks. The mother of the ducklings went down to the moat with all her little ones. Splash! and into the water she jumped. "Quack, quack!" she called out, and in the ducklings jumped, one after

"MAKE HASTE AND BOW YOUR HEADS TO THE OLD DUCK. SHE IS THE OLDEST OF THEM
ALL HERE. SHE IS OF SPANISH BLOOD!"

the other. The water closed over their heads, but the next moment they came up again and were swimming about most beautifully, their legs going of themselves. They were all in the water; even the ugly gray youngster was swimming about with them.

"No, he is not a turkey," she said; "look how well he uses his legs, and how erect he carries himself. He is one of my own ducklings. He is not so ugly, after all, when you look at him properly. Quack, quack! Come along with me and I will take you all out into the world and present you in the duck-yard; but keep close to me, so that no one shall tread upon you, and beware of the cat!"

"And then they came into the duck-yard, where there was a terrible noise; two families were fighting over the head of an eel, which the cat got, after all.

"Ah, just look! that's the way of the world," said the mother, licking her beak, for she would have liked to have the eel's head herself.

"Now use your legs," she said; "just try and make haste and bow your heads to the old duck yonder. She is the grandest of them all here. She is of Spanish blood; that is

"PEEP, PEEP!" SAID THE YOUNGSTER AS HE ROLLED OUT OF THE SHELL.

why she is so fat, and you see she has a red rag round her leg. That's something particularly fine and the greatest distinction that any duck can get; it means that they don't want to lose her. Be quick! don't turn in your toes! A well-bred duckling places his legs well apart from each other, just like your father and mother. Now then. Just like this. Now bow with your neck and say, Quack!"

And this they did; but the other ducks round about looked at them and said quite loudly: "Hem! Now we shall have to put up with that riff-raff as well. Just as if there were not enough of us already: and, fie! what an ugly duckling! We sha'n't stand him!" And a duck flew right at him and bit him in the neck.

"Leave him alone," said the mother; "he won't hurt anybody."

"No, but he is too big, and is so different from the others," said the duck who had bitten the duckling; "and therefore he must be pecked."

"These are pretty children of yours," said the old duck with the rag round her leg; "all of them are pretty, except that one; he has not turned out a success. I wish you would try again."

"That can't be done, your grace," said the mother of the duckling. "He is not pretty, but he is very good-natured, and swims as beautifully

THINGS GOT WORSE AND WORSE, AND THE POOR DUCKLING WAS CHASED AND BITTEN BY THEM ALL.

as any of the others, and even a little better, I venture to say. I think he will grew pretty, or in time he may grow smaller. He has been lying too long in the egg, and that 's why he has n't got a proper figure." And she nipped him in the neck, and smartened up his downy coat a bit with her beak. "Besides, he is a drake," she said; "and so it does n't matter much. I think he 'll be a strong bird, and that he 'll manage to get on in the world."

"The other ducklings are very nice," said the old duck; "now just make yourselves at home, and if you find an eel's head, you may bring it to me."

And so they made themselves quite at home.

But the poor duckling who had come out of his shell last of all and looked so ugly was bitten, pushed, and jeered at both by the ducks and the fowls. "He is too big," they all said; and the turkey-cock, who was born with spurs and therefore believed he was an emperor, puffed himself out like a vessel in full sail, went straight for him, and began gobbling till he grew quite red in the face. The poor duckling did not know which way to turn or go; he felt very miserable because he was so ugly and was the laughing-stock of the whole duck-yard.

In this way the first day passed, and afterward things got worse and worse. The poor duckling was chased by them all. Even his brothers and sisters behaved badly to him, and were always saying: "If the cat would only catch you, you ugly fright!" And the mother wished him far away, while the ducks snapped at him, and the fowls pecked at him, and the girl who fed the poultry kicked him with her foot.

So he ran away and flew over the hedge. The little birds among the bushes flew up in great fright. "That's because I am so ugly," thought the duckling, and shut his eyes; but he ran and ran till he came out on the great marsh where the wild ducks lived. Here he remained the whole night, he was so very tired and miserable.

In the morning the wild ducks flew up and then saw their new comrade. "Who are you?" they asked. The duckling turned round in all directions, and bowed to them the best he could.

"You are terribly ugly," said the wild ducks, "but that is all the same to us, so long as you do not marry into our family."

Poor thing, he was not likely to think of getting married! If he could only be allowed to lie among the rushes and drink a little of the marsh water!

There he remained for two whole days; then there came two wild geese, or, rather, wild ganders, for they were two male birds. It could not have been long since they came out of the egg, and that's why they were so frisky.

"Just listen, comrade," said they. "You are so ugly that we are almost inclined to like you. Will you come along with us and be a bird of passage? Close by, in another marsh, there are some sweet, darling wild geese, all of them spinsters, who can say, 'Quack!' You may be able to make your fortune there, ugly as you are."

"Pop! pop!" was heard just above them at this moment, and both the wild ganders fell down dead among the rushes, and colored the water red. "Pop! pop!" was heard again, and whole flocks of wild geese flew up from the rushes and then there

SUDDENLY A TERRIBLE DOG, WITH HIS TONGUE HANGING OUT, STOOD RIGHT IN FRONT OF HIM.

were more reports. A great shooting party had arrived on the spot, and the sportsmen were lying all over the moor; some were even sitting in the trees which stretched out their branches far over the rushes. The blue smoke floated in the air like clouds between the dark trees, and extended far over the water; the dogs bounded right into the mud, splash, splash! Rushes and reeds swayed to and fro in all directions; the poor duckling was in a terrible fright; he turned his head to put it under his wing, when suddenly a terrible big dog, with his tongue hanging far out of his mouth and his eyes glaring wildly, stood right in front of him; he thrust his open jaws right against the duckling, showing his sharp teeth, when, splash! off he went without touching him.

"Thank Heaven," said the duckling, "I am so ugly that even the dog does not care to touch me."

And so he lay quite still, while the shots were whistling through the rushes and report after report went off.

It was late in the day before everything became quiet, but the poor youngster did not as yet venture to move; he still waited for some hours before he looked around him, and then he hurried off from the moor as fast as he could. He ran across fields and meadows in the face of such a wind that he had great difficulty in getting on.

Toward evening he came to a poor little farm-house; it was in such a miserable state that it did not know to what side it would tumble down, and therefore it remained standing. The wind blew so hard against the duckling that he was obliged to sit down to keep up against it, but it grew worse and worse. He then noticed that one of the hinges of the door had given way, and that in consequence the door hung in such a slanting position that he was able to slip through the opening into the room, which he did.

In this house lived an old woman with a cat and a hen. The cat, which she called Sonny, could raise his back and purr, and his coat would even bristle with sparks, but then one had to stroke him the wrong way. The hen had quite small, short legs, and was therefore called Henny Shortlegs; she laid good eggs, and the woman loved her as if she were her own child.

In the morning they at once noticed the stranger duckling, and the cat began to purr and the hen to cluck.

"What 's this?" said the woman, looking around her; but she could not see well, and so she believed the duckling was a fat duck that had lost her way.

"Why, what a rare catch!" she said; "I can now get duck's eggs, if only it is n't a drake. I must find out."

And so the duckling was taken on trial for three weeks, but there came no eggs. The cat was the master of the house and the hen was the mistress, and they always used to say, "We and the world," for they believed that they were one half of it, and by far the better half. The duckling thought it might be possible to hold a different opinion, but the hen would not stand that.

IN THIS HOUSE LIVED AN OLD WOMAN WITH A CAT AND A HEN.... "WHAT'S THIS?" ASKED THE WOMAN. SHE COULD NOT SEE WELL, AND SO SHE BELIEVED THE DUCKLING WAS A FAT DUCK.

"Can you lay eggs?" she asked.

"No."

"Well, you must hold your tongue, then."

And the cat asked: "Can you raise your back, or purr, or make sparks?"

"No."

"Well, then, you must n't have any opinion when sensible folk are talking."

And the duckling sat in a corner, very much dispirited. He began thinking about the fresh air and the sunshine, and got such a wonderful longing to be floating on the water that at last he could not help telling it to the hen.

"What is the matter with you?" she asked. "You have nothing to do, and that 's why you get such silly ideas. Lay eggs, or purr, and they will pass away."

"But it is so delightful to swim about in the water !" said the duckling; "so delightful to get in over your head and dive down to the bottom."

"That must be a great pleasure, indeed !" said the hen. "You must be going mad! Ask the cat—he is the wisest creature I know—if he likes to float on the water, or dive under it, to say nothing of myself. Just ask our mistress, the old woman, who is wiser than any other person in the world. Do you think she would like to float about and get the water over her head?"

"You don't understand me," said the duckling.

THE DUCKLING HAD TO KEEP HIS LEGS CONSTANTLY MOVING, SO THAT THE HOLE IN THE ICE SHOULD NOT CLOSE UP.

"Well, if we don't understand you, who is likely to understand you? I don't suppose you think that you are wiser than the cat or the old woman, not to speak of myself? Don't be conceited, child, and be thankful to Heaven for all the kindness you have received. Have you not got a warm room, and nice company, where you can learn something? But you are a chatterer, and it is n't pleasant to be in your company. Believe me, I only speak for your own good. I say unpleasant things to you, but by that you may know your true friends. Now just set about laying eggs and learning to purr or make sparks!"

"I think I 'll go out into the wide world," said the duckling.

"Yes, do by all means," said the hen.

And off went the duckling; he swam about on the water and he dived, but he was shunned by all other creatures on account of his ugliness.

Autumn was now setting in; the leaves of the forest were turning yellow and brown, and the wind caught them up and set them dancing and whirling about.

The air was turning cold and the clouds hung heavily laden with hail and snow. On the fence sat the raven and cawed, "Caw! caw!" from sheer cold. It made one shiver at the mere thought of it; the poor duckling was indeed in bad straits.

One evening, as the sun was setting in all its beauty, a whole flock of large beautiful birds came out of the bushes; the duckling had never seen such lovely birds before. They were dazzlingly white, with long, curved necks; they were swans. They uttered quite a strange sound, and spreading out their splendid broad wings, they flew away from those cold regions to warmer climes, to the open lakes; they mounted higher and higher, and a feeling of sadness came over the ugly little duckling; he turned round and round in the water like a wheel, stretched his neck high up in the air after them, and uttered a cry so loud and strange that he became frightened at it himself. Oh! could he ever forget these beautiful, happy birds? As soon as they were out of sight he dived straight down to the bottom, and when he came up again he was quite beside himself. He did not know what the birds were called, or whither they were flying, but still he loved them as he had never loved anything before; he was not at all envious of them; how could he think of wishing for such beauty for himself? He would have been quite happy if only the ducks would have allowed him to remain with them; poor, ugly little thing!

And the winter was growing cold — oh, so cold! The duckling had to swim about in the water to prevent it from being frozen over; but every night the opening in which he was swimming grew smaller and smaller. It was freezing so hard that the ice creaked and cracked; the duckling had to keep his legs constantly moving so that the hole should not close up. At last he became exhausted; he lay quite still, and soon became frozen in the ice.

Early in the morning a peasant came by and saw him; he went out on the ice and broke it in pieces with his wooden shoe, and carried the duckling home to his wife. There he came to himself again.

The children wanted to play with him, but the duckling thought they would hurt him, and rushed in a great fright straight into the milk-bowl, so that the milk splashed all over the room. The woman screamed and held up her hands when the duckling flew into the trough where the butter was kept, and then into the flour-barrel and out of it again. What a sight he was! The woman screamed and tried to hit him with the fire-tongs, and the children tumbled against one another in trying to catch the duckling, while they laughed and screamed. It was lucky that the door stood open; he slipped out and rushed in among the bushes in the new-fallen snow, and here he lay down almost insensible.

But it would be too sad to tell you about all the sufferings and misery he had to endure during the severe winter. He was lying among the rushes on the marsh when the sun again began to send forth its warm rays; the larks were singing, and everything around told of a beautiful spring.

"ONLY KILL ME!" SAID THE POOR CREATURE AS HE BENT HIS HEAD DOWN AGAINST THE SURFACE OF THE WATER.

Then all at once he lifted his wings; they beat the air more strongly than before and carried him rapidly away, and before he knew of it he found himself in a large garden where the apple-trees were in bloom, and where the fragrant lilacs were hanging on their long green boughs right down to the winding canals. Oh, how lovely everything looked in the freshness of the spring! And out of the thicket right in front of the duckling came three beautiful white swans; they rustled with their feathers as they gracefully floated past on the water. The duckling recognized the beautiful creatures and was seized with a strange fit of sadness.

"I will fly over to these royal birds and they will kill me because I, who am so ugly, dare to approach them. But I do not care! It is better to be killed by them than to be snapped at by the ducks, pecked by the hens, kicked by the girl who looks after the poultry-yard, and to suffer hardships in the winter." And he jumped into the water and swam toward the beautiful swans. As soon as they saw him they rushed at him with rustling wings.

"Only kill me!" said the poor creature as he bent his head down against the surface of the water, waiting for death—but what did he see in the clear water? He saw under him his own image in the water, but he was no longer a clumsy dark-grayish bird, ugly and hideous to behold, but a beautiful swan!

It matters but little to be born in the duck-yard when one comes from a swan's egg!

He felt extremely happy at having gone through all the sufferings and hardships he had endured; now he fully understood his good fortune, and all the loveliness he saw around him. The big swans swam round him and stroked him with their beaks.

Some little children came into the garden and threw bread and corn into the water. The youngest of them cried out:

"There is a new one!" and the other children shouted for joy. "Yes, a new one has come!" and they clapped their hands and danced about, and ran to fetch their father and mother. Bread and cakes were thrown into the water, and they all said: "The new one is the prettiest! so young and so beautiful!" and the old swans bowed their heads to him.

He felt quite bashful, and hid his head under his wings; he did not know what to do; he was extremely happy, but not at all proud, for a good heart is never proud. He was thinking how he had been persecuted and despised, and now he heard all say that he was the most beautiful of all beautiful birds. And the lilac-trees bent their branches right into the water to him, and the sun shone so warm and so pleasantly. Then he rustled his feathers and curved his graceful neck, and with joy he shouted: "So much happiness I did not dream of when I was an ugly duckling!"

THE FLYING TRUNK

IT WAS A WONDERFUL TRUNK! AS SOON AS YOU PRESSED THE LOCK
THE TRUNK COULD FLY.

THE FLYING TRUNK

THERE was once upon a time a merchant who was so rich that he could have paved the whole street with silver coins, and even have enough over for a narrow lane; but he did not do anything of the kind. He knew how to make use of his money in quite a different way; if he paid out a shilling, he got back a dollar. That was the kind of merchant he was—and then he died.

The son now got all this money, and began to lead a merry life; he went to masquerades every night, made paper kites out of dollar notes, and played ducks and drakes across the lakes with gold coins instead of stones, and money soon comes to an end in this way, which it did. At last he had only four pennies left, and no other clothes than a pair of slippers and an old dressing-gown. His friends no longer cared for him, as they could not very well be seen with him in the streets; but one of them, who was of a kind disposition, sent him an old trunk with the message, "Pack up." That was all very well, but he had nothing to pack, and so he sat down in the trunk.

It was a wonderful trunk! As soon as you pressed the lock, the trunk could fly. He pressed the lock, and off the trunk flew with him, up through the chimney and high above the clouds, farther and farther away. The bottom of the trunk began to creak, and he was afraid it would go to pieces. What a curious descent that would be! Heaven preserve him!

219

And so he came to the land of the Turks. He hid the trunk in the forest under some dried leaves and then went into the town. He could very well do that, for in Turkey everybody goes about in dressing-gowns and slippers, just as he did.

He then met a nurse with a little child. "I say, you Turkish nurse!" he said, "what big palace is that close to the town, with the windows placed so high?"

"The princess lives there," she said. "It has been foretold that she will be unfortunate in love. And therefore nobody is allowed to come near her unless the king and the queen are present."

"Thank you," said the merchant's son; and so he went back to the forest, sat down in the trunk, flew to the roof of the palace, and crept through the window into the princess's room.

She was lying asleep on the sofa; she was so beautiful that the merchant's son could not resist kissing her. She awoke, and was very much frightened, but he said he was the god of the Turks, who had come down to her through the air, at which she was much pleased.

So they sat down, side by side, and he began telling her stories about her eyes: they were the most beautiful dark lakes, in which her thoughts were swimming about like mermaids. And he told her about her forehead: it was a snowy mountain with the most magnificent halls and pictures. And he told her about the stork who brings the sweet little children.

Yes, they were really delightful stories. And so he asked the princess if she would marry him, and she said "Yes" at once.

"But you must come here on Saturday," she said; "the king and queen will then be here to tea. They will be very proud to hear that I am going to marry the god of the Turks, but mind you are prepared with a really beautiful fairy tale, for my parents are particularly fond of stories. My mother prefers those with a moral and some romance, and my father the merry ones which make one laugh."

"Very well. I shall bring no other wedding present than a fairy tale," he said, and then they parted; but the princess gave him a saber which was mounted with gold coins, and these especially would come in very useful.

He then flew away, bought a new dressing-gown, and then sat in the forest, making up the fairy tale. It had to be ready by Saturday, so it was not an easy task.

By the time he had finished it, it was Saturday.

The king, the queen, and the whole court were at tea with the princess, waiting for him. He was most graciously received.

"I hope you will tell us a fairy tale," said the queen—"one that is profound and instructive."

"But one that we can laugh at," said the king.

THE KING, THE QUEEN, AND THE WHOLE COURT WERE TAKING TEA WITH THE PRINCESS.

"With pleasure," he said, and so he began. We must now listen attentively.

"There was once a bundle of matches that were exceedingly proud because of their high degree. Their genealogical tree—that is to say, the big fir-tree of which each was a little piece—had been a big old tree in the forest. The matches were now lying on the shelf between a tinder-box and an old iron pot, to whom they were telling all about their early days. 'Yes, when we were green branches,' they said, 'we were indeed well off. Every morning and evening we had diamond tea,—that's what we called the dew,—and all day we had sunshine whenever the sun was shining, while all the little birds had to tell us stories. We could easily tell that we were well off, for the other trees wore leaves only in the summer, while our family could afford green clothes both summer and winter. But then came the wood-cutter, like the great revolution, and our family was split up. The head of the family got an appointment as mainmast on a splendid ship, which could sail round the whole world if it liked; and the other branches of the family came to different places, and we were now consigned to the task of providing light for the lower classes; that's the reason we people of high degree came to be here in the kitchen.'

"'Well, my fate has been quite a different one,' said the iron pot, near which the matches were lying. 'From the very first I have been scoured and have cooked ever so many meals. I look after the material welfare of the household and am really of first importance in the house. My only pleasure is, when dinner is over, to lie clean and bright on my shelf and have a good talk with my comrades. With the exception of the water-pail, which now and then is taken down into the yard, we all spend our life indoors. Our only messenger that brings news from the outer world is the market-basket, but she talks so violently about the government and the people! Why, the other day an old pot became so frightened at her talk that he fell down and broke in pieces! She is very outspoken, I must tell you—'

"'You talk a good deal too much!' said the tinder-box, and the steel struck the flint a blow so that the sparks flew about. Come, let us have a merry evening.'

"'Yes, let us discuss who is of the best family,' said the matches.

"'No, I don't like to talk about myself,' said the earthen pot; 'let us get up an entertainment. I will begin—I will tell you about something which has happened to all of you, so that you can easily enter into it, and then it is all the more amusing: On the shores of the Baltic, in the shelter of the Danish beeches—'

"'That's a very pretty beginning!' said all the plates; 'that is sure to be a story we shall like.'

"'Well, there I spent my youth with a quiet family; the furniture was polished and the floors washed, and clean curtains were put up every fortnight.'

"'What an interesting way you have of telling stories!' said the broom. 'One can hear at once it is a lady who is telling stories, there is something so true about it all.'

"'Yes, one can feel that,' said the water-pail; and in his joy he made a jump and the water splashed all over the floor.

"And the pot went on with her story and the end was as good as the beginning.

"All the plates rattled with delight, and the broom took green parsley from the sand-hole and crowned the pot with it, for he knew it would amuse the others, and 'If I crown her to-day,' he thought, 'she will crown me to-morrow.'

"'I want to have a dance,' said the fire-tongs, and began dancing. Good heavens! How the tongs kicked high in the air! The old chair-cover over in the corner split at the sight. 'Ought I not to be crowned too?' said the fire-tongs, and so this was done.

"'They are a common lot, after all!' thought the matches.

"The tea-urn was now going to sing, but she had a cold, she said, and could not sing except when she was at boiling-point; but it was only affectation. She would not sing unless she was standing on the table in the parlor.

"Over in the window lay an old quill pen which the servant-girl used to write with; there was nothing remarkable about him except that he had been dipped too far into the inkstand, but of this he was very proud. 'If the tea-urn won't sing,' he said, 'she may leave it alone! Outside in a cage hangs a nightingale who can sing; he has not learned much, but we won't say anything disparaging about that this evening.'

"'I think it most improper,' said the tea-kettle, who was singer to the kitchen utensils and half-sister to the tea-urn, 'that a foreign bird should be allowed to sing. Is it patriotic? I shall let the market-basket decide the point.''

"'I am very much annoyed,' said the market-basket; 'I am more annoyed than any one can imagine. Is this the proper way to spend an evening? Would it not be more sensible to put the house in order? Every one should then be in his proper place, and I would manage the whole affair. Then things would be quite different.'

"'Yes, let us make a disturbance,' they all cried. Just at that moment the door opened. It was the servant-girl, and so they all became silent; no one muttered a sound. But there was not a pot among them who did not know what he could have done and how grand he was. 'If I had had my way,' they all thought, 'we should have had a really merry evening.'

"The servant-girl took the matches and lighted the fire with them. Gracious me! How they sputtered and blazed up!

"'Well, now,' they thought, 'all can now see that we are of the first importance.   How we shine!   What a light we give!'—and then they went out.''

"What a capital story!'' said the queen, "I felt just as if I were in the kitchen with the matches.   Well, thou shalt have our daughter.''

"Yes, of course!'' said the king.   "Thou shalt marry our daughter on Monday.''   They called him "thou'' now that he was going to be one of the family.

HE PUT THE FIREWORKS ON HIS TRUNK AND FLEW UP INTO THE AIR WITH IT.   CRACK! OFF WENT THE FIREWORKS, SPURTING IN ALL DIRECTIONS.

The wedding was thus settled, and the evening before the whole town was illuminated.   Buns and fancy bread were thrown among the people; the street boys stood on tiptoe and shouted, "Hurrah!'' and whistled through their fingers.   It was altogether very fine.

"Well, I suppose I shall have to do something as well,'' said the merchant's son, and so he bought some rockets, crackers, and all the fireworks he could think of, put them on his trunk and then flew up into the air with it.

Crack!   Off went the fireworks, spurting and flashing in all directions. All the Turks were delighted and jumped so high that their slippers flew about their ears. Such a vision in the sky they had never seen before. Now they could understand that it was the god of the Turks himself who was going to marry the princess.

As soon as the merchant's son had descended into the wood with his trunk he thought to himself: "I will go into the town and hear what people think of it all!" And it was only natural he should like to know.

How the people were talking! Every one he inquired of had seen it in his own way, but all thought it was a splendid sight. "I saw the god of the Turks myself," said one; "his eyes were like glittering stars, and his beard like a falling waterfall."

"He flew away in a cloak of fire," said another; "the loveliest cherubs were peeping out from among its folds."

Yes, he heard the most wonderful things, and the following day he was to be married.

He then went back to the forest to sit in his trunk—but where was it? The trunk was burned. A spark from the fireworks had set fire to the trunk, which was burned to ashes. He could not fly any more and could not get to his bride any more.

She stood the whole day on the roof waiting for him. She is still waiting for him; but he goes about all over the world telling stories, though they are no longer as funny as that he told about the matches.

THE STORKS

ON THE LAST HOUSE IN A LITTLE VILLAGE A PAIR OF STORKS
HAD BUILT THEIR NEST.

THE STORKS

ON the last house in a little village a pair of storks had built their nest. Mother Stork sat in it with her four little young ones, who stretched out their heads and their little black beaks, for they had not yet become red. A little way off on the ridge of the roof stood Father Stork, erect and stiff; he had drawn up one of his legs, in order to show he was putting himself to some inconvenience in standing as sentry. One would think he was carved out of wood, so still did he stand. "I think it must look quite grand for my wife to have a sentry by her nest," thought he; "they can't know that I am her husband; they must think I have been ordered to stand here. It looks quite grand." And so he continued to stand on one leg.

In the street below a lot of children were playing about, and when they saw the storks one of the boldest of the boys began to sing the old verse about the stork, and afterward all the others joined in, but they sang it just as he could remember it:

> "Storkey, storkey, sty oh!
> Swiftly homeward fly, oh!
> For your wife lies safe at rest,
> With four fledglings in the nest:
> The first, he shall be hanged!
> The second shall be spitted through!
> The third, he shall be roasted brown!
> The fourth shall be turned upside down!"

"Just listen to what those boys are singing," said the young storks; "they say we shall be hanged and roasted."

"Never mind what they are singing," said Mother Stork; "don't listen to them, and then it won't matter."

But the boys went on singing, and pointed their fingers at the storks. Only one of the boys, whose name was Peter, said it was a shame to make fun of the birds, and would not join in with the others. Mother Stork comforted her young ones and said: "Don't mind them! Just look how quietly your father takes it, standing there on one leg."

"We are so frightened!" said the young ones, and drew back their heads into the nest.

Next day, when the children came again to play and saw the stork, they began their song again:

> "The first, he shall be hanged!
> The second shall be spitted through!"

"But we are not going to be hanged and spitted through, are we?" asked the young ones.

"No, of course not!" said the mother. "You are going to learn to fly, and I 'll look after your training! Then we shall go into the fields and pay visits to the frogs; they will make their bow to us in the water, and sing, 'Croak, croak!' And then we shall eat them. It will be great fun!"

"And what then?" asked the young storks.

"Then all the storks all over the country will assemble, and the autumn manœuvers will commence. Every one must be able to fly properly; that is of great importance, for the general will kill with his beak all those who cannot fly. So mind you learn as well as you can when the training begins!"

"Then we shall be killed, after all, just as the boys said; and just listen, now they are singing it again!"

"Listen to me, and not to them," said Mother Stork. "After the great manœuvers we fly to the hot countries — oh, ever so far from here, across mountains and forests. We shall fly to Egypt, where there are three-cornered stone houses which end in a point above the clouds; they are called pyramids, and are older than any stork can imagine. And there is a river there, which overflows its banks and leaves the land covered with mud. You walk about in the mud and eat frogs."

"Oh, my!" said all the young ones.

"Yes, it is so delightful! One does nothing but eat all day, and while we are enjoying ourselves down there, there is not in this country a green leaf on the trees, and it is so cold here that the clouds freeze to pieces and fall down in little white rags." It was the snow she referred to, but she could not explain it any better.

"Do the naughty little boys also freeze to pieces?" asked the young storks.

"No, they do not freeze to pieces. But they are not very far from it; they have to sit indoors in dark rooms, and mope and shiver. You, however, can fly about in foreign countries, where there are flowers and warm sunshine."

Some time had now passed, and the young storks were already so big that they could stand up in the nest and look around, and Father Stork came flying home every day with nice frogs, little snakes, and all kinds of dainties for storks which he could find. And how he amused them with all sorts of tricks! He would twist his head right round his tail,

FATHER STORK CAME FLYING HOME EVERY DAY WITH NICE FROGS, LITTLE SNAKES,
AND ALL KINDS OF DAINTIES FOR STORKS.

and clatter with his beak as if it were a rattle, and then he would tell them stories all about the swamps.

"Now you must learn to fly!" said Mother Stork one day; and so all the four young ones had to go out on the ridge of the roof. How they reeled! They had to balance themselves with their wings, and yet they were nearly falling down.

"NOW YOU MUST LEARN TO FLY!" SAID MOTHER STORK ONE DAY.

"Look at me!" said the mother. "This is the way to hold your head. And your feet this way. One, two! one, two! That's the way to help yourselves on in the world." And then she flew a little way. The young storks made a little clumsy jump, when—bump!—there they lay, for they were too heavy in the body.

"I don't want to fly," said one of the young storks, and crept back into the nest; "I don't care to go to the hot countries."

"Do you want to freeze to death here when the winter comes? Do you want the boys to come and hang you and spit you and roast you ? I will just call them!"

"Oh, no!" said the young stork; and then he hopped out on the roof again to the others. On the third day they were able to fly a little, and then they thought they could also soar into the air, and this they tried to do, but — bump! — down they fell, and so they had to use their wings again. The boys down in the street began singing their song :

"Storkey, storkey —"

"Shall we fly down and peck their eyes out?" said the young storks.

"No, leave them alone," said the mother; "only listen to me — that's more important. One, two, three! Now to the left round the chimney. That was well done. The last stroke with the wings was done so beautifully and correctly that you shall have permission to come with me to the swamp to-morrow. There are several nice stork families coming there with their children. Let them see that mine are the nicest; so mind you hold yourselves erect; it looks well and commands respect."

"But are we not going to have our revenge on those naughty boys?" asked the young storks.

"Let them scream as much as they like. You are going to fly up to the clouds, and will come to the land of the pyramids, while they have to remain here shivering, without seeing a green leaf or a sweet apple."

"Yes, we will be revenged," they whispered to one another; and so they went on practising.

Of all the boys in the street no one was more persistent in singing the mocking verse than the one who had begun it, and he was quite a little fellow, not more than six years old. The young stork thought of course he was a hundred years old, for he was so much bigger than their mother and father, and what did they know about children's ages and how big human beings can be?

All their revenge was to fall upon this boy; he had first begun it, and he was always going on with it. The young storks were very angry, and as they grew bigger they were less likely to tolerate it; their mother had at last to promise them that they should have their revenge, but not till the last day when they were leaving the country.

"We must see, first, how you get on at the great manœuver. If you don't acquit yourselves well, the general will run you through with his beak, and then the boys will be right, after all, at least in one respect. Now let me see you try."

"That you shall!" said the young ones; and so they set to work with a good will and practised every day till they could fly so nicely and lightly that it was a pleasure to look at them.

Then the autumn came. All the storks began to assemble before they flew away to the hot countries for the winter.

The manœuver was a trial of strength; the young storks had to fly over forests and towns to see how well they could fly, for it was a long journey they had before them. The young storks did so well that they got "excellent" as their mark, and frogs and snakes as prizes. This was the very highest award, and as for the frogs and snakes, they were to eat them, which the young storks did.

"Now we 'll be revenged!" they said.

"Yes, of course," said Mother Stork. "What I have been thinking over is just the right thing. I know where the pond is in which all the little children are lying till the storks come to fetch them to their parents. There the pretty little babies lie sleeping and dreaming so sweetly as they never will again. All parents like to have a little child, and all children like to have a sister or brother. We will now fly over to the pond and fetch one to each of the children who have not sung the wicked song and made fun of the storks. None of the other children shall have any."

"But the boy who began the song — that naughty, wicked boy," cried the young storks, "what shall we do to him?"

"In the pond there lies a little dead baby, who has dreamed itself to death. We will take this baby to him, and then he will cry because we have brought him a dead little brother. But what about the good boy? Surely you have not forgotten him who said, 'It is a shame to make fun of the birds.' We will bring him both a brother and a sister, and as his name was Peter, all of you shall also be called Peter."

And what she said came to pass, and all the storks were called "Peter," and that is what they are still called.

SILLY HANS

THE PRINCESS HAD PUBLICLY ANNOUNCED THAT SHE WOULD MARRY
THE PERSON WHO COULD SPEAK BEST FOR HIMSELF.

SILLY HANS

OUT in the country there was an old mansion, and in it lived an old squire and his two sons, who were so witty that they were really too clever by half; they wanted to woo the king's daughter, which they were quite at liberty to do, for she had publicly announced that she would marry the person who could speak best for himself.

The two brothers took eight days to prepare themselves—that was all the time they could give to it; but that was quite sufficient, for they possessed a good deal of elementary knowledge, and that comes in useful. One of them knew the whole of the Latin dictionary, and the contents of the newspaper of the city for the last three years, by heart; in fact, he could say it just as well backward as forward. The other one had studied the rules and regulations of all the guilds and everything that an alderman ought to know, so he thought he should be able to talk of the affairs of the state; and besides this he could also embroider braces, for he was of a gentle nature and very nimble with his fingers.

"I shall win the king's daughter," said both of them; and then their father gave each of them a beautiful horse: the one who knew the dictionary by heart got a coal-black horse, and he who knew all about the guilds and the aldermen and could embroider received a milk-white horse. And then they rubbed the corners of their mouths with cod-liver oil, so that they might be able to talk more glibly. All the servants were in the courtyard to see them mount their horses, and just then came the third brother,— for there were three,— but no one took him into account as one of the brothers, for he did not know as much as they, and he was only called "Silly Hans."

"Where are you going to, since you have got your fine clothes on?" he asked.

"To the palace to woo the king's daughter. Have n't you heard what the drummer is announcing all over the country?" And then they told him.

"My word! then I 'll go too," said Silly Hans; and the brothers laughed at him and rode away.

"Father, let me have a horse," said Silly Hans. "I should like so much to get married.   If she takes me, she takes me; and if she does n't take me, I will take her for all that."

"What nonsense!" said his father; "I sha'n't give you a horse.   Why, you can't talk properly.   No; your brothers are fine specimens of what young fellows ought to be."

"If I can't have a horse," said Silly Hans, "I 'll take the billy-goat; he 's mine, and he carries me very well."   And so he jumped astride the billy-goat, stuck his heels into its side, and set off along the highroad. "Heigh! what a pace! I am coming," said Silly Hans, and sang away till you heard him far and wide.

But the brothers rode quietly on in front; they did not speak a word; they were thinking over all the clever sayings with which they would have to be prepared, for they intended to be so very smart, you know.

"HULLO!" SHOUTED SILLY HANS.   "JUST LOOK WHAT I HAVE FOUND!" AND HE
SHOWED THEM A DEAD CROW HE HAD FOUND.

"Hullo!" shouted Silly Hans, "here I am.   Just look what I have found in the highroad!" and he showed them a dead crow which he had found.

"Blockhead!" they said, "what are you going to do with that?"

"I 'll make a present of it to the king's daughter."

"Yes, do so by all means," they said, as they laughed and rode on.

"Hullo! here I am! Just look what I have found now; you don't find that every day in the highroad."

And the brothers turned round again to see what it was.

"Blockhead!" they said, "that 's an old wooden clog, and the upper leather is gone.   Is the king's daughter going to have that as well?"

"That she shall," said Silly Hans; and the brothers laughed and rode on, and got a long way ahead.

"HERE'S MY COOKING APPARATUS," SAID SILLY HANS, AND SO HE PULLED OUT THE OLD
WOODEN CLOG AND PLACED THE CROW ON IT.

"Hullo! here I am!" shouted Silly Hans; "I am really in luck's way. Heigh-ho! This is really wonderful!"

"What have you found now?" asked the brothers.

"Oh," said Silly Hans, "it is hardly worth mentioning, but how pleased the king's daughter will be!"

"Ugh!" said the brothers; "why; that's mud just thrown up from the ditch."

"Yes, that's what it is," said Silly Hans; "and it is of the finest sort—so fine that you can't hold it between your fingers;" and so he filled his pocket with it.

But the brothers rode on as fast as their horses' legs could carry them, and thus they arrived at the city gate an hour earlier than Hans. Here the suitors received numbers in the order in which they arrived, and were then placed in rows of six each, and placed so closely that they could not even move their arms, which was a very good thing, for otherwise they would have cut each other's backs to pieces, for the one was standing in front of the other.

All the other inhabitants of the country stood round about the palace, right up to the windows, to see the king's daughter receive the suitors. As they entered the room, one by one, the power of speech seemed to desert them.

"No good," said the king's daughter. "Away with you!"

Now came the turn of the brother who knew the dictionary by heart, but he had forgotten it all while standing in the row; the floor creaked at each step he took, and the ceiling was of looking-glass, so that he could see himself standing on his head, and at every window there were three clerks and an alderman, who wrote down everything that was said, so that it could get into the papers at once, and be sold for a penny at the street corner. It was really terrible, and, moreover, they had put so much fire in the stove that the drum was red-hot.

"It's dreadfully hot in here," said the suitor.

"Yes, that's because my father is roasting chickens to-day," said the king's daughter.

Bah! there he stood; he had not expected to be spoken to in that way; he did not know what to say, although he wanted to say something clever. Bah!

"No good," said the king's daughter. "Go away;" and so he had to go. Next came his brother.

"There's a dreadful heat in here," he said.

"Yes, we are roasting chickens to-day," said the king's daughter.

"Beg your par—" he said; and all the clerks wrote down "Beg your par—."

"No good," said the king's daughter. "Go away."

Then came Silly Hans, riding his billy-goat right into the room. "What a sweltering heat!" he said.

"That's because I am roasting chickens," said the king's daughter.

"That's lucky," said Silly Hans. "I suppose I can get a crow roasted here, then?"

"That you may," said the king's daughter; "but have you got anything to roast it in, for I have neither pot nor pan."

"That I have," said Silly Hans. "Here's a cooking apparatus with a tin handle;" and so he pulled out the old wooden clog and placed the crow on it.

"That's enough for one meal," said the king's daughter; "but where shall you get the dripping from?"

"I have it in my pocket," said Silly Hans. "I have got so much that I don't mind if I spill some of it;" and so he took a little of the mud out of his pocket and basted the crow with it.

"That's what I like," said the king's daughter. "You can give one an answer, at any rate, and you can speak; and so I will have you for my husband. But do you know that every word we say and have said is written down, and will appear in the paper to-morrow? At every window you will see three clerks and an old alderman, and the alderman is the worst of all, for he does n't understand anything." She said this to frighten Hans, and all the clerks giggled and upset the ink on the floor.

"Oh, these are the gentlemen, are they?" said Silly Hans; "then I suppose I must give the alderman the best;" and so he turned out his pocket and flung the mud right into his face.

"That was clever," said the king's daughter; "I could not have done it. But I shall learn it right enough."

And so Silly Hans was made king, and got a wife and a crown, and sat on a throne, all of which we have read about in the alderman's paper — and that's one you can't depend upon.

THE WILD SWANS

THE PRINCES WERE TURNED INTO ELEVEN BEAUTIFUL WILD SWANS.

THE WILD SWANS

FAR away from here, in the land where the swallows fly to when we have winter, lived a king who had eleven sons and one daughter, whose name was Elisa. The eleven brothers, who were all princes, went to school with a star on their breast and a saber by their side; they wrote on golden slates with diamond pencils, and knew their lessons by heart just as well as if they had read them from a book. One could see at once that they were princes. Elisa, the sister, sat on a small footstool of plate glass and had a picture-book which cost as much as half the kingdom.

Yes, those children led indeed a happy life, but it was not always to be so.

Their father, who was king of the whole country, married a wicked queen, who was not at all kind to the poor children. On the very first day this became apparent to them. There were great festivities all over the palace, and the children were playing at "having company," but instead of their getting, as usual, all the cakes and roasted apples that could be had, the queen gave them only sand in a tea-cup and said they might pretend it was something nice.

The following week she sent their little sister, Elisa, away to some peasants in the country, and before long she succeeded in getting the king to believe all sorts of things about the poor princes, so that he did not trouble himself any more about them.

"Fly out into the world and shift for yourselves!" said the wicked queen; "fly away like great birds without the power of speech!" but she could not, however, carry out her bad intentions as far as she wished, for the princes were turned into eleven beautiful wild swans. With a strange cry they flew out through the palace windows and away over the park and the forest.

It was still quite early in the morning when they passed the peasant's cottage where their sister lay asleep; here they hovered over the roof, twisting their long necks and flapping their wings, but nobody heard or saw them; they had to set out again, high up toward the clouds, till they came to a great, gloomy forest which reached right down to the shore.

Poor little Elisa was standing in the peasant's parlor, playing with a green leaf, the only plaything she had; she made a hole in the leaf, looked up at the sun through it, and fancied she saw the bright eyes of her brothers, and every time the warm sunbeams shone upon her cheek she thought of all their kisses.

One day passed just like another. When the wind blew through the big hedges of roses outside the cottage, it would whisper to the roses, "Who can be more beautiful than you?" But the roses shook their heads and said, "Elisa!" And when the old woman on a Sunday sat in the doorway reading her hymn-book, the wind would turn over the leaves and say to the book, "Who can be better than you?" "Elisa!" answered the hymn-book; and it was the real truth that the roses and the hymn-book had said.

When she was fifteen years old she was to return home; and when the queen saw how beautiful she was, she became filled with anger and hatred against her. She would have liked to turn her into a wild swan like her brothers, but she dared not do so at once, as the king would, of course want to see his daughter.

Early in the morning the queen went into the bath, which was built of marble and adorned with soft cushions and the most beautiful carpets, and she took three toads, kissed them, and said to one of them, "Sit on Elisa's head when she gets into her bath, so that she may become lazy like yourself!" "Sit upon her forehead," she said to the other, "so that she may become ugly like yourself, and her father will not recognize her!" "Rest close to her heart," she whispered to the third; "let her heart become wicked, so that she may suffer through it!" She then put the toads into the clear water, which at once turned a greenish color. She called Elisa, undressed her, and let her go into the water, and as she ducked her head, one of the toads settled itself in her hair, the other on her forehead, and the third on her breast; but Elisa did not seem to notice them. As soon as she stood up, three red poppies were floating on the water; had the animals not been poisonous and had they not been kissed by the queen, they would have been turned into red roses; but they became flowers, however, through resting on her head and near her heart. She was too good and innocent for the witch-craft to have any power over her.

When the wicked queen saw this, she took some walnut juice and rubbed Elisa with it till she became quite brown, besmeared her pretty face with a nasty-smelling salve, and ruffled her lovely hair, so that it was impossible to recognize the beautiful Elisa.

When her father saw her he became quite frightened and said that she was not his daughter. Nobody but the bandog and the swallows would acknowledge her; but they were only humble animals and were of no importance.

Poor Elisa then began to cry and think of her eleven brothers, who were all lost to her. Greatly distressed in mind, she stole out of the palace and walked the whole day across fields and moors till she came to the big forest. She did not know where she wanted to go, but she felt so sad and longed so much for her brothers. No doubt they, like herself, had also been driven out into the world, and she made up her mind she would try to find them.

She had been only a short time in the forest when night set in; she had strayed away from the roads and paths, and so she lay down on the soft moss, said her evening prayers, and leaned her head up against the stump of a tree. All was still and quiet, the air was so mild; and round about, in the grass and on the moss, hundreds of glow-worms were shining like green fire. When she gently touched one of the branches above her, the shining insects fell down to her like shooting-stars.

The whole night long she dreamed about her brothers. They were again playing as children, writing with diamond pencils on golden slates, and looking at the most beautiful picture-book, which cost as much as half the kingdom. But they did not write strokes and pot-hooks as before —no, they wrote about the most valiant deeds which they had performed, and about everything they had seen and gone through. In the picture-book everything was alive — the birds were singing and the people came walking out of the book and spoke to Elisa and her brothers, but when she turned over the leaf, they ran back to their places, so that the pictures should not be disarranged.

When she awoke the sun was already high in the heavens; she could not exactly see it, as the lofty trees spread their branches closely and firmly above her, but its beams were playing through them like a fluttering veil of gold. There came a fragrance from the verdure around her, and the birds almost perched on her shoulder. She heard the splashing of the water from the many springs, which all fell into a lake that had the most beautiful sandy bottom. There were thick bushes growing all round the lake, but in one place the stags had dug out a large opening, and here Elisa got to the water, which was so clear that had not the wind put the branches and bushes into motion, she must have believed that they had been painted on the bottom of the lake, so plainly were all the leaves reflected, both those through which the sun shone and those which were quite in the shade.

As soon as she saw her own face she became quite frightened, so brown and ugly was it; but on wetting her little hand and rubbing her eyes and forehead, the white skin soon shone through. She then took off all her clothes and went into the fresh water, and a lovelier royal child than she could not be found in this world.

When she was dressed again and had plaited her long hair, she went to the sparkling spring, drank out of the hollow of her hand, and wandered farther into the forest, without knowing whither she went. She thought of her brothers and of the kind God, who surely would not desert her. He let the wild forest apples grow, so that the hungry might be satisfied; he showed her such a tree, the branches of which were bent beneath the weight of the fruit, and there she made her midday meal. After having propped up the branches of the tree she walked off into the darkest parts of the forest. It was so quiet that she heard her own footsteps, heard every little dry leaf being crushed under her foot; not a bird was to be seen, nor could any sunbeam penetrate through the great close branches of the trees. The lofty trunks stood so close to one another that when she looked straight before her it appeared as if one barrier of logs close upon another encircled her. Oh, such a solitude she had never known before!

The night was very dark, and not one single little glow-worm glittered in the moss. Quite distressed, she lay down to sleep. She then thought she saw the branches part above her and our Lord looking down upon her with eyes full of tenderness, while little angels peeped out above his head and from under his arms.

When she woke in the morning she did not know whether she had been dreaming, or whether it had all really happened.

She had not gone many steps when she met an old woman with a basket of berries, of which the woman gave her some. Elisa asked her if she had not seen eleven princes riding through the forest.

"No," said the old woman; "but yesterday I saw eleven swans, with golden crowns on their heads, swimming down the river close by."

And she led Elisa some distance farther till they came to a slope, at the bottom of which a river wound its way. The trees on its banks stretched their long, leafy branches across the water to each other, and where they, according to their natural growth, could not reach the other side, the roots had been torn up from the soil, and hung out over the water, with the branches entwined in each other.

Elisa bade farewell to the old woman, and walked along the river till it flowed out into the great, open sea.

The great, glorious ocean lay before the young maiden; but not a sail was to be seen out there, not a boat was in sight. How was she to continue her journey? She looked at the countless little pebbles on the shore; the water had worn them quite round. Glass, iron, stones, everything that had been washed up by the sea had been shaped by the water, and this was even far softer than her delicate hand.

"It rolls on and on persistently, and the hardest substance must in the end yield to it. I will be just as persistent. Thanks for the lesson you have given me, you clear, rolling waves! One day, my heart tells me, you will carry me to my dear brothers."

Among the sea-weeds that had been washed ashore lay eleven white swans' feathers, which she gathered into a bunch. There were drops of water on them, but whether they were dew-drops or tears, no one could say. It was very lonely there on the shore, but she did not feel it, for the sea was perpetually changing, and presented, in fact, a greater variety of aspects in a few hours than the fresh-water lakes could show in a whole year. If a large black cloud appeared, it was as if the sea meant to say, "I too can look black," and then the wind would begin to blow and the waves to show their white crests; but if the clouds were bathed in the red sunlight and the winds had gone to rest, the sea was like a rose-leaf; now it was green, now white, but however calmly it might rest, there was always a slight motion near the shore; the sea heaved gently, like the breast of a sleeping child.

Just as the sun was setting, Elisa saw eleven wild swans with golden crowns on their heads flying toward land, one behind the other; they looked like a long white sash. Elisa went up the slope and hid herself behind a bush; the swans settled down close to her, and began flapping with their large white wings.

The moment the sun sank below the water's edge the swans' plumage fell off the birds, and there stood eleven handsome princes, Elisa's brothers. She uttered a loud cry, for although they had changed greatly, she knew it was they, she felt it must be they; she ran into their arms and called them by their names, and they became so happy and delighted when they saw her and recognized their little sister, who was now so tall and beautiful. They laughed and they cried, and they soon came to understand how cruel their stepmother had been to them all.

"We brothers," said the eldest, "must fly about as wild swans as long as the sun is in the heavens; when it has gone down we resume our human shape; at sunset we must therefore always take care to be near a resting-place, for if at that time we were to fly toward the clouds, we should, as human beings, be plunged into the depths of the sea. We do not live here; yonder, across the sea, lies a country just as beautiful as this, but the way thither is long; we have to cross the wide sea, and there is no island on the way, on which we could rest for the night; only a lonely little rock which rears its head in the midst of the ocean out there, but it is only just large enough for us all to rest upon it when we sit side by side. If the sea goes high, the water splashes high over us; still we are thankful to the Lord for it. There we pass the night in our human form; without it we should never be able to visit our beloved country, for it takes two of the longest days in the year to accomplish the journey. Only once a year are we allowed to visit our paternal home, and then we can remain here for only eleven days, when we fly over this big forest, from which we can see the palace where we were born and where our father lives, and the lofty tower of the church where our mother lies buried. Here we feel as if we were related to every tree and bush, here the wild horses are running across the plains, just as we saw them in our childhood; here the charcoal-burners are singing the old songs to which we danced as children; here is our native country, to which we are drawn; and here we have found you, our dear little sister. Only two more days can we remain here, and then we must cross the sea to a beautiful country, but it is not our own country. How shall we take you with us? We have neither ship nor boat."

"How shall I be able to save you?" asked the sister.

And so they went on talking together nearly the whole night, and only for a few hours did they get any sleep.

Elisa awoke at the sound of the rustling of the wings as the swans were soaring above her. Her brothers had again been turned into swans and were flying in large circles above her head, till at last they flew far away and out of sight. But one of them, the youngest, remained behind; he laid his head on her lap, while she stroked his white wings, and thus they remained together the whole day. Toward evening the others came back, and when the sun had disappeared they assumed their natural shape.

"To-morrow we must fly away from here, and we dare not return for a whole year; but we cannot leave you thus. Have you the courage to accompany us? My arm is strong enough to carry you through the forest. Should not, then, all our wings be strong enough to fly with you across the sea?"

"Yes, take me with you," said Elisa.

"They spent the whole night in making a big, strong net of the pliant willow bark and the tough sedges; on this Elisa lay down, and when the sun rose and her brothers had been changed into wild swans, they seized the net with their beaks and flew high up toward the clouds with their dear sister, who was still asleep. The sunbeams fell right on her face, and one of the swans therefore flew over her head, so that his broad wings could afford her shade.

They were far away from land when Elisa awoke; she thought she was still dreaming, so strange did it seem to her to be carried high up in the air across the sea. By her side lay a branch with delicious ripe berries

ELISA SAW HER BROTHERS STANDING ROUND HER, ARM IN ARM, WHILE THE SEA
DASHED AGAINST THE ROCK.

and a bunch of savory roots, which her youngest brother had gathered and placed at her side. She smiled gratefully to him, for she knew it was he who flew right over her head and shaded her with his wings.

They were so high up that the first ship they saw below them looked like a white sea-gull lying upon the water. A great cloud stood behind them, just like a big mountain, and across it Elisa saw the shadow of herself and the eleven swans, quite gigantic in size, as they sailed through the air. It was quite a picture, prettier than any she had ever seen; but as the sun rose higher, and the cloud was left further and further behind, the floating shadow-picture gradually vanished.

Like a whizzing arrow they shot through the air the· whole day, although their progress was somewhat slower than usual, as they now had their sister to carry. Dark clouds began gathering toward the evening, and Elisa anxiously saw the sun sinking, and yet there was no sign of the lonely rock in the ocean. It appeared to her as if the swans were making greater efforts with their wings. Alas! she was the cause of their not being able to get on fast enough; when the sun had gone down they would become human beings and fall into the sea and be drowned. She then prayed to our Lord from the bottom of her heart, but no rock could as yet be seen. The black cloud came nearer; the violent gusts of wind foretold a storm; the clouds gathered in one great, threatening wave, which moved forward like a solid mass of lead, while one flash of lightning followed upon another.

The sun was now close to the edge of the ocean. Elisa's heart trembled; the swans then darted downward so suddenly that she thought she must fall out of the net, but soon they sailed on again through the air. The sun was half-way under the horizon, and just then she caught sight of the little rock below them; it did not appear larger than the head of a seal above water. The sun was sinking rapidly; now it seemed no larger than a star, and then her foot touched the firm ground; the sun went out like the last spark in a piece of burning paper. She saw her brothers standing round her, arm in arm, but there was only just room enough for them all. The sea dashed against the rock and descended upon them like a heavy shower of rain; the heavens were continually lighted up with flashes of fire, and peal after peal of thunder followed each other; but sister and brothers held each other by the hands and sang a psalm, from which they received both comfort and courage.

At daybreak the air was pure and quite still. As soon as the sun rose the swans flew away with Elisa from the rock. The sea was still high, and, to them, who were so high up in the air, the white foam on the dark green waves appeared like millions of swans swimming on the waters.

When the sun had risen higher Elisa saw before her, half floating in the air, an alpine country with glittering masses of ice on the mountains, in the midst of which lay a palace almost a mile long, with one colonnade daringly piled above another, while below were forests of waving palms and luxurious flowers as large as mill-wheels. She asked if this was the country whither she was going, but the swans shook their heads, for what she saw was nothing but the magnificent and ever-changing aërial castle of Fata Morgana; thither they dared not bring any human being. Elisa was still gazing at it when the mountains, forests, and palace all tumbled together, and in their place stood twenty stately churches, all alike, with high steeples and pointed windows. She thought she heard the sound of an organ, but it was the sea she heard. Now she was quite close to the churches, when they changed into a whole fleet of ships that were sailing below her. She looked down and found it was only clouds of sea-mist

ELISA SAW A PALACE ALMOST A MILE LONG, WITH ONE COLONNADE DARINGLY
PILED ABOVE ANOTHER.

floating over the ocean.   Yes, she saw continual changes before her eyes, and now, at last, she saw the real country she was going to, with its beautiful blue mountains, cedar-woods, cities, and palaces.   Long before the sun had set she was sitting on the mountain before a large cave which was overgrown with delicate green creepers looking like embroidered carpets.

"Now we shall see what you will dream about here to-night," said the youngest brother, and showed her to her bedchamber.

"Heaven grant I may dream how I shall be able to save you!" she said, and this thought took entire possession of her mind.

She prayed so fervently to God for help that even in her sleep she went on praying.   She thought she was flying high up in the air to Fata Morgana's palace; the fairy herself came to meet her; she was so beautiful and gorgeously attired, and yet she was very much like the old woman who had given her the berries in the forest, and told her about the swans with the golden crowns.

"Your brothers can be saved," she said; "but have you the courage and perseverance?   Water, as you know, is softer than your delicate hands, but still it can change the shape of the hardest stones; but it does not feel the pain that your fingers will feel; it has no heart and does not suffer from the anxiety and anguish that you will have to endure.   Do you see the nettle which I hold in my hand?   Of this kind a great many grow round about the cave in which you sleep, but, mark you, only those which grow there and on the graves of the churchyards can be used; these you must gather, although they will blister your hands; tread the nettles with your feet and they will turn into flax, and this you must twist and then knit eleven shirts of mail with long sleeves.   Throw these over the eleven swans, and the spell will be broken.   But you must remember particularly that from the moment you begin your task till it is finished, even though it may take you years, you must not speak; the first word you speak will go like a deadly dagger to your brothers' hearts and kill them; on your silence depend their lives.   Remember all this!"

And then she touched Elisa's hand with the nettle, which was like burning fire, and caused her to wake.   It was broad daylight, and close to where she had slept lay a nettle like the one she had seen in her dream. She then fell on her knees, thanked the Lord, and went out of the cave to begin her task.

With her delicate hands she took hold of the nasty nettles, which were like fire and blistered her hands and arms; yet she was quite willing to suffer it all, if only she were able to save her dear brothers.   She trod every nettle with her bare feet and twisted the green flax from it.

When the sun had gone down her brothers came back; they grew frightened when they found her so silent, and thought it was some new witchery of the wicked stepmother's; but when they saw her hands they understood what she was doing for their sake.   The youngest brother wept, and where his tears fell on her hands the pain ceased and the burning blisters vanished.

She worked all night, for she could not rest till she had set free her dear brothers. During the whole of the following day, while the swans were away, she sat all alone, and the time had never flown so quickly. One shirt was already finished, and now she had begun another.

Just then a hunting-horn was heard among the mountains and startled Elisa. The sound came nearer; she heard the barking of dogs. She took refuge in the cave in great fright, tied the nettles she had gathered and hackled into a bundle, and sat down on it.

At that moment a big dog jumped out from the thicket, and immediately afterward he was followed by another, and still another; they barked loudly, ran back, and then returned again. In a few minutes all the huntsmen were there outside the cave, and the handsomest among them was the king of the country. He went up to Elisa, for he had never seen a more beautiful girl in his life.

"How did you come here, you lovely child?" he said. Elisa shook her head; she dared not speak, for her brothers' deliverance and lives depended upon it. She hid her hands under her apron, so that the king should not see what she had to suffer.

"Come with me," he said; "you must not remain here. If you are as good as you are beautiful I will dress you in silks and velvet, and place the golden crown upon your head and you shall live in my grandest palace!" And he lifted her on to his horse. She wept and wrung her hands, but the king said: "I think only of your happiness. One day you will thank me for it all." And so he dashed off across the mountains, holding her before him on his horse, and the huntsmen came rushing on behind.

Toward sunset the magnificent royal city with its churches and cupolas lay before them. The king led her into the palace, where large fountains were playing in the lofty marble halls, and where walls and ceilings were resplendent with paintings, but she had no mind for such things. She wept and mourned and passively allowed the women to dress her in regal robes, plait pearls in her hair, and put delicate gloves on her blistered fingers.

As she stood there in all her splendor, she was so dazzlingly beautiful that all the court bowed still lower before her. And the king chose her for his bride, although the archbishop shook his head and whispered that the pretty maiden from the forest was, in all probability, a witch who had dazzled their eyes and bewitched the king's heart.

But the king would not listen to this; he ordered the music to strike up, the most costly dishes to be served, and the loveliest girls to dance around her. She was conducted through fragrant gardens to most magnificent halls, but not a smile could be seen on her lips or in her

THERE, ON ONE OF THE LARGEST TOMBSTONES, ELISA SAW SOME UGLY WITCHES
BUSY TAKING OFF THEIR RAGS.

eyes. Sorrow seemed to be imprinted upon her as her everlasting heritage.

The king now opened the door to a small chamber close to the one in which she was to sleep; the floor was decked with costly green carpets, but the room was otherwise exactly like the cave in which she had been living; on the floor lay the bundle of flax which she had spun out of the nettles, and from the ceiling hung the shirt of mail which she had finished,— all of which one of the huntsmen had brought with him as curiosities.

"Here you can imagine yourself back in your late home," said the king. "Here is the work you were busy with there; and now in the midst of all the splendor around you it will amuse you to recall that time to your mind."

When Elisa saw that which was so dear to her heart, a smile played round her mouth, and the blood came back into her cheeks; she thought of her brothers' deliverance, and kissed the king's hand; he pressed her to his heart and ordered all the church bells to be rung to announce their wedding festivities. The beautiful dumb maiden from the forest was to be the queen of the land.

The archbishop then whispered wicked words into the king's ears, but they did not penetrate to his heart; the wedding was to take place, and the archbishop himself had to place the crown on her head. He maliciously pressed the narrow ring so tightly down upon her forehead that it hurt her, but a heavier ring lay around her heart, and that was the grief for her brothers, so that she did not feel the bodily pain. Her mouth was sealed,—one single word would cost her brothers their lives; but her eyes told of the deep love she bore for the kind, handsome king, who did everything to make her happy. She loved him with her whole heart and became more and more fond of him every day. Oh, if she only could have dared to confide in him, to tell him of her sufferings! But she must remain dumb, and as dumb she must complete her task. She therefore stole away from his side at night, went into the little private room which was fitted up like the cave, and knitted one shirt of mail after another; but when she began the seventh she had no flax.

She knew that the nettles which she had to use grew in the churchyard, but she herself must gather them; how should she be able to get there?

"Oh, what is the pain in my fingers compared to the anguish which my heart suffers?" she thought; "I must venture upon it. The Lord will not forsake me." With a heart heavy with fear and anxiety, as if she were bent upon some evil deed, she stole down into the garden in the clear moonlight night, walked through the long avenues of trees and along the lonely streets to the churchyard. There, on one of the largest tombstones, she saw some ugly witches sitting in a ring and busy taking off their rags, as if they were going to bathe, whereupon they began digging up the freshly made graves with their long, bony fingers, pulling out the corpses and eating their flesh. Elisa had to pass close by them, and they glared at her with their evil eyes, but she said her prayers, gathered the stinging nettles, and carried them home to the palace.

Only one human being had seen her, and that was the archbishop; he had been up while the others slept. Now he was convinced that there was something wrong with the queen: she was a witch, and that explained how she had been able to bewitch the king and the whole of the people.

He told the king in the confessional what he had seen and what he feared, but as the terrible words came from his lips the carved images of saints shook their heads as if they wanted to say: "It is not true; Elisa is innocent." The archbishop, however, had quite a different explanation: he said that they bore witness against her, and that they shook their heads at her sins. A couple of bitter tears rolled down the king's cheeks, and he went home with doubt in his heart. That night he pretended to sleep, but no peaceful slumber closed his eyes; he saw how Elisa got up from her bed, and every night afterward she did the same. Every time he followed quietly after her, and saw her disappear in her private room.

Day by day his brow became darker. Elisa noticed this, but she could not understand the reason. It made her anxious, however, and increased the suffering she endured on her brothers' account. Her hot tears flowed down upon the royal velvet and purple, and lay there like sparkling diamonds, and all who saw the splendor that surrounded her wished to be a queen. She would soon be finished with her work: only one shirt was wanting; but she had no more flax, and not a single nettle. Once more, and only this once, would she have to go to the churchyard and gather a few handfuls of nettles. She thought with dread of the lonely walk and the horrible witches, but her will was as firm as was her trust in the Lord.

Elisa went, but was followed by the king and the archbishop. They saw her disappear through the iron gate of the churchyard, and when they came up to it they saw the witches sitting on the tombstone, just as Elisa had seen them. The king turned away at the thought that she, whose head had rested on his breast that very evening, might be amongst them.

"The people must judge her," he said. And the people gave judgment that "she was to be burned by the devouring fire."

From the magnificent halls of the royal palace she was conducted to a dark, damp dungeon, into which the wind whistled through the grated windows; instead of velvet and silks they gave her the bundle of nettles she had gathered to rest her head upon. The hard, stinging shirts of mail which she had knitted were to serve her as mattress and coverlet, but they could not have given her anything she could have prized more. She began her work again and prayed to God, while outside the boys in the street were singing mocking ditties about her. Not a soul came near her to comfort her with a kind word.

Toward evening she heard the rustling of a swan's wings near the window grating; it was the youngest of her brothers who had discovered his sister. She sobbed loudly for joy, although she knew that the coming night would probably be her last, but now her work was almost completed, and her brothers were near her.

ELEVEN WILD SWANS CAME FLYING AND SETTLED DOWN AROUND HER ON THE CART,
FLAPPING THEIR LARGE WINGS.

The archbishop came to remain with her during her last hour — this he had promised the king; but she shook her head — yes! — and begged him by looks and signs to go away. She must finish her work that night, otherwise everything would be in vain — everything — her sufferings, her tears, and her sleepless nights. The archbishop left her with angry words, but poor Elisa knew that she was innocent, and went on with her work.

The little mice ran about on the floor and dragged the nettles to her feet, wanting to be of some help to her, and a thrush settled itself near the window grating and sang the whole night as merrily as it could, so that she should not lose courage.

The day was only just breaking; it was about an hour before sunrise when the eleven brothers appeared at the gate of the palace and asked to be conducted to the king, but they were told it could not be done. It was still night, the king was asleep, and they dared not wake him. The brothers begged and prayed and threatened; the guard appeared, and even the king came out and asked what was the matter. But just at that moment the sun rose and there were no princes to be seen, but over the palace eleven wild swans were seen flying away.

All the inhabitants were streaming out through the gate of the town to see the witch being burned. A miserable horse drew the cart on which Elisa sat; she had been given a gown of coarse sackcloth to wear, her beautiful long hair hung loosely about her lovely head; her cheeks were as pale as death, her lips moved slowly, while her fingers were twisting the green flax: even on her way to death she would not give up the work she had begun. The ten shirts of mail lay at her feet, and she was now busy knitting the eleventh, while the mob was scoffing at her.

"Look at the witch, how she is mumbling to herself! She has n't got a hymn-book in her hand,—no! There she sits with some of her wicked witchery. Let us tear it into a thousand pieces!"

And all the people rushed at her and wanted to tear the shirts to pieces, when the eleven wild swans came flying and settled down around her on the cart, flapping their large wings. At this the crowd drew back in terror.

"It 's a sign from heaven! She must be innocent!" many whispered; but they did not venture to say it aloud.

The executioner now took her by the hand, when suddenly she threw the eleven shirts over the swans, and there stood eleven handsome princes; but the youngest had a swan's wing instead of one of his arms, because one of the sleeves, which she had not been able to finish, was missing in his shirt.

"Now I may speak!" she said. "I am innocent!"

And the people, who had seen what had taken place, bowed before her as before a saint; but she sank insensible into her brothers' arms, overcome by all the excitement, anxiety, and grief she had gone through.

"Yes, she is innocent!" said the eldest brother; and now he related everything that had happened, and while he spoke a perfume as from millions of roses filled the air, for every log in the pile had taken root and put forth branches till they formed a fragrant hedge, broad and high, with red roses, above which bloomed a white, bright flower that shone like a star. This the king plucked and placed in Elisa's bosom when she awoke with peace and happiness in her heart.

And all the church bells began ringing of themselves, and the birds came flying into the town in great flocks. Such a wedding procession as that which returned to the palace no king had ever seen.

WHAT THE OLD MAN DOES IS ALWAYS RIGHT

THE FARMER CHANGED HIS HORSE FOR A COW, AND SO ON DOWN TO A BAG OF ROTTEN APPLES.

WHAT THE OLD MAN DOES IS ALWAYS RIGHT

I WILL now tell you a story which I heard when I was a little lad, and every time I have thought of it since it seems to become more and more delightful, for it is with stories as with many people — they become more and more delightful the older they grow; and that is so pleasant.

You have been in the country, of course. You have seen a real old farm-house with thatched roof, where moss and grass grow of themselves; there is a stork's nest on the ridge of the roof, for one cannot do without the stork. The walls are crooked and the windows low; only one of them can be opened; the baking-oven projects far into the room, and the elder bush leans over the hurdle, where there is a little pool of water with a

263

duck and some ducklings under the knotty willow tree. And then there is a yard dog, which barks at everybody.

There was just such a farm-house out in the country, and in it lived an old couple, a farmer and his wife. Although they did not possess much, there was one of their belongings which they thought they could do without, and that was a horse which managed to live upon the grass that grew in the ditch beside the highroad. The old man used to ride it to town, and the neighbors borrowed it, and for this they rendered him services in return; but the old couple thought it would be more serviceable for them to sell the horse, or change it for something or other which would be more useful to them. But what should it be?

"You understand that best, father," said the woman; "there is a fair in Copenhagen now; ride there and get money for the horse, or change it for something good. What you do is always right, so ride to the fair."

And she tied his neckerchief for him, for she understood that better than he; she tied it in a double bow and made him look quite smart. Then she brushed his hat with her flat hand and gave him a hearty kiss, and so he set out on the horse which was to be sold or changed. Yes, her old man understood that all right.

The sun shone hotly; there were no clouds to be seen. The road was dusty, for a number of people were on the way to the fair, either driving, riding, or walking. The heat from the sun was terrible, and there was no shelter to be found on the way.

Just then a man came along the road, driving a cow to the fair. The cow was as fine a creature as any cow could be.

"She is sure to give good milk," thought the farmer; "it would be a good thing if I could get her in exchange for the horse."

"I say, you with the cow!" he shouted; "we two ought to have a talk. You see, a horse costs more than a cow, as you know, but that does not matter. I have more use for the cow; shall we change?"

"All right," said the man with the cow; and so they changed animals.

The farmer had now done his business, and he might just as well have turned back; but since he had made up his mind to go to the fair, he would go there, if only to look on, and so he set out with his cow. Both he and the cow walked at a brisk pace, and soon they came up to a man who was driving a sheep. It was a fine sheep, in good condition and with plenty of wool on its back.

"I should like to have it," thought the farmer. "There would be enough grass for it on the sides of the road, and in the winter we could keep it in the room with us. It would really be better for me to keep a sheep than a cow. Shall we change?"

Yes, the man with the sheep would not mind that, and so they changed animals, and the farmer set out with his sheep along the highroad. Over by the stile he saw a man with a big goose under his arm.

"SHALL WE HAVE A BET?" SAID THE ENGLISHMEN TO THE FARMER.
"WE HAVE GOLD BY THE BARREL!"

"That is a big bird you have there," said the farmer; "it has a lot of feathers and plenty of fat. She would look well in our little pool at home. That would be something for mother to save up her parings for. She has often said: 'If only we had a goose!' Now she can get it and she shall have it. Will you change with me? I give you the sheep for the goose and my thanks into the bargain."

Yes, the man was quite willing, and so they changed animals, and the farmer got the goose. He was close to the town and the road was getting more and more crowded. It swarmed with people and cattle. They walked along the road and in the ditch alongside it, and right up into the toll-keeper's potato-field, where his hen was tied up so that she should not lose herself if she took fright and wanted to run away. She was a bob-tailed hen, and stood winking with one eye, but looked in good condition. "Cluck, cluck!" she said. What she meant by it I cannot say, but the farmer, when he saw her, thought: "She is the finest hen I have ever seen. She is finer than the parson's brood hen. I should like to have her. A hen can always find a grain or two. She can almost keep herself. I think it would be a good thing if I could get it for the goose."

"Shall we change?" he asked. "Change!" said the toll-keeper; "yes, that would n't be a bad thing," and so they changed animals and the toll-keeper got the goose and the farmer got the hen.

He had now got through a good deal of business on his way to town. It was warm and he was beginning to feel tired. He wanted a dram and a mouthful of bread. He had now arrived at the inn, and he was just about to enter it when the potman, who was coming out, ran up against him in the doorway, carrying a bagful of something on his back.

"What have you got there?" asked the farmer.

"Rotten apples," answered the potman; "a whole sackful for the pigs."

"That 's a terrible lot. I should like mother to see this sight. Last year we had only one apple on the old tree by the turf-shed. That apple was to be kept, and it was left on the cupboard till it went bad. 'It 's always a sign of prosperity,' mother said. Now, here she could see plenty of prosperity. Yes, I would like her to see it."

"Well, what will you give?" asked the potman.

"Give? I 'll give you my hen for it," and so he gave him the hen for the apples and went into the inn right up to the bar. The bag of apples he placed against the stove, but he did not notice that it was lighted. There were many strangers in the room—horse-dealers, cattle-dealers, and two Englishmen. The latter are generally so rich that their pockets are bursting with gold money and they are always making bets. Now you shall hear.

"Hiss—s—s! hiss—s—s!" What noise was that near the stove? The apples were beginning to frizzle.

"What 's that?" they all asked. Well, they soon got to know, as well as the whole story about the horse, which had been changed for the cow and so on down to the rotten apples.

"Well, your old woman will give it you when you get home," said the Englishmen; "there will be a row in the house."

"She 'll give me kisses, not kicks," said the farmer; "mother will say that what the old man does is the right thing."

"Shall we have a bet?" they said; "we have gold by the barrel. A hundred pounds to a hundredweight."

"WELL, NOW I MUST KISS YOU!" SAID THE WOMAN; "THANK YOU, MY OWN HUSBAND," AND SHE KISSED HIM RIGHT ON THE MOUTH.

"That will fill a bushel," said the farmer; "I can only fill it with apples, but I will throw in myself and the old woman. That 's piling up the measure, I should say."

"Done! We agree," they said, and so the bet was made.

The innkeeper's carriage was brought out, and the Englishmen and the farmer got into it, taking with them the bag of rotten apples, and so they arrived at the farmer's house.

"Good morning, mother."

"The same to you, father."

"Well, I have changed the horse."

"Ah, you know what you are about," said the woman, and put her arm round his waist, forgetting both the strangers and the bag.

"I changed the horse for a cow."

"Heaven be praised for the milk we shall get!" said the woman; "now we can have milk, butter, and cheese on the table. That was well done."

"Yes, but I changed the cow for a sheep."

"Ah, that 's better still," said the woman. "You are always very thoughtful. We have just enough of grass for a sheep. Now we can have sheep's milk, and sheep's cheese, and woolen stockings, and even woolen shirts. The cow could not give us that; her hairs are not good for anything. Well, you are a thoughtful man!"

"But I changed the sheep for a goose!"

"Shall we, then, really have goose for Michaelmas this year, father dear? You always think of pleasing me. It 's so very kind of you! The goose we can keep in tether and let her get still fatter for Michaelmas."

"But I have changed the goose for a hen," said the man.

"A hen! Well, that was a good exchange," said the woman; "the hen lays eggs and hatches them; we shall have a regular poultry-yard—just what I have been wishing for so long."

"Yes, but I changed the hen for a bag of rotten apples."

"Well, now I must kiss you!" said the woman. "Thank you, my own husband; I have got something to tell you. When you were gone I thought of making a nice little dish for you, a savory omelet with chives. So I went over to the schoolmistress's, where I know they have chives. I asked her to lend me some. 'Lend you?' she said. 'Nothing grows in our garden, not even a rotten apple,' which I could lend her. Now I can lend her ten—aye, a bagful! Well, it is great fun, father!" and she kissed him right on the mouth.

"That 's what I like!" said both the Englishmen. "Always going down hill, and still be just as content. That 's worth the money!" and so they paid a hundredweight of gold to the farmer who got kisses and no kicks.

Yes, it is always best that a wife should maintain that her husband is the wisest, and that what he does is the right thing.

Well, this is the story I heard when I was a little lad, and now you have heard it too, and know that what the old man does is always right.

THE OLD HOUSE

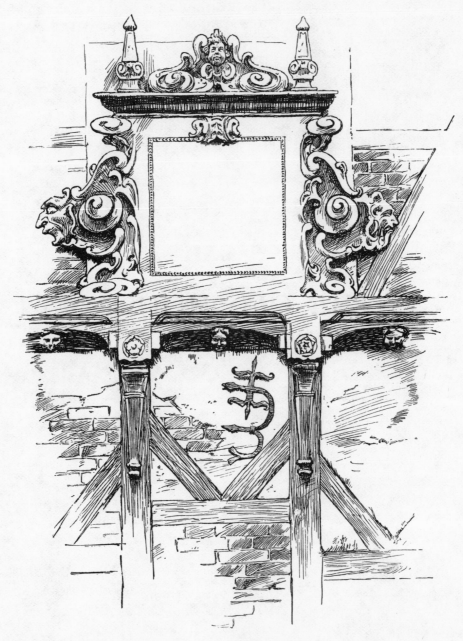

ROUND THE CORNER IN THE NEXT STREET STOOD AN OLD, OLD HOUSE.

THE OLD HOUSE

ROUND the corner in the next street stood an old, old house; it was almost three hundred years old, as any one might read on the beam, where the date was carved out, together with hyacinths and branches of hop vine; there were whole verses spelled as in olden days, and over the windows were carved faces making all sorts of grimaces. One story projected considerably over the other, and just under the roof was a leaden gutter with a dragon's head; the rain-water should have run out of its mouth, but it ran out of its stomach, for there was a hole in the gutter.

All the other houses in the street were quite new and fresh, with large window-panes and smooth walls. One could see they did not want to have anything to do with the old house. They were no doubt thinking: "How long is that ramshackle thing going to stand there as a disgrace to the street? And the bow-window projects so far into the street that no one can see from our windows what is going on in that direction; the door-steps are as broad as the staircase of a palace and as high as the stairs

271

of a church tower. The iron railing looks like the gate of an old family vault, and has brass knobs as well. It makes one feel quite ashamed."

Just opposite were also some new and fresh-looking houses, and they were of the same opinion as the others, but here at the window of one of them sat a little boy with fresh, rosy cheeks and clear, bright eyes. He liked the old house best of all, both by sunshine and by moonlight, and when he looked over at the wall where the plaster had fallen off, he would sit and imagine the most wonderful pictures of what the street had looked like in former days, with steps, bow-windows, aad pointed gables; he could see soldiers with halberds, and gutters and spouts that looked like dragons and serpents. That was certainly a house worth looking at! Over there lived an old man who wore shag trousers, a coat with large brass buttons, and a wig which any one could see was a real one. Every morning an old man came to the house to clean the rooms and go errands, otherwise the old man in the shag trousers was quite alone in the old house. Sometimes he would come to the windows and look out, when the little boy would nod to him, and the old man nodded in return, and thus they were acquainted and became friends, although they had never spoken to each other; but that was of no consequence.

The little boy heard his parents say: "The old man over there is very well off, but he must be terribly lonely."

Next Sunday the little boy wrapped up something in a piece of paper, went down to the gate, and when the man who went errands came past he said to him, "Here! will you give this to the old man over there from me? I have two tin soldiers, and this is one of them; he shall have it, for I know he is so terribly lonely."

And the old man looked quite pleased, nodded his head, and carried the tin soldier across to the old house. Afterward a message came asking if the little boy would not like to come across himself on a visit; and this he got permission from his parents to do, and thus it was he came to enter the old house.

And the brass knobs on the railing leading up the steps shone much brighter than usual; one would think they had been polished in honor of the visit, and it seemed as if the trumpeters standing on tulips which were carved on the door were blowing with all their might, their cheeks looking much rounder than usual. They blew: "Taratantarra! the little boy is coming! taratantarra!"—and then the door was opened. The whole of the hall was hung with old portraits—knights in armor and ladies in silk gowns; the armor rattled and the silk gowns rustled. And then came some more steps which led up, and then a few steps which led down, and then one came to a balcony which was in rather a rickety condition with large holes and long crevices, through all of which grass and leaves were growing, for the wall and the whole of the balcony which

"THANK YOU FOR THE TIN SOLDIER, MY LITTLE FRIEND!" SAID THE OLD MAN,
"AND THANKS FOR COMING TO SEE ME."

projected from the house into the yard were covered with so much foliage that it looked like a garden, but it was only a balcony. Old flower-pots with faces and asses' ears stood round about, and the flowers grew just as they pleased. In one pot with carnations the sprouts were hanging all over the sides, and seemed plainly to say:

"The breeze has patted us, the sun has kissed us and promised us a little flower on Sunday—a little flower on Sunday."

And so the little boy came into a room where the walls were covered with pigskin on which flowers were stamped in gold.

> "Gilding soon may perish,
> But pigskin forever will flourish,"

said the walls.

Round the room stood chairs with high backs and arms on both sides, all beautifully carved. "Sit down, sit down!" they said. "Ugh, how I am creaking! I suppose I shall get rheumatism, just like the old cupboard. Rheumatism in the back, ugh!"

And then the little boy came into the parlor with the bow-window, where the old man was sitting.

"Thank you for the tin soldier, my little friend," said the old man. "And thanks for coming over to see me."

"Thanks, thanks!" or "Creak, creak!" groaned all the furniture; there was so much of it that the various pieces got into each other's way in trying to see the little boy.

And in the middle of the wall hung a picture of a beautiful lady, quite young and cheerful in appearance, but dressed like people in the olden times with powdered hair and stiff clothes. She said neither "Thanks" nor "Creak," but looked with her mild eyes at the little boy, who at once asked the old man, "Where have you got her from?"

"From the old-furniture dealer round the corner," said the old man. "Many pictures are hanging there which no one knows or cares anything about, because the persons are all buried, but many years ago I knew this lady; she has now been dead and gone half a century."

And below the picture, under glass, hung a bouquet of withered flowers; they also seemed to be half a century old, so old did they look. And the pendulum of the big clock went to and fro, and the hand went round, and everything in the room began to look still older, but they did not seem to notice it.

"They say at home," said the little boy, "that you are so terribly lonely."

"Well," was the answer, "old memories, and what they can carry with them, come and visit me, and now you have also come! I am very comfortable."

And then he took from the shelf a book with pictures; there were great long processions with the most wonderful carriages, which one does not see nowadays, with soldiers dressed like the knave of clubs and citizens with flying banners; the tailors had one with a pair of shears supported by two lions, and the shoemakers had one without a boot, but with an eagle that had two heads, as the shoemakers must have everything so arranged that they can say, "Here is a pair." Yes, it was a wonderful picture-book!

And the old man went into the other room to fetch sweetmeats, apples, and nuts; it was really very pleasant in the old house.

"I cannot stand it," said the tin soldier, who stood on the chest of drawers; "it is so lonely and dull here. When one has been accustomed to family life one cannot get used to this state of things. I cannot stand it! The day itself is long enough, but the evening is still longer. It is not at all like your house, where your father and mother were always talking so pleasantly together, and where you and all the other dear children were making such a delightful noise. How lonely the old man is here! Do you think he gets any kisses? Do you think he gets any kind looks or a Christmas tree? He 'll get nothing, except a funeral. I cannot stand it!"

"You must not take things so sadly," said the little boy. "I think it is lovely here; and, besides, old memories and what they can carry with them come and visit you."

"But I don't see them, and I don't know them," said the tin soldier. "I can't stand it!"

"But you must!" said the little boy.

And the old man came back with the pleasantest of faces, with the most lovely sweetmeats, apples, and nuts; and then the little boy thought no more of the tin soldier.

The little boy went home happy and delighted; days and weeks passed by, and the nodding went on to and from the old house, and so the little boy went over there again.

And the carved trumpeters blew their "Taratantarra! Here is the little boy! Taratantarra!" And the swords and armor on the pictures of the old knights rattled, and the silk gowns rustled, the pigskin talked, and the old chairs had rheumatics in their back and said, "Ugh!" It was just like the first occasion, for over there one day or one hour was just like another.

"I cannot stand it!" said the tin soldier; "I have wept tears of tin! It is really too melancholy here. Rather let me go to the wars and lose my arms and legs! That would be a change, at any rate. I cannot stand it! Now I know what it is to receive visits from one's old memories and what they can carry with them. I have had visits from mine, and I can tell you it 's no pleasure in the long run; I was just on the point of jumping from the chest of drawers. I saw all of you in the house

IN THE EVENING A CARRIAGE STOPPED AT THE DOOR, INTO WHICH THEY PUT
THE OLD MAN'S COFFIN.

opposite as plainly as if you had been really here; it was that Sunday morning—you know which I mean. All you children were standing in front of the table singing the hymn you sing every morning; you were standing devotedly with folded hands, and your father and mother were just as solemn. Then the door was opened and your little sister Maria, who is n't two years old yet, and who always will dance when she hears music or singing, no matter what kind, was brought into the room,—which ought not to have been done,—and then she began to dance, but she could not keep the right time, for the music was too slow, and then she stood first on one leg and bent her head right forward, and then on the other leg with her head in the same position, but she could not get into right time. You all looked very serious, although it was difficult enough to keep from laughing, but I laughed inwardly till I fell down from the table and got a bump which I still have, for it was n't right of me to laugh. All of it stands again vividly before me, as well as everything else I have gone through; and those must be the old memories and what they can carry with them. Tell me if you still sing on Sundays. And tell me something about little Maria. And how is my comrade, the other tin soldier? Ah, he is really happy! I cannot stand it any longer."

"But you have been given away as a present," said the little boy; "you must remain where you are; don't you understand that?"

And the old man came in with a drawer, in which there were many things to look at: there was "the white house," and "the balsam-box," and old playing-cards, so large and richly gilt as one never sees nowadays. And many other drawers were opened. Later on the old man opened the piano. It was one of those with a landscape on the inside of the lid. He sat down to play on it, but it was very much out of tune, and then he hummed a song.

"Yes, she could sing that," he said, and nodded to the portrait he had bought of the old-furniture dealer, and the old man's eyes shone brightly.

"I want to go to the wars! I want to go to the wars!" cried the tin soldier as loud as he could, and threw himself down on the floor.

What had become of him? Both the old man and the little boy searched for him, but he was lost and gone. "I shall find him," said the old man, but he never found him. The flooring was so open and full of holes that the tin soldier had fallen through one of the chinks, and there he lay in an open grave.

And the day passed, and the little boy went home; and the week passed, and many more weeks passed. The windows were quite frozen over, and the little boy had to sit and breathe on the panes to get a peephole through which he could look over at the old house. The snow had covered up all the ornaments and inscriptions and the steps were full of snow, just as if there was no one at home.

Neither was there any one at home, for the old man was dead.

In the evening a carriage stopped at the door, into which they put his coffin.   He was to be laid out at some place in the country before being buried.   And so he was driven away, but there was no one to follow him; for all his friends were dead.   The little boy kissed his hand after the coffin as the carriage drove away.

Some days later the old house was sold by auction.   From his window the little boy could see how they carried away the old knights and the old ladies, the flower-pots with the long ears, the old chairs and ancient cupboards.   Some things went one way and some another way.   Her portrait, which the old man had bought at the old-furniture dealer's, came back to him again, and there it remained, for no one knew her any more, and no one cared for the old picture.

In the spring the house itself was pulled down, for it was a tumbledown shanty, people said.   One could see from the street right into the parlor with the pigskin on the walls, which was slashed and torn in all directions; and the green foliage on the balcony hung in wild disorder round the falling beams.   And then the ground was cleared.   "What a good riddance!" said the neighbors.

.   .   .   .   .   .

And a fine house was built, with large windows and white, smooth walls; but in front of it, on the site where the old house had really stood, a small garden was laid out, and up against the walls of the neighboring house grew wild vines.   Before the garden was a large iron railing with an iron gate, which looked quite stately.   People stopped before it and looked through the railings.   The sparrows hung by the score on to the vine and chattered away to each other as fast as they could, but it was not about the old house, for they could not remember that.   So many years had passed that the little boy had grown into a man, and had proved himself to be a fine fellow whom his parents might well be proud of.   He had just been married and had moved with his little wife into this house with the garden round it.   He was now standing by her while she was planting a wild flower which she considered so pretty.   She planted it with her little hands and pressed the soil up against it with her fingers.   Ah, what was that?   She had pricked herself.   There was something sharp sticking up out of the soft soil.

Only think!   It was the tin soldier, the one that was lost in the old man's house, and had been tumbling about between the timbers and the rubbish, and finally had been buried in the ground, where he had been lying for many years.

And the young wife dried the soldier, first with a green leaf and then with her soft handkerchief, which was so delicately perfumed.   It seemed to the tin soldier as if he came out of a trance.

"Let me see him," said the young man, with a smile and a shake of the head. "Well, I don't suppose it can be he, but I remember an adventure I had with a tin soldier when I was a little boy." And so he told his wife about the old house and the old man, and about the tin soldier which he had sent across to him because he was so terribly lonely. And he told it exactly as it had happened, so that the young wife had tears in her eyes over the story of the old house and the old man.

"It may be that it is the same tin soldier," she said; "I should like to keep it and remember all you have told me. But you must show me the old man's grave."

"I don't know where it is," he said, "and no one knows. All his friends were dead, nobody looked after it, and I was only a little boy."

"How terribly lonely he must have been!" she said.

"Terribly lonely!" said the tin soldier; "but it is delightful not to be forgotten!"

"Delightful!" something close by exclaimed, but nobody except the tin soldier saw that it was a bit of the pigskin hangings. All the gilding had gone off it, so that it looked like wet soil; but it had one opinion, and that it expressed:

> "Gilding soon may perish,
> But pigskin will forever flourish."

But the tin soldier did not believe it.

THUMBELINE

IN THE MIDDLE OF THE FLOWER SAT A TINY LITTLE GIRL.

THUMBELINE

THERE was once upon a time a woman who wanted so much to have a tiny child, but she did not know where she could get one, so she went to an old witch and said to her: "I would like so very much to have a little child! Will you tell me where I can get one?"

"Oh, yes! that can easily be managed!" said the witch. "Here is a barleycorn, but it is not of the sort that grows in the farmers' fields or the fowls get to eat. Put that into a flower-pot, and then you will see something!"

"Thank you!" said the woman, and gave the witch sixpence. She then went home and planted the barleycorn, and immediately a large, beautiful flower grew up, which was quite like a tulip, but its petals were tightly closed, just as if it were still a bud.

"What a beautiful flower!" said the woman, and kissed its lovely red and yellow petals; but just as she kissed the flower, it gave a loud report and opened its petals. It was a real tulip,—one could see that,—but in the middle of the flower, on the green stamens, sat a tiny little girl, most delicate and beautiful to look at. She was scarcely half the size of one's thumb, and therefore she was called Thumbeline.

For a cradle she had a pretty, lacquered walnut shell, for mattresses blue violet leaves, and for a coverlet a rose leaf. There she slept at night, but in the daytime she played about on the table where the woman had put a plate with a wreath of flowers around it, their stalks reaching down into the water. On this a large tulip leaf was floating about, and on this Thumbeline sat and sailed from one side of the plate to the other. She used two white horse-hairs to row with. It was a pretty sight! She could also sing, and her song was so sweet and beautiful that nothing like it had ever been heard before.

One night as she lay in her pretty bed an ugly toad jumped in through the window, in which there was a broken pane. The toad, a very ugly, big, and wet creature, jumped down on the table where Thumbeline lay asleep under the red rose leaf.

"That would be a beautiful wife for my son!" said the toad, and so she took the walnut shell in which Thumbeline was sleeping, and jumped through the window down into the garden with her.

Through the garden ran a broad stream; near its banks the ground was marshy and muddy, and here the toad lived with her son. Ugh! How ugly and hideous he was, just like his mother! "Croak, croak!" was all he could say when he saw the lovely little girl in the walnut shell.

THE TOAD TOOK THE WALNUT SHELL
IN WHICH THUMBELINE WAS
SLEEPING.

"Don't talk so loud, or else she will wake up," said the old toad; "she might easily run away from us, for she is as light as swan's-down. We will put her in the stream on one of the large leaves of the water-lily. It will be like an island to her, for she is so small and light. She cannot run away from there while we are getting the best room ready under the marsh, where you two shall settle down and keep house."

Out in the stream there grew a great many water-lilies, with the large green leaves which appeared to be floating on the water. The leaf which was farthest out was also the largest of all, and to this the old toad swam out and put the walnut shell with Thumbeline on it.

The tiny little creature awoke quite early next morning, and when she saw where she was she began to cry most bitterly, for there was water on all sides of the great green leaf, so that she could not get ashore.

The old toad was sitting down in the mud decorating her room with rushes and the yellow brandy-bottle, for she wanted to make the place look pretty for her new daughter-in-law. She then swam out with her ugly son to the leaf where Thumbeline was standing; they had come to fetch her pretty bed, which was to be placed in the bridal chamber before she went there herself. The old toad courtesied deeply in the water before her and said: "Here is my son! He is going to be your husband, and you two will be very comfortable down there in the mud!"

"Croak, croak!" was all that her son could say.

They then took the pretty little bed and swam away with it; but Thumbeline sat quite alone on the green leaf and cried, for she did not want to live with the ugly old toad

THE OLD TOAD COURTESIED TO THUMBELINE AND SAID,
"HERE IS MY SON!"

or have her hideous son for a husband. The small fishes which were swimming about in the water must have seen the toad and heard what she said, and so they put their heads above the water, just to have a look at the little girl. As soon as they saw how beautiful she was, they felt sorry that she should have to go down to the ugly toad. No, that should never happen. They assembled round the green stalk which supported the leaf on which she stood, and gnawed it through with their teeth, so that the leaf drifted down the stream, carrying Thumbeline along with it, far away where the toad could not reach her.

Thumbeline sailed past many places, and the little birds who sat on the bushes and saw her sang, "What a lovely little maiden!" The leaf carried her farther and farther away, and thus Thumbeline came to foreign lands.

A beautiful little white butterfly kept fluttering round about her, and at last he settled down on the leaf, because he had taken such a fancy to Thumbeline, who was also much pleased, for now the toad could not reach her, and everything around her where she sailed was so beautiful; the sun was shining on the water, which glittered like the brightest gold. She then took her girdle and tied one end to the butterfly and the other she fastened to the leaf, which then glided onward much faster with Thumbeline standing on it.

Just then a big cockchafer came flying past and saw her; the next moment he had caught hold of her round her slender waist with his claws and flew up with her into a tree, while the green leaf floated down the stream and the butterfly flew with it, for he was fastened to the leaf and could not get away.

HE FLEW UP WITH HER INTO A TREE.

Oh, how frightened poor Thumbeline was when the cockchafer flew up into the tree with her! But she was greatly distressed about the beautiful white butterfly, whom she had tied fast to the leaf. If he could not get away from it, he must starve to death. But the cockchafer did not trouble himself about that. He sat down with her on the largest green leaf on the tree, gave her the sweet part of a flower to eat, and told her she was very beautiful, although she was not at all like a cockchafer. Later on the other cockchafers who lived in the tree came to pay a visit and to have a look at Thumbeline. The young lady cockchafers turned up their feelers and said, "She has got only two legs. What a miserable thing!" "She has no feelers," some said. "How thin her waist is! Fie! she looks like a human being. How ugly she is!" said all the lady cockchafers. And yet Thumbeline was very beautiful. That is what the cockchafer who had caught her thought, but as all others said that she was ugly, he at last also believed it, and would have nothing more to do with her. She might go where she liked. They flew down with her from the tree and put her on a daisy, where she began to cry, because she was so ugly that the cockchafers would not have her, and yet she was the most beautiful being one could imagine, as delicate and tender as the loveliest rose leaf.

Poor Thumbeline lived quite alone in the great forest all through the summer. She plaited a bed with blades of grass for herself, and hung it under a large burdock leaf to protect herself from the rain. She sucked the honey from the flowers and drank the dew which she found on the leaves every morning, and in this way the summer and the autumn passed; but now came the winter—the cold, long winter. All the birds who had sung so beautifully to her flew away, and the trees and the flowers began to wither. The large burdock leaf under which she had lived shriveled up and there was only a yellow, withered stalk left. She felt the cold terribly, for her clothes were in tatters, and she herself was so tender and small—poor Thumbeline!—that she might easily freeze to death. It began to snow, and every flake that fell on her was to her the same as a whole shovelful would be when thrown over us, for we are great, big people, and she was only an inch in height. She then wrapped herself in a dry leaf, but it did not keep her warm, and she shivered with cold.

Just outside the forest she came to a large corn-field, but the corn had been harvested long ago; only the bare, dry stubble was left on the frozen ground. It looked to her like a big forest which she had to struggle through. Oh, how she trembled with cold! Then she came to the door of a field-mouse's house. It was a little hole under the stubble, where the field-mouse lived in comfort and ease. She had the whole parlor full of corn, and had, besides, a nice kitchen and larder. Poor Thumbeline stood at the door like any poor beggar-girl and asked for a small piece of barley-corn, for she had not had any food for two days.

"Poor little creature!" said the field-mouse, who was really a kind old creature, "come inside my warm room and have some food with me."

As she took a liking to Thumbeline, she said, "You may stop with me this winter, but you must keep my room neat and clean, and tell me stories, for I am very fond of them;" and Thumbeline did what the kind old field-mouse asked her, and had a very pleasant time of it.

"We shall soon have visitors," said the field-mouse; "my neighbor generally visits me once a week. He is even better off than I; he has large rooms and goes about in such a beautiful black, velvety fur coat. If only you could get him for a husband, you would be well provided for. But he cannot see you. You will have to tell him all the prettiest stories you know.''

But Thumbeline did not care for all this. She would not have the neighbor, for he was a mole. He came on a visit in his black, velvety fur coat. "He is very rich and very learned," said the field-mouse; "his house is twenty times bigger than mine, and he possesses a great deal of knowledge, but he does not like the sun and beautiful flowers. He speaks contemptuously of them, for he has never seen them." Thumbeline had to sing, and she sang both "Cockchafer, fly, fly away" and "The monk goes in the meadows," so that the mole fell in love with her all on account of her beautiful voice, but he did not say anything, he was such a prudent person.

He had just dug a long passage through the ground from his house to theirs, and the field-mouse and Thumbeline had permission to take their walks there whenever they liked. But he asked them not to be afraid of the dead bird which lay in the passage. It must have died quite lately, when the winter began, and had been buried just where the mole had dug his passage.

The mole took a piece of decayed wood in his mouth, for this shines like fire in the dark, and went before them, lighting them on their way through the long, dark passage. When they came to where the dead bird lay, the mole put his broad nose up against the roof and pushed the soil up, so that he made a great hole, through which the day-light could fall.

THE MOLE HAD DUG A PASSAGE FROM HIS HOUSE TO THEIRS, AND THE FIELD-MOUSE AND THUMBELINE HAD PERMISSION TO TAKE THEIR WALKS THERE.

In the middle of the floor lay a dead swallow, with his beautiful wings firmly pressed to his sides, while his legs and the head were drawn up under his feathers. The poor bird must have died of cold. Thumbeline was very sorry for this, for she loved little birds so much; they had sung and twittered for her so beautifully all the summer. But the mole pushed him aside with his short legs and said : "He won't sing any more now. It must be a hard fate to be born a little bird. Heaven be praised that none of my children have become that ! Such a bird has nothing but his 'Tweet, tweet !' and must starve to death in the winter."

"Yes, you, who are a sensible person, may well say that," said the field-mouse. "What does a bird get in return for all his 'Tweet, tweet' when the winter comes? He has to starve and freeze, but perhaps that is considered grand, too !"

Thumbeline did not say anything, but when the other two turned away from the bird, she bent down, pushed aside the feathers which covered his head, and kissed his closed eyes. "Perhaps he is the bird who sang so prettily to me during the summer," she thought. "How much pleasure he gave me, the dear, pretty bird !"

The mole now stopped up the hole through which the sun shone, and accompanied the ladies home. But Thumbeline could not sleep that night, so she got up from her bed and plaited a large beautiful coverlet of hay, which she carried down into the passage and wrapped round the dead bird, and put some cotton-wool, which she had found in the field-mouse's room, on each side of the bird, so that it might keep him warm as he lay on the cold ground.

"Good-by, you pretty little bird !" she said; "good-by, and thanks for your beautiful song last summer, when all the trees were green and the sun shone so warmly upon us." She then put her head close to the bird's breast, but the next moment she was startled at hearing something beating inside the bird. It was his heart. The bird was not dead; he lay in a torpor, and now that he began to feel warm he soon revived. The swallows always fly away to the hot countries in the autumn, but if any of them are prevented from following the others, they will feel the cold so much that they fall to the ground as if they were dead, and the cold snow covers them up where they fall.

Thumbeline was so frightened that she trembled all over, for the bird was, of course, much bigger than she, who was only an inch long; but she took courage, put the cotton-wool still closer round the poor swallow, and brought a mint leaf that she had used as coverlet, and put it over the bird's head.

The next night she again stole down to the bird, and he was then alive, but so weak that he could open his eyes only a moment, when he saw Thumbeline, who stood there with a piece of decayed wood in her hand, for she had no other light.

"Many thanks, you pretty little child !" said the sick swallow; "I feel so beautifully warm. I shall soon get back my strength and be able to fly again out into the warm sunshine."

"Oh," she said, "it is so cold outside ! It is snowing and freezing. Stay in your warm bed and I will nurse you."

She then brought the swallow some water in the petal of a flower, and he drank it and told her how he had torn one of his wings in a bramble-bush, and therefore could not fly as fast as the other swallows, who were soon far on their way to the hot countries. He had at last fallen to the ground, but he could not remember anything more, and did not know in the least how he had got there.

The swallow remained down there the whole winter, and Thumbeline was kind to him and came to love him very much. Neither the mole nor the field-mouse knew anything about it, for they did not care in the least for the poor swallow.

THE FIELD-MOUSE HIRED FOUR SPIDERS TO SPIN AND WEAVE, AND THE MOLE
CAME EVERY EVENING ON A VISIT.

As soon as the spring came and the sun began to warm the ground, the swallow said good-by to Thumbeline, who opened the hole which the mole had made in the ground above the passage. The sun shone in upon them so brightly, and the swallow asked Thumbeline if she would not go away with them. She could sit on his back, and they would fly away far into the green forest. But Thumbeline knew the old field-mouse would be much grieved if she left her in this way.

"No, I cannot," said Thumbeline.

"Farewell, farewell, you kind and pretty girl!" said the swallow, and flew out into the sunshine. Thumbeline stood looking after him, and the tears came into her eyes, for she was very fond of the poor swallow.

"Tweet, tweet!" sang the bird as he flew away into the green forest.

Thumbeline was very sad at heart. She was not allowed to go out into the warm sunshine. Besides, the corn that had been sown in the field over the field-mouse's house had grown to a great height. It seemed quite a thick forest to the poor little girl, who was only an inch high.

"You must begin and get your outfit ready this summer," said the field-mouse to her; for their neighbor, the tiresome mole in the black, velvety fur coat had now asked for Thumbeline's hand. "You must have both woolen and linen clothes. You must have things to wear and things to lie upon when you are the mole's wife."

Thumbeline had to spin on the distaff, and the field-mouse hired four spiders to spin and weave day and night. Every evening the mole came on a visit, and he was always saying that when the summer came to an end the sun would not shine nearly so hot, while now it was baking the earth almost to a hard stone. Yes, when the summer was over, then he and Thumbeline should get married. But she was not at all contented, for she did not care in the least for the tiresome mole. Every morning when the sun rose, and every evening when it set, she stole out to the door, and when the wind blew the corn aside, so that she could see the bright sky above, she thought how light and beautiful it would be out there, and wished so much that she could see her dear swallow again. But he never came back — he must have flown far away into the beautiful green forest.

When the autumn came Thumbeline had the whole of her outfit ready.

"In four weeks the wedding will take place," said the field-mouse. But Thumbeline cried, and said she would not have the tiresome old mole.

"What nonsense!" said the field-mouse; "don't be obstinate, or I shall bite you with my white tooth. Why, you will have a fine fellow for a husband! Even the queen has not a black, velvety fur coat like his! His kitchen and his cellar are well stored. You ought to be thankful to get him!"

And so the wedding was to take place. The mole had already arrived to fetch Thumbeline. She was to live with him far under the ground, and would never be allowed to go out into the warm sunshine, for he did not like it. The poor child was so distressed at the thought of having to say farewell to the beautiful sun, which she, at any rate, had been allowed to look at from the door-steps while she was with the field-mouse.

"Good-by, you bright sun!" she said, and stretched her arms toward it as she went a few steps away from the field-mouse's house, for the corn had now been reaped and only the dry stubble was left. "Good-by, good-by!" she said, and threw her little arms around a small red flower close by her. "Give my love to the dear swallow, if you should see him."

Just then she heard the twittering of a bird over her head, and she looked up; it was the swallow, who happened to be flying past. He was so pleased at seeing Thumbeline, who now told him how unwilling she was to marry the ugly old mole, and that she would have to live far under the ground, where the sun never shone. She could not help crying at the thought of it.

"The cold winter is now approaching," said the swallow; "I am going to fly away to the hot countries. Will you come with me? You can sit on my back. You need only tie yourself fast with your girdle, and then we will fly away from the ugly old mole and his dark room, far away over the mountains to warmer climes, where the sun shines more brightly than here, where there is always summer and beautiful flowers. Only fly with me, sweet little Thumbeline,—you who saved my life when I lay frozen in the dark cellar under the ground."

THUMBELINE SEATED HERSELF ON THE SWALLOW'S BACK, AND THEN THE BIRD FLEW HIGH UP IN THE AIR WITH HER.

"Yes, I will go with you," said Thumbeline, and seated herself on the bird's back with her feet on his outstretched wing, and tied her girdle fast to one of his strongest feathers, and then the swallow flew high up in the air over forests and lakes, high over the big mountains, which are always covered with snow. And Thumbeline then began to suffer from the cold, but she crept in under the bird's warm feathers and only put out her little head to look at all the splendor below her.

And so they came to the hot countries. There the sun shone much brighter than here, the sky was twice as lofty, and in the ditches and the hedges grew the most lovely green and purple grapes. In the woods hung lemons and oranges, and the air was fragrant with myrtle and mint, and on the roads pretty children ran about, playing with big, gay butterflies. But the swallow flew on still farther, and everything became more and more beautiful. Under the magnificent green trees by the blue sea stood a dazzling white marble palace of the olden times; the vines clustered round its high pillars and on the top were a number of swallows' nests, and in one of these lived the swallow who had carried Thumbeline.

"This is my home," said the swallow; "but if you will choose one of the prettiest flowers which grow down there I will put you on it, and you shall be as happy as you wish."

"How splendid!" she said, and clapped her little hands.

Down in the garden lay a great white marble pillar which had fallen to the ground and was broken in two places; but between the pieces grew the most lovely white flowers. The swallow flew down with Thumbeline and put her on one of the large petals of one of the flowers; but what a surprise awaited her! She saw a little man sitting in the middle of the flower, so white and transparent, as if he had been made of glass, with the most lovely golden crown on his head, and the most beautiful, clear wings on his shoulders, while he himself was no bigger than Thumbeline. He was the angel of the flower. In every flower there lived such a little man or woman, but this one was the king of them all.

"Oh! How beautiful he is!" whispered Thumbeline to the swallow. The little prince became greatly frightened at the swallow, for he was, of course, quite a gigantic creature compared to him, who was so small and tender; but when he saw Thumbeline he became so pleased, for she was the most beautiful girl he ever had seen. He therefore took off his golden crown and placed it on her head, and asked her what her name was, and if she would become his wife, and she should be queen over all the flowers. He was indeed a husband for her, quite different to the son of the toad and to the mole with the black, velvety fur coat. She therefore said "Yes" to the lovely prince, and out of every flower came a lady and a cavalier so beautiful that it was a pleasure to look at them. All of them brought Thumbeline a present, but the best of them all was a pair of lovely wings of a large white fly. These were fastened to Thumbeline's back, and then she was able to fly from flower to flower. There was much rejoicing, and the swallow sat up in his nest and sang to them as well as he could, although at heart he was very sorry, for he was very fond of Thumbeline and would have liked never to part from her.

"You must not be called Thumbeline," said the angel of the flower to her; "it is an ugly name, and you are beautiful. We will call you Maja."

"Good-by, good-by!" said the swallow, and he flew away from the hot countries back to Denmark, where he had a little nest over the window in the house where the man lives who can write fairy tales. To him he sang, "Tweet, tweet!" and from him we have the whole story.

THE STORM SHIFTS THE
SIGN BOARDS

SUCH A STORM HAS NEVER RAGED IN OUR DAY.

THE STORM SHIFTS THE SIGN-BOARDS

I N the old days, when grandfather was quite a little boy and wore red trousers and a red jacket, a scarf around his waist and a feather in his cap (for that was the way in which little boys were dressed in the days of his childhood when they wore their best clothes)—at that time so many things were different from what they are now. There were often grand sights in the streets which we do not see, for they have all been done away with, as they were getting so old-fashioned; but it is delightful to hear grandfather tell about them.

It must have been a great sight to see the shoemakers change their signs when they moved into their new guild-hall.

On their silk banner, which was waving in the air, was painted a large boot and an eagle with two heads; the youngest of the journeymen carried the "cup of welcome" and the "casket" of their guild, and wore flowing red and white ribbons on their shirt-sleeves; the older ones carried drawn swords with a lemon stuck on the point. There was a full band of music, and the finest of the instruments was the "bird," as grandfather called the great pole with the half-moon at the top, and all kinds of jingling gewgaws—quite Turkish music. It was lifted aloft and swung to and fro, and it jingled and tinkled, and it hurt one's eyes to look at all the gold and silver and brass on which the sun was shining.

In front of the procession ran a harlequin dressed in clothes made of patches of every possible color, with a black face, and bells on his head like a sledge-horse. He struck the people with his wand, which made a loud noise without hurting them, and the people crushed against each other in trying to get backward or forward; little boys and girls tumbled over one another and fell right into the gutter; old women pushed their way with their elbows, looked cross, and kept on scolding. Some laughed and others talked; there were people on all the door-steps and in the windows, and even on the roofs. The sun was shining brightly; then it began to rain a little also, but that was good for the farmers, and when the people were thoroughly drenched the rain was a blessing to the country.

Ah, how grandfather could tell stories! As a little boy he had seen all these grand sights in their greatest splendor. The oldest journeyman of the guild made a speech from the scaffolding where the sign was to be hung up, and the speech was a versified one, just as if it had been poetry, which it was; in fact, there had been three people busy composing it, and they had first drunk a whole bowl of punch in order to make the speech really good. And the people shouted and cheered the speech, but they shouted and cheered still more when the harlequin came on the scaffolding and made faces at them. The buffoon was great at playing the fool, and drank mead out of dram-glasses, which he threw among the people, who caught them in the air.

Grandfather had one of these glasses, which the mason who mixed the mortar had caught and presented to him. It was all very amusing, and the sign on the new guild-hall was hung with flowers and foliage.

"Such a sight one never forgets, no matter how old one gets," said grandfather; nor did he forget it, although he had seen many other sights and splendors, which he told us about. But what amused us most was to hear him telling about the shifting of sign-boards in the big town where he went to live.

THE PEOPLE SHOUTED AND CHEERED STILL MORE WHEN THE HARLEQUIN CAME ON
THE SCAFFOLDING AND MADE FACES AT THEM.

Grandfather had remained there with his parents when he was a little boy; he had never before seen the biggest town in the country. There were so many people in the street that he thought they were going to move the sign-boards, and there were a good many to move: a hundred rooms could have been filled with pictures, if they had been hung indoors instead of outside. Thus there were all sorts of clothes painted on the tailors' sign-boards: they could make shabbily dressed people into quite grand folks; there were sign-boards outside the tobacco manufacturers' with the most delightful little boys smoking cigars, just as in real life; there were sign-boards on which were painted butter and salted herrings, parsons' ruffs and coffins, with inscriptions and announcements of all kinds. One could easily spend a whole day in going up and down the streets, looking at the pictures till one got tired of it, and at the same time one could learn what sort of people lived in those houses where they had hung out sign-boards; and, as grandfather said, it was a good thing, and very instructive as well, to know who lived in all the houses in a big town.

But just as grandfather came to town what I am about to tell you happened to the sign-boards. He has told me all about it himself, and he was not chaffing me, as mother said he always did when he wanted to "palm off" anything upon me; he looked as if you could rely upon every word he said.

The night he arrived in the big town the weather was the most terrible one had ever read about in the papers—such weather as no one within the memory of man had experienced. The air was filled with tiles; old palings were blown down; there was even a wheelbarrow which ran up the street just to save itself. The wind howled in the air; it whined and shook everything it came in contact with. It was indeed a terrible storm. The water in the canals splashed over the sides; it did not know what to do with itself. The storm swept over the town, carrying the chimneys along with it. More than one of the noble old church steeples had to lean over, and has never got straight since.

Outside the house of the old, respected captain of the fire brigade, who always arrived at a fire with the last engine, stood a sentry-box. The storm begrudged the captain this little box and blew it off its pivot. It rolled down the street, and, strange to say, it righted itself and was left standing outside the house of the foolish carpenter who had saved three lives in the last fire. But the sentry-box did not give that a thought.

The barber's sign, the great brazen dish, was torn off and thrown right into the window recess of the judge's, and it seemed almost as if it was done out of malice, said the whole neighborhood, for they and the most intimate friends of the judge's wife called her "the razor," she was so sharp. She knew more about people than they knew themselves.

Then flew a sign-board with a dried codfish painted on it. It stuck over the door of a house where there lived a man who wrote in a newspaper. It was a foolish joke on the part of the storm. It did not recollect that a newspaper writer is not at all to be trifled with. He is king in his own paper and in his own opinion.

The weathercock flew across to the neighbor's roof opposite, and there it stood, the very picture of blackest malice, said the neighbors.

The cooper's barrel got fixed under a sign, "Ladies' trimmings."

The bill of fare at the cookshop, which hung near the door in a heavy frame, was pitched by the storm above the entrance of the theater, which nobody went to. It was a funny bill: "Horse-radish soup and stuffed cabbage." But then plenty of people came to the theater.

The fox-skin of the furrier, the honorable sign of his trade, was shifted to the bell-pull of a young man who always went to early church service, and who looked like a shut-down umbrella, and was always searching for truth, and was a "model young man," as his aunt said.

The inscription, "Institute for Higher Education," was blown over to the billiard club, and the institute itself got another sign-board in exchange: "Children reared here by the bottle." This was not at all witty, only rude; but the storm had done it, and one cannot control the storm.

It was a terrible night, and in the morning — just fancy! — nearly all the sign-boards in the town had been shifted, and at some places it was done with such malice that grandfather would not talk about it; but, I noticed, he laughed to himself, and it is possible he was up to some mischief.

The unfortunate inhabitants of the big town, and especially the strangers, went wrong altogether when they tried to find people. Nor could they do otherwise, since they went by the sign-boards. Some people were going to a very solemn meeting of elders, where most important things were to be settled, and they found themselves in a noisy boys' school, where the boys were just about to jump on the tables.

There were people who mistook the church for the theater, and that was really too terrible!

Such a storm has never raged in our days. It is only grandfather who has experienced such a one, and that was when he was quite a little boy. Such a storm may not occur in our time, but perhaps it may in that of our grandchildren, and we can only hope and pray that they will keep indoors while the storm is shifting the sign-boards.

THE SHEPHERDESS AND THE CHIMNEY-SWEEP

CLOSE TO THEM STOOD ANOTHER FIGURE, AN OLD CHINAMAN WHO COULD
NOD HIS HEAD.

THE SHEPHERDESS AND THE
CHIMNEY-SWEEP

HAVE you ever seen a really old wooden cupboard, quite black with age, and covered with carvings of scrolls and foliage? Just such a cupboard was standing in a parlor; it had been left to the family by the great-grandmother. It was ornamented with carved roses and tulips from top to bottom, and between these quaint ornaments protruded small stags' heads and antlers, but in the middle of the cupboard was carved the full-length figure of a man which made one grin to look at it; he, at any rate, was grinning, for it could not be called laughing. He had goat's legs, small horns on his head, and a long beard. The children always called him "Major-and-lieutenant-general-war-commander-sergeant of the Billy-goat-legs," which was a difficult name to pronounce, besides being a title which many did not receive; but to get him carved must have been a difficult piece of work.

But there he was, and he was always looking toward the table under the mirror, for there stood a lovely little shepherdess of porcelain. Her shoes were gilt and her dress was fastened up with a rose, and then she had a gilt hat and shepherd's crook. She was really lovely. Close to her stood a little chimney-sweep, black as coal, but also made of porcelain. He was quite as clean and nice as anybody. As to his being a sweep, that was of course because he had been made to represent one; the workmen might just as well have made a prince of him at once.

There he stood with his ladder, looking quite handsome, with a face as white and red as a girl's, which, of course, was really a mistake, for he might as well have been a little blackened. He was standing close to the shepherdess. They had both been placed where they stood, and having been so placed, they became engaged, for they suited each other very well, and they were both young people and were made of the same porcelain, and equally liable to be broken.

Close to them stood another figure which was three times as big as they; it was an old Chinaman who could nod his head. He was also made of porcelain, and used to say that he was grandfather of the little shepherdess; but I don't think he could prove that. He would, however, insist that he had some influence over her, and that was the reason he had been nodding to the Major-and-lieutenant-general-war-commander-sergeant of the Billy-goat-legs, who was courting the little shepherdess.

"Now there is a husband for you," said the old Chinaman; "a man, who, I think, is actually made of mahogany. He can make you Lady-major-and-lieutenant-general-war-commander-sergeant of the Billy-goat-legs. He has got the whole cupboard full of silver, besides what he has in his secret drawers."

"I don't want to go into the dark cupboard," said the little shepherdess. "I have heard say he has eleven porcelain wives in there!"

"Then you can be the twelfth," said the Chinaman. "To-night, as soon as the old cupboard begins to creak, you two shall be married, as true as I am a Chinaman!" And then he nodded his head and fell asleep.

But the little shepherdess wept and looked at the beloved of her heart, the porcelain chimney-sweep.

"I think I must ask you," she said, "to go with me out into the wide world, for we cannot remain here."

"I will do everything you want me to do," said the little sweep. "Let us go at once. I think I shall be able to make a living by my profession."

"I wish we were safely down from the table," she said. "I shall not be happy till we are out in the wide world."

And he comforted her and showed her how she could place her little foot on the carved edges and the gilt foliage down along the leg of the table, and he also made use of his ladder; but when they looked in the direction of the old cupboard everything seemed to be in a state of confusion. All the carved stags stretched their heads still farther out, rearing their antlers aloft and twisting their heads. The Major-and-lieutenant-general-war-commander-sergeant of the Billy-goat-legs jumped into the air and shouted across to the old Chinaman: "They are running away! they are running away!"

This frightened them, and they jumped up into the drawer of the window seat.

Here were three or four packs of cards which were not complete, and a small toy theater which had been put up as well as could be; a play was being acted, and all the queens of diamonds and hearts, clubs, and spades were sitting in the first row, fanning themselves with their tulips, and behind them stood all the knaves, showing they had heads both at top and bottom, as playing-cards generally have. The play was about two lovers who were not allowed to marry, and the shepherdess cried because it was just like her own story.

"I cannot bear it," she said; "I must get out of this drawer." But when they got down on the floor and looked up at the table, the old Chinaman had awakened and all his body was rocking to and fro, although the bottom of him was a heavy lump.

"The old Chinaman is coming!" cried the little shepherdess, and fell down on her porcelain knees, so great was her distress.

"I have an idea," said the sweep; "let us creep into the great jar with potpourri, which stands in the corner; there we can lie on roses and lavender, and throw salt in his eyes when he comes."

"That will not do," she said; "besides, I know that the old Chinaman and the potpourri jar were once engaged, and there always remains a little kindly feeling between those who have stood in this relation to one another. No, there is no help for it; we must go out into the wide world."

"Have you really courage to go with me out into the wide world?" asked the sweep. "Have you considered how big it is, and that we can never come back here again?"

"Yes, I have," she said.

And the sweep looked fixedly at her, and then said: "My way lies through the chimney. Have you really courage to creep with me through the stove, both through the drum and the pipe? Then we get into the chimney, and there I know my way well. We shall climb up so high that they cannot reach us, and at the top there is a hole leading out to the wide world."

And he led her to the door of the stove. "It looks dark in there," she said, but she went with him for all that, both through the drum of the stove and through the pipe, where it was pitch dark.

"Now we are in the chimney," he said; "and see! look at the beautiful star that is shining just above us!"

And it was a real star in the sky which shone down on them, as if it wanted to show them the way. And they crawled and crept on, and a terrible way it was, so high, so very high; but he lifted her and supported her. He held her and showed her the best places where she should put her little porcelain feet, and thus they reached right up to the top of the chimney, where they sat down, for they were really tired, and no wonder.

The sky with all its stars was just above their heads, and below them lay all the roofs of the city. They could see far around them, far out into the wide world. The poor shepherdess had never thought it was anything

THEY REACHED THE TOP OF THE CHIMNEY, WHERE THEY SAT DOWN AND LOOKED
AROUND THEM, FAR OUT INTO THE WIDE WORLD.

like this. She leaned her little head against her chimney-sweep, and cried till the gilding was washed off her girdle.

"Oh, this is too much for me!" she said; "I cannot bear it. The world is too big. I wish I were back again in the little table under the mirror. I shall never be happy until I am there again. Now that I have followed you out into the wide world, you may as well go back with me if you care at all for me."

And the sweep tried to reason with her; he spoke of the old China-man and the major-and-lieutenant-general-war-commander-sergeant of the

Billy-goat-legs, but she sobbed so bitterly and kissed her little chimney-sweep, so that he could not do anything but humor her, although it was wrong.

And so, with great difficulty, they crawled down the chimney again; they crept through the drum and the pipe, which was anything but pleasant, and at last they stood inside the dark stove. They stopped behind the door to listen to what was going on in the room. They peeped out — alas! there, in the middle of the floor, lay the old Chinaman. He had fallen down from the table when he tried to run after them, and lay there broken into three pieces. The whole of his back had come off in one piece, and the head had rolled over into a corner. The major-and-lieutenant-general-war-commander-sergeant of the Billy-goat-legs stood where he had always stood, and seemed to be buried in thought.

"It is terrible," said the little shepherdess; "my old grandfather is broken to pieces and it is all our fault! I shall never survive it!" And then she wrung her tiny little hands.

"He can still be mended," said the sweep. "He can very well be riveted — only take things quietly. If they cement his back and give him a strong rivet in the neck, he will be as good as new, and be able to say a good many unpleasant things to us."

"Do you think so," she said. And they climbed up again on to the table where they had stood before.

"Well, this is as far as we have got," said the chimney-sweep; "we might as well have saved ourselves all the trouble."

"If only we had old grandfather mended!" said the shepherdess. "Would it be very expensive?"

And he was mended. The people in the house had his back cemented and he got a strong rivet in the neck, and he was as good as new, but he could no longer nod.

"You seem to have become rather proud since you broke in pieces," said the major-and-lieutenant-general-war-commander-sergeant of the Billy-goat-legs; "but I don't think it is anything to be so proud of. Shall I have her, or shall I not?"

And the chimney-sweep and the little shepherdess looked so pathetically at the old Chinaman. They were afraid he would nod his assent; but he could not, and besides it was unpleasant to him always to have to tell strangers that he had a rivet in his neck, and so the little porcelain people were left to themselves, and they blessed the rivet in grandfather's neck and loved one another till they broke to pieces.

DADDY DUSTMAN

(OLE LUKÖIE)

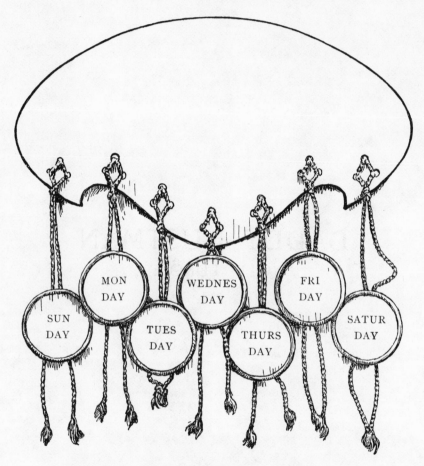

NOBODY IN THE WHOLE WORLD KNOWS SO MANY
STORIES AS DADDY DUSTMAN.

DADDY DUSTMAN

(OLE LUKÖIE[1])

THERE is nobody in all the world who knows so many stories as Daddy Dustman. And he does know how to tell stories.

When it is getting near bedtime, and the children are sitting comfortably round the table or on their little footstools, in comes Daddy Dustman. He comes so softly up the stairs, for he walks in his stocking-feet. He opens the door quietly, and, whist! he squirts sweet milk into their eyes, so little, oh, so very little, but always enough to prevent them from keeping their eyes open, and that's why they cannot see him. He steals up behind them, breathes gently on their necks, and this makes their heads heavy. But it does not hurt them, for Daddy Dustman means well

[1] Ole Luköie (literally Olaf the Eye-shutter) is the Dutch equivalent for the legendary character known to English children as " The Dustman."

311

by the children. He only wants them to be quiet, and the best way to do this is to get them to bed. They must be quiet, so that he can tell them stories.

As soon as the children are asleep, Daddy Dustman sits down on the bed. He is nicely dressed; his coat is of silk, but it is impossible to say what color it is, for it looks green, red, or blue, according to how he turns round. He carries an umbrella under each arm. One of them, with pictures inside, he spreads over the good children, and then they dream the most beautiful stories the whole night; but the other umbrella, which has no pictures, he puts over the naughty children, who fall into a heavy sleep, and awake in the morning without having dreamed anything.

We shall now hear how Daddy Dustman came every evening for a whole week to a little boy, whose name was Hjalmar, and what he told him. There are altogether seven stories, for there are seven days in the week.

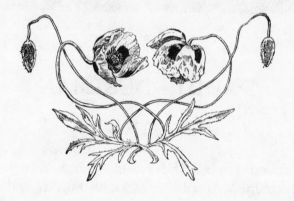

MONDAY

"Just listen!" said Daddy Dustman in the evening, when he had got Hjalmar into bed. "I will make the room pretty!" And all the flowers in the flower-pots became large trees, which stretched their long branches under the ceiling and along the walls, so that the whole room looked like the most lovely bower. The branches were covered with flowers, all of which were much prettier than any rose, and just as fragrant; and if any one had wanted to eat them, he would have found them sweeter than jam. The fruits glittered like gold, and there were buns cram full of raisins; it was simply wonderful! But just at that moment there came a terrible wail from the drawer in the table, in which Hjalmar kept his lesson-books.

"What's the matter now?" asked Daddy Dustman, and went over to the table and opened the drawer. It was the slate, which felt oppressed and crushed because a wrong figure had got into the sum, so that it was nearly falling to pieces. The slate-pencil jumped up and tugged at its string as if it were a little dog; it wanted to put the sum right, but could not. And Hjalmar's copy-book began to wail; it was really terrible to listen to. Down along each page stood all the capital letters, each with the small letter at its side,—quite a long row of letters down the page, which had to be copied; and by their side stood again some letters which thought they were just like them,—for Hjalmar had written these letters; but they all leaned over to one side, as if they had stumbled over the pencil-line upon which they were to stand.

"Look here! This is the way you should hold yourselves up," said the printed letters; "see, this way,—with a smart flourish."

"Oh, yes; we should be so glad to do it," said Hjalmar's letters, "but we cannot,—we don't feel well."

"Then you must have a powder," said Daddy Dustman.

"Oh, no!" cried the letters, and then they stood so straight and erect that it was a pleasure to look at them.

"Well, we shall have no time for stories now," said Daddy Dustman; "I shall have to put them through their paces. Left, right! Left, right!" and so he went on drilling the letters till they stood as upright and as fine-looking as any of the printed ones. But when Daddy Dustman had gone and Hjalmar looked at them in the morning they were as bad as ever.

TUESDAY

As soon as Hjalmar was in bed, Daddy Dustman touched all the pieces of furniture in the room with his magic squirt, and they began at once to talk and chatter. All of them talked about themselves, with the exception of the spittoon, who was annoyed and remained silent, because they were so conceited as only to talk about themselves, only to think about themselves, and had no thoughts for the spittoon, which stood in all humility in the corner and let itself be spat into.

Over the chest of drawers hung a large painting in a gilt frame. It represented a landscape with lofty old trees, flowers in the grass, and a big lake, from which flowed a river that passed round behind the forest, and past many castles far out into the open ocean.

Daddy Dustman touched the picture with his magic squirt, and the birds in it began to sing, the branches of the trees moved to and fro, and the clouds drifted across the sky. One could see their shadows passing over the landscape.

Daddy Dustman now lifted little Hjalmar up into the frame, and Hjalmar put his feet into the painting, right on the high grass, and there he stood, the sun shining down upon him through the branches of the trees.   He ran to the lake and sat down in a little boat which was lying there.   It was painted red and white and the sails shone like silver, while six swans, all with golden crowns round their necks and a bright blue star on their foreheads, towed the boat past the green forests, where the trees talked about robbers and witches, and the flowers about the little elves and about what the butterflies had told them.

The most beautiful fishes with silver and gold scales swam after the boat.   Now and then they would make a spring out of the water and, with a splash, fall back into it, while the birds, red and blue, large and small, flew after the boat in two long rows.   The gnats danced and the cockchafers sang " Boom, boom !"   All wanted to follow Hjalmar and all had a story to tell.

What a splendid sail !   In some places the forests were thick and dark, in others they looked like the most beautiful gardens, with sunshine and flowers.   Along the shore lay large palaces of glass and marble, and on the balconies stood princesses, all of whom were little girls that Hjalmar knew well and had played with.   They held out to him in their hands the nicest sugar-pigs that any sweet-stuff woman ever sold, and Hjalmar, as he sailed, seized hold of one end of the sugar-pigs, while the princesses held tightly on to the other, so that all got a piece, the princesses the smallest, and Hjalmar all the biggest.   At every palace little princes kept guard.   They presented arms with golden swords, and let it rain with raisins and tin soldiers.   They must be real princes!

At one moment Hjalmar sailed through forests, at another through large halls or through the middle of a town.   He also passed through the town where his nurse lived, the nurse who had been so fond of him, and she nodded and beckoned to him, while she sang the pretty verse she herself had written and sent to Hjalmar:

> " I think of you both long and oft,
>   Hjalmar, my own, my posy !
> I 've kissed your pretty cheeks so soft,
>   Forehead, and lips so rosy.
> I heard your lispings long ago;
>   Since then we 've said good-by.
> The good Lord bless you here below,
>   My angel from on high."

And all the birds joined in, the flowers danced on their stalks, and the old trees nodded, just as if Daddy Dustman were telling stories to them also.

WEDNESDAY

Dear, oh, dear! How the rain did pour down! Hjalmar could hear it in his sleep, and when Daddy Dustman opened the window the water had reached right up to the window-sill; outside was a great sea, and a fine ship was lying close to the house.

"Will you have a sail, little Hjalmar?" asked Daddy Dustman. "During the night you can see many foreign lands, and be back here again in the morning."

All at once Hjalmar, dressed in his best clothes, stood on the deck of the ship, and the weather immediately became fine   They sailed through the streets and turned round the corner by the church, and then they had the great ocean before them.   They sailed on till at last no land could be seen, and they saw a flock of storks, who also had left their home and were on their way to the hot countries.   The storks were flying one behind the other, and had already been flying such a long distance that

317

one of them was so tired his wings could not carry him any longer; he was the last in the line, and before long he was a long way behind the others.   At last he began to sink lower and lower on his outstretched wings.   He flapped his wings once or twice, but all in vain; his legs were now touching the rigging of the ship, and then he glided down along the sail, and plump! there he stood on the deck.

The ship's boy took him and put him into the hen-coop with the fowls, ducks, and turkeys.   The poor stork felt quite out of place in this company.

"What's that thing?" said all the fowls.

And the turkey-cock puffed himself out as much as he could and asked the stork who he was, while the ducks waddled backwards, pushing one another aside and crying, "quack, quack!"

Then the stork began telling them about Africa and how warm it was there, about the pyramids, and the ostrich, who raced like a wild horse across the desert; but the ducks did not understand what he said, and pushed against one another, saying: "Let's agree about one thing.   He is a fool!"

"Of course he is a fool!" said the turkey-cock, and went on gobbling. The stork then became silent and thought of his home in Africa.

"Those are thin, handsome legs of yours!" said the turkey-cock. "How much a yard?"

"Quack, quack, quack!" grinned all the ducks, but the stork pretended not to hear anything.

"You might laugh as well," said the turkey-cock to him, "for it was very wittily said; or, perhaps, it was not high enough for you.   Alas! he is not very versatile.   Let us continue to amuse one another all by ourselves."   And the fowls clucked and the ducks quacked: "Quick, quack! Quick, quack!"   How terribly amusing they all thought it was.

But Hjalmar went to the hen-coop, opened the door, and called the stork, who jumped out on the deck to him.   He had now rested himself, and, as he spread out his wings to fly away to the hot countries, it seemed as if he nodded to Hjalmar to thank him, while the fowls clucked and the ducks quacked and the turkey-cock became quite red in his face.

"To-morrow we shall make soup of you all!" said Hjalmar; and then he awoke and found himself lying in his little bed.   That was a wonderful journey which Daddy Dustman had let him take that night.

THURSDAY

"Look here!" said Daddy Dustman, "but don't be afraid! Here's a little mouse." And he held out his hand to him with the pretty little creature. "She has come to invite you to a wedding. There are two little mice who are going to get married to-night. They live down under the floor of your mother's larder, and they say it is such a nice place!"

"But how shall I be able to get through the little mouse-hole in the floor?" asked Hjalmar.

"Leave that to me," said Daddy Dustman, "I will make you small enough!" And then he touched Hjalmar with his magic squirt, who at once began to grow less and less, and at last he was no bigger than one's finger. "You can now borrow the tin soldier's clothes, which I think will fit you. It looks so smart to wear a uniform when you go to a party!"

"Yes, of course!" said Hjalmar; and in a moment he was dressed like the smartest tin soldier.

"Won't you be good enough to take a seat in your mother's thimble," said the little mouse, "and I shall have the honor to drive you!"

"Goodness gracious! Are you yourself, Madam, going to have all this trouble?" said Hjalmar, as they drove off to the wedding of the mice.

First they came into a long passage under the floor, which was hardly of sufficient height to allow any one in a thimble to drive through it. The whole of the passage was illuminated with touchwood.

"Isn't there a delicious smell here?" said the mouse who was driving Hjalmar; "the whole passage has been rubbed with bacon-rind. Nothing could be more delicious!"

They now arrived in the room where the wedding was to take place. On the right hand side stood all the little lady-mice, whispering and tittering, just as if they were making fun of one another, and on the left stood all the gentlemen-mice, stroking their mustaches with their paws; but in the middle of the floor could be seen the bridal couple, standing in a hollowed-out cheese-rind, kissing each other most lovingly before the eyes of everybody, for they were now engaged, and were just going to be married.

More and more guests were arriving, till they were nearly treading each other to death. The bridal couple were standing in the middle of the doorway, so that one could hardly get in or out. The whole of the room had been rubbed over with bacon-rind, just like the passage; this was all the refreshments there was to be, but as dessert a pea was shown round, in which a little mouse belonging to the family had bitten the name of the bride and the bridegroom — that is to say, the first letters of their names; it was something quite out of the common.

All the mice said it was a beautiful wedding, and that the conversation had been most delightful.

And so Hjalmar drove home again; he had, no doubt, been in very grand company, but he had certainly had to make himself very small, and get into the tin soldier's uniform.

FRIDAY

"It is incredible how many old people there are who want to get hold of me," said Daddy Dustman; "especially those who have done something wicked. 'Good little Daddy,' they say to me, 'we cannot close our eyes, and so we lie awake all the night and see all our wicked deeds, like horrible little imps, sitting on the edge of the bed and squirting hot water over us. Do come and drive them away so that we can get a good night's rest,' and then, with a deep sigh, they add: 'We should like so much to pay you. Good night, Daddy. The money is lying in the window.' But I don't do this for money," said Daddy Dustman.

"What shall we do this evening?" asked Hjalmar.

"Well, I don't know if you would like to go to a wedding again to-night—a different kind from the one you went to yesterday. Your sister's big dolly, the one who looks like a man, and who is called Herman, is going to be married to the doll we call Bertha. Besides, it is her birthday, and there will be a lot of presents."

"Yes, I know all about that," said Hjalmar; "whenever my sister wants new clothes for her dolls she always lets them have birthday parties or weddings. That has happened at least a hundred times."

"Yes, and the wedding to-night will be the hundred and first, and when one hundred and one is reached then everything comes to an end, and therefore this will be a grand affair.   Just look!"

And Hjalmar looked at the table: there stood the little cardboard house with lights in all the windows, and all the tin soldiers outside presenting arms.   The bride and the bridegroom sat on the floor leaning against the leg of the table, both looking quite thoughtful, which was only reasonable, while Daddy Dustman, dressed in grandmother's black skirt, performed the marriage ceremony.   When it was over, all the furniture in the room joined in singing the following pretty song, which was written by the lead-pencil, and set to the tune of the military tattoo:

"Our song shall burst into the room;
The bridal pair shall hear it — boom!
They stand erect, straight as a broom,
Fresh as a new glove, how they bloom!
Hurrah, hurrah, for bride and groom!
Our song must be loud, piercing storm, wind, and gloom!"

And now came the presents; but the bride and bridegroom had requested that no eatable should be sent, as they had sufficient of love to live upon.

"Shall we go somewhere in the country or go abroad?" asked the bridegroom.   The swallow, who had traveled a great deal, and the old farm-hen, who had hatched five broods of chickens, were consulted on the subject.   The swallow told about lovely countries, where the air was mild and the mountains a color of which we have no idea.

"But you don't find our spring cabbage there," said the hen.   "I went into the country one summer with all my chickens.   We had a gravel-pit there, all to ourselves, where we could go and scratch up the ground all day; and we also had leave to go into a garden where there was spring cabbage.   Oh, how green it was!   I cannot think of anything more delightful."

"But one cabbage stalk looks very much like another," said the swallow; "and then you have often such bad weather here."

"Yes, but one gets accustomed to that," said the hen.

"But you have so much frost and cold in this country."

"That's good for the cabbages," said the hen.   "Besides, we have warm weather as well.   One summer it was so hot one could scarcely breathe.   And then we have none of the poisonous creatures that are found abroad.   And we are free from robbers.   He is a wretch who does n't think our country the most beautiful.   He does n't deserve to be allowed to live here," said the hen, with tears in her eyes.   "I, too, have traveled.   I once drove over fifty miles in a tub!   There is no pleasure at all in traveling."

"Yes, the hen is a sensible person," said Bertha, the bride.   "Nor do I like traveling over mountains either.   It is always up and down.   No, let us be off to the gravel-pit and take our walks in the cabbage garden."

And that settled it.

SATURDAY

"Shall I have any stories to-night?" said little Hjalmar, as soon as Daddy Dustman had got him into bed.

"We have no time for that to-night," said Daddy, and opened the pretty umbrella over him; "look at these Chinamen." And the whole umbrella looked like a great Chinese bowl with blue trees and pointed bridges, with tiny Chinamen on them, who stood nodding their heads. "We must have the whole world brightened up by to-morrow," said Daddy, "for it is a holy day, it is Sunday. I have to go over to the church tower to see if the little brownies are polishing the bells, so that they may sound all the more beautiful. I have to go into the fields to see if the wind has blown the dust off the grass and the flowers, and then there is the biggest job of all — I have to take down all the stars and polish them. I put them all in my apron; but they must first be numbered, as well as the holes into which they fit, so that they can be put back again in their right places.   Otherwise they would not stick fast, and we should have too many falling stars, for they would be tumbling down one after another.''

"I say, Mr. Dustman,'' said an old portrait, which was hanging on the wall in Hjalmar's bedroom, "I am Hjalmar's great-grandfather.   I am much obliged to you for telling the boy stories, but you must not confuse his ideas of things.   The stars cannot be taken down and polished.   The stars are planets, like our globe, and that 's just the beauty of them.''

"Thank you, old great-grandfather,'' said Daddy Dustman; "I am much obliged to you.   You are the head of the family — an ' old head,' in fact.   But I am older than you.   I am an old heathen.   The Romans and the Greeks called me the Dream God.   I have always visited the best of families and do so still.   I understand how to associate both with rich and poor.   And now you can tell stories yourself,'' said Daddy Dustman, and went away, taking the umbrella with him.

"So, one is not allowed to speak his mind any more,'' said the old portrait.

And then Hjalmar awoke.

SUNDAY

"Good evening," said Daddy Dustman, and Hjalmar nodded; but first he went over and turned the great-grandfather's portrait to the wall, so that it should not begin talking as it did yesterday.

"Now you must tell me some stories about 'the five green peas that lived in a shell,' and 'Cocky Locky, who made love to Henny Penny,' and about 'the darning-needle who was so conceited that she thought she was a sewing-needle.'"

"One may have too much of a good thing," said Daddy Dustman. "You know I would rather show you something. I will now show you my brother. His name is also Daddy Dustman, but he never comes to any one more than once, and when he comes, he takes you on his horse and tells you stories. He knows only two. The one is so wonderfully beautiful that no one in the world can imagine anything more beautiful,

325

and the other is so grim and terrible — well, it is impossible to describe it." And Daddy Dustman lifted little Hjalmar up into the window, and said: "There you see my brother, the other Daddy Dustman. They also call him Death. You see, he does not look as bad as in the picture-books, where he is represented as a skeleton. No, he has silver embroidery on his coat. It is the most lovely hussar's uniform. A cloak of black velvet flies behind him over the horse. Do you see how he gallops along?"

And Hjalmar saw how this Daddy Dustman rode off, taking both young and old people with him on the horse. Some he placed in front, and some at the back of him, but he always asked first of all, "What about your mark-book?" "Very good," they all replied. "Well, let me see for myself," he said; and then they had to show him the book, and all those who had "very good" and "excellent" were put in front of him, and were told the beautiful story. But those who had "tolerably good" and "indifferent" had to sit behind and listen to the horrible story. They trembled and cried, and wanted to jump off the horse, but they could not, for they had suddenly grown fast to it.

"But death is a most pleasant Daddy Dustman," said Hjalmar; "I am not afraid of him."

"Nor should you be," said Daddy Dustman; "only take care to have a good mark-book."

"Well, there is something instructive in that," muttered the portrait of the great-grandfather; "there is some use, after all, in speaking one's mind," and so he was satisfied.

This is the story of Daddy Dustman. He can now tell you some more stories himself this evening.

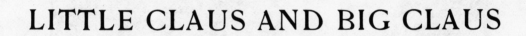

LITTLE CLAUS AND BIG CLAUS

THERE WERE TWO MEN IN A TOWN WHO HAD THE SAME NAME.

LITTLE CLAUS AND BIG CLAUS

THERE were two men in a town who both had the same name; both of them were called Claus, but one owned four horses, and the other only one. In order to distinguish the one from the other, he who had four horses was called Big Claus, and he who had only one horse Little Claus. Now you shall hear how the two fared, for this is a true story.

During the whole of the week Little Claus had to plow for Big Claus, and lend him his one horse; but then Big Claus helped him in return with all four—but only once a week, and that was on a Sunday. Houp-la! how Little Claus cracked his whip over all the five horses; they were now as good as his own, for that one day! The sun shone brightly and all the bells in the church tower were ringing; the people were dressed in their best, and, with their prayer-books under their arms, were on their way to hear the clergyman preach. They looked at Little Claus, who was plowing with the five horses, and he was so pleased that he cracked his whip and called out: "Gee up, all my horses!"

"You must not say that," said Big Claus, "only one of the horses is yours!"

But when some people again were passing on their way to church Little Claus forgot that he must not say it, and shouted: "Gee up, all my horses!"

"Now you 'll just have to stop that," said Big Claus; "for if you say it once again I 'll strike your horse on the forehead, so that he drops down dead on the spot, and it will be all over with him!"

LITTLE CLAUS CLIMBED UP TO THE TOP OF THE SHED,
WHENCE HE COULD SEE INTO THE ROOM.

"I shall not say it any more!" said Little Claus; but when people came by and they nodded "Good day" to him, he became so pleased, and thought it looked so grand to have five horses to plow his field, that he cracked his whip and shouted: "Gee up, all my horses!"

"I 'll gee up your horses!" said Big Claus, and took a hammer and struck Little Claus's only horse on the forehead, so that it fell down dead.

"Oh dear, now I have no horse at all!" said Little Claus, and began to cry. Afterward he flayed the horse, took its hide, dried it well in the wind, and put it in a sack which he took on his back and set out to town to sell the hide.

He had a long way to go, and had to pass through a great, gloomy forest, when a terrible storm arose; he lost his way, and before he got on the right road again, the evening came on, and it was too far to reach the town or his home before the night set in.

Close to the road he saw a large farm-house, the shutters outside the windows were closed, but the light shone out at the top. "I suppose I can get permission to stop here for the night," thought Little Claus, and went up to the door and knocked.

The farmer's wife opened the door, but when she heard what he wanted, she said he must go his way; her husband was not at home and she could not receive any strangers.

"Well, then, I must lie down outside," said Little Claus, and the farmer's wife shut the door upon him.

Close by stood a large haystack, and between it and the house was a small shed with a flat thatched roof.

"I can lie up there!" said Little Claus, when he saw the roof; "that will make a fine bed. I hope the stork won't fly down and bite my legs." For he saw a stork on the roof, where it had its nest.

Little Claus now climbed up to the top of the shed, where he lay and turned to and fro to make it comfortable to lie on.

The wooden shutters before the windows did not fit at the top, so he could look straight into the room.

There was a long table laid out with wine, a joint of meat, and such a fine fish. The farmer's wife and the deacon were seated at the table, and no one else; and she poured out the wine and helped him to some fish, as it was a favorite dish of his.

"If one could only get some of it," said Little Claus, and stretched his head toward the windows. Goodness gracious! what a splendid cake he saw standing on the table! Yes, that was a feast indeed!

Just then he heard some one riding along the highroad toward the house. It was the woman's husband who was returning home.

He was a good man, but he had the remarkable failing that he never could bear to see a deacon. If he caught sight of a deacon he would fly into a violent rage. This was the reason that the deacon had gone to the house to wish the woman good day, because he knew that the husband was not at home; and the good woman had put all the best food she had before him. When they heard the husband coming they became frightened, and the woman asked the deacon to creep into a large empty chest which stood over in the corner. This he did, for he knew, of course, that the poor husband could not bear to see a deacon. The woman quickly put away all the nice food and wine into her baking oven, for if her husband should see it he would be sure to ask what it meant.

"Ah, well!" sighed Little Claus up on the shed when he saw all the food disappearing.

"Is there any one up there?" asked the farmer, looking up at Little Claus. "Why are you lying there? You had better come with me into the parlor."

Little Claus then told him how he had lost his way, and asked if he might stay there for the night. "Yes, of course," said the farmer; "but first we must have something to eat."

The woman received them both very kindly, laid the cloth on a long table, and put a large dish of porridge before them. The farmer was hungry and ate with a good appetite, but Little Claus could not help thinking of the nice fish and the cake that he knew were in the oven.

Under the table at his feet lay his sack with the horse's hide, for we know he had gone away from home to get it sold in town. The porridge was not to his taste, and so he pressed the sack with his foot till the dried hide began to creak quite loudly.

"Hush!" said Little Claus to his sack, but he pressed it again at the same time, so that it creaked louder than before.

"Whatever have you got in your sack?" asked the farmer.

"Oh, it 's a wizard," said Little Claus; "he says we ought not to eat porridge. He has filled the whole oven with meat and fish and cake for us."

"You don't say so!" exclaimed the farmer; and in all haste he opened the oven door, where he saw all the nice food which his wife had hidden, and which he believed the wizard in the bag had conjured up for them. The woman dared not say anything, but put the things at once on the table; and so they both ate of the fish and the joint and the cake. Little Claus then again pressed the sack with his foot and made the hide creak.

"What does he say now?" asked the farmer.

"He says," said Little Claus, "that he has conjured three bottles of wine for us, and that they also are standing in the oven." The woman had now to bring out the wine she had hidden, and the farmer drank and became quite merry. Such a wizard as Little Claus had in his sack he would very much like to possess.

"Can you conjure up the devil as well?" asked the farmer. "I should like to see him, for I feel so jolly now."

"Oh, yes," said Little Claus; "my wizard can do everything I tell him. Is n't that so?" he asked, and pressed the sack till it creaked. "Can you hear? He says, 'Yes,' But the devil is so terrible to look at that you may not like to see him."

"Oh, I am not at all afraid. What do you think he looks like?"

"Oh, he looks exactly like a deacon."

"Ugh!" said the farmer, "that 's horrible! You must know I can't bear to see deacons. But it does n't matter now. I know it 's the devil, and so I shall bear it all the better. My courage is up now, but he must n't come too near me."

"I 'll tell the wizard," said Little Claus, pressing the sack and listening.

"What does he say?"

"He says that you can go over and open the chest which stands in the corner, and you 'll see the devil sitting moping there; but you must keep the lid down so that he does not slip out."

"Will you help me to keep it down?" said the farmer, and went over to the chest in which the woman had hidden the real deacon, who sat there, trembling with fear.

The farmer lifted the lid a little and peeped under it. "Ugh!" he cried, and sprang back. "Yes, I saw him, and he looks just like our deacon! Oh, it 's horrible!"

After this they must have a drink; and so they went on drinking till far into the night.

"You must sell me that wizard," said the farmer. " Ask anything you like for him. I will give you a whole bushel of money for him at once."

"No, I can't do that," said Little Claus. "Just fancy what use I can make of this wizard!"

"Oh, but I would so like to have him," said the farmer, and went on begging.

"Well," said Little Claus at last, "since you have been so good to me and given me shelter for the night, I sha'n't mind. You shall have the wizard for a bushel of money, but it must be heaped-up measure."

"That you shall have," said the farmer; "but you must take that chest with you as well. I won't have it another hour in my house. Who knows if he isn't sitting in there still."

Little Claus gave the farmer his sack with the dried hide, and got a whole bushel of money, and good measure, too, for it. The farmer even made him a present of a large wheelbarrow to wheel away the chest and the money.

"Farewell," said Little Claus. And so he went off with his money and the big chest, in which the deacon was still hiding.

On the other side of the forest was a broad, deep river, where the water flowed so rapidly that one could scarcely swim against the current. A big new bridge had been built across it, and when Little Claus stopped in the middle of it he said quite loudly, so that the deacon in the chest might hear it:

"Whatever shall I do with this silly chest? It is as heavy as if there were stones in it. I shall be quite knocked up if I wheel it any longer. I will throw it into the river, and if it sails home to my place, it is all well and good; and if it does n't, well, it is no matter."

He then took hold of the chest with one hand, and lifted it up a little, as if he intended to plunge it into the water.

"No; stop, stop!" cried the deacon in the chest; "let me get out first."

"Oh," said Little Claus, pretending to be frightened; "he is still in there, so I had better throw it into the river at once and drown him."

"No, no," cried the deacon; "I will give you a whole bushel of money if you let me out."

"Oh, that 's another matter," said Little Claus, and opened the chest. The deacon crept out as quickly as he could, pushed the empty chest into the water, and went off to his house, where Little Claus got a whole bushel of money, and with the one he had already received from the farmer he had now his wheelbarrow full of money.

"Well, I have been rather well paid for that horse, I must say," he said to himself when he got home to his own room, and turned out all the money into a heap in the middle of the floor. "It will annoy Big Claus when he gets to know how rich I have become through that one horse of mine, but I sha'n't tell him exactly all about it."

He then sent a boy to Big Claus to borrow a bushel measure.

"What can he want it for, I wonder?" thought Big Claus, and he smeared some tar under the bottom, so that something of whatever was to be measured should stick to it, which really happened, for when the measure was returned to him there were three silver sixpences sticking to it.

"What's this?" said Big Claus, and ran off at once to Little Claus. "Where have you got all that money from?"

"Oh, that's what I got for the hide of my horse. I sold it last night."

"That was a good price, I must say," said Big Claus, and he ran home, took an ax, killed all his four horses, flayed them, and drove to town with the hides.

"Hides, hides! Who'll buy hides?" he cried through the streets.

All the shoemakers and tanners came running, and asked how much he wanted for them.

"A bushel of money for each of them," said Big Claus.

"Are you mad?" said they all; "do you think we have money by the bushel?"

"Hides, hides! Who'll buy hides?" he cried again, and all who asked what the hides cost were told: "A bushel of money."

"He is making a fool of us," they all said; and the shoemakers took their straps, and the tanners their leather aprons, and began beating Big Claus.

"Hides, hides!" they shouted mockingly at him; "yes, we'll give you a hiding that will make your bones ache. Out of the town with him!" they cried. And Big Claus had to take to his heels as fast as he could; he had never had such a thrashing in his life.

"Well, Little Claus shall pay for this," he said when he came home. "I'll kill him for it."

But at Little Claus's house the old grandmother had died. She had been rather cross and hard upon him, but still he was sorry. He took the dead woman and put her in his warm bed, to see if she might not come to life again. There she was to lie all night, while he sat over in the corner and slept in a chair, as he had often done before.

As he sat there during the night the door opened, and in came Big Claus with his ax; he knew where little Claus's bed was, and went straight up to it and struck the dead grandmother on the forehead, thinking it was little Claus.

"There, now," he said; "you won't make a fool of me any more"; and so he went home again.

"He must be a bad, wicked man," said Little Claus, "to want to kill me. It was a good thing for old granny that she was dead already, else he would have taken her life."

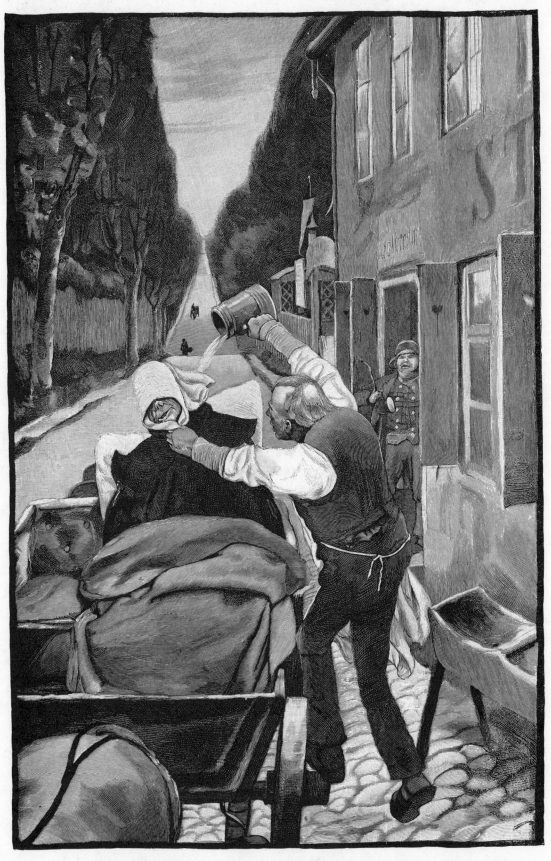

THE INNKEEPER THREW THE MEAD RIGHT INTO THE DEAD WOMAN'S FACE, AND SHE
FELL BACKWARD IN THE CART.

So he dressed his old grandmother in her Sunday clothes, borrowed a horse from his neighbor, put it to the cart, and placed the old grandmother up against the back seat, so that she should not fall out when the cart gave a jerk, and so they drove off through the wood.

At sunrise they came to a large inn, where Little Claus pulled up and went in to get something to eat.

The innkeeper was very, very rich, and also a good man, but with a temper as hot as pepper.

"Good morning," he said to Little Claus; "you 've got early into your Sunday clothes to-day."

"Yes," said Little Claus, "I am going to town with my old grandmother. She is sitting out there in the cart, and I can't get her to come into the parlor. Won't you take her a glass of mead? But you must talk pretty loudly to her, for she is hard of hearing."

"Yes, that I will," said the innkeeper, and poured out a large glass of mead, with which he went out to the dead grandmother, who had been placed upright in the cart.

"Here 's a glass of mead from your son!" said the innkeeper. The dead woman did not speak a word, but sat quite still.

"Don't you hear?" cried the innkeeper, as loud as he could. "Here 's a glass of mead from your son!"

Once more he cried out the same, and again once more; but as she did not move a muscle he flew into a passion, and threw the glass right in her face, so that the mead ran down her nose, and she fell backward in the cart, for she was only placed upright, and not tied fast to the cart.

"Hullo!" cried Little Claus, as he rushed out at the door and seized the innkeeper by the throat; "you have killed my grandmother! Just look, there is a great cut in her forehead."

"Oh, what a misfortune!" cried the innkeeper, wringing his hands; "that all comes from my hasty temper! My dear Little Claus, I 'll give a whole bushel of money, and I 'll bury your grandmother as if she were my own. Only keep quiet, or else they will cut off my head, and that is so unpleasant!"

So Little Claus got a whole bushel of money, and the innkeeper gave the old grandmother a burial as if she had been his own.

As soon as Little Claus got home with all the money, he sent his boy across to Big Claus to ask if he might have the loan of a bushel measure.

"What 's this?" said Big Claus. "Did n't I kill him? I must see to this myself!" and so he went across with the measure to Little Claus.

"Where have you got all this money from?" he asked, opening his eyes wide at the sight of all that had now been added.

"It was my grandmother you killed, and not me!" said Little Claus; "I have now sold her, and got a bushel of money for her."

"That was a good price, I must say!" said Big Claus, and hurried

home, took an ax, and killed his old grandmother without any loss of
time, put her into his cart, drove into the town to the apothecary's, and
asked him if he would buy a dead body.

"Who is it? and where did you get it from?" asked the apothecary.

"It is my grandmother!" said Big Claus. "I have killed her to sell
her for a bushel of money!"

"Heaven preserve us!" said the apothecary. "You must be raving
mad! Don't go on talking like that, else you'll lose your head."

And then he told him plainly what a wicked deed he had done, and
what a bad man he was, and that he ought to be punished. Big Claus got
such a fright that he ran right out of the apothecary's shop, jumped into
his cart, whipped up his horse, and drove off furiously; but the apothecary
and all the people thought he was mad, and let him, therefore, drive
whither he would.

"You shall pay for this!" said Big Claus, when he had got out on the
highroad. "Yes, you shall pay for this, my Little Claus!" And as soon
as he came home he took the largest sack he could find, went across to
Little Claus, and said: "You have made a fool of me again! First I
killed my horses, then my old grandmother. It is all your fault, but you
shall never make a fool of me again!" And so he seized Little Claus
round the body and put him into his sack, threw it across his back, and
cried out to him: "Now I'm going to drown you!"

It was a long way to go before he got to the river, and Little Claus
was no light weight to carry. The road passed close by the church, where
the organ was playing and the people were singing so beautifully. So
Big Claus put down his sack with Little Claus in it close to the church
door, and thought it might do him good to go in and listen to a hymn
before he went any farther. Little Claus could not, of course, get out of
the sack, and all the people were in church; so he went in.

"Oh dear! oh dear!" sighed Little Claus in the sack, as he turned
and twisted about in it, but it was not possible for him to get the string
undone. Just then an old cattle-drover, with snow-white hair and a large
staff in his hand, came past; he was driving a whole herd of cows and
oxen before him, and they ran against the sack in which Little Claus was
sitting, and overturned it.

"Oh, dear!" sighed Little Claus. "I am so young, and yet I have to
go to heaven!"

"And I, poor fellow!" said the drover, "I am so old, and yet I can't
get there!"

"Open the sack!" cried Little Claus. "Creep into it instead of me,
and you will soon get to heaven!"

"Yes, that I will willingly do!" said the drover, opening the sack for
Little Claus, who jumped quickly out of it.

"You will look after the cattle for me?" said the old man, and crept into the bag which Little Claus tied up and so went his way with all the cows and oxen.

A little while after Big Claus came out of church and took the sack on his back again; he thought, however, it was much lighter, for the old drover was not half so heavy as Little Claus.

"How light he is to carry now!" he said. "Well, that's because I have been listening to the singing, I suppose!" So he went off to the river, which was broad and deep at that place, threw the sack with the old cattle-drover into the water and shouted after him, thinking of course it was Little Claus in the sack:

"Now, then, you sha'n't make a fool of me any more!"

And so he went homeward; but when he came to where the cross-roads met, he saw Little Claus, who was driving all his cattle before him.

"What's this?" cried Big Claus. "Did n't I drown you?"

"Yes, of course," said Little Claus; "you threw me into the river scarcely half an hour ago."

"But where have you got all these fine cattle from?" asked Big Claus.

"They are sea-cattle!" cried Little Claus. "I'll tell you all about it. But I must thank you for drowning me. I am well off now; I am quite rich, I can tell you! I was so frightened as I lay in the sack, and the wind was whistling about my ears when you threw me from the bridge down into the cold water. I sank at once to the bottom, but I did not hurt myself, for down there grows the finest, softest grass imaginable. I fell right on this, and soon afterward the sack was opened. A most beautiful maiden, in snow-white robes and with a green wreath in her wet hair, took me by the hand and said: "Are you there, Little Claus? Well, here are some cattle for you to begin with, but a mile farther on up the road a whole herd stands, which I will make you a present of."

"I now saw that the river was a big highway for the mermen down there. They were walking and driving along the bottom, right out from the sea up into the country where the river ends. It was very delightful; there were flowers and the freshest of grass, and the fish which swam about in the water were stealing round about my ears just like the birds in the air up here. What nice people there were down there, and what a lot of cattle were grazing in the ditches and along the hedges!"

"But why did you come up to us again?" asked Big Claus. "I should n't have done that if it was so nice down there."

"Well, you see," said Little Claus, "it was just a little trick of mine. You heard me say that the mermaid told me that a mile farther along the road,— and by the road, of course, she meant the river, for she can't get away to any other place,— a whole herd of cattle was still waiting for me. But I know the big windings the river makes, now here, now there; it would be a regular roundabout way. No, one makes a short cut when one can, and by coming up here on land and making right across for the river again I shall save nearly two miles and get quicker to my sea-cattle."

"Well, you are a lucky fellow," said Big Claus. "Do you think I shall get any sea-cattle if I go down to the bottom of the river?"

"Yes, I should think so," said Little Claus; "but I can't carry you in the sack as far as the river. You are too heavy for me. If you will walk there yourself and then creep into the sack I'll throw you in with the greatest pleasure."

"Thank you," said Big Claus; "but if I don't get any sea-cattle when I get down there I'll give you a good thrashing, you may be sure!"

"Oh, no! don't be so hard on me!" said Little Claus; and so they went down to the river. When the cattle, which were thirsty, saw the water they ran as fast as they could to drink.

"See what a hurry they are in," said Little Claus. "They are longing to get down to the bottom again."

"Yes, but help me first," said Big Claus, "or else I'll thrash you!" And so he crept into the big sack which was lying across the back of one of the oxen.

"Put a stone in with me, else I may not sink," said Big Claus.

"No fear of that," said Little Claus. Still he put a large stone into the sack, tied the string tightly, and gave the sack a push. Plump! down fell Big Claus into the river, and sank at once to the bottom.

"I'm afraid he won't find those cattle," said Little Claus, and so he drove home what he had.

THE SHIRT COLLAR

THE SHIRT COLLAR

THERE was once upon a time a stylish gentleman whose only goods and chattels were a boot-jack and a comb; but he had the finest shirt collar in the world, and it is about this collar I am now going to tell you a story. The collar was now old enough to think about getting married, and then it happened that he and a garter met one day in the same wash-tub.

"Well," said the collar, "I have never seen any one so slender and elegant, so soft and neat, before. May I be permitted to ask your name?"

"I shall not tell you," said the garter.

"Where do you come from?" asked the collar.

But the garter was very shy, and thought it was a very strange question.

"You are a waistband, I presume," said the collar; "a kind of inside waistband. I can see you are both useful and ornamental, my little lady."

"You must n't speak to me," said the garter; "I do not think I have given you any encouragement."

"Oh, when one is as beautiful as you," said the collar, "that is encouragement enough."

"Don't come so near to me," said the garter. "You look so masculine."

"Yes, I am quite a gentleman," said the collar. "I possess a boot-jack and a comb" (which, of course, was not true, as they belonged to his master; but he was very fond of boasting).

"Do not come near me," said the garter; "I am not used to it."

"What a prude!" said the collar, just as he was being taken out of the wash-tub. He was next starched and hung across the chair in the sunshine, and was then put on the ironing-board, when the hot iron was passed over him.

"Madam," said the collar, "little widow, I begin to feel quite warm. I feel a change coming over me; I am quite losing my head; you are burning a hole right through me! Ah! Will you be mine?"

"Rag!" said the iron, and passed proudly over the collar. She imagined that she was a steam-engine going along the railway, dragging carriages after her.

"Rag!" she repeated.

The collar was a little frayed at the edges, and so the scissors were brought out to cut off the ragged ends.

"Oh," said the collar, "you are a première-danseuse, I presume. How you can stretch your legs! I have never seen anything so beautiful! No human being could do that."

"I know that!" said the scissors.

"You deserve to be a countess," said the collar. "I am a gentleman, and all I possess is a boot-jack and a comb. If only I were a count!"

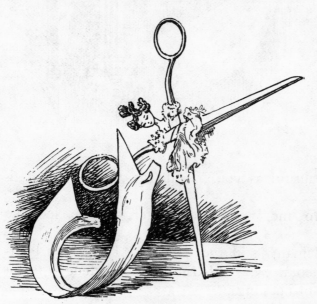

"Is that meant as a proposal?" said the scissors angrily, and gave the collar such a nasty cut that he was ruined forever.

"I must propose to the comb," said the collar. "It is really wonderful how well your teeth are preserved, my little lady. Have you never thought of getting engaged?"

"Yes, of course!" said the comb. "I am engaged to the boot-jack."

"Engaged!" exclaimed the collar. Now there was no one left to propose to, and so he looked with contempt upon courting and such like.

A long time passed, and then the collar came into a bag and was sent to the paper-mill. There was a grand company of rags, the fine ones in a heap by themselves, and the common ones in another, as was only right. They had all a lot to say, especially the collar; he was a regular braggart!

"I have had a terrible lot of sweethearts," said the collar; "I was never left in peace. But I was quite a gentleman, you must know, starched up to the nines! I kept both a boot-jack and a comb, which I never used. You should have seen me at the time when I was turned down! I shall never forget my first sweetheart; she was a waistband, so fine, so soft, so beautiful; she threw herself into a wash-tub for my sake. Then there was a widow, who was head and ears over in love with me, but I left her to herself to remain in her weeds. Then there was a première-danseuse; she gave me the gash you see me with—she was a fury! My own comb was in love with me; she lost all her teeth through disappointed love. Yes, I have gone through a lot of such experiences. But I am most sorry for the garter—the waistband I mean, who jumped into the wash-tub. I have a great deal on my conscience; it is really time I was made into white paper!"

And all the rags were made into paper; the collar became the very piece of white paper before me, on which this story is printed—all in punishment for having boasted so dreadfully of what had never happened. We ought to take warning by this, and try to behave better, for one never knows what may happen; we might find ourselves one day in the bag with rags, and be made into white paper, and then have the whole story of our life, even the most secret part of it, printed upon the paper, and have to run about and tell it, just like the shirt collar.

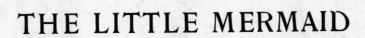

THE LITTLE MERMAID

DOWN BELOW THE SURFACE OF THE SEA LIVE THE MERMEN
AND THE MERMAIDS.

THE LITTLE MERMAID

FAR out at sea the water is as blue as the petals of the most beautiful cornflower, and as clear as the purest crystal, but it is very deep — deeper than any cable can reach. Many church towers would have to be placed one on the top of another to reach from the bottom to the surface of the sea. Down there live the mermen and the mermaids.

Now you must not think that there is only the bare, white sandy bottom down there. No, the most wonderful trees and plants grow there, the stalks and leaves of which are so pliable that the least movement of the water sets them in motion, just as if they were alive. All the fishes, big and small, glide in and out among the branches, just as the birds do up above in the air. In the deepest place of all lies the palace of the Sea King, the walls of which are of corals and the long, pointed windows of clearest amber, but the roof is made of mussel shells, which open and shut with the motion of the water. It is a lovely sight, for in each shell lie pearls, a single one of which would be a great gem in a queen's crown.

The Sea King had been a widower for many years, but his old mother kept house for him. She was a wise woman, but very proud of her noble rank, and therefore she used to wear twelve oysters on her tail, while other grand folks were allowed to wear only six.

In other respects she deserved great praise, especially because she was so very fond of the sea princesses, her granddaughters. They were six beautiful children, but the youngest was the most beautiful of them all. Her skin was as clear and as delicate as a rose-petal, and her eyes as blue as the deepest sea, but, like all the others, she had no feet. Her body ended in a fish's tail.

All day long they played in the large halls of the palace, where living flowers grew out of the walls. The large amber windows were opened, and the fishes then swam into them, just as the swallows fly in to us when we open the windows; but the fishes swam right up to the little princesses, ate from their hands, and let themselves be stroked.

Outside the palace was a large garden with fiery-red and dark-blue trees; the fruits beamed like gold and the flowers like burning flames, because they continually moved their stalks and leaves to and fro. The ground itself was of the finest sand, but as blue as sulphur flames. A strange blue light shone upon everything down there. It was easier to believe that one was high up in the air, with only the blue sky above and beneath one, than that one was at the bottom of the sea.

In calm weather one could see the sun, which looked like a purple flower from the cup of which all the light streamed forth.

Each of the young princesses had her own little plot in the garden, where she might dig and plant as she pleased. One gave her flower-bed the shape of a whale, another preferred hers to resemble a little mermaid; but the youngest made hers quite round like the sun, and grew only flowers that gleamed red like the sun itself. She was a strange child, quiet and thoughtful; and when her other sisters decked themselves out with the most wonderful things which they obtained from wrecked ships, she cared only for her flowers, which were like the sun up yonder, and for a beautiful marble statue, a beautiful boy hewed out of pure white stone, which had sunk to the bottom of the sea from a wreck. She planted close by the statue a rose-colored weeping willow, which grew luxuriantly, and hung its fresh branches right over it down to the blue, sandy ground. Its shadow was violet and moved to and fro like its branches. It looked as if the top and the roots played at kissing one another.

Nothing gave her greater joy than to hear about the world above and its people. Her old grandmother had to tell her all she knew about ships and towns, about human beings and animals. What seemed to her particularly strange and beautiful was that up on the earth the flowers gave out a fragrance which they did not do at the bottom of the sea, and that the woods were green, and the fish, which were to be seen there among the branches, could sing so loudly and beautifully that it did one's heart good to hear them. It was the little birds that her grandmother used to call fishes, for otherwise the mermaids would not have understood her, as they had never seen a bird.

"When you are fifteen years old," said her grandmother, "you will be allowed to rise to the surface of the sea and sit on the rocks in the moonlight and look at the big ships which sail past; and forests and towns you shall also see."

The following year one of the sisters would be fifteen, but the others —well, each of them was a year younger than the other, so the youngest would have to wait five long years before she could venture up from the bottom of the sea and have a look at the world above. But they promised to tell one another what they had seen on the first day and found to be most beautiful; for their grandmother had not told them enough, there was so much they wanted to know more about.

No one longed more that her time should come than the youngest, who had the longest time to wait, and who was so quiet and thoughtful.

Many a night did she stand at the open window, looking up through the dark-blue water, where the fishes were beating about with their tails and fins. She could see the moon and the stars shining, although somewhat indistinctly, but through the water they appeared much larger than to our eyes. If something like a black cloud passed between her and the moon, she knew it was either a whale swimming above her, or a ship sailing past with many people on board; they could have no idea that a lovely little mermaid was standing below them, stretching her white hands up toward the keel of their ship.

The eldest princess was now fifteen years of age, and might venture up to the surface of the water. When she came back, she had hundreds of things to tell; but the loveliest of all, she said, was to lie in the moonlight on a sand-bank when the sea was calm, and see the big city close to the coast, where the lights were twinkling like hundreds of stars, to hear the music and the noise and rattle of the carriages and people, to see the many church towers and steeples, and hear the bells ringing. Just because she could not get there, she longed most of all for this.

Oh, how the youngest sister listened to every word! And when, later on in the evening, she stood by the open window and looked up through the dark-blue water, she thought of the large city with all its noise and bustle, and then she thought she could hear the church bells ringing down where she was.

The year after the second sister was allowed to go to the surface and to swim about where she pleased. She emerged above the water just as the sun was setting, and this sight she found to be the loveliest of all. The whole of the heavens looked like gold, she said; and the clouds—well—she could not sufficiently describe their glory! Red and purple, they had sailed past above her head, but much more rapidly than the clouds flew a flock of wild swans, like a long white veil, over the water toward where the sun stood; she swam toward it, but it sank below the horizon, and the rosy hue on the water and the clouds vanished.

The year after the third sister came up to the surface; she was the boldest of them all, and swam up a broad river which ran into the sea. She saw beautiful green hills, covered with vines; palaces and houses peeped out between the mighty trees of the forests, and she heard how all the birds were singing. The sun shone so warm that she often had to dive under the water to cool her burning face. In a little bay she came across a whole flock of children, who ran and splashed about, quite naked, in the water; she wanted to play with them, but they ran away in great fright, when a little black animal—it was a dog, but she had never seen one before—began barking so terribly at her that she became frightened and made her way back to the open seas. But she could never forget the mighty forests, the green hills, and the beautiful children who could swim about in the water, although they had no fish's tail.

The fourth sister was not so daring; she remained far out at sea among the wild waves; and there, she said, was certainly the loveliest place one could see for many miles around, and above rose the heavens liks a big glass bell. She had seen ships, but they were far away and looked like sea-gulls; the lively dolphins had made somersaults, and the great whales had spouted water from their nostrils till it seemed as if there were a hundred fountains all around.

Now came the fifth sister's turn; her birthday was in the winter, and therefore she saw what the others had not seen the first time. The sea looked quite green, and great icebergs were floating about, each looking like a pearl, she said, and yet they were much larger than the church towers built by men. They were of the most wonderful shapes, and glittered like diamonds. She had settled herself on one of the largest of them, and all the ships with their terror-stricken crews eluded the place where she sat, and let the wind play with her long hair. But toward evening the sky became overcast with clouds; it thundered and lightened, and the dark waves lifted the big ice blocks high up, while they shone brightly at every flash of lightning. All the ships' sails were reefed, the minds of those on board were filled with fear and anxiety; but she sat quietly on her floating iceberg, and saw the blue flashes of forked lightning strike down into the glittering sea.

When the sisters came to the surface of the water the first time, they were always delighted with all the new and beautiful sights they saw; but now, when they, as grown-up girls, were allowed to go up when they liked, they became indifferent and longed to be home again, and after a month had passed they said it was best, after all, down at their place, and, besides, it was much more pleasant at home.

Many an evening the five sisters would take one another by the arm and ascend together to the surface. They had beautiful voices—more beautiful than any human being; and when a storm was gathering, and they expected ships would be wrecked, they swam in front of the ships, and sang so sweetly of the delights to be found at the bottom of the sea, and told the sailors not to be afraid of coming down there. But the sailors could not understand their language: they believed it was the storm. Nor did they ever see the splendors down there; for when the ships went down the men were drowned, and reached the palace of the Sea King only as corpses.

When, in the evenings, the sisters thus rose, arm in arm, high up through the water, the little sister would stand all alone looking after them, feeling as if she could cry; but a mermaid has no tears, and therefore she suffered all the more.

"Oh, if I were only fifteen! she said. "I know I shall love the world up above, and all the people who live and dwell there."

At last she was fifteen years old.

"Well, now you are off our hands," said her grandmother, the old queen-dowager. "Come here, let me deck you like your other sisters." And she put a wreath of white lilies in her hair; every leaf in the flowers was half a pearl. The old lady ordered eight large oysters to hang on to the princess's tail, to show her high rank.

"But it hurts so!" said the little mermaid.

"Well, one has to suffer for appearances," said the old lady.

Oh, how gladly would she not have shaken off all this finery and put aside the heavy wreath! The red flowers in her garden would have suited her much better, but she dared not make any change now. "Farewell!" she said, and rose through the water as light and bright as a bubble.

The sun had just set as she lifted her head above the sea, but all the clouds still gleamed like roses and gold, and in the middle of the pale-red sky the evening star shone bright and beautiful. The air was mild and fresh, and the sea calm.

A large ship with three masts was lying close to her, with only one sail set. Not a breath of wind stirred, and the sailors were lying idly about among the rigging and across the yards. There was music and song aboard, and as the evening became darker hundreds of gaily colored lanterns were lighted. It looked as if the flags of all nations were waving in the air. The little mermaid swam right up to the cabin window, and every time the waves lifted her up she could look in through the polished panes and see many finely dressed people standing in the cabin. But the handsomest of all was the young prince with the large black eyes. He could not be more than sixteen years old. It was his birthday which was being celebrated with all these festivities. The sailors were dancing on deck, and when the young prince stepped out a hundred rockets shot up into the air, making everything look as bright as by daylight, so that the little mermaid became quite frightened and dived under the water. But she soon put her head above the water again, and it then seemed to her as if all the stars of heaven were falling down upon her. Such showers of fire she had never seen before.

Large suns whizzed round and round, and gorgeous fiery fishes flew about in the blue air, while everything was reflected in the calm, smooth sea. The ship was so brilliantly lighted up that even the smallest ropes could be seen distinctly, and the people on board still more so. How handsome the young prince was! He pressed the hands of the men and laughed and smiled, while the music rang out in the beautiful night.

It was late, but the little mermaid could not turn her eyes away from the ship and the handsome prince. The brightly colored lanterns were being extinguished, the rockets did not rise any more into the air, nor were any more cannons fired; but below in the sea a rumbling and buzzing sound was heard. The little mermaid sat rocking up and down on the waves so that she could look into the cabin. But the ship was beginning to make greater headway; one sail after another was unfurled, and the billows now rose higher and higher; large clouds were gathering, and far away flashes of lightning were seen. Oh, what terrible weather was coming on! The sailors had now to take in the sails; the big ship rushed at full speed through the wild seas; the waves rose like big black rocks, as if they would throw over the masts; but the ship dived just like a swan between them, only to be lifted up again on the top of the towering billows.

The little mermaid thought this was fine sport, but the sailors were of a different opinion. The ship creaked and groaned, the massive planks gave way to the violent shocks of the seas against the ship, the masts snapped in two just like reeds, and the ship rolled to and fro, while the seas penetrated into the hold. The little mermaid now understood that the ship was in danger, and she herself had to beware of the beams and fragments of the ship that were drifting about in the water. At one moment it was so pitch-dark that she could not see a single object; but the next, when it lightened, she could see so clearly again that she recognized all the people on the ship. All were looking out for themselves as best they could. She looked anxiously for the young prince, and she saw him just as the ship was going down, sinking into the deep sea. She was at first greatly pleased, for now he would come down to her; but then she remembered that human beings cannot live in the water, and that it would only be his dead body that could come down to her father's palace. No, he must not die; and she therefore swam about among the beams and planks that were drifting about in the water, quite forgetting that they might have crushed her to death. She dived down deep under the water, and rose again high up among the waves. She came at last to the young prince, who could hardly swim any longer in the stormy sea. His arms and legs began to fail him, his beautiful eyes closed, and he would have met his death had not the little mermaid come to his assistance. She kept his head above water, and let the waves drift with her and the prince whither they liked.

In the early morning the bad weather was over, and not a splinter was to be seen of the ship. The sun rose red and shining out of the water, and it seemed to bring back life to the prince's cheeks; but his eyes remained closed. The mermaid kissed his high, fair forehead, and stroked back his wet hair. She thought he was like the marble statue down in her garden. She kissed him and wished that he might live.

THE SHIP WAS BEGINNING TO MAKE GREATER HEADWAY; LARGE CLOUDS WERE GATHERING
AND FLASHES OF LIGHTNING WERE SEEN.——THE LITTLE MERMAID NOW
UNDERSTOOD THAT THE SHIP WAS IN DANGER.

She now saw in front of her the mainland, with lofty blue mountains, on the top of which the white snow looked as bright as if large flocks of swans had settled there. Down by the shore were beautiful green forests, in front of which lay a church or a convent, she did not know which, only that it was a building. Lemon- and orange-trees grew in the garden, and before the gate stood lofty palm-trees. The sea formed here a little bay, where the water was quite smooth and calm, but of great depth right up to the rocky shore where the fine white sand had been washed up. Thither the little mermaid swam with the handsome prince, and placed him on the sand, taking great care that his head should lie raised in the sunshine.

The bells in the large white building now began ringing, and a number of young girls came out into the garden. The little mermaid then swam some distance farther out to a place behind some high rocks which rose out of the water, and covered her head and her shoulders with sea foam, so that no one could see her little face; and from here she watched to see who would discover the poor prince.

She had not long to wait before a young girl came to the place. She seemed quite frightened, but only for a moment; then she fetched some people, and the mermaid saw how the prince came back to life, and that he smiled to all around him; but he did not send a smile in her direction, for how could he know that she had saved him? She became very sad, and when he was brought into the great building she dived under the water and returned to her father's palace, greatly distressed in mind.

She had always been quiet and thoughtful, but now she became more so than ever. Her sisters asked her what she had seen on her first visit up above, but she would not tell them anything.

Many an evening and morning she visited the place where she had left the prince. She saw how the fruits in the garden ripened and were plucked, she saw how the snow melted on the lofty mountains; but the prince she did not see, and therefore she always returned home still more sorrowful than before. Her only comfort was to sit in her little garden and throw her arms round the beautiful marble statue which resembled the prince. She neglected her flowers, which soon grew, as if in a wilderness, over the paths, and twined their long stalks and leaves around the branches of the trees till the place became quite dark.

At last she could endure it no longer, and told her story to one of her sisters, and then all the other sisters got to know it; but no one else knew anything except themselves and a couple of other mermaids, who did not speak about it to any one except to their nearest and dearest friends. One of these knew who the prince was. She had also seen the festivities on board the ship, and knew where he came from, and where his kingdom lay.

"Come along with us, little sister," said the other princesses, and with their arms around each other's shoulders they ascended to the surface in front of the place where the prince's palace lay.

It was built of a kind of light-yellow shining stone, with large flights of marble stairs, one of which went right down to the sea.

Magnificent gilt cupolas rose above the roof, and between the columns which surrounded the whole building stood marble statues which looked as if they were alive. Through the clear glass in the lofty windows one could see into the most magnificent halls, with costly silk curtains and tapestries. On the walls hung large paintings, which it was a pleasure to look at. In the middle of the largest hall a big fountain was playing, its jets reaching right up into the glass cupola of the ceiling, through which the sun shone on the water, and on the beautiful plants which grew in the large basin.

Now she knew where he lived, and many an evening and night did she come there. She swam much nearer the shore than any of the others had dared to do; she even went right up the narrow canal under the splendid marble balcony which threw a long shadow out over the water. Here she would sit and look at the young prince, who believed he was all alone in the bright moonlight.

Many an evening she saw him sailing in his magnificent boat, with music and waving flags on board, while she peeped out from among the green rushes; and if the wind caught hold of her long silver-white veil, any one who saw it thought it was a swan which was spreading out its wings.

Many a night when the fishermen were out at sea fishing by torch-light, she heard the many good things they said about the young prince, and she rejoiced to think she had saved his life when he was floating half dead on the billows, and she called to mind how heavily his head had rested on her bosom, and how passionately she had kissed him; but he knew nothing at all about this, and could not even dream of her.

More and more she came to love human beings; more and more she wished to be able to be among them. Their world, she thought, was far larger than hers. They could fly across the seas in their ships, and they could climb the lofty mountains, high above the clouds; and the countries they possessed, with forests and fields, stretched farther than her eyes could reach. There was so much she wanted to know, but her sisters could not answer everything; so she asked the old grandmother, who knew the upper world well, as she rightly called the countries above the sea.

"If human beings are not drowned," asked the little mermaid, "can they go on living forever? Do they not die as we die down here in the sea?"

"Yes," said the old lady, "they must also die, and their term of life is even shorter than ours. We can live to be three hundred years old; but when we then cease to exist we only become foam on the water, and have not even a grave down here among our dear ones. We have not an immortal soul; we shall never live again. We are like the green rushes:

when once cut down we can never live again.   Human beings, however, have a soul which lives forever — which lives after the body has become dust: it rises up through the clear air, up to all the shining stars.   Just as we rise up out of the sea and see the countries of the world, so do they ascend to unknown beautiful places which we shall never see."

"Why did we not receive an immortal soul?" asked the little mermaid in a sad tone.   "I would give all the hundreds of years I have to live to be a human being only for a day, and afterward share the joys of the upper world!"

"You must not go on thinking of that," said the old lady; "we are much happier and better off than the human beings up there."

"So I must die and float as foam upon the sea!   I shall not hear the music of the billows, or see the beautiful flowers and the red sun!   Can I, then, do nothing at all to win an immortal soul?"

"No," said the old queen-dowager.   "Only if a man came to love you so much that you were more to him than his father or mother, if he clung to you with all his heart and all his love, and let the parson put his right hand into yours with a promise to be faithful to you here and for all eternity, then his soul would flow into your body, and you would also partake of the happiness of mankind.   He would give you his soul and still retain his own.   But that can never happen.   What we here in the sea consider most beautiful, our fish's tail, they would consider ugly upon earth.   They do not understand any better.   Up there you must have two clumsy supports which they call legs to be considered beautiful."

Then the little mermaid sighed, and looked sadly at her fish's tail.

"Let us be satisfied with our lot," said the old lady; "we will frisk and leap about during the three hundred years we have to live in.   That is surely long enough.   After that one can rest all the more contentedly in one's grave.   This evening we are going to have a court ball."

No such display of splendor has ever been witnessed on earth.   The walls and ceiling in the large ball-room were of thick but transparent glass.   Several hundreds of colossal mussel-shells, pink and grass-green, were placed in rows on each side, with blue fires, which lighted up the whole hall and shone through the walls, so that the sea outside was quite lit up.   One could see all the innumerable fishes, great and small, swimming up to the glass walls.   On some the scales shone in purple, and on others they appeared to be silver and gold.

Through the middle of the hall flowed a broad stream, in which the mermen and mermaids danced to their own song.   Such beautiful voices the inhabitants of the earth never possessed.   The little mermaid sang the most beautifully of all, and they clapped their hands to her, and for a moment she felt joyful at heart, for she knew that she had the loveliest voice of any to be found on earth or in the sea.   But soon she began again to think of the world above.   She could not forget the handsome prince, and her sorrow at not possessing an immortal soul like his. She therefore stole out of her father's palace, and while everybody was merry and singing she sat sad at heart in her little garden. Suddenly she heard the sound of a bugle through the water, and she thought to herself, "Now he is out sailing — he whom I love more than father and mother, he to whom my thoughts cling, and in whose hands I would place the happiness of my life. I will risk everything to win him and an immortal soul. While my sisters are dancing in my father's palace I will go to the sea witch, of whom I have always been so frightened. She may advise and help me."

The little mermaid then went out of her garden toward the roaring whirlpools behind which the witch lived. She had never been that way before. Neither flowers nor seaweed grew there. Only the bare, gray sandy bottom could be seen stretching away to the whirlpools where the water whirled round like roaring mill-wheels, tearing everything they got hold of down with them into the abyss below. She had to make her way through these roaring whirlpools to get into the sea witch's district, and for a long distance there was no other way than over hot, bubbling mud, which the witch called her turf-moor. Behind it lay her house, in the middle of a weird forest. All trees and bushes were polyps, half animal, half plant. They looked like hundred-headed snakes growing out of the ground. All the branches were long slimy arms with fingers like wiry worms, and they moved, joint by joint, from the root to the outermost point. They twisted themselves firmly around everything they could seize hold of in the sea, and never released their grip. The little mermaid stood quite frightened before all this, her heart beat with fear, and she was nearly turning back, but then she thought of the prince and man's immortal soul, and this gave her courage. She twisted her long, flowing hair tightly round her head, so that the polyps should not seize her by it, crossed both her hands on her breast, and then darted forward as rapidly as fish can shoot through the water, in between the polyps, which stretched out their wiry arms and fingers after her. She noticed how they all held something which they had seized—held with a hundred little arms as if with iron bands. The white skeletons of people who had perished at sea and sunk to the bottom could be seen firmly fixed in the arms of the polyps, together with ships' rudders and sea chests, skeletons of land animals, and a little mermaid whom they had caught and strangled. This was the most terrible sight of all to her.

She now came to a large slimy place in the forest, where great fat water snakes were rolling about, showing their ugly whitish-yellow bellies. In the middle of the open space stood a house built of the white bones of the people who had been wrecked. There the sea witch was sitting, while a toad was eating out of her mouth, just as a human being lets a little canary bird eat sugar from his mouth. The ugly, fat water snakes she called her little chickens, and allowed them to crawl all over her bosom.

THE SEA-WITCH WAS SITTING, WHILE A TOAD WAS EATING OUT OF HER MOUTH AND
THE WATER-SNAKES WERE CRAWLING OVER HER BOSOM.

"I know what you want," said the witch; "it is very stupid of you. But you shall have your way, for it is sure to bring you unhappiness, my pretty princess. You want to get rid of your fish's tail and to have two stumps instead to walk upon, like human beings, so that the young prince may fall in love with you, and that you may get him and an immortal soul." And then the witch laughed so loudly and horribly that the toad and the snakes fell down to the ground, where they rolled about.

"You come only just in time," said the witch, "for after sunrise to-morrow I should not be able to help you till another year had passed. I will make a drink for you, with which you must proceed to land before the sun rises, and then sit down on the shore and drink it, when your tail will be parted in two and shrink to what human beings call pretty legs; but it will cause you great pain—you will feel as if a sharp sword went through you. Every one who sees you will say you are the most beautiful human child they have seen. You will keep your graceful walk, no dancer will be able to float about like you; but at every step you take you will feel as if you stepped on a sharp knife, and as if your blood must flow. If you will suffer all this, I will help you."

"Yes," said the little mermaid, in a trembling voice, thinking only of the prince and of winning an immortal soul.

"But remember," said the witch, "when once you have assumed the human form, you can never become a mermaid again. You will never be able to descend through the water to your sisters, or to your father's palace, and if you do not win the prince's love so that he forgets his father and mother for your sake and clings to you with all his heart, and lets the parson join your hands making you man and wife, then you will not receive an immortal soul. The first morning after he has married another your heart will break, and you will become foam on the water."

"I will do it," said the little mermaid, and turned as pale as death.

"But you will have to pay me as well," said the witch; "and it is not a trifle I ask. You have the loveliest voice of all down here at the bottom of the sea, and with that you think of course you will be able to enchant him, but that voice you must give to me. I will have the best thing you possess for my precious draught. I shall have to give you my own blood in it, so that the draught may become as sharp as a double-edged sword."

"But if you take away my voice," said the little mermaid, "what have I then left?"

"Your beautiful form," said the witch, "your graceful walk, and your expressive eyes. With these you can surely infatuate a human heart. Put out your little tongue and I will cut it off as my payment, and you shall then have the powerful draught."

"So be it,' said the little mermaid; and the witch put the caldron on the fire to boil the magic draught. "Cleanliness is a virtue!" she said, and took the snakes and tied them in a knot to scour out the caldron with. She then slashed her chest and let her black blood drop into the caldron. The steam formed itself into the most fantastic figures, so that one could not help being frightened and scared. Every moment the witch threw some new ingredients into the caldron, and when it began to boil it sounded like the weeping of a crocodile. At last the draught was ready, and it looked like the purest water.

"There it is," said the witch, and cut off the little mermaid's tongue. She was now dumb, and could neither sing nor speak.

"If the polyps should get hold of you when you pass through my forest," said the witch, "then throw just a single drop of this draught over them, and their arms and fingers will be rent in a thousand pieces." But there was no need for the little mermaid to do so, for the polyps drew back from her in fear when they saw the sparkling draught which shone in her hand as if it were a glittering star. Thus she quickly got through the forest, the marsh, and the roaring whirlpools.

She could see her father's palace. The lights in the great ball-room were extinguished. All were now, no doubt, asleep; but she did not venture to go with them now that she was dumb and was going away from them forever. It seemed as if her heart would break with sorrow. She crept into the garden and took a flower from each of her sisters' flower-beds, threw a thousand kisses with her hand to the palace, and swam up through the dark blue waters.

The sun had not yet risen when she saw the prince's palace and arrived at the magnificent marble steps, but the moon was shining bright and clear. The little mermaid drank the strong and fiery draught; she felt as if a two-edged sword went through her delicate frame; she fell down in a swoon, and lay like one dead. When the sun began to shine across the waters she came to herself and felt a burning pain. But right in front of her stood the handsome young prince. He looked at her so fixedly with his coal-black eyes that she cast down her own, and then discovered that her fish's tail had vanished, and that she had the prettiest little white feet that any young girl could possess. But she was quite unclothed, and she therefore wrapped herself in her long, luxuriant hair. The prince asked her who she was, and how she got there; and she looked at him so mildly and yet so sadly with her dark blue eyes, for speak she could not. He then took her by the hand and led her into the palace. As the witch had told her, each step she made was as if she was treading on the points of awls and sharp knives; but she bore it gladly. Holding the prince's hand, she walked as lightly as a soap-bubble, and he and all the people at court were surprised at her graceful walk.

Costly clothes of silk and muslin were now brought to her, in which she arrayed herself. She was the most beautiful of all in the palace, but she was dumb, and could neither sing nor speak. Lovely female slaves, dressed in silk and gold, appeared and sang before the prince and his royal parents. One of them sang more beautifully than all the others, and the prince clapped his hands and smiled at her. This made the little mermaid sad, for she knew that she had been able to sing far more beautifully, and thought to herself: "Oh, if he could only know that I have given away my voice forever to be near him!"

The slaves now began dancing graceful aërial dances to the most lovely music. Then the little mermaid lifted up her lovely white arms, raised herself on the tips of her toes, and glided over the floor, dancing as no one yet had danced. At each movement her beauty became more apparent, and her eyes spoke more deeply to the heart than the song of the slave girls.

All were delighted with her, especially the prince, who called her his little foundling; and she went on dancing more and more, although each time her feet touched the ground she felt as if she were treading on sharp knives. The prince said she should always remain with him, and she was allowed to sleep on a velvet cushion outside his door. He had a male costume made for her, so that she could accompany him on horseback. They rode through the fragrant forests, where the green branches brushed against her shoulders and the little birds sang behind the fresh leaves. She climbed the lofty mountains with the prince; and although her tender feet bled so that the others could see it, she only laughed and followed him until they could see the clouds floating below them as if they were a flock of birds flying away to foreign lands.

At night, when all the others at the prince's palace slept, she went down to the broad marble steps, where it cooled her burning feet to stand in the cold sea-water, while she thought of all dear to her far down in the deep.

One night her sisters came arm in arm, singing most mournfully as they glided over the water. She beckoned to them, and they recognized her, and told her how sad she had made them all. After that they visited her every night; and one night she saw far away her old grandmother, who had not been to the surface for many years, and the sea king with his crown on his head. They stretched out their hands toward her, but did not venture so near land as her sisters.

Day by day the prince became more fond of her. He loved her as one loves a good, dear child, but he never thought of making her his queen. She would have to become his wife, otherwise she would not receive an immortal soul, and would be turned into froth on the sea on the morning of his wedding-day.

"Do you not love me most of them all?" the eyes of the little mermaid seemed to say when he took her in his arms and kissed her beautiful forehead.

"Yes, you are most dear to me," said the prince, "for you have the best heart of all of them. You are the most devoted to me, and you are like a young girl whom I once saw, but whom I fear I shall never find again. I was on board a ship which was wrecked, and the waves washed me ashore close to a holy temple, where several young maidens were in attendance. The youngest of them found me on the shore and saved my life. I saw her only twice. She was the only one I could love in the world; but you are like her, and you have almost driven her image out of my mind. She belongs to the holy temple, and therefore my good fortune has sent you to me. We shall never part."

"Alas! he does not know that I saved his life," thought the little mermaid. "I carried him across the sea to the forest where the temple stands. I sat behind the foam and watched for some one to come. I saw the beautiful maiden whom he loves more than me." And the mermaid sighed deeply, since she could not cry. "The maiden belongs to the holy temple, he told me. She will never come out into the world. They do not see each other any more. I am with him, and see him every day. I will cherish him, love him, and give my life for him."

But then she heard that the prince was to be married to the beautiful daughter of the neighboring king, and that was the reason he was fitting out such a splendid ship. The prince was going to visit the countries of the neighboring king, it was said; but it was to see the king's daughter, and he was going to have a great suite with him. But the little mermaid shook her head and smiled. She knew the prince's thoughts better than all the others.

"I must go," he had said to her. "I must see the beautiful princess. My parents demand it; but they will not compel me to bring her home as my bride. I cannot love her. She is not like the beautiful girl in the temple, whom you are so like. If, some day, I were to choose a bride, I would rather choose you, my dumb foundling with the eloquent eyes." And he kissed her rosy lips, played with her long hair, and laid his head on her heart, while she dreamed of human happiness and an immortal soul.

"You are not afraid of the sea, my dumb child," said he, as they stood on board the noble ship which was to carry him to the country of the neighboring king; and he told her about storms and calms, about strange fishes in the deep, and what the divers had seen there; and she smiled at his stories, for she knew, of course, more than any one else about the wonders of the deep.

In the moonlight night, when all were asleep except the steersman who stood at the helm, she sat on the gunwale of the ship, looking down into the clear water. She thought she saw her father's palace, and in the uppermost part of it her old grandmother, with the silver crown on her head, gazing up through the turbulent current caused by the keel of the ship.

Just then her sisters came up to the surface, staring sorrowfully at her and wringing their white hands. She beckoned to them, smiled, and wanted to tell them that she was well and happy, but the ship's boy came up to her, and the sisters dived down, so that he remained in the belief that the white objects he had seen were the foam on the sea.

The following morning the ship sailed into the harbor of the beautiful city of the neighboring king. All the church bells were ringing, and from the lofty towers trumpets were being blown, while the soldiers were standing with flying colors and glittering bayonets. Every day there was a festival. Balls and parties followed one another; but the princess had not as yet appeared. She was being brought up at a holy temple far away, they said, where she learned every royal virtue. At last she came.

The little mermaid was very anxious to see her beauty, and she had to acknowledge that a more beautiful being she had never seen. Her skin was so fine and clear, and from behind her long dark eyelashes shone a pair of dark blue, faithful eyes.

"It is you," said the prince—"you who saved my life when I lay like a corpse on the shore." And he folded his blushing bride in his arms.

"Oh, I am far too happy!" he said to the little mermaid. "My highest wish, that which I never dared to hope for, has been fulfilled. You will rejoice at my happiness, for you love me more than all of them." And the little mermaid kissed his hand, and felt already as if her heart were breaking. His wedding morning would bring death to her, and change her into foam on the sea.

All the church bells were ringing, and heralds rode about the streets proclaiming the betrothal. On all the altars fragrant oil was burning in costly silver lamps. The priests swung jars with incense, and the bride and bridegroom joined hands and received the blessing of the bishop. The little mermaid stood dressed in silk and gold, holding the bride's train, but her ears did not hear the festive music, and her eyes did not see the holy ceremony. She was thinking only of the approaching night, which meant death to her, and of all she had lost in this world.

The very same evening the bride and the bridegroom went on board the ship, the cannons roared, all the flags were waving, and in the middle of the deck a royal tent of purple and gold, with the most sumptuous couches, had been erected. There should the bridal pair rest during the quiet, cool night.

The sails swelled in the wind, and the ship glided smoothly and almost motionless over the bright sea.

When it grew dark gaily colored lanterns were lighted, and the sailors danced merry dances on the deck. The little mermaid could not help thinking of the first time she rose out of the sea and saw the same splendor and merriment, and she joined in the dance, whirling round and round like the swallows when they are pursued. All applauded her. Never

before had she danced so charmingly.   Her tender feet felt as if they were
being pierced by sharp knives, but she did not feel this; her heart suffered
from a far more terrible pain.   She knew it was the last evening she should
see him for whom she had left her relations and her home, for whom she
had given up her beautiful voice, and had daily suffered infinite agonies, of
which he had no idea.   It was the last night she would breathe the same
air as he, and see the deep sea and the starlit sky.   An eternal night
without thoughts and dreams awaited her, who had no soul, who could
never gain one.   On board the ship the rejoicings and the merriment
went on until far beyond midnight.   She laughed and danced while the
thoughts of death were uppermost in her mind.   The prince kissed his
lovely bride, and she played with his black locks, and arm in arm they
went to rest in the magnificent tent.

Everything then became quiet on the ship, only the steersman was
standing at the helm, and the little mermaid laid her white arms on the
gunwale and gazed toward the east for the first blush of the morning.   The
first ray of the sun, she knew, would be her death.   Then she saw her
sisters rising from the sea.   They were as pale as she, and their long, beautiful hair no longer waved in the wind.   It had been cut off.

"We have given it to the witch, that she might help you, that you
may not die this night.   She has given us a knife; here it is.   See how
sharp it is!   Before the sun rises you must plunge it into the prince's heart,
and when his warm blood touches your feet they will grow together to a
fish's tail, and you will become a mermaid again, and can go down with us
into the sea and live your three hundred years before you become the dead
salt froth on the sea.   Make haste!   He or you must die before the sun
rises.   Our old grandmother is mourning so much for you that her white
hair has fallen off, just as ours fell under the scissors of the witch.   Kill
the prince and come back with us.   Make haste!   Do you see the red
streak on the sky?   In a few minutes the sun will rise, and then you must
die."   And the sisters gave a strange, deep sigh and vanished in the waves.

The little mermaid drew back the purple curtain of the tent, and saw
the beautiful bride asleep with her head resting on the prince's breast.   She
bent down, kissed him on his beautiful forehead, and looked at the sky,
where the gleam of the morning was growing brighter and brighter.   She
glanced at the sharp knife, and again fixed her eyes on the prince, who
just then whispered the name of his bride in his dreams.   He thought only
of her.   The knife trembled in the hand of the little mermaid—then she
suddenly flung it far away into the waves, which gleamed red where it fell.
The bubbles that rose to the surface looked like drops of blood.   Once
more she looked with dimmed eyes at the prince, and then threw herself
from the ship into the sea.   She felt her body dissolving itself into foam.

The sun now rose above the horizon, its rays falling so mild and warm
on the deadly cold sea foam that the little mermaid did not feel the pangs

of death. She saw the bright sun, and above her floated hundreds of beautiful transparent beings, through whom she could see the white sails of the ships and the red clouds in the sky. Their voice was melodious, but so spiritual that no human ear could hear it, just as no human eye could see them. They had no wings, but soared lightly through the air. The little mermaid now discovered that she had a body like theirs, and that she was gradually rising out of the foam.

"Where am I going?" she asked. And her voice sounded like that of the other beings, so spiritual that no earthly music could reproduce it.

"To the daughters of the air," replied the others. "A mermaid has not an immortal soul, and can never gain one unless she wins the love of a man. Her eternal existence depends upon the power of another. Neither have the daughters of the air any immortal soul, but they can win one by their good deeds. We fly to the warm countries, where the close, pestilent air kills human beings. There we waft cool breezes to them. We spread the perfume of the flowers through the air, and distribute health and healing. When for three hundred years we have striven to do all the good we can, we receive an immortal soul, and can share in the eternal happiness of mankind. You, poor little mermaid, have with all your heart striven to reach the same goal as we. You have suffered and endured, and raised yourself to the world of spirits. Now you can, by good deeds, obtain an immortal soul after three hundred years."

And the little mermaid lifted her transparent arms toward the sun, and for the first time she felt tears coming into her eyes.

On the ship there was again life and merriment. She saw the prince with his beautiful bride searching for her. Sorrowfully they looked at the bubbling foam, as if they knew that she had thrown herself into the sea. Invisibly she kissed the bride's forehead. She gave the prince a smile, and rose with the other children of the air on the rosy cloud which sailed through space. "After three hundred years we shall thus float into the kingdom of heaven."

"We may yet get there earlier," whispered one of them. "Invisibly we float into the houses of mankind, where there are children; and for every day on which we find a good child who brings joy to his parents and deserves their love, our time of probation is shortened. The child does not know when we fly through the room, and when we smile with joy at such a good child, then a year is taken off the three hundred. But if we see a bad and wicked child, we must weep tears of sorrow, and for every tear a day is added to our time of trial."

IT IS QUITE TRUE!

THERE IS A HEN WHO HAS PLUCKED OUT ALL HER FEATHERS
FOR THE SAKE OF THE COCK!

IT IS QUITE TRUE!

"IT is a terrible story!" said a hen who belonged to a quarter of the town where the affair had not happened. "It is a terrible story from a poultry-yard! I dare not sleep by myself to-night. It is a good thing there are so many of us together on the perch." And then she began telling the story, which made the feathers of the hens stand on end and the cock drop its comb. It is quite true!

But we will begin at the beginning, and that took place in another part of the town, in a poultry-yard. The sun had set, and the fowls had gone to roost. Among them was a white hen with rather short legs, who laid eggs regularly, and was, for a hen, most respectable in every way. As she settled down on her perch she pecked herself with her beak, and then a little feather fell from her.

"There it goes!" she said; "the more I peck myself the prettier I become." And she only said this in fun, for she was the merry one among the hens; but otherwise, as already said, highly respectable. And then she went to sleep.

It was quite dark all round them. The hens sat side by side on the perch; but the hen who sat next to the white hen was not asleep. She could hear, and she could not hear (as one has to do in this world if one wants to live in peace); but she could not help telling her neighbor: "Did you hear what was said just now? I sha'n't mention names, but there is a hen here who wants to pluck out all her feathers in order to look fine. If I were a cock I should look with contempt upon her."

And just above the hens sat an owl, with her husband and children. They have sharp ears in that family, and they heard every word which the hen below them had said. They rolled their eyes, and Mother Owl fanned herself with her wings and said: "Don't listen to her; but very likely you heard what she said. I heard it with my own ears. One has to hear a great deal before they fall off. There is one of the hens who has so far forgotten what is befitting for a hen that she sits plucking out all her feathers while the cock sits looking at her."

"Prenez garde aux enfants," said Father Owl. "That is not a story for children to hear."

"I must tell it to my neighbor opposite. She is such a respectable owl to associate with." And off flew Mother Owl.

"Hooh! hooh! oohooh!" they hooted to each other, so that it could be heard right down among the pigeons in the pigeon-house of the neighbor opposite.

"Have you heard the news? Have you heard it? Hooh! hooh! There is a hen who has plucked out all her feathers for the sake of the cock. She will freeze to death, if she is not dead already. Hooh! oohooh!"

"Where, where?" cooed the pigeons.

"In the house opposite. I have as good as seen it myself. It is almost too improper a story to tell, but it is quite true."

"We believe it; we believe every word of it!" said the pigeons, and cooed down to the poultry in the yard: "There is a hen — well, some say there are two, who have plucked out all their feathers so as not to look like the others, and so attract the attention of the cock. It is a dangerous thing to do; one can catch a cold and die of fever; and they are both dead!"

"Wake up! wake up!" crowed the cock, and flew up on the paling. His eyes were still heavy with sleep, but he went on crowing for all that: "There are three hens which have died of a broken heart. They were all in love with the cock, and had plucked out all their feathers. It 's a terrible story! I don't want to keep it to myself. Pass it on!"

"Pass it on!" squeaked the bats; and the hens clucked and the cocks crowed: "Pass it on! Pass it on!" And thus the story went from poultry-yard to poultry-yard, and at last it came back to the place from which it had started.

"There are five hens," so the story ran, "who have plucked out all their feathers to show which of them had become thinnest for love of the cock; and then they pecked each other till they bled and fell down dead, to the shame and disgrace of their family and the great loss of their master."

And the hen who had lost the loose little feather did not, of course, recognize her own story, and, being a respectable hen, she said: "I have the greatest contempt for those hens. But there are many more of that sort. Such things must not be hushed up, and I will do my best to get the story into the papers, so that it may get known all over the country. It will serve those hens right, and their family too."

And it got into the newspapers; it was in print, so it must be quite true! *A little feather may easily become five hens.*

THE LITTLE MATCH GIRL

THE GOOSE JUMPED FROM THE DISH WITH KNIFE AND FORK IN ITS BACK.

THE LITTLE MATCH GIRL

I T was terribly cold; the snow was falling, and the dark evening was
setting in; it was the last evening of the year — New Year's Eve. In
this cold and uncomfortable darkness a poor little girl, bareheaded
and barefooted, was walking through the streets. She had certainly had
some sort of slippers on when she left her home, but they were not of
much use to her, as they were very large slippers. Her mother had

used them last, so you can guess they were large ones. As the little girl ran across the street just as two carriages were passing at a terrible rate, she lost the slippers. One of the slippers could not be found, and the other a boy ran away with. He said he would use it for a cradle when he got children of his own.

There was the little girl walking about on her naked little feet; they were red and blue with cold. In an old pinafore she had some bundles of matches, and in her hand she carried one of them. No one had bought anything of her the whole day, and no one had given her a penny. Hungry and shivering, she passed on, poor little girl, looking the very picture of misery. The snowflakes fell on her long yellow hair, which curled itself so beautifully about her neck; but of course she had no thoughts for such vanities. Lights were shining in all the windows, and there was such a delicious smell of roast goose in the street. "Ah! it is New Year's Eve," she thought.

Over in a corner between two houses—the one projected a little beyond the other—she crouched down, with her little feet drawn up under her; but she felt colder and colder, and she dared not go home, for she had not sold any matches or got a single penny; her father would beat her, and, besides, it was just as cold at home. They certainly had a roof over their heads, but through this the wind whistled, although they had stopped the largest cracks with rags and straw. Her little hands were quite benumbed with cold. Ah! a match might do some good. If she only dared to take one out of the bundle and rub it against the wall, and warm her fingers over the flame! She took one out—ratch!—how it spurted, how it burned! It was a warm, clear flame, just like a little candle, when she held her hand round it. It was a wonderful light; the little girl thought she was sitting right before a great iron stove with bright brass feet and brass mountings. How beautiful the fire burned! How it warmed her! But what was that? The little girl stretched her feet out to warm them also, and the flame went out—the stove vanished—she had only the small stump of the burned match in her hand. A new match was rubbed against the wall; it burned, it gave a beautiful light, and where the light fell on the wall it became transparent like a veil. She could see right into the room, where the table was covered with a bright white cloth, and on it a fine china dinner service; the roast goose, stuffed with prunes and apples, was steaming beautifully. But, what was still more delightful, the goose jumped from the dish and waddled along the floor, with knife and fork in its back, straight toward the poor girl, when the match went out, and there was only the thick, cold wall to be seen. She lighted a new match. Then she was sitting under a beautiful Christmas-tree; it was still larger and more decorated than that she had seen through the glass door at the rich merchant's last Christmas. Thousands of candles burned upon the green branches, and colored pictures, like those that you see in

SHE LIGHTED A NEW MATCH. THEN SHE WAS SITTING UNDER A BEAUTIFUL CHRISTMAS TREE,
WITH THOUSANDS OF CANDLES BURNING UPON THE GREEN BRANCHES.

the shop windows, were looking down upon her. The little girl stretched both her hands toward them—and the match went out. The light seemed to go farther and farther away from her. She saw now that they were the bright stars. One of them fell down, leaving a long train of fire after it.

"Now some one is dying," said the little one. Her old grandmother, who was the only one who had been good to her, but was now dead, had told her when a star falls a soul goes to God.

She rubbed a match again on the wall. It gave such a light, and in its luster stood the old grandmother—so clear, so bright, so mild, so blessed!

"Grandmother," cried the little one, "oh, take me with you! I know you will be gone when the match goes out—gone, just like the warm stove, the beautiful roast goose, and the great, beautiful Christmas tree." And she rubbed quickly all the remaining matches in the bundle,—she would not lose her grandmother,—and the matches burned with such a splendor that it was brighter than in the middle of the day. Grandmother had never before been so beautiful, so grand. She took the little girl in her arms, and they flew away in brightness and joy, so high—high, where there was no cold, no hunger, no fear—they were with God!

But, next morning, in the corner by the house sat the little girl with red cheeks and a smile about her mouth, dead—frozen to death on the last evening of the old year. The sun of New Year's morning rose up on the little corpse, with the matches in the pinafore, and one bundle nearly burned. "She wanted to warm herself," said the people. No one knew what beautiful visions she had had, and in what splendor she had gone into the New Year's joy and happiness with her old grandmother.

TWELVE BY THE MAIL

THE WEATHER WAS SHARP AND FROSTY, THE SKY
GLITTERED WITH SPARKLING STARS.

TWELVE BY THE MAIL

THE weather was sharp and frosty, the sky glittered with sparkling stars, and not a breath of wind stirred the air. "Bump!" there went a pot against the door.[1] "Bang!" went a gun in honor of the new year. It was New Year's Eve, and the clock was now striking twelve.

"Taratantarra!" There comes the mail. The big mail-coach halted at the town gate. There were in all twelve passengers. The coach could not hold more. All the places had been taken.

"Hurrah! Hurrah!" they shouted in all the houses where the people were keeping New Year's Eve, and had just stood up with filled glasses to drink success to the new year.

"Health and happiness in the new year!" they shouted. "A pretty wife, plenty of money, and no worries!"

And thus they drank success to one another, and clinked their glasses, while the mail-coach stood at the town gate with the stranger guests, the twelve travelers.

Who were they? They had passports and luggage with them, even presents for you and me and all the people in the town. Who were the strangers? What did they want, and what did they bring with them?

"Good morning," they said to the sentry at the gate.

"Good morning," said he, for the clock had just struck twelve.

"Your name? Your profession?" the sentry asked the first who stepped out of the coach.

[1] It is an old Danish custom to bang an earthen pot against the doors on New Year's Eve.

383

"Look at the passport," said the man. "That is I." He was a great big fellow, dressed in a bearskin coat and fur boots. "I am the man in whom so many persons place all their hopes. Come to-morrow, and you shall have a New Year's present. I throw coppers and silver dollars about, I give presents, and I give balls—altogether thirty-one balls.

THEY WERE KEEPING NEW YEAR'S EVE, AND WERE DRINKING SUCCESS TO THE NEW YEAR.

I have no more nights to spare. My ships are frozen fast in the ice, but it is nice and warm in my office. I am a merchant, and my name is January. I have got only bills with me."

Then came the next. He was a merry fellow. He was the manager of the theaters, of the masquerade balls and all the amusements you can think of. His luggage was a great barrel.

"We 'll get more fun out of that at Shrovetide than out of the cat," said he. "I want to amuse others as well as myself, for I have the shortest time to live of the whole family. I can become only twenty-eight. Sometimes they put on an extra day, but that makes no difference. Hurrah!"

"You must n't shout so loud," said the sentry.

"Of course I must," said the man. "I am Prince Carnival, and travel under the name of February."

Now came the third. He looked the image of Lent, but carried his head high, for he was related to "the forty knights," and was a weather prophet; but it is not a very fat living, and that 's why he praised the lenten time. His decoration was a bunch of violets in his button-hole, but the flowers were very small.

"March! March!" cried the fourth, and gave the third a push. "March! March! Let 's go into the guard-room; there 's punch there; I can smell it." But it was n't true; he wanted to make an April fool of him; that 's how the fourth began. He seemed to be a smart fellow; he did n't do much work, but kept a lot of holidays. "It makes one's temper very changeable," he said. "Rain and sunshine, moving in and moving out. I am also agent for furniture removals.[1] I go round and ask people to funerals; I can both laugh and cry. I have my summer clothes in the portmanteau, but it would be foolish to begin to wear them. Here I am. For show I go out in silk stockings, and carry a muff."

Then a lady stepped out of the coach. "Miss May," she said, announcing herself. She was dressed in summer clothes, and had galoshes on her feet. She wore a silk dress the color of the green beech leaves, and anemones in her hair, and she brought such a perfume of sweet woodruff with her that the sentry began to sneeze. "God bless you!" she said; that was her greeting. How lovely she was! She was a singer: not at the theaters, but in the woods; not at fairs, but in the fresh green woods, where she wandered about and sang for her own amusement. In her work-bag she carried Christian Winter's[2] "Woodcuts," for they are just like the beechwood, and Richardt's "Minor Poems," which are like woodruff.

"Now our young mistress is coming!" they cried in the coach, and then Mistress June stepped out. She was young and delicate, proud and charming. One could see at once she was born to keep the feast of the Seven Holy Sleepers. She gave a party on the longest day of the year, so that the guests might have time to partake of all the dishes on her table. She could well afford to drive in her own carriage, but she traveled by the mail-coach like the rest, for she wanted to show she was not proud. She did not travel alone, for she was accompanied by her younger brother, July.

[1] In Denmark most removals take place in April.
[2] Winter and Richardt, now dead, are well-known Danish lyrical poets.

He was a strong, big fellow, dressed in summer clothes and a Panama hat. He had very little luggage with him, for it gave one such a lot of trouble in the hot weather. He had only a bathing cap and drawers with him, which was not much.

Then came old mother August in a big crinoline. She was a wholesale dealer in fruit, the owner of many fish-ponds and a farm. She was fat, and looked very warm; she took part in all kinds of work, and went herself with the beer-keg to the people in the fields. "In the sweat of your brow you shall eat your bread," she said. "That's in the Bible. Afterward we can give a dance in the wood and a harvest festival."

Now a man came out of the coach. He was a painter by profession, —a master of colors,—which the woods soon got to know. The leaves soon had to change color, but he could do it so beautifully when he liked. The woods would soon begin to glow in red, yellow, and brown. The master whistled like the black starling, was a diligent worker, and hung the brownish, greenish hop-vine around his beer-jug; it looked ornamental, and he had an eye for the decorative. Here he now stood with his pot of colors, which was all the luggage he had.

Now came the squire who was thinking of October, of plowing and tilling his fields, and also a little of the pleasures of the chase. He had a dog and a gun with him, and nuts in his bag—crick, crack! He had an awful lot of luggage, amongst which was an English plow. He talked about agricultural affairs, but one could not hear very much for all the coughing and hawking that was going on. It was November that was coming.

He had a cold in his head,—a terrible cold,—so that he had to use sheets instead of handkerchiefs; and yet he had to accompany the servant girls to their situations, he said. But the cold would soon get better when he began cutting firewood; and this he was anxious to do, for he was the master of the guild of sawyers. He spent his evenings in cutting out skates. He knew that before many weeks were over this pleasure-giving foot-gear would be in great demand.

Now came the last passenger, good old mother December, with her warming-pan. She felt very cold, but her eyes beamed like two bright stars. She carried a flower-pot with a small fir-tree. "I will look after it and tend it, so that it will be a big tree by Christmas Eve, and reach right from the floor up to the ceiling. It will be decorated with lighted candles, gilt apples, and garlands of colored paper. The warming-pan warmed like a stove. I take the fairy-tale book out of my pocket and read aloud, so that all the children in the room become quiet; but the dolls on the tree become alive, and the little wax angel at the top of the tree shakes her gold tinsel wings, and flies from the green top to kiss young and old in the room, even the poor children who are standing outside singing Christmas carols about the Star of Bethlehem."

THEN A LADY STEPPED OUT OF THE COACH. "MISS MAY," SHE SAID,
ANNOUNCING HERSELF.

"Now the coach may drive away," said the sentry.   "Now we have all twelve.   Let the next coach drive up."

"First let the twelve get in all right," said the captain, who was on duty. "One at a time! I shall keep the passport; it holds good for a month for each of you. When the month is over I will write on the back of it and say how you have behaved yourselves. Mr. January, will you please step in?"

And so in he went.

When a year has passed I will tell you what the twelve have brought to you, to me, and to all of us. I don't know now, nor do they know themselves, I think — for they are wonderful times we live in.

THE GARDEN OF PARADISE

"WE SHALL SOON REACH THE GARDEN OF PARADISE," SAID THE EAST WIND.

THE GARDEN OF PARADISE

THERE was once upon a time a king's son. No one had so many and such pretty books as he. Everything that had happened in this world he could read about in them and see depicted in splendid pictures. He could find out everything about all the pictures and countries in the world. But as to where the Garden of Paradise was to be found not a word was mentioned, and that was the very thing he was thinking most about.

His grandmother had told him, when he was quite a little boy and just beginning to go to school, that every flower in the Garden of Paradise was a most delicious cake, and that the pistils were filled with the finest wine. On some of them history was inscribed, on others geography or tables, and one needed only to eat cakes in order to learn one's lesson. The more one ate, the more one knew of history, geography, and tables.

That was what he believed at that time; but as he grew older and got to know more, and became wiser, he could understand that the delights in the Garden of Paradise must be something quite different.

"Oh, why did Eve pick of the Tree of Knowledge? Why did Adam eat of the forbidden fruit? If it had been I, it would not have happened. Sin should never have entered the world." That is what he said at that time; and he said so still when he was seventeen years old. The Garden of Paradise filled all his thoughts.

One day he was reading in the forest. He was alone, for that was his greatest pleasure.

The evening set in, the clouds gathered, and it began to rain as if the windows of heaven were opened and were pouring forth their waters. It was as dark as it is at night at the bottom of the deepest well. At one moment he slipped on the wet grass, and the next he stumbled over the bare stones which stuck out of the rocky ground. All his clothes were dripping wet. There was not a dry thread on the poor prince. He had to crawl ever large boulders, where the water oozed out of the thick moss. He was on the point of fainting when he heard a strange hissing sound, and in front of him he saw a cavern all alight. In the middle of it was burning a fire big enough to roast a whole stag, which was actually being done — the finest stag imaginable, with its long horns, was stuck upon the spit, and was being turned slowly round between the trunks of two pine-trees that had been felled.

An elderly woman, as tall and strong as if she were a man in disguise, sat by the fire, busy throwing one log after another upon it.

"Just come nearer," she said; "sit down by the fire, and get your clothes dried."

"There is a great draught here," said the prince, as he sat down on the ground.

"It 'll be worse than it is when my sons come home," answered the woman. "You are in the cavern of the winds. My sons are the four winds of the world. Do you understand that?"

"Where are your sons?" asked the prince.

"It is not easy to answer a stupid question," said the woman. "My sons are their own masters. They are playing at rounders with the clouds up yonder in the grand parlor." And then she pointed up in the air.

"Oh, indeed!" said the prince. "But you talk rather harshly, and you are not quite as gentle as the women I generally see about me."

"I suppose they have nothing else to do. I am obliged to be harsh to keep my boys in order. But I do it, although they are pretty headstrong. Do you see the four sacks which are hanging on the wall? They are just as afraid of them as you have been of the rod behind the looking-glass. I can double up the boys, I can tell you, and then I put them in the bag. We make no ceremony about it. There they stop, and cannot get out to gad about till it suits me. But here comes one of them."

It was the North Wind who came in and brought an icy chill with him. Big hailstones bounded along the ground, and the snowflakes flew all round the room. He was dressed in bearskin trousers and jacket. A hood of sealskin came down over his ears, while long icicles hung from his beard, and hailstones were rolling down from the collar of his jacket, one after the other.

"Don't go near the fire so soon," said the prince. "You can easily get your face and hands frost-bitten."

"Frost-bitten!" said the North Wind, with a loud laugh. "Frost-bitten! Why, frost is just my greatest delight. But what sort of a stripling are you? How did you get into the cavern of the winds?"

"He is my guest," said the old woman, "and if you are not satisfied with that explanation you'll soon find yourself in the bag. Now you know my opinion."

Well, that settled matters, and the North Wind told them where he had come from, and where he had now been for nearly a whole month.

"I come from the Polar Sea," said he. "I have been on Beeren Island with the Russian walrus-hunters. I sat asleep at the helm as they sailed away from the North Cape. When I happened from time to time to awake, the fulmars would be flying about my legs. They are very funny birds; they give a sudden flap with their wings, and then they keep them stretched out and quite motionless, and sail through the air at full speed."

"Don't spin it out too long," said the mother of the winds. "And so you got to Beeren Island?"

"Ah, that's a fine place. There's a floor for you to dance upon as flat as a pancake. Half-thawed snow, moss, sharp stones, and skeletons of walruses and ice-bears were lying all about, looking like giants' arms and legs covered with greenish mold. You would think the sun had never shone upon them. I puffed away some of the mist in order to see the shed. There was a house built of wreck-wood and covered with walrus hides, the fleshy side of which was turned outward and looked both red and green.

"On the roof a live ice-bear sat growling. I went along the shore, looked at the birds' nests, and saw the unfledged youngsters, which were screeching and gaping with their beaks open. I blew down in the thousand throats and taught them to close their mouths. Farthest away the walruses were rolling about like live intestines or giant maggots with pigs' heads and teeth an ell long.'

"You are a good story-teller, my boy," said the mother. "It makes my mouth water to listen to you."

"Then the hunting began. The harpoon was thrown right into the walrus's breast, and the reeking jets of blood rose like a fountain above the ice. Just then I thought of my own sport. I began to blow hard. I let the mountain-high icebergs hem in the boats. Ho! how they howled and how they screamed! But I howled louder than them all. The carcasses of the dead walruses, the sailors' chests, and the tackle were thrown out upon the ice. I blew the snowflakes about their ears, and let those on board the ice-bound vessels drift with their catch to the south to taste salt water. They will never come back to Beeren Island."

"Then you have done something wicked," said the mother of the winds.

"What good I have done the others can tell," he said; "but here comes my brother from the West. I like him best of all, for there is a smell of the seas and a bracing freshness about him."

"Is it little Zephyr?" asked the prince.

"Yes, of course it is Zephyr," said the old woman; "but he is not so little as you imagine. In the days of old he was a handsome boy, but now that is all over."

He looked like a wild man, and he wore a padded hat, so that he should not hurt his head. In his hand he held a mahogany club, hewn in the American mahogany forests. Nothing less would do.

"Where do you come from?" asked his mother.

"From the wild forests," he said, "where the prickly lianas make hedges between trees, where the water snakes lie in the wet grass, and where human beings seem out of place."

"What did you do there?"

"I looked at the deep river. I saw how it rushed over the cliff, how it became spray and flew toward the clouds to support the rainbow. I saw the wild buffalo swimming in the river; but the current carried him away. He drifted with a flock of wild ducks, which flew up into the air where the water rushed over the precipice. The buffalo was carried along with it. That pleased me, and I raised such a storm that it tore up ancient trees, which sailed down the river and were smashed into bits."

"And have you done nothing else?" asked the old woman.

"I have turned somersaults in the Savannahs, I have stroked the wild horses and shaken down cocoanuts. Yes, yes; I have lots of stories to tell. But one must not tell everything one knows. You know that, mother."

And then he kissed his mother so violently that she nearly fell on her back. He was really a wild young fellow.

Just then came the South Wind in a turban and a flowing Bedouin cloak.

"It's very cold in here," said he, and threw some fuel on the fire. "One can feel that the North Wind came back first."

"It is hot enough here to roast an ice-bear," said the North Wind.

"You are an ice-bear yourself," said the South Wind.

"Do you want to be put into the bags?" asked the old woman. "Sit down on the stone there and tell us where you have been."

"In Africa, mother," he answered. "I went lion-hunting with the Hottentots in the land of the Kafirs. Oh, what grass grows on the plains there — as green as olives! There the gnus danced about, and there the ostrich ran a race with me; but I was the fastest, after all. I came to the desert — to the yellow sand which looks like the bottom of the sea. I met a caravan. They killed their last camel to get water to drink but it was only a little they got. Above the sun was scorching, and below the sand was roasting. There were no bounds to that vast desert. I gamboled about in the fine loose sand, and sent it whirling up into great pillars. What a dance! You should have seen how cowed the dromedary stood, and how the merchant pulled his caftan over his head. He threw himself down before me as before Allah, his god. Now they are buried. A pyramid of sand covers them all. One day, when I blow it away, the sun shall bleach their white bones. Then travelers will see there have been people there before, otherwise they would not have believed it."

"So you have done nothing but wicked deeds," said the mother. "Just march into the bag." And before he knew of it, she had seized the South Wind by the waist and put him in the bag. He rolled about on the floor, but she sat down upon him, and then he had to lie quiet.

"You have some lively boys," said the prince.

"Yes, indeed," she answered; "and I know how to manage them. Here comes the fourth."

It was the East Wind, and he was dressed like a Chinaman.

"So you come from that quarter," said the mother. "I thought you had been to the Garden of Paradise."

"I am going there to-morrow," said the East Wind; "to-morrow it will be a hundred years since I was there. I come from China now, where I have danced round about the porcelain tower till all the bells began to tinkle. Down in the streets the officials were being punished. Bamboo canes were thrashed to pieces across their shoulders, and they were people of the first to the ninth degree. They cried, 'Many thanks, my fatherly benefactor,' but they did not mean anything by it, and I rang the bells and sang, 'Tsing, tsang, tsu.'"

"You are in a gay mood," said the old woman. "It is a good thing you are going to the Garden of Paradise to-morrow; it always improves your manners. Drink plentifully from the fountain of wisdom, and bring a small bottle with you for me."

"That I will," said the East Wind. "But why have you put my brother from the south into the bag? Let him out. He must tell me about bird Phœnix. The princess in the Garden of Paradise always wants to hear about that bird when I pay her a visit every hundredth year. Open the bag. There 's a good mother, and I will make you a present of two pocketfuls of tea, just as green and fresh as when it was picked on the spot."

"Well, for the sake of the tea, and because you are my pet boy, I will open the bag." This she did, and the South Wind crept out; but he looked rather abashed, because the strange prince had seen everything that had happened.

"Here is a palm-leaf for the princess," said the South Wind. "This leaf the old bird Phœnix — the only one there was in the world — has given me. With his beak he has inscribed on it the whole history of his life during the hundred years he lived, and now she can read it herself. I saw how bird Phœnix set fire to his nest himself, and sat there while he was burned, just like a Hindu's widow. How the dry twigs crackled! What a smoke and what a fragrance there was! At last everything burst out into flame; the old bird Phœnix was reduced to ashes; but his egg lay red-hot in the fire; it broke with a loud report, and the young bird flew out. Now it is ruler over all birds, and the only bird Phœnix in the world. He has bitten a hole in the palm-leaf I gave you. That is his greeting to the princess."

"Let us now get something to eat," said the mother of the winds, and then all sat down to eat of the roasted stag. The prince sat next to the East Wind, and therefore they soon became good friends.

"Just tell me," said the prince, "what sort of a princess it is you are talking so much about, and where is the Garden of Paradise?"

"Ho, ho!" said the East Wind; "if you want to go there, you must fly with me to-morrow. But I had better tell you that no human beings have been there since the days of Adam and Eve. You know them, of course, from your Bible history."

"Yes, of course," said the prince.

"Well, when they were driven away from the Garden of Paradise, it sank into the earth, but it retained its warm sunshine, its balmy air, and all its magnificence. The queen of the fairies lives there. There lies the Island of Happiness, where death never comes, where it is delightful to dwell. Sit on my back to-morrow, and I will take you with me. I think it can be managed. But now you must not talk any more, for I want to go to sleep."

And so they all went to sleep.

It was early morning when the prince awoke, and he was not a little bewildered to find that he was already high up above the clouds. He was sitting on the back of the East Wind, who stuck to him faithfully. They were so high up in the air that forests and fields, rivers and seas, looked just as they do on a large colored map.

"Good morning," said the East Wind. "You might just as well have slept a little longer, for there is not much to be seen in the flat country below us, unless you would like to count the churches. They stand out just like chalk spots down on the green-board." It was the fields and meadows he called the green-board.

"It was rude of me not to say farewell to your mother and brothers," said the prince.

"When one is asleep one must be excused," said the East Wind; and then they flew on faster than ever. One could notice it by the tops of the trees. When they swept past them there was a violent rustling among the branches and the leaves. You could hear it on the sea and the lakes, for wherever they flew the waves rose higher and higher, and the large ships dipped down into the water like swimming swans.

Toward evening, as it grew dark, it was most interesting to watch the great towns. Lights were burning here and there down below. They looked just like the many little sparks of fire you see rushing about when you have burned a piece of paper, just like children running home from school. And the prince clapped his hands with joy; but the East Wind asked him to let that alone, and rather to hold on fast, else he might easily fall down and find himself hanging on to a church steeple.

The eagle of the dark forests flew fast enough, but the East Wind flew still faster. The Cossack on his little steed dashed swiftly along the plains, but the prince swept along quite differently.

"Now you can see the Himalayas," said the East Wind. "They are the highest mountains in Asia. We shall soon reach the Garden of Paradise." They then turned more to the south, and soon they noticed a fragrance of spices and flowers in the air. Figs and pomegranates grew wild, and the wild vines were hung with blue and red grapes. Here they both alighted and stretched themselves on the soft grass, where the flowers were nodding to the wind as if they wanted to say: "Welcome back again!"

"Are we now in the Garden of Paradise?" asked the prince.

"No, of course not," answered the East Wind; "but we shall soon be there now. Do you see the mountain side yonder, and the big cavern where the vines are hanging down like large green curtains? We shall have to pass through there. Wrap yourself in your cloak. Here the sun is scorching, but one step further and it is icy cold. The bird which flies past the cavern has one wing in the warm summer out here, and the other in the cold weather in there."

"So this is the way to the Garden of Paradise?" asked the prince.

They then went into the cavern. Ugh! how icy cold it was! But it did not last long. The East Wind spread out his wings, which gleamed like the brightest fire. But what a cavern! The large blocks of stone from which the water was dripping hung above them in the most wonderful shapes. Sometimes the passage was so narrow that they had to creep on their hands and knees, and at other times they came into spaces so lofty and extensive that they might have been in the open air. The places looked like chapels for the dead, with silent organ pipes and petrified banners.

"We seem to be going through the Valley of Death to the Garden of Paradise," said the prince. But the East Wind did not not answer a word, but pointed forward, where the most lovely light was shining in dazzling brightness. The blocks of stone above their heads became more and more faint and misty in appearance, till at last they looked like white clouds on a moonlight night.

They were now in the most delightful mild air — fresh as if it had come from the mountains, and as fragrant as from among the roses of the valley.

They then came to a river which was as clear as the air itself, and where the fishes were like silver and gold. Scarlet eels, which emitted blue sparks of fire at every movement, were playing about down in the water, and the broad leaves of the water-lilies shone in all the colors of the rainbow. The flower itself was a reddish-yellowish burning flame, which was fed with water just as a lamp is always kept burning by oil. A bridge of solid marble of most artistic and delicate workmanship, as if it were made of lace and crystal pearls, led across the water to the Isle of Happiness, where the Garden of Paradise flourished.

The East Wind took the prince in his arms and carried him across. There the flowers and leaves were singing the most lovely melodies of his youth, but more exquisitely than any human voice could ever sing.

Were they palm-trees or gigantic water-plants that grew here? The prince had never beheld such large and sappy trees. The most wonderful creepers hung in long festoons between the trees in such a way as can only be seen depicted in colors and gold in the margin of old missals, or twisted round the letters of the chapters. It was the most weird combination of birds, flowers, and flourishes.

On the grass close by a flock of peacocks was standing with their gorgeous tails spread out. Yes; surely that must be so! But no; when the prince touched them he saw they were not birds, but plants. They were large burdocks which here were as radiant as the beautiful tail of the peacock. A lion and tiger were running about like agile cats among the green hedges, the fragrance of which was like that of the flowers of the olive-tree. Both the lion and the tiger were tame. The wild wood-pigeon, which shone as the brightest pearl, struck the lion on the mane with his wings as he flew past, and the antelope, which is usually so shy, stood nodding his head as if he also wanted to gambol with them.

Then the Fairy of Paradise appeared. Her clothes shone like the sun, and her face was as kind and as gentle as that of the joyous Madonna in

THEN THE FAIRY OF PARADISE APPEARED. SHE WAS YOUNG AND BEAUTIFUL, AND WAS
ACCOMPANIED BY THE MOST BEAUTIFUL MAIDENS.

the picture where she is represented as being extremely happy over her Child. She was young and beautiful, and was accompanied by the most beautiful maidens, each with a shining star in her hair.

The East Wind gave her the palm-leaf with the inscribed words from bird Phœnix, which made her eyes sparkle. She took the prince by the hand and conducted him into her palace, where the walls were of the color of the most splendid tulip-leaf when held up to the sun. The ceiling itself was one large radiant flower, and the longer you gazed up into it the deeper did its cup appear. The prince stepped to a window and looked out through one of the panes, when he saw the Tree of Knowledge with the Serpent, and Adam and Eve standing close by. "Were they not banished?" he asked. And the fairy smiled, and explained to him that upon each pane time had burned its pictures, but not as we are accustomed to see pictures. No; there was life in each one. The leaves on the trees moved; people came and went just as the reflected pictures we see in a mirror. Then he looked through another pane, and there he saw Jacob's Dream, where the ladder reached right up to heaven, and angels with large wings were soaring to and fro. Yes; everything that had happened in this world lived and moved on these panes; such wonderful pictures time only could produce.

The fairy smiled, and conducted him into a large and lofty hall, the walls of which consisted of transparent paintings with faces the one more beautiful than the other. They were millions of happy beings, who smiled and sang till their song melted into one melody. The uppermost were so small that they appeared smaller than the smallest rosebud when drawn as little dots on paper.

And in the middle of the hall stood a large tree with luxuriant hanging branches, on which golden apples, large and small, hung like oranges among the green leaves.

It was the Tree of Knowledge, of the fruit of which Adam and Eve had eaten. From every leaf fell a bright red dewdrop, as if the tree was weeping tears of blood.

"Let us now get into the boat," said the fairy. "There we will have our repast while out on the billowy water. The boat will roll, but it will not move away from the spot. Meanwhile all the countries of the world will glide past before our eyes."

And it was a wonderful sight to see how the whole coast moved past.

There came the lofty snow-clad Alps, with clouds and dark pine-trees. The horn sounded so melancholy and the shepherd was yodeling so merrily in the valley. And now the banana-trees bent their long, drooping branches over the boat, coal-black swans glided about on the water, and the strangest of animals and flowers were to be seen on the shore. It was New Holland, the fifth part of the world, which with its background of blue mountains glided past. They heard the song of the priests, and saw the dance of the savages to the sound of drum and bone trumpets.

The pyramids of Egypt, reaching up to the clouds, overturned columns, and Sphinxes, half buried in the sand, sailed past them. The Northern lights glittered over the glacial mountains of the North — no fireworks could come up to this display.

The prince was highly delighted. He saw, of course, a hundred times more than what we are relating here.

"And can I always remain here?" he asked.

"That depends upon yourself," answered the fairy. "If, unlike Adam, you do not let yourself be tempted to do what is forbidden, then you can remain here forever."

"I shall not touch the apples on the Tree of Knowledge," said the prince. "Here are thousands of fruits just as beautiful as they."

"Examine yourself, and if you do not feel strong enough, return with the East Wind, who brought you here. He is now going to fly back, and will not be here again for a hundred years. That time will here pass as quickly as if it were only a hundred hours, but it is a long time if one is exposed to temptation and sin.

"Every evening, when I leave you, I must cry out to you, 'Come with me!' I shall have to beckon to you with my hand, but you must remain behind. Do not follow, for if you do your longing will increase with every step you take. You will come into the hall where the Tree of Knowledge is growing. I shall be asleep under its fragrant, drooping branches. You will bend over me, and I shall smile; but if you press a kiss upon my lips Paradise will then sink deep into the earth and be lost to you. The cutting wind of the desert will sweep past you; the cold rain will drip from your hair. Sorrow and tribulation will be your inheritance."

"I shall remain here," said the prince. And the East Wind kissed him on his forehead and said, "Be strong, and we shall meet here again in a hundred years. Farewell, farewell!" And the East Wind spread out his large wings. They shone like the sheet-lightning in the autumn, or the Northern lights in the cold winter.

"Farewell, farewell!" resounded from flowers and trees. Storks and pelicans flew after him in a long row like streaming ribands, and followed him to the boundary of the garden.

"Now the dancing will begin," said the fairy. "Toward the end, when I shall be dancing with you, you will see me beckoning to you just as the sun is sinking. You will hear me calling out to you, 'Come with me!' But do not do it. For a hundred years I must repeat it. Each time when that period is over you will gain more strength, and at last you will never think of it. To-night is the first time, and I have warned you."

The fairy then conducted him into a large hall of white, transparent lilies.

THERE SHE WAS LYING ASLEEP AND LOOKING AS BEAUTIFUL AS ONLY THE FAIRY IN THE
GARDEN OF PARADISE CAN LOOK.

The yellow stamens of each flower made a miniature golden harp, which resounded with delicious music, as if from both strings and flutes. The most lovely maidens, with slender, graceful figures, and robed in wavy gauze, through which one could see their lovely limbs, floated past them in the dance, and sang of the happiness of life—how they would never die, and how the Garden of Paradise would flourish forever.

When the sun went down the whole sky became one sheet of gold, and shed the hue of the loveliest roses upon the lilies, and the prince drank of the foaming wine which the maidens handed him, and felt a bliss he never before had experienced. He saw how the background opened: beyond stood the Tree of Knowledge in a halo of luster which dazzled his eyes. The singing that reached his ears was soft and beautiful as his mother's voice, and it seemed as if she were singing, "My child, my beloved child!"

The fairy then beckoned to him and called out lovingly, "Come with me, come with me!" And he rushed after her, forgetting his promise—forgetting it on the very first evening; and she went on, beckoning and smiling to him. The spicy fragrance in the air became stronger and stronger, the harps sounded lovelier, and it seemed as if the millions of faces on the walls of the hall where the tree grew nodded and sang, "One should know all; man is the lord of the earth." It was no longer drops of blood that fell from the leaves of the Tree of Knowledge; they appeared to him to be red, glittering stars.

"Come with me! come with me!" went on the trembling tones, and at every step the cheeks of the prince burned more hotly, and his blood flowed more quickly.

"I must," he said. "It is no sin; it cannot be. Why not pursue beauty and joy? I must see her asleep! No harm will come of it if I only do not kiss her. And that I shall not do. I am strong; I have a firm will."

And the fairy threw aside her dazzling robe, bent back the branches, and in a moment was hidden beneath them.

"I have not yet sinned," said the prince, "and I will not;" and then he pushed the branches aside. There she lay already asleep, and looking as beautiful as only the fairy in the Garden of Paradise can look. She smiled in her dreams. Bending over, he saw tears trembling on her eyelashes.

"Do you weep for me?" he whispered. "Do not weep, thou loveliest of women! Now only do I understand the happiness of Paradise. It courses through my blood, through my thoughts. I feel the strength and the eternal life of the cherub in my mortal body. Let eternal night come! One moment like this is reward enough!" And he kissed the tears from her eyes; his mouth touched her lips. Just then came a loud and terrible clap of thunder such as had never before been heard by any one, and everything tumbled together. The beautiful fairy, the lovely Paradise sank; everything sank deeper and deeper.

In the darkness of the night the prince saw it sinking till at last he could only see it beaming like a little glittering star in the far distance. A deadly chill shot through his limbs. He closed his eyes, and lay long like one dead.

The cold rain fell upon his face and the cutting wind blew about his head when he came to himself. "What have I done?" he sighed. "I have sinned, like Adam! Sinned, so that Paradise has sunk far beyond me!" And he opened his eyes. The far-away star — the star that had glittered like the sunken Paradise — he could still see. It was the morning star in the sky.

He sat up and found himself in the big forest close to the cavern of the winds, with the mother of the winds sitting by his side. She looked angry, and was just going to lift her arms against him.

"And the first evening, too!" she said. "I thought as much. Well, if you were my boy I should put you into the bag."

"And into it he shall go!" said a voice. It was Death. He was a tall old man with a scythe in his hand, and with large black wings. "In the coffin he shall be put, but not just yet. I shall only put my mark upon him, and shall let him wander about in the world yet a while to atone for his sin and become a better man. But I shall come some day. When he least expects it I shall put him into the black coffin, and take it on my head and fly up toward the star. There also blossoms the Garden of Paradise, and if he is good and pious he shall be allowed to enter it; but if his thoughts be wicked, and his heart still be full of sin, then he shall sink with his coffin still deeper than he saw the Garden of Paradise sink, and only once in every thousandth year shall I fetch him again, either to sink still deeper or to remain in the star — the star up yonder."

THE WIND TELLS ABOUT VALDE-
MAR DAA AND HIS DAUGHTERS

BY THE SHORE OF THE GREAT BELT STANDS AN OLD MANSION
WITH THICK RED WALLS.

THE WIND TELLS ABOUT VALDEMAR DAA[1]
AND HIS DAUGHTERS

WHEN the wind sweeps over the grass the meadow ripples like a lake, and when it sweeps over the corn the whole field moves in waves like the sea; it is the dance of the wind—but listen to him telling stories. He sings them out loudly; among the trees in the forest it sounds quite different to when it blows through holes, cracks, and crevices in the walls. Do you see how the wind up there is chasing the clouds as if they were a flock of sheep? Do you hear how the wind down here is howling through the open gate, as if it were a watchman blowing his horn? With strange sounds it whistles down the chimney and into the fireplace. The fire flares up and sends out sparks, and throws a light far into the room, where it is so snug and pleasant to sit and listen to it. Only let the wind speak. He knows more fairy tales and stories than all of us put together. Just listen to what he is telling: "Whew!—ugh!—whew! Rush along!" is the burden of his song.

"By the shore of the Great Belt stands an old mansion with thick red walls," begins the wind. "I know every stone of it; I have seen them

[1] Pronounced in Danish as "Daw."

before, when they formed part of Marsk Stig's castle on the promontory, but it had to be pulled down. The stones were used again for the walls of a new mansion and another place, which became Borreby House, and still stands there. I have seen and known the noble barons and ladies of many generations, who one after another had lived there; but now I am going to tell you about Valdemar Daa and his daughters.

"He carried himself proudly, for he was of royal descent. He could do something more than hunt a stag or empty a beaker; things will come all right in the end, as he used to say.

"His wife, dressed in gold-embroidered robes, walked proudly across her brightly polished parquet floors; the tapestries were magnificent, the furniture most costly and artistically carved. He had brought gold and silver plate with him to the house; in the cellar was German beer, when there was any, and in the stables black, spirited horses were neighing; there was abundance of wealth at Borreby House, when wealth was there.

"There were three children—three fair maidens, Ida, Johanne, and Anna Dorthea; I still remember the names.

"They were rich, fine folks, born and bred in luxury. Whew!—ugh! —whew! Rush along!" said the wind; and so he went on again.

"I did not see here, as in other old mansions, the high-born lady sitting in the great hall, with her maidens around her turning the spinning-wheel; she played on the sonorous lute and sang thereto, not always the old Danish ballads, but songs in foreign languages. There was feasting and merriment; there came grand folks from near and far, the music sounded, the beakers clinked; I could not drown the noise," said the wind. "Here ruled pride in all its ostentatious display; but the fear of the Lord was not there.

"And so it happened one May-day evening," said the wind, "that I came from the west, after having seen ships being crushed and wrecked on Jutland's western shore; I rushed on over the heath and wood-girt coast, and over the Island of Fünen; I had just come across the Great Belt's panting and blowing.

"I then settled down to rest on Zealand's coast, close to Borreby House, where the forest with its magnificent oak-trees was still flourishing.

"The young men from the district came out here to gather twigs and branches, the largest and driest they could find, which they took with them into the village; here they put them into a heap and set fire to them, while the lads and lasses danced round and round.

"I lay still," said the wind, "but I gently touched one branch—the one which the handsomest lad had put on the pile; his fagot flared up, its flames shooting higher than the others. He was the favored one, received the pet name, became the cock-of-the-walk, and was the first to choose his little pet lamb among the lasses. There were rejoicings and merriment far greater than at the wealthy Borreby House. And the noble lady and her three daughters came driving toward the mansion in a gilded coach drawn by six horses. The daughters were young and beautiful—three delicate flowers, the rose, the lily, and the pale hyacinth. The mother herself was a gorgeous tulip; she did not return the salutations of any in the whole crowd, who paused in their sport to drop courtesies and go on their knees before her; one would have thought the good lady's neck had been made as brittle as glass. The rose, the lily, and the pale hyacinth! Yes, I saw them all three. Whose pet lamb would they one day become? thought I. Their lord and master will be a gallant knight, perhaps a prince. Whew! —ugh!—whew! Rush along! Rush along!

"The carriage rolled away with them, and the peasants ran back to their dancing. They went a-maying to Borreby, to Fjæreby, and to all the villages in the neighborhood.

"But in the night, when I arose," said the wind, "the grand lady lay down to rise no more; death overtook her, as it will overtake us all— there is nothing new in that. Valdemar Daa remained grave and thoughtful for a time; the strongest tree can be twisted but not broken, said something within him; the daughters cried, and at the mansion all were drying their tears; but Lady Daa had rushed away—and I rushed away! Whew!—ugh!—whew!" said the wind.

"I came back again—I came back often across the Island of Fünen and the waters of the Belt; I rested down by Borreby shore, by the noble oak forest, where the osprey, the wood-pigeon, the blue raven, and even the black stork built their nests. It was early in the year; some were sitting on their eggs, some had nestlings. How they fluttered, how they cried! The sound of the ax was heard, blow upon blow; the forest was to be cut down. Valdemar Daa wanted to build a big ship, a man-of-war, a three-decker, which the king would be sure to buy; and therefore the forest—the sailors' landmark, the home of the birds—was doomed. The shrike flew away frightened—its nest was destroyed; the osprey and all the birds of the forest lost their home, and flew wildly about, crying in fear and anger. I understood them well. Crows and jackdaws croaked jeeringly: 'From the nest! From the nest! Croak! croak!'

"And in the midst of the forest, among the crowd of workmen, stood Valdemar Daa and his three daughters, and all were laughing at the wild cries of the birds; but the youngest daughter, Anna Dorthea, felt grieved in her heart, and when they were going to fell a tree that was nearly dead, upon the naked branches of which the black stork had built his nest, and from which the young nestlings stretched out their necks, she prayed, with tears in her eyes, for them; and so the tree with the nest of the black stork was allowed to remain standing. It was not of much consequence.

"Trees were cut and logs were sawn; they were building the big ship, the three-decker. The master shipbuilder was of low birth, but of noble mien; his eyes and forehead spoke of great intellect; and Valdemar Daa used to listen with pleasure to his stories, and so did little Ida, his eldest daughter, now fifteen years old. While he was building the ship for the father he built a castle in the air for himself, where he and little Ida should preside as man and wife; all of which might have happened if the castle had been one built of stone, with ramparts and moats, forests and gardens. But with all his talents, the master shipbuilder was only a poor man, after all; and what business has a sparrow among the cranes, as the saying is? Whew!—ugh!—whew! I flew away, and so did he, for he dared not remain; and little Ida got over it—there was no help for it.

"The black horses were neighing in the stables; they were noble steeds, well worth looking at, and grand folk came to see them. The admiral, who was sent by the king to inspect the new man-of-war and to arrange about its purchase, spoke in great praise of the high-spirited horses. I heard it all," said the wind; "I followed the grand folk through the open door, and strewed stalks of straw like bars of gold before their feet. Valdemar Daa wanted gold, and the admiral wanted the horses, for he was always praising them; but Daa did not understand the hint, and so the ship was not purchased, either.

"There it stood on the beach, bright and new. It was then covered over with boards, and looked like a Noah's ark which was never to take to the water. Whew!—ugh!—whew! Rush along! Rush along! Oh, it was a pity!

"During the winter," said the wind, "when the fields were covered with snow, and the belts choked with drift ice which I drove up against the coast, there came large flocks of ravens and crows, the one blacker than the other, which settled down on the desolate, lonely ship on the beach, and screamed hoarsely, looking for the forest which was no more, and for the many cozy nests which had been destroyed. Poor, homeless birds, old and young! And all this for the sake of that big piece of lumber, the noble ship which was never to sail on the sea!

"I whirled up the snowflakes around it till they lay like a sea of snow over it all. I let it hear my voice, so that it might know what a storm has got to say; I know I did my best to give it a lesson in seamanship. Whew!—ugh!—whew! Rush along!

"And the winter passed; winters and summers have passed, and will continue to pass away, just as I pass away and rush along, like the drifting snow, like the apple blossoms and the falling leaves. Rush along! Rush along! Rush along! Men and women pass away, too!

"But the daughters were still young; little Ida was a rose, fair and beautiful to behold, just as when the master shipbuilder saw her. I often caught hold of her long brown hair when she stood buried in thought by

A FIRE WAS ALWAYS BURNING ON HIS HEARTH; THE DOOR TO HIS CHAMBER WAS LOCKED,
AND THERE HE WORKED FOR DAYS AND NIGHTS.

the apple-tree in the garden and did not notice that I sprinkled flowers on her hair, which became disheveled, and while she gazed at the red sun and the golden sky through the dark trees and bushes in the garden.

"Her sister Johanne was fair and erect as a lily; she bore herself well and held her head high, and, like her mother, little inclined to bend her neck. She was fond of walking up and down in the large hall where the family portraits were hanging; the ladies were painted in dresses of velvet and silk, with tiny little hats, embroidered with pearls, on their plaited hair. They were beautiful women. Their husbands were to be seen clad in armor or costly cloaks lined with the fur of squirrels, and with the blue ruff. The sword was buckled round their thigh, and not round the loin. Where would her own portrait hang some day, and what would her noble husband be like? Such were the thoughts that occupied her mind. I heard her talking half aloud to herself about it as I rushed along the passage into the hall and turned round on my way out.

"Anna Dorthea, the pale hyacinth, was only a child fourteen years old, quiet and thoughtful. Her large, deep-blue eyes were dreaming, but a childlike smile still played round her mouth. I could not blow it away, and I did not wish to do so, either.

"I met her in the garden, in the narrow lanes, and in the fields where she was gathering herbs and flowers. She knew her father used them for making drinks and household drugs which he knew how to distil. Valdemar Daa was proud and haughty, but he was also learned and possessed great knowledge,— one could not help noticing that,— and all sorts of rumors were afloat in consequence. A fire was always burning on his hearth, even in the summer time. The door to his chamber was locked, and there he worked for days and nights; but he did not talk much about it. The elements of nature must be conquered in the dead of night. Soon he would discover the greatest secret of all—that of making the red gold.

"That was the reason why the smoke rose from the chimney, why the fire was burning and crackling on the hearth. Yes; I was there," the wind said. "'Let it be, let it be!' I sang through the chimney; 'it will all end in smoke, embers, and ashes. You will burn yourself. Whew!—ugh! —whew! Let it be, let it be!' But Valdemar Daa did not let it be.

"What has become of the splendid horses in the stable? of the old silver and gold plate in the cupboards and closets? of the cow in the fields? of house and home? Yes; they melt—they all melt in the crucible, but they have not yet yielded any gold.

"The barns and storehouses, the cellars and larders, were empty. The less people the less mice. One window broke, another cracked. I need not wait to get in through the door," said the wind. "Where smoke rises from the chimney there's roasting going on; but the smoke that came from this chimney devoured food, and all for the sake of the red gold.

"I blew through the gateway like a watchman blowing his horn, but no watchman was there," said the wind. "I turned the vane on the spire; it grated as if the watchman was snoring in the tower, but there was no watchman. There were rats and mice. Poverty laid the table-cloth; poverty sat in the wardrobe and in the larder. The doors fell off their hinges; cracks and crevices appeared everywhere; I could go in and out," said the wind, "and that is how I know all about it.

"In smoke and in ashes, in sorrow and sleepless nights, his beard and hair became gray, his skin furrowed and yellow, while his eyes searched greedily for the gold—the much longed for gold.

"I blew the smoke and ashes into his face and beard. Debts increased, but no gold came. I sang through the broken panes and open cracks; I blew into the daughters' wardrobe, where their clothes lay faded and threadbare, for they had to last for a long time. That was not the kind of song which had been sung at their cradles. A life of luxury had become one of penury. I was the only one who sang merrily in the mansion," said the wind. "I snowed them up. Snow makes a place snug, they say. Of firewood they had none. The forest whence they should fetch it had been cut down. It was bitterly cold. I rushed in through holes and crevices and along the passages, over gables and walls, to keep myself in practice, while within the daughters of high degree kept their bed because of the cold, and the father crouched under his fur coverlet. Nothing to eat, no fire on the hearth; what a life for people of high degree! Whew!—ugh!—whew! Rush along! But the lord of the manor could not do that.

"'After winter comes spring,' said he. 'After hard times come good; but they are a long time coming. Everything is mortgaged. We are at our last extremity, and then the gold will come—at Easter.'

"I heard him mumbling to the spider in his web: 'You diligent little weaver! You are teaching me to hold out. If your web is torn, you begin again and make it whole. If torn again, you patiently set to work again from the beginning—from the beginning. That is what one must do; and then comes the reward.'

"It was Easter morning. The bells were ringing and the sun was shining brightly in the sky. In feverish excitement he had watched, melted, mixed, and distilled. I heard him sigh like a soul in despair; I heard him pray; I noticed he held his breath. The lamp had burned out, but he did not notice it. I fanned the embers, which threw a reddish glare over his white face. His eyes were sunk deep in their sockets, but now they grew bigger and bigger, as if they would burst.

"Look at the alchemist's glass! Something glitters in it. It seems to glow, it is pure, it is heavy. With trembling hands he lifts it up. With a quivering voice he exclaimed, 'Gold! gold!' He grew dizzy at the sight. I could easily have blown him over," said the wind, "but I only

THEY WALKED ALONG THE ROAD WHERE THEY USED TO DRIVE IN THEIR CARRIAGE; NOW
THEY WENT FORTH WITH THEIR FATHER AS BEGGARS.

fanned the glowing embers and followed him through the door to where his daughters lay shivering. His robe was covered with ashes; they were clinging to his beard and his tangled hair. He drew himself up and held aloft the brittle glass with his great treasure.

"'Found! found! Gold!' he shouted, holding the glass still higher as it glittered in the rays of the sun. The hand trembled; the alchemist's glass fell on the floor and broke into a thousand pieces. The last bubble of his wealth had burst. Whew!—ugh!—whew! Rush along! And away I rushed from the goldmaker's abode.

"Late in the year, when the days are short up here in the North, and when the fog comes with its misty veil and drops dew on the red berries and the leafless branches, I felt in good spirits, stirred up the air, swept the sky clear, and broke off all the rotten branches; it is no great task, but it has to be done. At Valdemar Daa's Borreby House there was another kind of clearing out. His enemy, Ove Ramel, from Basnas, had arrived with the mortgages on the estate, and on all the goods and chattels, which he had bought up. I drummed at the dilapidated doors and whistled through all the cracks and crevices: Whew!—ugh! Master Ove should not take a fancy to live there! Ida and Anna Dorthea cried bitterly; Johanne stood pale and erect, biting her thumb till it bled. Of what did it avail? Ove Ramel offered Valdemar Daa leave to remain on the estate during his lifetime, but he did not even receive thanks for his offer. I listened to them; I saw the homeless master lift his head still higher and toss it back proudly; I sent such a gust against the house and the old linden trees that one of the thickest branches broke—one that was not rotten. It lay in front of the gate like a big broom, if any one should want to sweep out the place; and a great sweeping out there was. I thought there would be! It was a trying day, a difficult time to maintain one's dignity; but the soul was hardened, the will was obstinate.

"They possessed nothing but the clothes they had on, except the alchemist's glass, which had just been bought and filled with the spillings that had been scraped up from the floor—the treasure which had promised so much, but failed to keep its promise. Valdemar Daa hid it in his bosom and took his staff in his hand; and the once wealthy nobleman, with his three daughters, walked out of Borreby House. I blew cold gusts against his flushed cheeks, I patted his long white hair, and I sang as best I could. Whew!—ugh!—whew! Rush along! Rush along! That was the end of all the wealth and splendor.

"Ida and Anna Dorthea walked one on each side of him; Johanne turned round at the gateway; but what was the good? Their luck was not likely to turn. While looking at the red stones of Marsk Stig's castle did she think of his daughters?

"The eldest took the youngest by the hand,
And wandered far into the world.

"Was she thinking of the old ballad? They were three, and their father was also with them. They walked along the road where they used to drive in their carriage; now they went forth with their father as beggars to Smidstrup field, to the mud hut which they had rented for ten marks a year. This was to be their new mansion, with empty walls and empty jars. Crows and jackdaws flew over them croaking, as if jeering at them, 'From the nest! from the nest! Caw! caw!' as the birds had done in Borreby forest when the trees were cut down.

"Valdemar Daa and his daughters understood them well. I whistled round about their ears; it was not worth listening to.

"So they entered the mud hut in Smidstrup field, and I rushed along over marshes and fields, through bare bushes and leafless trees, to the open water, to other lands. Whew!—ugh!—whew! Rush along! Rush along! Year after year."

How did it fare with Valdemar Daa, and how did it fare with his daughters? The wind will tell us.

"The one I saw last was Anna Dorthea, the pale hyacinth; she was then old and crooked; it was fifty years afterward. She lived the longest, and she knew all about it.

"Over yonder on the heath, close to Viborg town, lay the dean's new and handsome house, built of red stone and with pointed gables. The smoke curled thickly out from the chimney. The gentle mistress of the house and her beautiful daughters sat in the bay-window and looked out over the hanging box-thorn to the brown heath. What were they looking at? They were looking at the stork's nest on the tumbledown hut over there. The roof, as far as there was any roof, consisted of moss and house-leek; that which covered the greatest part of the hut was the stork's nest, and that was the only part of it which was looked after, for the stork kept it in order.

"It was a house only to be looked at, not to be touched. I had to be careful," said the wind. "The house was allowed to stand for the sake of the stork's nest, although it was a disgrace to the heath. The dean would not drive the stork away, so the old shed was left standing, and the poor body inside it was allowed to live there. She had to thank the Egyptian bird for that, or was it not a return for her kindness when she interceded for the nest of his wild black brother in Borreby forest? She was then, poor thing, a young child, a delicate pale hyacinth in the noble garden. She, Anna Dorthea, remembered it all.

"'Alas! alas!' she sighed; for people can sigh, just as the wind sighs among the reeds and rushes. 'Alas! no bells were rung when you were buried, Valdemar Daa! The boys from the charity school did not sing when the late master of Borreby was laid to rest. Alas! everything comes to an end, even misery. Sister Ida became a peasant's wife; that was the hardest trial our father had to go through. His daughter's husband, a miserable serf, whose master could make him mount the wooden horse,—I suppose he is underground by this. And you too, Ida. Alas! alas! It is not ended yet—poor miserable body that I am! Oh, release me, kind Jesus!'

"That was Anna Dorthea's prayer in the wretched hut, which was allowed to stand only for the sake of the stork.

"I did what I could for the bravest of the sisters," said the wind; "she cut her coat according to her cloth.

"She dressed as a lad and went to a skipper and got a berth on his ship; she was chary of words, and sullen in appearance, but willing at her work. But she could not climb the rigging—so I blew her overboard before anybody knew she was a woman; and I think I did the right thing," said the wind.

"It was on an Easter morning, just like the one when Valdemar Daa thought he had discovered the red gold, that I heard a hymn being sung under the stork's nest within the rickety walls. It was Anna Dorthea's last song. There was no window—only a hole in the wall. The sun came like a bright lump of gold and shone through it. What a luster! Her eyes were growing dim; her heart was breaking. That would have happened even if the sun had not shone in upon her that morning.

"The stork had provided her with a roof till her death. I sang at her grave," said the wind—"her father's grave. I know where he lies and where she lies. Nobody else knows.

"New times, other ways. The old road has become a plowed field. Over the peaceful graves runs the busy highroad, and soon the railway with its train of carriages will come and rush over the graves, which will be forgotten like their names. Whew!—ugh!—whew! Rush along!

"This is the story of Valdemar Daa and his daughters. Tell it better, any of you, if you can," said the wind, and turned about. And then it was gone.

THE GALLANT TIN SOLDIER

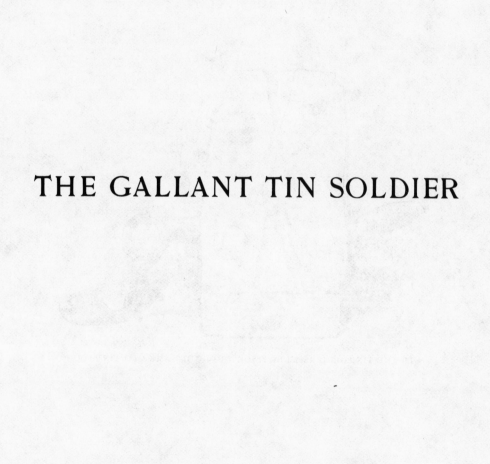

ALL THE TIN SOLDIERS WERE MADE FROM THE SAME OLD TIN SPOON.

THE GALLANT TIN SOLDIER

THERE were once five-and-twenty tin soldiers. They were all brothers, because they were born of the same old tin spoon. They all shouldered their muskets, they all looked straight before them, and they all had the same splendid uniform — red and blue. The first words they heard in this world, when the lid was taken off the box in which they were lying, were : "Tin soldiers!" It was a little boy who shouted this as he clapped his hands in delight at seeing the soldiers. They had just been given to him as a present, because it was his birthday. He began putting them on the table. They were all exactly alike, except one, and he had only one leg because he had been cast last of all, and there was not tin enough to fill the mold; but he stood just as firm on his one leg as the others on their two, and it was just this soldier who became famous.

On the table where they had been placed stood many other toys, but the most remarkable of all was a splendid castle made of cardboard. You could see right into the rooms through the small windows. In front of the castle some small trees were placed round a looking-glass which was to represent a lake. Swans made of wax swam on the lake and watched their reflection in it. It was altogether very pretty ; but the prettiest of all was a little lady who was standing right outside the open gate of the castle. She was also cut out of paper, but she had a skirt of the clearest gauze, and a little, narrow blue ribbon over her shoulders, just like a scarf, and in the middle of it was a bright spangle as big as her face. The little lady stretched out both her arms, — she was a dancer, — and she lifted one leg so high that the tin soldier could not see it, and he believed that she had only one leg like himself. "That's the wife for me," he thought ; "but she is very grand : she lives in a castle. I have only a box, and there are twenty-five of us in there already. It's no place for her. But I must try and get acquainted with her." And then he laid himself down at full length behind a snuff-box which was on the table. There he could

have a good look at the elegant little lady, who remained standing on one
leg without losing her balance.

Later on in the evening all the other tin soldiers were put back in
their box, and the people in the house went to bed. Then the toys
commenced to play and amuse themselves. They played at "visiting," at
"making war," and at "giving balls." The tin soldiers were making a
noise in their box because they wanted to join in the fun, but they could
not get the lid off. The nut-cracker turned somersaults, and the slate
pencil did all sorts of tricks on the slate. There was such a noise that the
canary woke up and began to chatter, and that in verse too. The only
two who did not stir from their places were the tin soldier and the little
dancer. She was standing on the tip of her toes, with both her arms
stretched out; he remained quietly behind the snuff-box. He never took
his eyes off her for a moment. The clock struck twelve and—bounce!
—the lid flew off the snuff-box; but there was no snuff in it at all, only
a little black goblin. It was a kind of Jack-in-the-box, you know.

"Tin soldier," shouted the goblin, "will you keep your eyes to yourself?" But the tin soldier appeared as if he did not hear it. "Just wait
till to-morrow," said the goblin.

When the morning came and the children were up, the tin soldier was
put in the window; but whether it was the goblin or the draught which
was the cause of it, the window flew open all of a sudden, and the soldier
fell head foremost from the third story. It was a terrible fall. There
he was, standing on his head, his bayonet sticking between two paving-
stones and his leg pointing up in the air. The servant girl and the
little boy ran down into the street at once to look for him; but although
they very nearly trod upon him, they could not see him. If the soldier
would only have cried out, "Here I am!" they could have found him;
but he thought it was beneath his dignity to shout aloud because he was
in uniform. It began to rain; the drops fell faster and faster till they
poured down. When the rain was over two boys came past. "Look!"
cried one of them, "there's a tin soldier! Let's give him a sail." They
made a boat out of a newspaper and put the soldier in it, and soon he was
sailing along the gutter, while the two boys ran alongside him, clapping
their hands. What a rough sea there was in that gutter, and what a strong
tide there was running! But then it had been raining in torrents. The
paper boat rocked up and down, and now and then it turned about so
rapidly that the tin soldier was very nearly shaken overboard; but he
stuck to it manfully, and did not even change countenance. He looked
straight before him, and grasped his musket. All of a sudden the boat
drifted into a drain, where it was just as dark as if he had been in his
box. "I wonder where I am off to now?" he thought. "Well, well, it
is all the doing of that goblin. Aha! if the little lady were only here
along with me in the boat, I would not mind if it were twice as dark."

A LITTLE LADY WAS STANDING RIGHT OUTSIDE THE OPEN GATE OF THE CASTLE WITH
BOTH HER ARMS OUTSTRETCHED.

Just then a large water-rat, who was living in the drain, saw him. "Have you got a pass?" asked the rat. "Give me your pass!" But the tin soldier did not answer, and grasped his musket still tighter. The boat rushed on, and the rat gave chase to it. How the rat gnashed his teeth! He shouted out to all the bits of wood and straw which were floating about in the drain, "Stop him! stop him! He has n't paid the toll! he has n't shown his pass!" But the rush of the water in

"STOP HIM! STOP HIM!" SHOUTED THE RAT, GNASHING HIS TEETH, "HE HAS N'T SHOWN HIS PASS!"

the drain carried the boat along faster and faster. The tin soldier could already see the bright daylight at the end of the drain, but he heard at the same time a roaring noise, which was enough to frighten even a bold man. Only think, at the end of the drain the water rushed out into a big canal! It was to him just as dangerous a passage as a big waterfall would be to us. He was now so near this point that he could not stop the boat. The boat darted out; the poor tin soldier summoned up all his courage, and kept himself steady—nobody should say of him that he moved a muscle. The boat whirled round three or four times—it was filling with water to the very edge—it must sink; the tin soldier stood up to his neck in water, the boat sank deeper and deeper, and the paper was gradually giving way.

The water had now reached up to the soldier's head; he thought of the beautiful little dancer, whom he should never see again; the old nursery rhyme was ringing in his ears:

> Danger, danger, warrior bold,
> Prepare to meet thy grave so cold!

At this moment the boat went to pieces, and the tin soldier was sinking to the bottom when a great fish snapped him up and swallowed him. What a dark place it was! It was even darker than in the drain, and there was so little room, too; but our gallant tin soldier did not flinch a bit; he lay at full length, shouldering his musket. The fish was rushing about, and was struggling fearfully. At last he became quiet; something like a flash of lightning passed through him. It was broad daylight, and somebody cried out, "A tin soldier!" The fish had been caught and brought to market, where he was sold, and had now been carried up into the kitchen, where the cook cut him open with a big knife. She took the soldier and carried him into the parlor, where everybody wanted to see the remarkable man who had traveled about in the stomach of a fish; but the tin soldier was not at all proud. They put him on the table, and there—but no!—what wonderful things will happen in this world!—the tin soldier was in the very room where he fell out of the window; he saw the same children, and the toys were all standing on the table; there was the beautiful castle, with the elegant little dancer. She was still standing on one leg, and kept the other high in the air. Had she been waiting for him? The tin soldier was so much moved that he nearly shed tears of tin, but it was not becoming. He looked at her and she looked at him, but they did not say anything. Then one of the little boys took the tin soldier and threw him right into the fire, without giving any reason for doing so; it must have been the goblin in the box who put this into his head.

The tin soldier stood there quite radiant; he felt a heat that was something terrible, but whether it was the heat from the fire or from his love, he was not quite sure. The colors had quite gone off him, but whether this had happened to him on his journey, or was caused by his grief, no one could tell. He looked at the little lady, and she looked at him; he felt he was melting, but he remained firm, shouldering his musket. Suddenly the door of the room flew open, the draft caught the dancer, and she flew like a sylph straight into the stove to the tin soldier; there was a blaze—and she was gone. The brave tin soldier melted down into a little lump, and when the servant girl took out the ashes next morning, she found him in the shape of a little tin heart. Of the beautiful dancer remained only the spangle, and that was burned as black as coal.

THE STORY OF A MOTHER

OVER IN THE CORNER THE OLD CLOCK WAS
WHIRRING ROUND.

THE STORY OF A MOTHER

A MOTHER was sitting by her little child. She was in great distress, for she feared it was going to die. It was so pale, its little eyes were closed. It breathed slowly, and sometimes so deeply, as if it were sighing; and the mother looked still more sadly at the little creature.

There was a knock at the door, and a poor old man came in. He was wrapped in something like a great horse-cloth. He was greatly in need of something to keep him warm, for it was cold winter. Everything out of doors was covered with ice and snow, and the wind blew so fiercely that it cut one's face.

And as the old man was shivering with cold, and the little child happened to be sleeping for a moment, the mother got up and put a small mug of beer on the stove to warm it for him. The old man sat down and rocked the cradle, and the mother took a seat on the chair close by, and looked at her sick child, which breathed so hard, and lifted its little hand.

"Don't you think I shall keep him?" she said. "God will not take him from me."

And the old man—it was Death himself—nodded to her in such a strange way, it might just as well mean yes as no. The mother cast down her eyes, while the tears rolled down her cheeks. Her head was so heavy, —for three nights and days she had not closed her eyes,—and soon she dropped asleep, but only for a moment. Then she started up, shivering with cold. "What is it?" she exclaimed, and looked round on all sides. But the old man was gone, and her little child was gone also. He had taken it with him. Over in the corner the old clock was whirring and whirring round; the heavy leaden weight ran right down to the floor —bump!—and the clock stopped also.

But the unhappy mother ran out of the house, calling for her child.

Out in the snow sat a woman in long black clothes, and she said: "Death has been into your room. I saw him hurrying away with your little child. He goes faster than the wind. He never brings back what he takes."

"Only tell me which way he went," said the mother. "Tell me the way, and I shall find him."

"I know it," said the woman in the black clothes. "But before I tell you, you must sing to me all the songs you have sung for your child. I love them; I have heard them before. I am Night, and I have seen your tears while you sang them."

"I will sing them all—all," said the mother. "But do not keep me, so that I may overtake him, and find my child."

But Night sat dumb and still. The mother wrung her hands, sang, and wept. There were many songs, but yet more tears, and then Night said: "Go to the right, into the dark pine forest. I saw Death take the road thither with your little child."

Far in the forest she came to a cross road, and she knew no longer which way to take. Close by stood a hawthorn bush, on which were neither leaves nor flowers, for it was cold winter time, and icicles hung from its branches.

" Have you seen Death go by with my little child? "

" Yes," said the hawthorn. " But I shall not tell you which way he went, unless you first warm me against your bosom. I am freezing to death. I shall soon be all ice."

And she pressed the hawthorn close to her bosom so that it might be thoroughly warm; but the thorns pierced her flesh, and her blood flowed in great drops. The hawthorn shot forth fresh green leaves, and flowers blossomed forth in the cold winter night—so warm is the heart of a sorrowing mother. The hawthorn then told her the way she should go.

At length she came to a great lake on which there was neither ship nor boat. The lake was not sufficiently frozen to carry her, nor was it open and shallow enough to allow her to wade across it, and across it she must get if she wanted to find her child. So she laid herself down to drink up the lake, which, of course, was impossible for a human being; but the distressed mother thought that a miracle might happen.

"No; that will never do," said the lake. "Let us rather make a bargain. I am fond of collecting pearls, and your eyes are the two brightest pearls I have seen. If you will cry them out for me I will carry you across to the big hothouse where Death lives and tends his flowers and trees, each of which is a human life."

"Oh, what would I not give to reach my child!" said the weeping mother. And she continued to weep still more, till her eyes sank to the bottom of the lake and became two precious pearls; and the lake lifted her up as if she sat in a swing, and carried her deftly to the shore on the other side, where there stood a wonderful house many miles long. One could not tell whether it was a mountain with forests and caverns, or whether it had been built; but the unhappy mother could not see it, for she had cried her eyes out.

"Where shall I find Death, who took away my little child?" she asked.

"He has not returned yet," said the old woman who went about tending the plants and flowers in Death's large hothouse. "How did you find your way here, and who has helped you?"

"God has helped me," she said. "He is merciful, and you must be merciful, too. Where shall I find my little child?"

"I do not know it," said the woman; "and you cannot see. Many flowers and trees have withered away during the night. Death will soon come and transplant them. You know, of course, that every human being has a life-tree or life-flower, according as one's fate has been decided. They look like other plants, but they have hearts which beat. Children's hearts also beat. Go and search for it. Perhaps you will know your child's; but what will you give me if I tell you what else you should do?"

"I have nothing to give," said the distressed mother ; "but I will go to the end of the world for you."

"I have nothing to do there," said the woman ; "but you can give me your long black hair. You know yourself it is beautiful, and I like it. You shall have my white hair instead, and that is something."

"Is that all you ask?" she said. "I give it you gladly." And she gave her her beautiful black hair, and received the old woman's snow-white hair in return.

They then went into the great hothouse of Death, where flowers and trees grew so strangely together. There were delicate hyacinths under glass shades, and large round peonies side by side ; there grew water-plants — some looked fresh, others sickly ; the water-sloes settled on them, and black crayfish clung to their stems. There were beautiful palm-trees, oaks, and plane-trees ; there were parsley and fragrant thyme. Every tree and every flower had its name, each of them representing the life of a human being, of people still alive, — some in China, some in Greenland, — all over the world. There were large trees in small pots. They looked quite stunted in their growth, while the roots were nearly bursting the pots. In several places there were also tiny sickly flowers in rich soil, with moss around the stem, well nursed and tended. But the sorrowing mother bent down over all the smallest plants, and heard the human heart beating within them, and, among millions, she recognized that of her child.

"Here it is!" she cried, and stretched out her hand over a little blue crocus which hung drooping to one side.

"Do not touch the flower," said the old woman, "but remain here, and when Death comes — he may be here before we know of it — do not let him pull up the plant ; threaten that you will do the same with the other flowers. That will frighten him, for he has to account to God for every one of them. None must be pulled up before he has given his permission."

All at once an ice-cold blast came rushing past them, and the blind mother could feel it was Death that had come.

"How did you find your way here?" he asked. "How could you travel faster than I?"

"I am a mother," she said.

And Death stretched out his long hand toward the little delicate flower ; but she kept her hands closely around it — so closely, and yet so anxious that she should not touch any of its leaves. Then Death breathed upon her hands. The breath was colder than the cold wind, and her hands sank down benumbed.

"You can do nothing against me," said Death.

"But God can," she said.

"I only do what he wills," said Death. "I am his gardener. I take

ON THE OTHER SIDE OF THE LAKE STOOD A WONDERFUL HOUSE,—IT WAS
DEATH'S LARGE HOT-HOUSE.

all his flowers and trees and plant them out in the great Garden of Paradise in the unknown land; but how they grow there and what it is like there, I dare not tell you."

"Give me back my child," said the mother, weeping and beseeching. Then all at once she seized hold of two flowers close to her with both her hands, and cried to Death:

"I will tear up all your flowers, for I am in despair."

"Do not touch them," said Death. "You say that you are unhappy, and now you would make another mother just as unhappy."

"Another mother!" said the poor woman, and let go both the flowers.

"There are your eyes," said Death. "I have fished them up out of the lake; they shone too brightly. I did not know they were yours; take them back,—they are now brighter than before,—and then look down into the well close to you. I will tell you the names of the two flowers which you were going to tear up, and you will see their whole future, the course of their whole human life. You will see what you wanted to disturb and destroy."

And she looked down into the well. It was a pleasure to her to see how the one became a blessing to the world, and how much happiness and joy grew up around it. And then she saw the life of the other. It was a life of sorrow and want, of fear and misery.

"Both are the will of God," said Death.

"Which of them is the flower of misfortune, and which is the blessed one?" she asked.

"I must not tell you that," said Death; "but this much you may know — one of the flowers was that of your own child. It was your child's fate, your own child's future you saw."

The mother uttered a shriek of terror, and cried: "Which of them was my child? Tell me! oh, tell me! Save the innocent being. Save my child from all that misery. Rather take it away. Carry it into the Kingdom of God. Forget my tears, forget all my prayers and everything I have said and done."

"I do not understand you," said Death. "Will you have back your child, or shall I take it to the place you know not of?"

The mother wrung her hands, fell on her knees and prayed to God: "Hear me not when I pray against thy will, which is always the best. Hear me not, hear me not!" And she buried her head in her lap, while Death carried away her child into the unknown land.

THE EMPEROR'S NEW CLOTHES

THE EMPEROR WAS SO FOND OF NEW CLOTHES THAT HE SPENT
ALL HIS MONEY ON DRESSES.

THE EMPEROR'S NEW CLOTHES

MANY years ago there lived an emperor who was so fond of fine new clothes that he spent all his money on finery and dresses. He did not care anything about his soldiers, nor did he care about going to the play, or driving in the park, except when he wanted to show off his new clothes. He had a dress for every hour of the day; and just as we should say of a king that he is in the council-room, so they always used to say the emperor was in his dressing-room.

In the great city where he lived there was always great merriment going on; every day a number of strangers arrived there. One day two vagabonds came to the city; they called themselves weavers, and said they knew how to weave the most splendid cloth one could imagine. Not only were the colors and the patterns something out of the common, but the clothes which were made from these materials possessed the wonderful property of becoming invisible to every one that was not fit for his office, or was hopelessly stupid.

"They must be fine clothes indeed!" thought the emperor; "by wearing them I could find out which men in my empire are not fit for their places. I should be able to know the wise from the stupid. Yes; I must have that cloth made for me at once." And he gave the two vagabonds a lot of money on account, so that they should begin with their work at once. They put up two looms, and pretended that they were working, but they had really nothing at all on the looms. They kept on ordering the finest silk and the costliest gold; this they put in their own bags, and worked away at the empty looms till late at night.

"I should like to know how much of the cloth they have ready now," thought the emperor; but he felt a little uneasy at the thought that whoever was stupid or not suited for his place could not see the cloth. He thought, of course, that he need not be afraid for his own part; but he would send somebody first to see how they were getting on. Everybody knew about the wonderful property which the cloth possessed, and all were anxious to find out how bad or stupid their neighbors were.

"I will send my old and honest minister to the weavers," thought the emperor; "he can best see what the cloth looks like, for he has sense, and no one knows his business better than he." Well, the old and trusty minister went into the room where the two vagabonds sat working at the empty looms. "Dear me!" thought the old minister, and opened his eyes; "I can't see anything!" But he did not say this aloud. The two vagabonds asked him to be so kind as to come nearer, and inquired if he did not like the fine pattern and the beautiful colors. They pointed to the empty looms; and the poor old minister opened his eyes still more, but he could not see anything, because there was nothing to see. "Dear, dear!" he thought, "am I really so stupid? I should never have thought it. Nobody must know it, however. Am I not fit for my place? No; it would never do to say I cannot see the cloth." "Well, you don't say anything about it," said one of the weavers. "Oh, it is really fine—quite charming," said the old minister, and looked through his eye-glasses; "what a pattern, and what colors! Yes; I shall tell the emperor that I am very much pleased with it." "Well, we are pleased to hear that," said the weavers; and they then called the colors by their names, and spoke about the wonderful pattern. The old minister listened to them very attentively, so that he could repeat what they said when he returned to the emperor; and this he did.

The vagabonds now asked for more money, and silk and gold, which they said they wanted to complete the work. However, they put everything in their bags; not a thread came on the looms, but they kept on weaving as before at the empty looms. The emperor soon sent another trusty councilor to see how the weaving was going on, and whether the cloth would soon be ready. It fared, however, with him as with the minister; he looked and looked, but there was nothing but the empty looms. He could see nothing at all.

"Well, is not this a fine piece of cloth?" said the two vagabonds; and

THEN THE EMPEROR WENT IN THE PROCESSION UNDER THE SPLENDID CANOPY.
"BUT HE HASN'T GOT ANYTHING ON!" CRIED A LITTLE CHILD.

they pretended to show him the cloth, and described to him the fine pattern which did not exist at all. "I am not stupid," thought the councilor; "it is my good office I am not fit for. It is very provoking, but I must not let it out!" So he praised the cloth, which he did not see, and expressed his delight at the beautiful colors and the splendid pattern. "Yes, it is very charming," he said to the emperor.

All the people in the town were talking about the splendid cloth. At last the emperor wished to see it himself while it was still on the loom. With a whole company of chosen men, amongst whom were the two honest councilors who had been there before, he proceeded to the two cunning vagabonds, who were now working away with all their might, but without any thread or materials whatever.

"Is it not magnificent?" said the two honest councilors. "Does your majesty see what a pattern and what colors?" And then they pointed to the empty looms, because they believed that the others were sure to see the cloth. "What can this be?" thought the emperor. "I see nothing. This is really dreadful. Am I stupid? Am I not fit to be emperor? This is the most terrible thing that could have happened to me. Oh, yes; it is very fine," said the emperor; "it has my entire approbation." And he nodded approvingly, and looked at the empty looms. He would not say that he could not see anything. The whole of his suite looked and looked, but could not see anything. They said, however, just like the emperor, "It is very fine," and they advised him to wear the new clothes made from the splendid stuff for the first time at the great procession which was to take place soon. "It is magnificent, splendid, excellent!" was echoed from mouth to mouth, and everybody seemed to be greatly delighted. The emperor gave each of the vagabonds a cross of a knightly order to wear, and gave them also the title of "Weavers to the Emperor."

The whole night before the day when the procession was to take place the vagabonds were sitting up working, and had more than sixteen candles lighted. The people could see they were busy getting the emperor's new clothes ready. They pretended to be taking the cloth off the looms. They were cutting in the air with large scissors; and were sewing with needles without any thread, and said at last: "See, there are the clothes ready."

The Emperor, with his most distinguished courtiers, came himself to their place, and the vagabonds would lift one arm as if they were holding something, and said, "See, here are the trousers; here is the coat; here is the cloak," and so on. "It is as light as a cobweb," they said; "one would think one had nothing on at all; but that's just the beauty of it." "Yes," said all the courtiers; but they could not see anything, because there was nothing. "Will your imperial majesty please to take off your clothes?" said the vagabonds; "and we will put the new clothes on your majesty here in front of the large looking-glass."

The emperor took off his clothes and the vagabonds pretended to give him piece by piece of the new clothes, which they were supposed to have ready. They appeared to be fastening something round his waist; that was the train to the cloak, and the emperor turned round in all directions before the looking-glass. "How well they look! how splendidly they fit!" said all. "What a pattern! what colors! That is a costly dress."

"They are waiting outside with the canopy which is to be borne over your majesty in the procession," said the master of the ceremonies.

"Yes, I am quite ready," said the emperor. "Does it not fit me well?" And then he turned round once more before the looking-glass, to make the people believe that he was really admiring his finery. The chamberlains who were to carry the train fumbled along the floor with their hands, as if they were gathering up the train of the cloak. They walked as if they were carrying something in their hands, because they were afraid that the people should think they could not see anything.

And thus the emperor went in the procession, under the splendid canopy. And all the people in the streets and in the windows said, "Dear me! what matchless new clothes the emperor has! What a splendid train he has to his cloak! How beautifully they fit him!" Nobody would admit that he saw nothing, because in that case he had not been fit for his office, or he must be very stupid. No other clothes of the emperor had been such a success.

"But he has n't got anything on!" cried a little child. "Dear me! just listen to what the little innocent says," said the father; and the people whispered to each other what the child had said. "He has n't got anything on!" shouted all the people at last. This made the emperor's flesh creep, because he thought they were right; but he thought, "I must keep it up through the procession, anyhow." And he walked on still more majestically, and the chamberlains walked behind and carried the train, which did not exist at all.

THE SNOW MAN

"IT'S SO DELIGHTFULLY COLD!" SAID THE SNOW MAN.

THE SNOW MAN

"I AM creaking all over, it's so delightfully cold," said the snow man. "This wind does blow life into one, and no mistake. How that glowing thing up there is staring at me!" It was the sun he meant; it was just about setting. "He shall not get me to wink; I can keep the bits right enough."

He had two large three-cornered bits of tile stuck in his head for eyes, and for mouth he had a piece of an old rake, which was his teeth.

He came into the world amidst the cheering of the boys, and was greeted with the tinkling of bells and cracking of whips from the passing sledges.

The sun went down and the full moon rose round and large, bright and beautiful, in the blue sky.

"There he is again from another quarter," said the snow man. He thought it was the sun that showed himself again.

"I have cured him of staring. Now he can hang there and give me light so that I can see myself. If I only knew how I could manage to move about! I should like so much to move about. If I could, I should now be sliding on the ice down yonder, as I have seen the boys doing; but I don't know how to run."

"Go! go!" barked the old yard-dog. He was somewhat hoarse; he had been so ever since he was a house-dog and lay under the stove. "The sun will soon teach you to run. I noticed that with your predecessor last year, and with his predecessors as well. Go! go! They are all gone."

"I do not understand you, comrade," said the snow man. "Will that thing up there teach me to run?" (He meant the moon.) "Well, I noticed he ran just now when I stared hard at him. Now he steals on us from another quarter."

"You don't know much," said the yard-dog; "but then you have only just been put together. What you now see is called the moon, and the one that you saw before was the sun. He will come back again to-morrow. He will soon teach you to run down into the ditch near the ramparts. We shall soon have a change in the weather. I can feel it in my left hind leg; there is a shooting pain in it. We shall have a change."

"I do not understand you," said the snow man; "but I have a presentiment that it is something unpleasant you mean. He that glowed and went down, whom you call sun, is not my friend, either; my instinct tells me that."

"Go! go!" barked the yard-dog, and walked round three times, and then went into his kennel and lay down to sleep.

There really came a change in the weather. In the early morning a thick clammy fog lay over the whole district. At dawn it began to clear up; but the wind was icy cold, and a regular frost seemed to have set in. What a sight it was when the sun rose! All the trees and bushes were covered with hoar-frost. They looked like a whole forest of white corals, as if all the branches were overloaded with sparkling white flowers. The innumerable delicate little shoots which we do not see in the summer time on account of the luxuriant foliage were now every one of them visible, and looked like sparkling white lace-work, and as if a bright luster streamed out from every branch. The weeping birch waved in the wind. There was life in it, as in the trees in summer time. It was wonderfully beautiful in the sunshine.

How everything sparkled! It seemed as if everything was powdered with diamond dust, and as if large diamonds were sparkling all over the snow that covered the ground; or one might imagine that innumerable little candles were burning with a light still whiter than the white snow.

"How wonderfully beautiful it is!" said a young girl, who stepped out into the garden in company with a young man, and stopped close to the snow man, where they stood looking at the glittering trees. "There is no finer sight to be seen in the summer," she said, and her eyes sparkled.

"And such a fellow as this one is not to be seen at all," said the young man, pointing to the snow man. "He is splendid!"

The young girl laughed, nodded to the snow man, and then danced away over the snow with her friend. The snow creaked under their feet, as if they walked on starch.

"Who were those two?" asked the snow man of the yard-dog. "You have been longer here than I have. Do you know them?"

"Of course I do," said the yard-dog. "She strokes me, and he gives me bones. I should not think of biting either of them."

"But what are they?" asked the snow man.

"Lover-r-rs," said the yard-dog. "They are going to move into the same kennel and gnaw bones together. Go! go!"

"Are those two as important as you or I?" asked the snow man.

"They belong to the family," said the yard-dog. "One does n't know much, of course, when one was born only yesterday. I can see that by you. I am old and experienced. I know everybody in this house, and I

"GO! GO!" BARKED THE OLD YARD-DOG. "THE SUN WILL SOON TEACH YOU TO RUN.
I NOTICED THAT WITH YOUR PREDECESSOR LAST YEAR."

remember the time when I did not stand here in the cold, chained up. Go! go!''

"The cold is delightful," said the snow man. "Go on with your story; go on! But you must not rattle so with your chain, for it makes me feel shaky."

"Go! go!" barked the yard-dog. "They tell me I was once a pretty little puppy. I lay on a velvet cushion, or in the ladies' laps. They kissed me on the nose, and wiped my paws with embroidered handkerchiefs. They called me 'Beauty' and 'Popsy Wopsy,' but then I grew too big for them, and they gave me to the housekeeper. I had to go to the basement. You can see right down there from where you are standing; you can look down into the room where I was the master; for that 's what I was at the housekeeper's. It was not, of course, such a grand place as upstairs, but it was much more comfortable down there; I was not mauled and dragged about by the children as upstairs. I had just as good food as before, and more of it. I had my own cushion, and then there was a stove, the finest thing in the world at this time of the year. I crept right under it and got out of the way. Ah, that stove — I still dream about it! Go! go!''

"Does a stove look so beautiful, then?" asked the snow man. "Is it at all like me?"

"No, it is just the reverse of you. It is black as coal, and has a long neck with a brass drum to it. It eats firewood till the flames reach right out of its mouth. Whether you are beside it, close to it, or under it, it gives no end of comfort. You can see it through the window from where you are standing."

And the snow man looked and saw a black polished object with a brass drum and the light shining out through an opening. The snow man felt a strange emotion within him; it was a feeling he could not account for, but which all people know who are not snow men.

"And why did you leave her?" said the snow man. He felt that the stove must belong to the female sex. "How could you leave such a place?"

"I was obliged," said the yard-dog; "they turned me out of doors and chained me up here. I had bitten the youngest boy in the leg, because he kicked away the bone I was gnawing. Bone for bone, thought I; but they took it in bad part, and from that time I have been standing here chained up, and have lost my voice. Just listen — how hoarse I am! Go! go! That was the end of it all."

The snow man did not listen any longer; he was continually looking down into the basement, into the housekeeper's room, where the stove was standing on its four iron legs. It was of the same size as the snow man.

"I feel such a strange crackling within me," he said. "Shall I never be able to get down there? It is an innocent wish, and our innocent wishes ought surely to be fulfilled. It is my highest wish, my only wish, and it would almost be unjust if it were not granted. I must get there, I must lean against her, even if I have to break the window."

"You 'll never get there," said the yard-dog; "and if you did get near the stove, you would be gone — gone!"

"I am as good as gone," said the snow man. "I am breaking up, I think."

The snow man stood the whole day looking in through the window. When the twilight had set in the room looked still more inviting; the stove threw out such a pleasant light — more pleasant than the moon, or even the sun, could throw out; such as only a stove can do when there is anything in it. When the door of the room was opened, the flame would dart out through the opening, as was its custom; the snow man's white face blushed crimson, while a red glare shone out from his bosom.

"I cannot stand it!" he said. "How it does suit her to stretch out her tongue!"

The night was long, but it did not appear so to the snow man; he stood buried in his own pleasant thoughts, and they froze till they crackled.

In the morning the window-panes in the basement were frozen over with the most beautiful ice flowers that any snow man could desire, but they shut out the stove from his sight. The ice on the panes would not thaw, and he could not see her. It creaked and it crackled; it was just the kind of frosty weather that would please a snow man, but he was not pleased; he could and ought to have felt happy, but he was not happy — he was stove-sick.

"That 's a dangerous complaint for a snow man," said the yard-dog. "I have suffered from it myself, but I have got over it. Go! go! Now we are going to have a change of weather."

And the weather changed; a thaw had set in. The thaw increased, the snow man decreased. He did not say anything, he did not complain, and that is a certain sign. One morning he fell to pieces. Something like a broomstick stuck out of the ground where he had stood. It was the one round which the boys had built him up.

"Now I can understand about his great longing!" said the yard-dog. "The snow man has had a stove-rake inside him; it was that which moved in him; now he has got over it. Go! go!"

And soon the winter was over too.

"Go! go!" barked the yard-dog; but the little girls in the house sang:

> "Shoot forth, sweet woodruff, so stately and fresh;
> Hang out, willow-tree, your long woolen locks;
> Come, cuckoo and lark, come hither and sing —
> Ere February's close we already have spring;
> I, too, will sing, 'Cuckoo! Quivit!'
> Shine, dear sun, come often and shine!"

And then nobody thought any more about the snow man.

"EVERYTHING IN ITS PROPER PLACE"

THEY WERE THE PORTRAITS OF THE PEDDLER AND THE GOOSE-GIRL, FROM
WHOM THE WHOLE FAMILY DESCENDED.

"EVERYTHING IN ITS PROPER PLACE"

IT is over a hundred years ago!   Behind the forest near the great lake
stood an old country mansion, around which was a deep moat where
rushes and reeds grew in abundance.   Near the bridge at the entrance
gate stood an old willow-tree which leaned over the reeds.

From the narrow way under the hill came the sound of bugles and
tramping of horses' feet, and therefore the little goose-girl hastened to get
her geese on one side of the bridge before the hunting party came galloping up.   They came at such a pace that she had to jump up quickly on to
one of the big stones near the bridge to avoid being ridden over.   She
was scarcely more than a child.   She was slightly and delicately built,

with a beautiful expression and two lovely bright eyes; but the baron took no notice of all this. As he galloped past her, he took hold of the top of his whip, and in rough play gave her a push with the butt-end, so that she fell backward into the ditch.

"Everything in its proper place," he shouted; "into the mud with you!" And then he laughed at what he thought was wit, and the rest of the company joined in. They shouted and screamed, and the dogs barked. In fact it was truly, "Rich birds come rushing." But goodness knows how rich he was. The poor girl, in trying to save herself as she fell, caught hold of one of the drooping branches of the willow-tree, by which she was able to keep herself from sinking into the mire, and as soon as the company and the dogs had disappeared through the gate she tried to drag herself out; but the branch broke off at the top, and she would have fallen back among the reeds if a strong hand from above had not seized her at the same moment. It was that of a peddler, who had seen what had happened some distance off, and now hastened to help her.

"Everything in its proper place," he said jokingly, mimicking the baron, as he pulled her up on to a dry place. The broken branch he put back against the place where it had been broken off; but "in its proper place" does not always answer, and so he stuck the branch into the soft ground. "Grow, if you can, and furnish a good rod for them up at the mansion yonder;" for he would have liked to see the baron and his companions running the gantlet in earnest. He then walked up to the mansion and went in; but he did not go into the grand rooms—he was too humble for that. He went to the servants' hall, where all the servants looked at his goods and bargained with him, while from the festive board upstairs came the sound of shouting and bawling, which was intended for singing. They were not in a state to produce anything better. Then followed laughter, accompanied by the howling of dogs. There was great feasting and carousing going on. Wine and old ale foamed in jugs and glasses. The dogs were allowed to feast with their masters; and some of them, after having their snouts wiped with their long ears, were even kissed by them. The peddler was asked to come up with his wares, but only to be made game of. The wine had entered their heads, and their senses had left them. They poured out ale into a stocking for him, so that he could drink with them; but he must drink quickly. This was considered very funny, and caused much merriment. Whole herds of cattle, farms, and peasants were staked and lost.

"Everything in its proper place," said the peddler when he had got safely away from the "Sodom and Gomorrah," as he called it. "The broad highway is my right place. I did not feel quite myself up there." And the little goose-girl, who looked after the geese, nodded to him from her place at the stile.

Days passed, and weeks passed, when it was found that the branch that had been broken off the willow-tree, and which the peddler had stuck into the ditch, remained fresh and green, and had even put forth fresh shoots. The little goose-girl could see that it had taken root, and she rejoiced greatly, for it was her tree, she thought.

The tree made good progress; but everything else at the mansion was going to ruin through riotous living and gambling — two wheels on which it is not easy to run securely.

Six years had scarcely passed when the squire had to wander forth, a beggar, with bag and stick in hand. The estate was bought by a rich peddler. It was the very man whom the baron had made game of, and to whom he had offered ale in a stocking; but honesty and industry are like favorable winds to a ship, and had helped the peddler, who was now master of the mansion. From that time card-playing was no longer permitted any more there. "They are bad reading," the master would say. "They are the devil's work. When he saw the Bible for the first time he wanted something to counteract it, and so he invented card-playing."

The new master took a wife, and who do you think she was? Why, the little goose-girl, who had always been so well-behaved, so pious and good. In her new clothes she looked just as grand and beautiful as if she had been of high birth. How did all this happen? Well, that's too long a story in these busy times; but it did happen, and the most important part of it has yet to be told.

There were now happy and prosperous times at the old mansion. The mistress managed all the household affairs, and the master the estate. Blessings seemed to overflow. Where there are riches, riches are sure to follow. The old mansion was repaired and painted, the moat was cleared out and fruit-trees were planted in it. Everything looked bright and cheerful. The floors were as clean as a kitchen dresser. In the large hall the mistress sat in the winter evenings, with all her maids around her, spinning woolen and linen yarn; and every Sunday evening the justice of the peace, for the peddler had been made one,—a dignity which had been conferred upon him only in his old age,—would read aloud from the Bible. The children grew up—for children had come—and were well educated; but they were not all equally gifted, which may be the case in every family.

But the willow branch outside had grown to be quite a fine tree, rearing its head aloft, free and undisturbed. "That is our genealogical tree," the old people said; "and that tree must be held in honor and respect." This they told to all their children, even to those who were not gifted with clever heads.

A hundred years had now rolled by. It was in our time. The lake had grown into a marsh, and the old mansion had almost disappeared. A long, narrow pool of water, with the remains of stone walls along the edges, was all that remained of the deep moat, and here still stood a fine old tree with its drooping branches. It was the "genealogical tree" which stood there, an example of how beautiful a willow-tree may become if left to itself. The trunk had certainly a big crack in it, right from the root to the crown, and the storm had given it a little twist; but it remained firm in its place, and in all the cracks and crevices into which the wind had blown earth grew grasses and flowers, especially near the top where the large branches shot out in all directions. There was a kind of miniature hanging garden, with raspberry bushes and chickweed, and even a little mountain ash had taken root there, and stood erect and elegant among the branches of the old willow-tree, which reflected itself in the dark water when the wind had driven all the duckweed into a corner of the pond. Close by a narrow path led across the fields to the manor.

High on the hill and close to the forest stood the new mansion. It was a large and magnificent building, with a beautiful outlook from the windows, the glass of which was so clear and transparent that one could hardly believe there were any panes in them at all. The large flight of steps in front of the door looked like a bower of roses and large-leaved plants. The lawn was as fresh and green as if every blade of grass had been tended morning and evening. In the drawing-room hung costly pictures; and there were chairs and sofas covered with silk and velvet which seemed to run on their own legs, tables with bright marble tops, and books in morocco bindings with gilt edges. Yes; they must really be wealthy people who lived here. They were people of position. Here lived the baron and his family.

Everything in the house was in harmony. The motto of the family was still, "Everything in its proper place." Therefore all the pictures which at one time were the honor and glory of the old house had now been hung in the passage leading to the servants' hall. They looked like old lumber, especially the two old portraits—the one of a man in a rose-colored coat and a wig, the other of a lady with powdered, high-dressed hair and a red rose in her hand, while both were surrounded with a wreath of willow leaves. There were a good many round holes in the two pictures, because the young barons were in the habit of using the two old folks as a target when shooting with their cross-bows. They were the portraits of the justice of the peace and his wife, from whom the whole family descended.

"But they did not properly belong to our family," said one of the young barons. "He was a peddler and she a goose-girl. They were not like papa and mama."

The pictures were only old lumber, and as the motto was, "Everything in its proper place," the great-grandfather and great-grandmother were sent to the passage leading to the servants' hall.

The son of the clergyman was tutor to the family. He was out walking one day with the young barons and their eldest sister, who had just been confirmed, when they followed the path that led down to the old willow-tree. As they walked on she gathered a bouquet of wild flowers of the field, "each in its proper place," so that the bouquet became altogether a thing of beauty.

At the same time she listened attentively to everything the clergyman's son said. She was pleased to hear him talk about the elements of nature and the great men and women in history. She was of a good and healthy disposition, and possessed great nobility of mind, and a heart which fully appreciated all that God had created.

They came to a halt down by the old willow-tree. The youngest of the barons wanted to have a flute cut for him, such as he had often had made from other willow-trees, and the clergyman's son therefore broke off a branch.

"Oh, don't do that," said the young baroness, but she spoke too late. "It is our famous old tree. I love it very much. And therefore they laugh at me at home, but I don't mind. There is an old tale attached to this tree."

And then she told him everything that we already know about the tree, about the old mansion, about the goose-girl and the peddler who first met here and became the ancestors of the grand family and the young baroness.

"They would not let themselves be ennobled, the good old folks!" she said. "They always used to say, 'Everything in its proper place,' and they did not think they would be in their proper place if they let themselves be exalted through money. It was their son, my grandfather, who was made a baron. He was a very learned man, and was much respected and appreciated by princes and princesses, and was present at all their festivals. The others at home think most of him; but to me — I don't know why — there is something about the old couple which draws my heart to them. It must have been so pleasant, so patriarchal in the old mansion, where the mistress of the house sat at the spinning-wheel with all her maids around her, and the venerable master read aloud from the Bible."

"They must have been excellent people — sensible people," said the clergyman's son; and then they began talking about nobility and commoners, and one would scarcely have thought he belonged to the latter by the way he spoke about the nobility.

"It is a good thing to belong to a family which has distinguished itself; to possess, so to speak, in one's blood the incentive to lead the way in what is great and noble. It is pleasant to bear the name of a family which is like a card of admission to the best circles. Nobility represents what is pure and lofty, and is a golden coin which has received the stamp that indicates its value. It is one of the mistakes of our day, into which many of our poets have naturally fallen, to proclaim that everything connected with nobility must be bad and stupid, and that among the poor, the lower you go, the more sterling qualities do you find. But that is not my opinion, for it is altogether wrong—quite wrong. In the higher classes you will find many beautiful and striking traits of character. My mother told me of one, and I could tell you of many more.

"She was on a visit to a grand house in town. I think my grandmother had nursed the lady of the house. My mother was in the room with the fine old baron when he noticed an old woman on crutches down in the courtyard. She used to come every Sunday to get a penny. 'There comes the poor old woman,' said the baron. 'She has great difficulty in getting about;' and before my mother could understand his intentions he was out of the door and down the stairs; he, the old excellency of seventy years, went down himself to the poor woman to save her the trouble of going up the troublesome stairs for the trifling assistance she came for. This is, of course, only a trivial incident, but, like the 'widow's mite,' it came from the bottom of the heart,—a voice from the very depths of humanity,—and that 's the moral the poet ought to point. Just in our times this is what he ought to sing about. It does good, it soothes and reconciles mankind. But when a person, because he is of good birth and has a pedigree, like the Arabian horses, prances on his hind legs and neighs in the streets, and says, on coming into his room after a commoner has been there, 'People from the street have been in here!' that shows nobility in its decay, for then it has become a mere mask of the kind which Thespis made for himself. Such a person people only laugh at and hand him over to satire."

This was the tutor's discourse. It was somewhat long, but in the meantime the flute had been cut.

There was a great party at the mansion. Many guests from the neighborhood and the capital were present. Some of the ladies were tastefully dressed, while others showed no taste at all. The great hall was quite full of people. The clergy of the district stood respectfully grouped together in a corner. They gave one the impression that there was going to be a funeral. All were, however, intent upon enjoying themselves. But the entertainment had not yet commenced.

A concert formed part of the program, and among the performers was the young baron, who had brought his willow flute with him, but he could not produce a note upon it, nor could his father; it was evidently quite useless.

There was music and there was song, but of the kind which the performers themselves enjoy most. Otherwise everything passed off nicely.

"You also play, I believe?" said a cavalier, whose only recommendation was that he was the son of his parents, addressing himself to the tutor. "You play the flute and make it yourself, I hear. It is genius

IT WAS A WONDERFUL FLUTE! IT WAS HEARD ALL OVER THE MANSION, IN THE GARDEN,
IN THE FOREST, AND FOR MANY MILES INTO THE COUNTRY.

which rules the world — which sits on the right side.   Heaven knows I try to follow the times.   You have to do that, you know.   You will delight us all with your little instrument, I 'm sure," he said, handing him the little flute which had been cut from the willow-tree down by the pool. Then he loudly announced that the tutor would oblige with a solo on the flute.

They evidently only wanted to make fun of him; so the tutor did not feel inclined to play, although he could perform very well on it.   But they pressed him and urged him, and at last he took the flute and put it to his lips.

It was a wonderful flute.   A tone was heard — a tone as sustained as that which one hears from a locomotive — yes, and even stronger.   It was heard all over the mansion, in the garden, and in the forest for many miles into the country.   And with the sound came a storm which roared, "Everything in its proper place!"   And then the baron flew, just as if he was carried by the wind, right out of the mansion and straight into the herdsman's cottage; and the herdsman flew up — not into the drawing-room: he could not get there — but up into the servants' hall, among the grand footmen who were strutting about in silk stockings.   And these proud fellows were almost paralyzed with horror on seeing such a common fellow daring to sit down at table among them.

But in the dining-hall the young baroness flew to the upper end of the table, where she worthily filled the seat of honor; and the clergyman's son got a seat next to her, and there the two sat as if they were a newly married couple.   An old count, one of the oldest families in the country, remained undisturbed in his seat of honor, for the flute was fair and just, as every one ought to be.

The witty cavalier, who was the cause of the flute having been played — he whose only recommendation was that he was the son of his parents — flew head over heels right among the poultry; but he was not the only one.

The flute was heard for a whole mile into the country, and many strange things happened.   A rich merchant and his family, who were driving in a coach and four, were blown right out of the coach, and could not even find a place behind it.   Two rich farmers who had grown too big to look after their fields were blown into the ditch.   It was a dangerous flute.   Fortunately, it burst at the first note, and that was a good thing.   It was put back in the player's pocket again, and "Everything was in its proper place."

The day after no one spoke of what had happened, and that is how we get the saying, "to pocket the flute."   Besides, everything was in its usual place again, with the exception of the two old pictures of the peddler and the goose-girl, which were now hanging in the drawing-room. They had been blown on to the walls there, and when one of the well-known connoisseurs said they were the works of a master, they were allowed to remain and were restored. They did not know before that they were worth anything, for how should they know?

Now they hung in a place of honor. "Everything in its proper place!" And that was now realized. Eternity is long—much longer than this story.

THE HAPPY FAMILY

THE SNAILS LIVE ON BURDOCK LEAVES, AND THAT IS WHY BURDOCKS
WERE PLANTED.

THE HAPPY FAMILY

THE biggest green leaf in our country is certainly the burdock leaf. If you hang one in front of you, it is almost large enough for an apron, and if you put it on your head, it would be just as useful in rainy weather as an umbrella, for it is so very big. A burdock never grows alone. No; where one grows there are many more. It is a lovely sight, and all this loveliness is, after all, only food for snails. In olden times grand folks made a fricassee of large white snails, which they thought tasted so delicious that they used to exclaim, "What a tasty morsel!" These snails lived on burdock leaves, and that is why burdocks came to be planted.

Now at the time of our story there was an old mansion where there lived people who did not eat snails any longer. The snails had quite died out, but the burdocks had not. They grew all over the walks and the beds in the garden till their growth could no longer be checked. It was a regular forest of burdocks. Here and there stood an apple-tree or a pear-tree; otherwise no one would have thought it was a garden. There were burdocks everywhere, and in among them lived two very old snails, the last survivors of the family.

They did not themselves know how old they were; but they could well remember that there had been many more of them, that they belonged to a family from foreign lands, and that the whole forest had been planted for them and theirs. They had never been outside the place, but they knew that there still existed something in the world which was called the mansion, and that up there one of them was boiled and became black, and was then placed on a silver dish; but what happened afterward they did not know. What it was like to be boiled and placed on a silver dish they could not very well imagine, but it was said to be very delightful and very grand. Neither the cockchafer, the toad, nor the earthworm, of whom they had made inquiries, could give any information. None of them had been boiled or placed on silver dishes.

The old white snails were the grandest beings in the world. This they knew. The forest had been planted for their sake, and the mansion existed so that they might be boiled and placed on a silver dish.

They lived very lonely and happily; and as they had no children of

465

their own, they had adopted a small, common snail, whom they brought up as their own child. But the little one would not grow, for he was only a common snail; but the old people, especially Mother Snail, thought she could see that he grew, and she asked Father Snail, in case he could not see it, if he would just feel the little snail's shell, which he did, and then he found that she was right.

One day it rained hard.

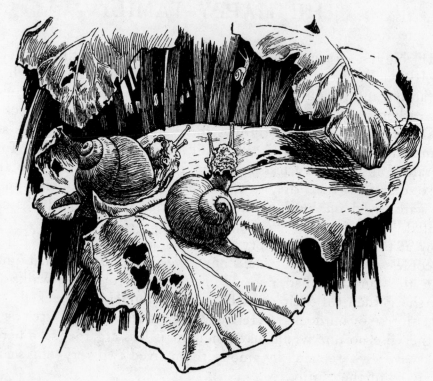

"I AM GLAD WE HAVE OUR OWN HOUSE," SAID MOTHER SNAIL, "AND THE LITTLE ONE
HAS ALSO HIS."

"Just listen to the pitter-patter on the burdocks," said Father Snail.

"And the drops are coming down," said Mother Snail. "They are running down along the stalk. You 'll see, we shall have the place wet. I am glad we have our own house, and the little one has also his. More has certainly been done for us than for all other creatures. One can see that we are the most important in the world. We have houses from our birth, and the burdocks are planted for our sake. I should like to know how far they extend and what there is beyond them."

"There is nothing beyond," said Father Snail. "It could not be better anywhere than here with us, and I have nothing to wish for."

"Well, yes," said Mother Snail. "I should like to go to the mansion, and be boiled and placed on a silver dish, just like all our ancestors. It is a great honor, you may be sure."

"The mansion is very likely in ruins," said Father Snail, "or it may be overgrown by burdocks, so that the people cannot get out. Besides, you need not be so impatient. You are always in such a hurry, and the little one is beginning to be just the same. Has he not for the last three days been trying to creep up that stalk? It makes me giddy when I look up at him."

"You must not scold us," said Mother Snail. "He is very careful how he creeps. He is sure to be a comfort to us, and we old people have nothing else to live for. But have you been thinking where we shall find a wife for him? Don't you think that far away in the burdock forest there may be some of our kin?"

"I think there are sure to be some black snails," said the old snail—"black snails without houses. But they are a very common lot, and very conceited besides. But we could commission the ants to do it. They are always running backward and forward, as if they had something to do, and they are sure to know of a wife for our little one."

"We know of a most lovely one for him," said the ants; "but we are afraid it would be of no use, for she is a queen."

"That does not matter," said the old ones. "Has she a house?"

"She has a palace," said the ants; "the most beautiful ant's palace, with seven hundred passages."

"Thanks," said Mother Snail. "Our son is not going into an ant-hill. If you know of nothing better, we shall commission the white gnats to find him a wife. They fly far and wide, in rain and sunshine, and they know the whole of the burdock forest."

"We have got a wife for him," said the gnats. "A hundred men's paces from here, on a gooseberry bush sits a little snail with a house. She is quite lonely, and old enough to be married. It is only a hundred men's paces from here."

"Well, let her come to him," said the old ones. "He has a whole forest of burdocks; she has only a bush." And so they fetched the little lady-snail. It took her eight days to get there; but that was just as it should be. One could then see she was one of the right sort. And then they had the wedding. Six glow-worms provided all the light they could. Otherwise it was a very quiet affair, for the old snail couple could not stand any carousing and merrymaking; but Mother Snail made a lovely speech, as Father Snail was too overcome to say anything. And so they gave the young couple the whole burdock forest as an inheritance, and said what they had always maintained: that it was the finest place in the world, and if they lived honestly and respectably, and multiplied themselves, they and their children might some day be taken to the mansion, and be boiled till they were black and placed on a silver dish.

After the speech had been made, the old couple crept into their house and never came out again. They slept the long sleep. The young snail

couple now ruled in the forest, and had a large progeny; but they were
never boiled, and were never placed on a silver dish. They therefore
came to the conclusion that the mansion was in ruins, and that all the
people in the world were dead; and, as nobody contradicted them, it must
be true. And the rain fell in heavy drops on the leaves of the burdocks,
in order to provide drum-music for their sake; and the sun shone, in order
to give the burdock forest color for their sake; and they were very happy,
and the whole family was happy, for that they really were.

THE SHADOW

THE SHADOW OF THE STRANGER FELL UPON THE WALL OF THE HOUSE OPPOSITE.

THE SHADOW

IN hot countries the sun can be very scorching indeed. The people there are as brown as mahogany, and in the very hottest countries they are black negroes. But the learned man from the cold regions, about whom you are now going to hear, had got only as far as the hot countries, where he thought he could roam about just as he did at home; but he soon found out his mistake. He and all sensible people had to keep indoors; shutters and doors were closed the whole day; one would have thought the whole house was asleep, or that there was nobody at home. The narrow street with the high houses, in which he lived, was so situated that the sun shone upon it from morning to night, till it became quite unbearable. The learned man from the cold regions, who was young and intelligent, felt as if he sat in a glowing oven. It soon began to tell upon him; he became quite thin. Even his shadow began to shrink, and grew much smaller than it had been at home; the sun seemed even to affect the shadow. They both seemed to revive in the evening, when the sun had gone down.

It was really a pleasure to see how the shadow, as soon as the light was brought into the room, stretched itself all the way up the wall and even along the ceiling, so long did it become; it had to stretch itself to gain strength. The learned man would sometimes go out on the balcony to stretch himself there, and as the stars began to appear in the bright, clear sky he felt life returning to him again. All the balconies—and in the hot countries every window has a balcony—were now filled with people, for air you must have, even if you have become accustomed to a heat that turns you as brown as mahogany. The streets in all directions became lively. Shoemakers and tailors—in fact everybody—moved out into the streets; tables and chairs were brought out, and candles—thousands of candles—were lighted; some would talk, others would sing, while the people walked up and down, and the carriages rolled past, and the donkeys with their tinkling bells pushed their way through the crowd. There were funerals with singing of hymns, the church bells rang, and the boys let off fireworks. Yes, there were indeed lively scenes in the streets.

Only in one house—in the one opposite to where the learned man lived—everything was quiet. Yet some one must be living there, for there were flowers on the balcony, which blossomed so beautifully in the sunshine, and this they could not have done unless they were watered; and as somebody would have to do this, there must be people in the house. Toward evening the door was opened; but the rooms were in darkness, especially the front room, while from the rooms farther in came the sound of music. The learned man from foreign lands thought the music was beautiful, but it may be it was only his imagination, for he thought that everything in the hot countries was beautiful; he only wished there had been no sun. His landlord said he did not know who had taken the house opposite; no people were to be seen there, and as for the music, he thought it was dreadfully monotonous. "It's just as if some one sat practising a piece which he could not master, and always the same piece. I suppose he thinks he will be able to master it at last; but he will never manage it, however long he may practise."

One night the stranger awoke; he was sleeping with the door leading to the balcony open, and the curtain before it was blown aside by the wind. He thought he saw a strange glare from the balcony of the house; all the flowers shone with the most lovely colors, and in the middle of them stood a beautiful, graceful maiden. It seemed as if a bright light also proceeded from her, which completely dazzled his eyes. But then he had opened them very wide indeed, and had only just awoke from his sleep. With one bound he was out of bed; he approached the window quietly, and peeped through the curtains; but the maiden was gone and the glare had disappeared; the flowers did not shine, but stood there as lovely as ever. The door was ajar, and from the inner rooms came the sounds of such soft and lovely music that one could not help falling into a sweet reverie; it all seemed like magic. Who lived there? Where was the real entrance? The whole of the ground floor was occupied by shops, and the people could not always be passing in and out through them.

One evening the stranger was sitting on his balcony; in the room behind him a light was burning, and so it was only natural that his shadow should fall upon the wall of the house opposite. Why! There it was sitting opposite to him among the flowers on the balcony, and whenever he moved the shadow also moved, which of course was only natural.

"I think my shadow is the only living thing one can see over yonder," said the learned man. "Look how comfortably it sits there among the flowers; the door is half open, the shadow might kindly go inside and look round the rooms, and then come and tell me what it had seen. Yes, you would be making yourself useful then," he said in fun. "Just step inside. Well, won't you?" he added, and nodded to the shadow, and the shadow nodded back to him. "Well, go then, but don't be long," he said, rising from his seat; and at the same time the shadow on the balcony opposite also rose. And when the stranger turned round to go in, the shadow also turned round; in fact, any close observer could plainly see that the shadow walked in through the half-open balcony door of the house opposite just as the stranger went into his room and drew down the long blinds.

Next morning the learned man went out to take his coffee and read the papers. "What is this?" he said, as he got out into the sunshine. "I don't appear to have any shadow. It must have left me last night and not come back. It's rather tiresome!"

It annoyed him, not so much because the shadow was gone, but because he knew that there was another story about a man without a shadow which everybody at home in the cold countries had heard of; and if the learned man now went back and told his story, they would say he was only palming off other people's stories as his own, and he did not care for that sort of thing. So he made up his mind not to say anything at all about it, which was only right and sensible.

In the evening he went out upon his balcony again; he had placed the light behind him, for he knew that a shadow always wants his master as a screen, but he could not lure it forth; he made himself little, he made himself big, but there was no shadow—no shadow appeared. He said "H'm! h'm!" but it was all of no use.

It was very annoying, but in hot countries everything grows so quickly, and after a week had passed by he noticed, to his great joy, that a new shadow was beginning to grow out of his legs when he came out into the sunlight, so that the root of it must have remained, after all. In three weeks he had quite a respectable shadow, which, when he set out homeward to the northern countries, grew more and more during the journey, till at last it became so long and big that half of it would have been sufficient.

The learned man returned home and began to write books about what is true in this world, and about what is good and what is beautiful; and days passed, and years passed—many, many years passed.

One evening, as he sat in his room, there came a gentle knock at the door.

"Come in!" he said; but no one came in. He then opened the door, and there stood before him such an exceedingly thin person that he felt quite uncomfortable. The stranger was, however, very elegantly dressed, so he thought he must be some great personage.

"To whom have I the honor of speaking?" asked the learned man.

"Ah! I thought as much," said the elegant person. "I thought you would not recognize me, I have gained so much body. I have actually gained flesh and clothes. You never thought you would see me so well off. Don't you know your old shadow? You never expected me to come back any more. I have got on remarkably well since last I was with you. I am well to do in every respect. If I want to buy myself free from service I can do it." And then he rattled a large bundle of valuable seals which were attached to his watch, and tugged at the massive gold chain he wore round his neck. How the diamond rings glittered on his fingers! And they were genuine.

"No, I cannot quite get over my surprise," said the learned man; "but what does it all mean?"

"Well, nothing of the ordinary kind," said the shadow; "but you yourself do not belong to ordinary folks, and I, as you know, have trodden in your footsteps since you were a child. As soon as you found I was old enough to go out alone in the world, I went my own way. I am now in the most brilliant circumstances; but a kind of longing came over me to see you once more before you die—for you must die, of course. I also wanted to see these parts again; for, after all, one does love one's native country. I know you have got another shadow in my place; have I got to pay him or you anything? If so, be good enough to let me know."

"No! Is it really thou?" said the learned man. "It is most remarkable. I should never have believed that one's old shadow could return again in the shape of a human being."

"But do tell me what I have got to pay you," said the shadow; "for I should not like to be in debt to any one."

"How canst thou talk like that?" said the learned man. "What debt can there possibly be to talk about? Be as free as any living being. I am exceedingly glad to hear of thy good fortune. Sit down, old friend, and tell me how it all happened, and what thou didst see in the house opposite where I lived in the hot countries."

"Yes, I don't mind telling you," said the shadow, and sat down; "but then you must promise me you will never tell any one in the town here, no matter where you may meet me, that I have been your shadow. I am thinking of getting engaged, for I have more than enough to support a family."

"Thou canst be quite easy on that point," said the learned man. "I will not tell anybody who thou really art. Here is my hand upon it. I promise it, and a man is as good as his word."

"And a shadow as good as his," said the shadow; for this was of course the right way for him to put it.

It was really very remarkable how much his appearance had become that of a man; he was dressed in black clothes of the very finest quality, and wore patent-leather boots and a hat which could be shut up so that you could see only the crown and the brim. Then there were the seals, the gold chain, and the diamond rings, which we already have mentioned. The shadow was in fact extremely well dressed, and it was just this which made him look so much like a human being.

"I 'll now begin my story," said the shadow, putting his feet with the patent-leather boots as firmly as he could upon the sleeve of the learned man's new shadow, which lay like a poodle at his feet. This was either

HE THEN OPENED THE DOOR, AND THERE STOOD BEFORE HIM SUCH AN EXCEEDINGLY
THIN PERSON THAT HE FELT QUITE UNCOMFORTABLE.

out of pride or to make the new shadow stick to his master, but it lay still and quiet in order to hear the better; it wanted to know how one could manage to become free and get on so well as to be one's own master.

"Do you know who lived in the house opposite to you?" asked the shadow. "Why, Poesy, the loveliest being in the world, lived there! I remained there three weeks, and it did me just as much good as if I had lived there a thousand years and read everything that was written in verse and prose; for, although I say it, it is the plain truth: I have seen everything, and I know everything!"

"Poesy!" cried the learned man. "Yes, yes! She often lives like a hermit in the great cities. Poesy! Yes, I saw her for one short moment, but my eyes were heavy with sleep. She stood on the balcony, radiant as the Northern lights. But tell me, do tell me! Thou wert on the balcony; thou didst enter through the door, and then——"

"Then I came into the anteroom," said the shadow. "You always used to sit and look across into it. There was no light there—only a kind of twilight; but one door after another stood open through a long suite of rooms and halls which were brilliantly lighted, and I should have been killed outright by the blaze of light if I had gone straight in to her ladyship; but I was prudent and took my time, and that is what one ought to do."

"And what didst thou see?" asked the learned man.

"I saw everything, and I will tell you all about it; but—and do not think it is pride on my part—as a free man, and with the knowledge I possess, not to speak of my good position and my affluent circumstances, I would rather you did not call me 'thou.'"[1]

"I beg your pardon," said the learned man. "It is an old habit which clings to me. You are quite right, and I shall remember. But now you must tell me everything you saw."

"Everything," said the shadow; "for I saw everything, and I know everything!"

"What was the innermost room like?" asked the learned man. "Was it like the cool forest? Was it like a sacred church? Were the rooms like the starlit sky when you stand on a high mountain?"

"Everything was there," said the shadow. "I did not go quite in; I remained in the anteroom in the twilight, but I had a very good place there. I saw everything, and I know everything! I have been to the Court of Poesy in the anteroom."

"But what did you see? Did all the gods of the ancients pass through the large halls? Did the heroes of old fight out their differences there? Did the sweet little children play about and tell their dreams?"

"I was there, as I have told you; and you will then understand that I

---

[1] In Denmark, as in many other Continental countries, only relations and intimate friends call each other "thou."

saw everything there was to be seen. If you had gone there you would not have become a human being; but I did. And at the same time I learned to know my innermost nature—what was born in me: my kinship to Poesy. During the time I was with you I did not think much about these things; but at sunrise and at sunset I always grew so wonderfully large, as you know, and in the moonlight I was almost more distinctly visible than yourself. I did not at that time understand my nature, but there, in the anteroom, it was revealed to me. I became a human being. When I went out, I had become mature; but you were no longer in the hot countries. I felt ashamed, as a human being, to go about in the state I was in. I wanted boots, I wanted clothes, and all the human varnish that makes the man. I betook myself to—well, I 'll tell you in all confidence, for you won't put it into any book—I betook myself to the sweet-stuff woman's petticoat, and under it I concealed myself. The woman little knew what she was concealing. I went out only in the evenings. I ran about the streets in the moonlight, I stretched myself up along the wall,—this tickles one's back so delightfully,—I ran up and down, and looked in through all the windows—through those highest up and on the drawing-room floor and in the roof. I looked in where no one else could look, and I saw what nobody ought to see. After all, the world is a wicked place. I would not be a human being if it were not an accepted fact that there is something in being one. I saw the most incredible things among the wives, among the husbands, among the parents, and among the darling little children. I saw," continued the shadow, "what nobody must know, but what all would so much like to know—about the evil doings of their neighbors. If I had written about it in a newspaper, how it would have been read! But I wrote direct to the persons themselves, and all the towns I came to became panic-stricken. The people were greatly afraid of me, and yet they were so exceedingly fond of me. The professors made me a professor; the tailors gave me new clothes, with which I am well supplied; the master of the mint coined money for me, and the women said I was very handsome. And then I became the man I am; and now I will say good-by. Here is my card. I live on the sunny side of the street, and I am always at home in rainy weather." And so the shadow took his leave.

"That was most remarkable," said the learned man.

Years and days passed by, and then the shadow called again.

"How are you getting on?" he asked.

"Alas!" said the learned man, "I am busy writing about what is true, about what is good, and what is beautiful, but nobody cares to hear anything about it. I am quite in despair, for I take it so much to heart."

"But I do not," said the shadow. "I am getting fat, and that is what one should try to become. You don't understand the world. You are making yourself ill over it. You must travel. I am going to take a trip this summer. Will you come with me? I should like to have a traveling companion. Will you come with me as my shadow? It would be a great pleasure to have you with me. I will pay all the expenses."

"This is rather too much," said the learned man.

"That is as you take it," said the shadow. "It will do you a great deal of good to travel. If you will be my shadow, you shall have everything free on the journey."

"This is really too much," said the learned man.

"But such is the way of the world," said the shadow; "and so it always will be." And so he left.

The learned man did not fare well at all. Sorrow and care pursued him, and what he said about the true, and the good, and the beautiful was no more valued by the majority of the people than a rose would be by a cow. And at last he fell ill.

"You look exactly like a shadow," people would say to him; and the learned man shuddered at the very thought of it.

"You must go to a watering-place," said the shadow, who had come to visit him; "there is no help for it. I will take you with me for old acquaintance' sake. I will pay the expenses, and you can write a description of it and amuse me a little on the journey. I must go to a watering-place. My beard does not grow as it should do. That is also an ailment, for one must have a beard. Be sensible now, and accept my offer. We shall travel like comrades, you know."

And so they set out on their journey. The shadow was now master, and the master was the shadow. They drove out together, they rode and walked together side by side or in front or behind one another, just as the sun stood in the sky. The shadow always knew how to look as the master, which the learned man did not seem to notice, for he was very good-natured, and of an exceedingly kind and gentle disposition. So he said one day to the shadow: "Since we have now become traveling companions, and have grown up together from our childhood, should we not drink to good-fellowship, and call each other 'thou'? It is far more sociable."

"There is something in that," said the shadow, who was now really the master. "It is very straightforward and well-meant of you to say so, and I will be just as well-meant and straightforward with you. You are a learned man, and you know all the vagaries of human nature. Some people cannot bear to touch brown paper because it makes them ill; others suffer terrible agonies if you scratch a nail against a pane of glass. I experience just the same sort of feeling on hearing you call me 'thou.' I feel as if I were crushed to the earth—very much the same as what I felt in my former relation to you. You see, it is a question of feeling, not of pride. I cannot very well let you say 'thou' to me, but I am quite willing to say 'thou' to you; and so I have met you half-way." And so the shadow addressed his former master as "thou."

"That is rather too bad," he thought, "that I must say 'you,' and he may call me 'thou.'" But he had now to put up with it.

So they arrived at a watering-place where there were many strangers, and among these there was a beautiful princess who was troubled with the complaint of being able to see too well, which makes one feel rather uneasy.

She discovered at once that the new arrival was quite a different personage from all the others. "He has come here to grow his beard, they say, but I can see the real reason—he is not able to cast a shadow."

She had now become quite curious about him, and so the next time she met him when taking her walk she entered at once into conversation with the stranger. As she was a princess, she was not obliged to stand on ceremony, but said straight out to him: "Your complaint is that you are not able to cast any shadow."

"Your royal highness must be on the highroad to recovery," said the shadow. "I know your complaint is that you see everything too well, but it has disappeared. You are cured. Now it happens that I have a shadow of quite an unusual kind. Have you not seen the person who always accompanies me? Other people have the usual kind of shadow, but I like something out of the common. We give our servants finer cloth for their liveries than we wear ourselves, and so I let my shadow dress up like a human being. You see, I have even given him a shadow. It is rather expensive, but I like to have something all to myself."

"What can he mean?" thought the princess. "Am I really cured? This watering-place is the best in the world. Water, in our times, does wonders. But I shall not leave here, for it is now beginning to get interesting, and I like this stranger exceedingly, if only his beard does not grow, for then he will go away."

In the evening the princess danced with the shadow in the great ball-room. She was light, but he was still lighter. Such a dancer she had never danced with before. She told him from what country she came; he knew it, and had been there himself, but she was not then at home. He had looked through the windows,—both the upper and lower ones,—and he had seen one thing and another, so he was able to answer the princess, and make such allusions that she was quite astonished. He must be the wisest man in the whole world, she thought, and she had the greatest respect for all his knowledge.

And then she danced with him again, and fell in love with him, which the shadow could very well see, for she was looking right through him. They then danced once more, and she was on the point of telling him of her love; but she was a prudent woman, and thought of her country and her kingdom, and of the many people she would one day rule over. "He is

THE PRINCESS AND THE SHADOW STEPPED OUT UPON THE BALCONY TO SHOW THEMSELVES,
AND TO HEAR THE PEOPLE SHOUT "HURRAH!" ONCE MORE.

a wise man," she said to herself, "and that is a good thing; and he dances beautifully, and that is also a good thing. But has he any profound knowledge? That is just as important. I shall have to examine him." And by and by she began, and asked him the most difficult questions—so difficult that she could not answer them herself, and the shadow made quite a wry face.

"You cannot give an answer to that," said the princess.

"Oh, I learned all that when I was a child," said the shadow. "I think that even my shadow over yonder by the door could answer them."

"Your shadow!" said the princess. "That would be most remarkable."

"Well, I will not say for certain," said the shadow, "but I should think so, since he has now followed me about for so many years and heard me speak so much—I should think so. But your royal highness must allow me to inform you that he is so proud of being taken for a human being that in order to put him into a good humor—and he must be that if he is to answer well—he must be treated just as if he were a human being."

"I must say I like that," said the princess.

And so she went over to the learned man near the door and spoke to him about the sun and the moon, and about men and women, about their outward and inward being; and he answered wisely and sensibly.

"What a man he must be who has such a wise shadow!" she thought. "It would be a real blessing to my people and my country if I chose him for my husband—and I shall do so."

And they soon came to an understanding, but no one was to know of it till she was back in her own kingdom.

"No one shall know—not even my shadow." And he had, no doubt, his own reasons for saying this.

And so they came to the country where the princess ruled.

"Just listen, my good friend," said the shadow to the learned man. "I am now as happy and as powerful as any one can be. I should now like to do something handsome for you. You shall always live with me at the palace, drive about with me in my royal carriage, and receive a hundred thousand dollars a year; but then you must let yourself be called shadow by one and all. You must not tell anybody you have ever been a human being, and once a year, when I sit on the balcony in the sunshine to show myself, you must lie at my feet as behoves a shadow. I may tell you I am going to marry the princess. This very evening the wedding will take place."

"No! This is really too bad!" said the learned man. "I will not and shall not do it. It would be deceiving the whole country, and the princess as well. I will tell everything—that I am the man and that you are the shadow; that you are only dressed up in men's clothes!"

"No one would believe you," said the shadow. "Be reasonable or I will call the guard."

"I will go straight to the princess," said the learned man.

"But I shall go first," said the shadow, "and you shall go to prison." And the learned man had to submit to this, for the guard obeyed the shadow, as they knew the princess was going to marry him.

"You tremble," said the princess when the shadow came into her presence. "Has anything happened? You must not make yourself ill, for we are going to have our wedding this evening."

"I have gone through the most terrible experience you can imagine," said the shadow. "Just fancy! Well, such a poor brain as that of a shadow cannot stand much. Only fancy! My shadow has gone mad. He thinks he is the man, and that I—just fancy!—that I am his shadow."

"It is terrible!" said the princess. "Has he been locked up?"

"He has. I am afraid he will never get well again."

"Poor shadow!" said the princess. "He must be very unhappy. It would be a mercy to relieve him of the bit of life he has left; and when I really come to think it over, I think it will be necessary to get rid of him quietly."

"It is a great pity, for he was a faithful servant," said the shadow, with something like a sigh.

"You have a noble character," said the princess.

In the evening the whole town was illuminated, and guns were fired—boom! boom!—and the soldiers presented arms. That was indeed a wedding! The princess and the shadow stepped out upon the balcony to show themselves and hear the people shout "Hurrah!" once more.

The learned man did not hear anything of all this, for they had made an end of him.

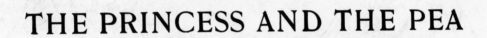

THE PRINCESS AND THE PEA

THE PRINCESS AND THE PEA

ONCE upon a time there was a prince. He wanted to marry a
princess, but she must be a real princess. So he traveled all
over the world to find such a princess, but everywhere there was
something in the way.

Princesses there were in abundance, but whether they were real
princesses he could not quite make out. There was always something
which was not quite right. So he returned home, and was so distressed,
for he wanted so much to find a real princess.

One evening a terrible storm set in.   It lightened and thundered, and the rain poured down in torrents.   It was really dreadful!   All at once there was a knock at the gate of the city, and the old king himself went to open it.

It was a princess who stood outside.   But, merciful heavens! what a sight she was, after all the rains and the terrible weather!   The water ran down her hair and clothes, and in at the toes of her shoes and out at the heels; and she told the king she was a real princess.

"Ah, well, we shall soon find that out," thought the old queen to herself; but she did not say anything.   She went into the bedroom, took off all the bedclothes, and put a pea at the bottom of the bed.   She then took twenty mattresses and put them on top of the pea, and next she put twenty eider-down beds on the top of the mattresses.

There the princess was to sleep that night.

In the morning they asked her how she had slept.

"Oh, horribly!" said the princess.   "I have scarcely closed my eyes the whole night.   Goodness knows what was in the bed.   I have been lying on something hard till I am blue and black all over my body.   It is really dreadful!"

Then they knew that she was a real princess, since she had felt the pea through the twenty mattresses and the twenty eider-down beds.   No one but a real princess could be so tender and delicate.

The prince then took her for his wife, for now he knew that he had got a real princess; and the pea was placed in the Art Museum, where it is still to be seen, if no one has stolen it.

Now, that's what I call a really good story!